Ballard Branch

# MIKHAIL
# AND MARGARITA

Julie Lekstrom Himes

# MIKHAIL
# AND MARGARITA

Europa
*editions*

Europa Editions
214 West 29th Street
New York, N.Y. 10001
www.europaeditions.com
info@europaeditions.com

This is a work of fiction. While many elements of the story are drawn
from the life of Mikhaíl Afanasievich Bulgakov, other details are purely fictional.

Library of Congress Cataloging in Publication Data is available
ISBN 978-1-60945-375-6

Lekstrom Himes, Julie
Mikhail and Margarita

Book design by Emanuele Ragnisco
www.mekkanografici.com

Cover photo © MLADEN ANTONOV/AFP/Getty Images

Stalin Epigram by Osip Mandelstam, reprinted with permission from the Osip
Mandelshtam Papers (C0539); 1900s–1970s, Manuscripts Division, Department
of Rare Books and Special Collections, Princeton University Library.

Excerpts from *The Master and Margarita*, reprinted with permission from
Andrew Nurnberg Associates, London, UK

Prepress by Grafica Punto Print – Rome

Printed in the USA

# CONTENTS

*For Len and Barbara*

# PART I
## ENTER THE HERO

# CHAPTER 1

History came late to Russia. Geography isolated her and isolation defined her. In the ninth century, pagan Vikings discovered her from the north; Muslim Khazars ruled her from the south. The Cyrillic alphabet, which was to craft her story, made its way across the Carpathian Mountains on the backs of Macedonian monks only in the winding years of the tenth century. Even nine centuries later, Pushkin and Tolstoy were yet inventing those words which in Russian did not exist: gesture and sympathy, impulse and imagination, individuality.

It would be the task of her subsequent writers to try to define them.

Mikhail Afanasievich Bulgakov sat with his back to an open window in the richly appointed restaurant of Moscow's All-Soviets Writers Union. It was late spring of 1933. His friend Osip Mandelstam leaned across their small table to emphasize a point, but Bulgakov wasn't listening. He was thinking instead of his friend's young lover, imagining how he might steal her from him.

The day preceding had been blisteringly hot. By midday the waitstaff had tied back the heavy damask curtains and pushed open the high, triple casing windows that encircled the polygonal room. A series of French doors opened onto a wide verandah that was likewise arranged with tables and chairs for dining. Repeatedly, the restaurant manager stood in the dining room, then on the painted planking of the verandah, then back again, considering the temperature and ventilation of each space. Finally, by late afternoon, he set the staff to move half a dozen additional tables from inside, through the open doors, and onto the already crowded verandah. He went from table to table with his meter-stick, measuring and ordering adjustments and measuring again. Shortly before dusk, dense green-grey clouds filled the sky and opened themselves upon the streets of Moscow. The heavy drapes floated up in the wind and slapped down against the window moldings. Enormous raindrops like errant birds flew through the open windows and between the broad porch columns, spotting the tablecloths and napkins and puddling on the polished wood floor. The sun returned only to dip below the darkening outlines of buildings, steam rose from the sizzled streets, and frantic waitstaff hustled about, blotting and wiping and mopping. By the time the restaurant opened at ten that night everything that needed to be dried or replaced had been considered, save one—not a single grain of salt could be coaxed from its shaker. After the second request for fresh salt, it was clear there was no more to be found either in the back storage closets or in the basement, and the manager sent one of the younger dishwashers out to procure some from a nearby restaurant with an extra ten-ruble note to pay for the speed of a cab. Not a block from the restaurant the dishwasher discharged the driver with a few kopeks and pocketed the rest. When the first did not return, the manager sent a second dishwasher on the same errand, only now, two washers short, dirty plates and glasses began to accumulate and service noticeably slowed. With the continuing requests, he set two of the waitstaff to dump several shakers' worth into a pestle and grind the grains apart, but the clumps reformed almost immediately. Meanwhile, the manager went from table to table apologizing and offering assurance they were only minutes from acquiring new salt that would be swiftly and equitably distributed. In any case, he told them, he hoped their meals were prepared to their satisfaction.

The manager paused from his rounds and stood in the doorway between the dining room and the verandah, scanning the guests. He recognized Mandelstam; otherwise there was no one of terrific consequence; the night could not be counted an utter disaster.

The air outside smelled of ozone, and, slightly cooled by the evening rain, it floated through the window behind Bulgakov. The squat alcohol lamps on each table were protected by small translucent shades and did not flicker. Other patrons, sweating in the dim light, moved little. The edges of conversations were muted as well. Several tables away, a young woman in a crumpled orange dress fed caviar to an older man with a poorly dyed goatee. To their right, another man, a minor poet, argued with his two companions, jabbing his finger into his palm, yet even this seemed vague and lacking conviction. Near the doors to the verandah, a band played a low and drifting melody.

Mandelstam sat back as though he'd made his point. The light from the lamp bloomed between them. Mandelstam's thinning dark hair ringed his scalp in an untidy damp fringe. His face was pale and moist in the heat. He was forty-two, only a year older than Bulgakov, yet he seemed more aged as if he'd lived in a different time or under more difficult circumstances. How he'd been able to attract the much younger Margarita Nikoveyena had occupied Bulgakov's thoughts on not a few occasions before this evening.

Bulgakov glanced over the room. Beyond the doors leading to the veranda there was the turn of a pale gown; a flicker of bare shoulders. A slender neck, then gone. Could she be here this evening? "Who the devil is that?" he murmured.

"You're not listening," said Mandelstam. It seemed more a weary reflection than an accusation. He maintained what Bulgakov would consider a too-generous gaze.

"That's true." Bulgakov smiled a little with this admission. He felt some guilt about this. They met infrequently these days. Their friendship had evolved from a mentorship of sorts, begun over a decade earlier when Bulgakov had moved to Moscow and started writing. Years later and now with some success of his own, their friendship had dwindled rather than strengthened. Bulgakov blamed himself generally. Their dinner tonight had been Mandelstam's suggestion. Bulgakov could not remember another meeting that had come at the poet's request. Even so, he had almost declined at the last moment, for no better reasons than the poor weather and the mediocre meal which was to be expected midweek at the Writers' Union. As he'd come across the room, unreasonably late and with an excuse forming, Mandelstam's gaunt face was so at odds with the room's richness that his first words were not a request for pardon but a pointed inquiry into the state of his health. Mandelstam assured him that he was fine, and yet it was the pleasure he showed at Bulgakov's arrival, and his willingness to set aside the annoyance he must have felt for being made to wait, which caused Bulgakov to consider that there was something Mandelstam required from him. This was the first time Bulgakov had ever thought such a thing.

Mandelstam's interest turned to Bulgakov's well-being.

"Why don't you get away? Go to Peredelkino—it's quite nice this time of year," said Mandelstam.

Six dachas—parceled out amongst three thousand writers. The privilege of Union membership for the politically connected. Bulgakov pretended this was a serious suggestion. "I've not had a turn."

"I've been a number of times." Bulgakov's reluctance to engage in Union politics was an old conversation. "It's not impossible. Who do you go to?"

Bulgakov laughed. "Who would have me?" His self-deprecation was false, but he had no desire for patronage. He preferred to remain in some way invisible. Not his work, of course, but for himself, this was fine; perhaps even best.

Mandelstam shook his head. "Everyone goes to someone. You don't have to live in that place of yours. You could do better. Committee members, they love writers—makes them feel cultured. I could introduce you."

Bulgakov glanced away again. "Is that Likovoyev? I haven't seen him in months."

"He's been at Peredelkino."

*Of course.* Bulgakov smiled. "And I thought he'd died."

Mandelstam lowered his head, whether from the heat or the conversation, it was difficult to say. He seemed disinclined to pursue other old topics: the necessity of placating critics, of transforming editors and directors and producers into advocates. Bulgakov was grateful, though he considered that in this, and possibly in other ways, too, he'd plumbed the limits of a friend's fortitude.

"Perhaps you should write poetry," said Mandelstam.

"Aren't you concerned I'd give you competition?" Bulgakov had intended this to be funny. He downed what remained of his vodka.

Mandelstam waited for his attention. "Only in this country is poetry respected," he said. "There's no place where more people are killed for it."

He was prone to speak in such a manner. Bulgakov found it tiresome; he did not share his friend's political discontent. This was not so much a stance, he told himself, as a lack of interest. He barely read the papers; he listened to the radio for its music. Yet because of this edge in Mandelstam a certain wariness was necessary, a constant recalibration of the space of their relationship. That was what was tiresome. He noticed that the poet had acquired a spot on his shirt since the start of their dinner. He was often careless, and Bulgakov found himself further annoyed by this. "One might argue, then, that writing poetry would not be such a good idea."

Mandelstam smiled. Perhaps this was so, he agreed.

Likovoyev moved from table to table, clasping hands as each patron rose from his seat. Only brief exchanges, and Bulgakov observed with mild interest as shifts in the Union's hierarchy were revealed. Likovoyev went next to the Art Theater's new librettist; then bent low to ingratiate himself with the man's young wife, a former countess, holding her hand for too long, ignoring her husband until she looked away, embarrassed. He was stork-like in his maneuverings; his awkwardness made him even more comedic. Bulgakov's lips parted.

"What is it?" said Mandelstam.

"Our beloved critic," said Bulgakov. "Among his many crimes, he is an appalling flirt."

"My wife seems to be immune to his advances."

"You are fortunate."

"In some ways, Nadya is like a nun. How is your Tatiana?"

The waiter appeared and replaced his drink. Bulgakov waited until he'd receded. "She's moved in with her sister and her husband."

Mandelstam seemed to check his surprise. It occurred to Bulgakov that this was already common knowledge. Their wives had been friends of a sort, sharing the burden of writer-husbands.

"Their apartment is larger," said Bulgakov. "And—they have a private bath."

Mandelstam nodded in feigned support of the wife. "I would leave you, too."

Likovoyev moved on from the librettist and was embracing a young poet. Bulgakov emptied his glass again. He remembered the precise moment he had fallen out of love with his wife. An acquaintance had introduced them at Bulgakov's request. For weeks she'd gently rebuffed his advances with teasing words he'd found endearing, then one evening, without explanation, she'd stayed. He remembered her sitting on the edge of his bed, the pearl-shaped buttons of her blouse between her fingers, undressing for him; he remembered the low angle of orange sunlight through the dirty window. He remembered watching his desire fall away as the chemise dropped from her shoulders. If only she would leave, he thought. Perhaps if she had, his desire would have returned; but she'd remained.

He'd married her anyway. He felt their lovemaking had been a kind of agreement to this. And he felt sorry for her, for being unloved. And she was fine, really. They got along well. She left him alone to write and was sufficiently distracting when the loneliness turned on him.

Likovoyev was standing by their table. Startled, Bulgakov laughed aloud. "I thought you were the waiter," said Bulgakov, lifting his empty glass.

Likovoyev bared his teeth in what might be called a smile.

Mandelstam interceded. "You look remarkable. Your time at Peredelkino served you well."

"It did," said the critic. "I banished all thoughts of this place, I must say, all—except—inexplicably, you." He nodded to Bulgakov.

"Then you must return, immediately, and try again," said Bulgakov. "I will petition the Union Chairman on your behalf, first thing tomorrow."

Likovoyev ignored this. "I understand you have a new play under production at the MAT. All is going smoothly, I pray?"

"We open at the end of the month." Bulgakov didn't bother to restrain a bit of swagger.

"So glad to hear. I'd heard mention of a delay." Likovoyev hesitated as though he might say more, then changed his mind. "I was obviously misinformed."

This was unexpected. "No," said Bulgakov, rather too quickly. "No. Not at all." Likovoyev looked again at Mandelstam as if for some sort of verification.

Bulgakov wanted to say that the play was progressing well, ahead of schedule, in fact, though this wasn't true. They were behind, but not irrevocably. Perhaps seven or eight days; certainly no more than two weeks. But the delay wasn't entirely his concern. The director, Stanislawski, had seemed to be avoiding him of late, locking himself in his office for hours until Bulgakov would bully his assistant to open it, only then to find that the director had somehow slipped away. Bulgakov had convinced himself this was all his imagining but now his worries bloomed afresh. He wanted to question Likovoyev further, but the other was already speaking.

"Frivolous gossip, then, no doubt. I knew it was nothing to heed."

"Stanislawski has made no mention—" Bulgakov began. Mandelstam frowned.

"Yes? I am so relieved," said Likovoyev. "And thankful to have spoken with you." He nodded. "I will look forward to *Moliere*'s opening—and to my humble review."

"Yes—to your review," Bulgakov echoed. Some part of him vaguely wished the critic would stay. For the first time, he looked forward to a *Likovoyev* review.

"I won't keep you from your meal." Likovoyev seemed more jovial than when he'd arrived, as though he'd extracted the better part of their good mood. "Please give my regards to your lovely wives." He bowed and turned away. Bulgakov watched him recede.

Mandelstam leaned forward. "He's not the reason for your—for Tatiana's—"

Bulgakov shook his head. "No, that was my fault." The critic was already several tables away. He bent low, to address some other writer's wife. At the woman's words, he dropped his head to the side, his eyes boring into hers. Bulgakov recognized the harmless gestures. Now he could almost forgive him for them.

He turned to Mandelstam. "What about a delay? Have you heard such rumors? Have you?"

Mandelstam was poking the remains of his dinner with his fork. "You've spoken with Stanislawski yourself. All is fine."

"Yes, we've spoken." Bulgakov tried to remember the last time they had. "I must speak with him again." He needed this production. Other recent efforts had been poorly received and short-lived.

"I'm surprised he's not here tonight," said Mandelstam. He considered a nondescript piece of meat. "Of course, it is a Tuesday."

Likovoyev kissed the hand of the writer's wife. Bulgakov watched him straighten and bow to her, then to the husband, helpless beside her. The woman lifted her eyes to the critic in a kind of wonderment; a combination of mild loathing and speculation. Bulgakov looked away.

He'd thought nothing of Likovoyev's flirtations with his wife. Nothing whatsoever, except some faint gratitude that the critic provided something which Bulgakov lacked all interest in supplying. That Likovoyev's stilted affectations might satisfy her in some small way. They, he and Tatiana, had laughed about him, yet perhaps, she had laughed not as much. He'd considered her secret satisfaction with the critic's attentions a kind of naïveté that should not have been surprising. He wasn't surprised and hadn't begrudged her those small pleasures.

There was no crime, no clandestine tryst that had come between them. Nothing save the briefest reluctance, the sparest of pauses, one afternoon as he'd stuttered through his regular tirade about him. For the first time she had not immediately agreed. For the first time she'd been quiet. And in that silence he saw her consideration for the critic, her alliance with him, and realized that this Likovoyev, though incapable of comprehending even the most lucid of writing, could nonetheless reveal in his boorish maneuverings a desolation in her far greater than some naïveté. Bulgakov turned to her for some explanation. She pressed her lips together and looked away as if something had passed their window.

Afterwards, he told himself she did not matter so much; it'd been a mistake from the start and it was easier to let her go. She did not leave right away, but drifted further and further, until one day her belongings slipped away as well. He came home that afternoon to those empty spaces. He left them that way for days, hangers in the wardrobe, the place by the door where her shoes had stood. He found reasons not to fill them; he told himself, though, it was not because she might return. It was not because her things might again need a place to stay.

He found his glass and tipped it forward to pool the remaining drops. He lacked the power to maneuver the world in his favor; he could not even will the waiter to sedate him with more drink. He started to lift it but found his hand restrained.

"Talk to Stanislawski," said Mandelstam. He nodded as if he understood the problem.

Bulgakov considered his glass. "I will," he said. Osip relaxed his hand and Bulgakov tipped back the last drops.

The musicians had begun to play again; they took up a jazz line. Music filled the spaces between conversations. Mandelstam frowned as if he'd been interrupted. Then he looked upward. Someone was by their table.

"Good evening, my dear," he said. He sounded slightly annoyed.

The pale gown from before was beside them. It was Margarita Nikoveyeva.

Bulgakov had seen her before, though not with the poet. They'd tried to conceal their affair although many, even

Mandelstam's wife, it was said, knew of it. There had been the time, the previous fall, at a party in this very room. He'd watched as she'd put off the advances of another man. At one point she'd looked about as though for some means of escape, and caught his gaze. Bulgakov had smiled, both sympathetic and duplicitous, and across that space they had shared an understanding. Or so he'd thought.

Tonight she was different, though. Indeed, all of her seemed unreasonably pale. Her hair pulled back in a chignon was silvery in the dim light; her ivory-colored dress, unadorned, fell in simple lines. He became aware of her breathing from its gentle motion. Her fingers rested on the edge of the tablecloth, as if to steady herself. Behind her, the band seemed muted. She nodded to both men but addressed only Mandelstam. Bulgakov expected him to compliment her appearance; the light of the room seemed to soak into her. But it wasn't this that gave her an unworldly appearance. She had the air of the ill-fated; of one about to step from a platform onto empty tracks, the sound of a train filling the air. Not with the purpose to end her life so much as to embrace the monstrosity. He wanted to pull her to safety and at the same time to stand back and watch her proceed. He stood to give her his chair; she smiled a little, shook her head, and returned her attention to Mandelstam. He had remained seated.

When Mandelstam spoke his voice had taken an edge.

"Who are you with tonight?" He spoke as a brother might, or a father. Someone responsible for her in some way. Or as an ex-lover. Reminding her that without a Union membership, she could not have gained entrance on her own merit. But perhaps more meaningfully, he was demonstrating his right to ask that question in that manner.

An embarrassed smile fluttered across her face; she provided a name. Bulgakov didn't recognize it, but Mandelstam nodded.

"You look well," she said. She sounded mildly hopeful in this.

"Perhaps in this lighting I do."

She continued with less certainty. "And Nadya?"

"She actually is quite well. But I don't think I'll tell her you asked."

He was condescending to the point of contempt, Bulgakov thought. He reached for Mandelstam's arm. She'd come to them, after all. Was there a need for this? Mandelstam moved his arm away.

"I simply wanted to say 'hello.'" She said this without apology or defense, as if a little tired.

"And so you have," he said flatly.

"I mean there's no reason for us to pretend we don't know each other," she said. She seemed not to lose courage, but hope.

Mandelstam frowned at the cloth and swept its crumbs aside as though he no longer had patience for them. They bounced lightly off the skirt of her gown.

"You are far too willing to overlook my shortcomings, my dear," he said. He smoothed the now-clean cloth with his hand.

Only her eyes revealed her distress, her unwillingness to believe his animosity and yet her acceptance of it. Her vulnerability was breathtaking. He wondered if Mandelstam saw this as well.

"Perhaps," she said quickly. "That would be my shortcoming." She turned to Bulgakov. "Please enjoy your meal," she said.

"We've finished," said Bulgakov, correcting her. "It wasn't particularly good."

"Ah, well then, enjoy—" She left her sentiment unfinished, unable to come up with a better idea of what they were to delight in. She'd already turned. He watched her recede, feeling as though he'd allowed her to escape.

Mandelstam watched her as well, his expression very different from the one just moments before. There was an old affection, perhaps one that had been retired, yet nonetheless remembered, and it occurred to Bulgakov that she was the reason they'd dined here this evening. She disappeared through one of the veranda doors and Mandelstam's gaze found his. "She should know better," Mandelstam said.

"I think she does now."

"I suspect not."

The door's opening maintained its velvety darkness. Bulgakov looked for her to reappear but it remained empty.

"We were speaking of your play," Mandelstam said.

Bulgakov thought that perhaps he'd rather talk about Margarita.

Mandelstam and Bulgakov left the restaurant together. The streets were wet and empty; the sky was low. Bulgakov felt the hum of alcohol out to his fingertips. He felt connected to the dense warm air that rose from the glistening asphalt. He wondered where Margarita might be at that moment. He imagined her alone, perhaps on a street like this one, then remembered she was with someone else. Was she holding his hand; his arm? Had he provided her comfort? He wondered how he might see her again.

Two uniformed men stepped into the street. Mandelstam stopped then immediately moved away from Bulgakov, and the four men stood apart, the points of some ill-formed square. Bulgakov was for a moment confused.

The gold threads of the police insignia glimmered in the light of a nearby streetlamp.

"Citizens. May we see your documents?" said the taller man.

Mandelstam provided a cache of papers. Bulgakov extended his as well and they were snatched up by the shorter of the two. This one mouthed the words as he silently read them.

"The poet Mandelstam," said the taller policeman. He sounded genuinely pleased.

"You never know who you might find roaming the streets at night," said the poet.

The other officer continued to review Bulgakov's papers as if disappointed he'd not caught a larger fish. "Are you together?" he asked finally. He handed the papers back.

"No," said Mandelstam. He seemed about to add something further then stopped. The taller officer studied Bulgakov with growing interest.

Bulgakov laughed. "You are Mandelstam?" he said. "I thought he was a much younger man." He swayed suddenly and stepped back to regain his balance. The shorter officer shined a flashlight in his face and the world disappeared in its glare. He heard, "Stand to, Citizen." The light moved and the street reappeared, muddled with spots. The shorter officer stepped closer. To Bulgakov it seemed this one was a clown's version of a policeman. He laughed aloud at the thought.

The shorter officer was about to speak but the other interrupted. "Comrade Poet, you give us a poem. We'd like that."

Mandelstam shook his head. "I can't think of one, friends. Perhaps another time."

The taller officer didn't move. It was clear he was unsatisfied with that answer.

"I know a poem," said Bulgakov. "One you will like. 'There once was a whore from Kiev.'" He paused. "No, Novgorod. Yes. 'There once was a whore from Novgorod.'"

The officers stiffened. Bulgakov noticed this in his blur but went on.

"No, it can't be Novgorod. The rhythm's all wrong. I can see you gentlemen are not enthusiasts of great literature."

Mandelstam spoke. "Enough."

"You're not so terribly funny," chimed the shorter officer.

"Perhaps you would like to be arrested for public drunkenness." He hooked his thumbs onto his belt.

"Oh but I am funny," said Bulgakov in a show of astonishment. "I am a satirist. Humor is my tool." He lowered his voice as if conspiratorial. "It is my weapon."

The policeman looked alarmed.

"But perhaps you think satire is a kind of fish that swims in the Volga."

"Enough." This time it seemed Mandelstam was speaking to the greater world. "I will give you a poem." He touched Bulgakov's sleeve.

The poet's manner had a dousing effect and Bulgakov was given to the uncomfortable sense that this was something Mandelstam had intended; and even if it was not precisely intended, then perhaps it was quite simply an opportunity he would take.

The streets were empty, as if Moscow had availed them some privacy. Mandelstam's voice rose as though he was speaking to a gathering of hundreds, as though this was his most beloved of works.

Mandelstam said:

*We live, deaf to the land beneath us,*
*Ten steps away no one hears our speeches,*

*All we hear is the Kremlin mountaineer,*
*The murderer and peasant-slayer.*

*His fingers are fat as grubs*
*And the words, final as lead weights, fall from his lips,*

*His cockroach whiskers leer*
*And his boots gleam.*

*Every killing is a treat*
*For the broad-chested Ossete.*

It was the shorter officer who made a sound, a sharp sigh.

Mandelstam licked his lips, as though he'd become parched. "I think even a *Bolshevik* can understand that much," he said.

With that Bulgakov staggered forward and threw his arms around Mandelstam's shoulders. He pressed the poet's head into his neck.

"He's drunk, Comrades. Can't you see? What a night we've had! His words—what words—I could barely understand such slurring. Can't you see—his wife left him, truly—just today. Left him for a younger man, a bookkeeper. The poor old goat. *And his daughter is pregnant.*" This he added in a whisper.

"Stand away," said the taller policeman. The baton was in his hand.

It seemed ridiculous—could this be happening? He clutched Mandelstam harder. "No, no, no—he's drunk, I tell you. I'll take him home. I'll tuck him in. The headache he'll have tomorrow. I should drive a car over his foot so he can forget the pain in his head." He looked from one officer to the other. He maneuvered Mandelstam past.

He broke into a jog, half-dragging the poet down the street. He imagined them following. They weren't far from the DRAMALIT house where Mandelstam shared an apartment with his wife.

He thrust them both through the front door. The street behind was silent. Only then did he release him.

"You should come by tomorrow," said Mandelstam. "There may be an apartment made newly available. A nice place, I hear." He appeared to enjoy his joke.

Bulgakov was shaking. "I don't think they followed us," he said.

Mandelstam shook his head. He seemed suddenly quite weary. "They're upstairs." He glanced at the ceiling. "Can you hear them? Roaches in the walls."

"Here? They cannot be here already."

The poet stepped back into the hall under the ceiling light. His scalp shone brightly. He looked upward. "She's alone with them," he said. He meant his wife. "They will have a time of it." He sounded mildly sympathetic.

"We must get you away. We'll go to my place. It's not far."

There was a distant thump, then the thinner crack of breaking wood. Mandelstam closed his eyes. "The sideboard. What we went through to haul that monstrosity up those stairs."

Bulgakov reached for the poet's arm. Tentatively, as if in this gesture he might disappear. "What can I do?" he said.

Mandelstam looked at him as though he'd not considered this before and Bulgakov saw in his face his sad realization: there was nothing Bulgakov could do; there was nothing anyone could do.

Mandelstam took hold of the stair rail. This slant of wood was his immediate future. He would follow it momentarily. All of his earlier passion seemed to have fled him. His face appeared to have aged even further and Bulgakov realized he was witnessing despair.

"Perhaps we've been fools to write." Mandelstam seemed to speak to all of that building's occupants. As if this was his revelation. As if they would have served better as window washers or carpet-layers. There would have been clean windows, straight carpets.

Bulgakov didn't know how to answer. He watched him ascend. He wanted to call him back.

The single bulb overhead whined. Moments later there was a distant rumble, a deeper disturbance. He put his ear to the plaster. Nothing, then a crash, a door slam—it seemed close. What did it mean that he stood there? What did it mean that he waited, listening as some poor widowed neighbor would listen? *What did it mean?* The building seemed to murmur a distant chorus. Could he stand there and do nothing? He pressed his hands to the wall. He held it dear. Yes, he could.

# CHAPTER 2

Bulgakov waited across the street in the shadows of a small apartment building. The road remained empty apart from a dark sedan. A streetlight crackled intermittently. Later, as the sky paled to gray, three secret police exited the DRAMALIT house. One carried a box; Mandelstam walked between the other two, his arms behind his back. They didn't notice Bulgakov. In an alley nearby, a trashcan was disturbed by a scavenging animal. They got into the car. It pulled away, turning at the end of the block. Bulgakov crossed the street.

At Mandelstam's apartment, the door was ajar and he entered. The lamps were extinguished. Grey light filtered from a window; beneath was a bookcase and nearby an upholstered chair and sofa. The light reached no further. Before him, in the semidarkness, shadowy, unrecognizable forms seemed strewn about the floor. He hesitated.

Across, a checked curtain was pushed aside and Mandelstam's wife emerged from a shallow hallway. She was thin and pale; her hair was short and very dark, cut at an angle across her face. She wore a loose cotton dress. She gazed past Bulgakov as if he was of no more consequence than a piece of furniture set out of place. She moved toward the window and knelt on the floor.

They'd known each other for years; he considered she was in shock.

"Nadya?" He stumbled against the leg of an overturned chair, then set it upright. Its seat and armrest were missing.

Objects around him seemed to emerge from the darkness. The floor was covered with books and papers; a large bookcase was upended and broken shelves hung loose. The fabled sideboard laid across the floor in a diagonal; broken glass glimmered dimly from the carpet. A desk chair sat across the room, upside down. Its legs turned slowly about its stem, as if its occupant had recently and quite absurdly departed.

Paper was everywhere. He picked up one. Notes in Mandelstam's hand.

"I can't find it," she said. "I know it's here. Here—" She pointed, between the floorboards. "A pin?" As if he was too dense to understand. "Do you know how hard it is to lay your hands on pins?" She looked up at him. "No, you wouldn't." Her expression was unreadable in the light.

He couldn't make sense of her tone; it bordered on contempt as though some part of this was his doing.

He turned on a lamp. In its light the devastation was complete. "Did they find what they were looking for?" he asked.

She shook her head. She sat back on her heels, her hands on her thighs, as if to say, *damn the pin*. They could live in a world without pins, for all her concern.

"He offered to write it out for them," she said. "So that even with their *myopic* vision, they could read it." Those were his words, of course. As she spoke, her anger went to incredulity then to sorrow. As if she couldn't believe she was saying these things; that they could even be said.

She crawled into the chair near the window. Through the wall came the faint sound of a man singing a popular tune. Bulgakov sat on the sofa near her. He picked up a displaced toy that lay at his feet; three carved horses wired together crudely and arranged on a small set of wheels. He moved one of them and the others bobbled up and down on their own, one after the other, as if galloping across the steppe. Bulgakov looked up and found she was watching him.

"Osip's?" he asked.

"It was mine," she said flatly.

She made no movement to take it, as if it'd belonged to a different and no longer relevant version of herself, and he set it on the floor again. A postcard stuck out from under the skirt of the sofa and he retrieved it. It was of the coastline of Yalta. It'd been written by Osip to Nadya's parents. He recognized the long looping strokes. The postmark was 1924.

He imagined a 1924 version of Osip. This one smiled square to the camera, his hands on his hips as if challenging it, with exuberant hair and teeth.

Nadya took the card from him.

"That was from our honeymoon," she said. "Well, we called it that." She studied the picture. "We stayed—there," and she pointed to a small jut of land, east of the city. "The place was terrible. Let by an older couple. I wouldn't let Osip sit on the bed until I'd boiled the sheets." She smiled. "There was a palm tree outside our door. Every morning, he'd kiss it. So silly. He'd do things to make me laugh. He was a wonderful man."

Then her face changed. "They're going to kill him, aren't they?" As if her utterance had set their decision. She began to cry.

"No, they're not." He covered her hand with his. "He's important, an important writer." He smiled to show how ridiculous this would be. "They wouldn't dare. I can't imagine it." He tried to appear convinced.

She wiped her face with her hands, then touched her hair. "What should we do?"

At first he was uncertain what she meant; as though their sitting together further endangered her husband. Then he understood: *what could they do?*

"Go to Bukharin," he said. "Tell him of—this." He didn't know what he would say, but it was something she could do, and immediately she nodded.

"He got us tickets to the Kirov last June. We didn't ask. They just came. I told him—Osip, of course. Well, it was nice, I told him. It was one nice thing. He could have given them to his housekeeper. The very least we could do was go."

The apartment door behind her opened and closed. Someone had entered. "Is it Anna?" she asked.

Although the light was dim, he could see it was Margarita. Why had she come?

Nadya turned to look, then got up abruptly and went to the checked curtain. He stood as she left. On the other side, in the bedroom, clothes and books had been tossed about; a terrible gash cut through a bare and overturned mattress. All disappeared as the curtain fell.

The room felt oddly crowded with now just the two of them. She nodded, as though acknowledging their recent encounter at the restaurant. He wondered if she was surprised to see him. He could only think of all of the reasons why she shouldn't have come. He hesitated to speak lest he start enumerating them for her.

She didn't seem surprised by the wreckage. Her hair was pulled back in a loose knot at the base of her neck. She wore trousers and a man's shirt, cinched at the waist. She lifted one hand for balance as she stepped through the remains of the sideboard.

He wondered whose shirt.

"Careful," he said. "There is glass."

She picked up some loose pages near her feet, then sat in the chair as Nadya had. In the better light he could see she'd been crying.

There was a noise from the bedroom but the curtain was still. He sat again.

"I'm surprised you're here," he said. It wasn't meant to be unkind.

He was nervous of Nadya's reaction.

Margarita looked over her shoulder as well.

She'd have known a Mandelstam different from his, perhaps even different from Nadya's. Seeing her face in this light he tried to imagine how the poet's hands would have touched her. Would he have used gestures different than those practiced on a wife of ten years?

But she was speaking. "Were you here when they came?"

"They were here when we got back," he said.

Perhaps she was wondering if she could have prevented these events. Would things have gone differently had she chosen different words? Worn a different dress? Would he have come home with her instead? Bulgakov imagined all of this as he watched her thoughts work, as his own worked in the same manner, searching for his own culpability. Suppose he had been a better friend? Had been attentive of Mandelstam's growing discontent? Could he have dissuaded him from taking action? There must have been something he could have done. Better to have been at fault than to have been powerless.

It occurred to him that in sitting with her, he was in some way colluding with the mistress. Nadya, he knew, would view it thusly. He could check on her; the other room was now quiet. He could begin to tidy the place. He could leave Margarita to her own accounting.

He continued to sit with her. He didn't know what to say.

"I'm sorry for the way he behaved in the restaurant," he said. He realized how odd it sounded. Was Nadya listening? He lowered his voice.

"What I mean is that I'm sorry you had to see that—I mean if it's the last time—*God*, I mean I'm certain that's not the way he feels." His words had become haphazard, going from odd to reckless.

She glanced at the pages, as though they might give better comfort.

The curtain pushed aside and Nadya appeared. They both stood and he moved between them as if he would mediate or divert her from examining the obvious.

Nadya's arms were crossed over her chest. She studied Margarita.

"I guess I'm not surprised," she said finally. Her voice lacked the earlier chilliness that he'd received. He found her calm unnerving. Her face was empty; something was about to happen there.

"I've wanted to see you," said Margarita. "I wish this was under different circumstances."

Nadya's face darkened slightly but her words were still assured. "Are you suggesting we could have arranged to meet for lunch? The way friends do?"

"I've missed you."

They knew each other. Perhaps even had been friends, and suddenly he knew, as though he'd been told, or really, as though he'd been witness: Nadya had introduced them to each other. Nadya, her arm through Margarita's, at some sort of gathering, had delivered to her husband his future mistress. Perhaps she'd read the desire in his eyes at that first encounter. In any case, she had known.

"A ladies' tête-à-tête?" Nadya's voice rose.

He thought to pull Margarita away. His hand edged to her arm, but she seemed not to notice. She had the same demeanor as in the restaurant the night before: there was something she needed to say.

"I know I've hurt you, Nadyusha."

"Slut." The word was well formed as though it had been waiting for its opportunity.

"I'm so sorry."

Nadya raised her hand to strike her. As though Margarita's regret was itself a kind of insult. As though some had rights to certain losses, to certain grievances, and some did not.

Bulgakov took Nadya's wrist. She pulled her arm away.

"I've hated you both," she said to Margarita. "Selfish— that's what you are—selfish—thoughtless." He could see her trying to get the words right. "No—I never hated him. It was you who made him selfish."

"He's not selfish," said Margarita. Nadya laughed.

"The wife knows 'selfish.'" She nodded. "The wife." She jabbed her fingers into her own chest. "Believe me. All of this." She gestured to the room. "All of this—he brought into being. Selfish."

"Nadya," he said. He knew he sounded reproachful. She turned on him with her anger and self-pity.

"The—wife—" She looked as if the need to explain this took something from her; particularly to explain to him, who should have known better. The wife who had suffered the humiliations of police searches. Who had borne the shame of gossip and curiosity. And now—an uncertain future. This was the currency of devotion measured against the currency of desire. They all should know better.

They had all become perpetrators of a kind, Mandelstam included. Their crimes might be different, but she was their victim. It was reflected in her face. Perhaps she had guessed it when Bulgakov had first appeared that morning: that he would fall in with them; that she would be alone, once again, as always; and he saw how she hated him for it.

She disappeared again behind the curtain.

Margarita didn't move. She looked at the fabric as though waiting for it to become something else.

The curtain stayed closed.

What else was there to do? Bulgakov set the desk upright, then the desk chair. He pushed the smaller bookcase back against the wall. Below was the wrecked sideboard. He swept the bits of glass onto a loose page. Everywhere were books and papers.

She pushed her sleeves up past her elbows, knelt, and began to return the books to their shelves. He worked at this too. Her hair slipped from its knot. She finally tucked it back and continued.

She smelled of soap.

Nadya appeared. She crouched and gathered as many papers as she could reach, then went back into the bedroom. There was something about her movements that made him follow.

A small stove extended from an older fireplace. It hummed. Nadya opened the grate and stuffed some papers into it. Next to her, a steamer's trunk sat open, filled with notebooks and more papers and letters. She watched, then slowly fed more to the flames.

The curtain moved and Margarita came up behind him.

"What are you doing?" he asked. He took the page in her hands. There were handwritten lines of verse. She pulled it back and pushed it through the grate.

He sensed some part of her was doing this to him, forcing him to watch. Asking who he thought the perpetrator was now.

"You're just angry," he said. "You're upset," he repeated, thinking to negotiate. "I understand. But you can't do this."

Nadya reached into the trunk for more papers. This seemed too easy for her.

"They're not yours to burn." He tried to keep his voice even.

She sneered. "They're yours?"

"Yes—perhaps. Yes—they could be."

"This will save him," she said. "Despite everything—because of everything. I will save him."

"But this—Nadya—it is his work," he said. She must be made to be reasonable.

Her face shimmered in the fire's light. He was suddenly afraid for himself.

She opened the grate again. "There are enough poets in this world," she said.

"I'll help you," said Margarita.

He turned in disbelief. She was already beyond the curtain. He followed her.

She was on her knees, turning over books and furniture, gathering pages from the floor. With the growing light, they seemed to be everywhere.

"What are you doing?" he whispered.

She considered the sheets in her hand. Slowly she paged through them. She pulled out several and hid them in her shirt. Not everything was verse.

He dropped to his knees and began to do the same.

Nadya appeared. Margarita gave her the assortment in her hands.

He paused and let the papers he held slowly fall to the floor. Nadya didn't seem to notice.

"You understand," she said to him. "This is his life we're talking about. His flesh and blood life. I cannot live without him." She spoke as if she was the first to ever say such things, the first to ever contemplate those feelings.

"I understand," he said. He couldn't look at her.

She disappeared behind the curtain.

"What about the trunk," he said.

Margarita looked pained but said nothing. She slipped more pages into her shirt.

He scrambled to collect others. One held a new poem. Its opening line rattled him. He shut his eyes.

Nadya took them from him and went into the bedroom.

*What were those words?* Their order became confused; then they dropped from his memory, first the smaller ones, then the larger ones followed. They were gone.

Margarita went to the desk and began to go through the drawers. He went to the bedroom again.

Nadya was kneeling next to the stove. The collection in the trunk had noticeably shrunk.

"He would not agree to this."

She stared through the open grate. "Get out of my apartment," she said.

"Please—"

She turned on him. "Get out. I will call the police. I will turn you over to them as a traitor. An enemy of the people." Her face loosened; the calm was gone. She was shaking. She went back to the stove. "I would hand you over in exchange for him."

He slid along the wall and passed through the curtain.

Margarita was kneeling on the floor. He took the pages from the corner of the bookcase as he went toward the door. Beyond it, as he rounded the upper landing, Nadya called to him.

"Never fear, Bulgakov! They will come for you too."

He clattered down the stairs, fleeing her. Only silence followed. The entry hall was cool and grey in the early light as though part of a different world. He looked at the pages.

A shopping list, a letter from the housing committee chairman, a memorandum from the Writers Union. He'd saved nothing. He struggled to remember the line taken by the flames.

He saw Mandelstam in a grey-green cell under the interrogator's light. *No one really wants you to write. Not even the ones who love you most. Did you not see how easily she'd burned them?*

Margarita appeared from around the stairway's landing. She descended to the bottom step. She carried a modest collection of loose pages. She measured him. He was an uncertain ally.

The fabric under her arm was dark with perspiration.

"I have to go back." She held out the pages. "Nadya moves quickly. She may realize I'm not as helpful as she thinks."

He took them and thumbed through. Stanzas flashed past. Phrases of new music. Something fresh and beating had been pulled from the wreckage. A life had been saved. It felt like it was his.

His eyes took to that darker place under her sleeve again. Somewhere above it floated shoulders and a head, but he stopped there. Here was enough. He didn't care whose shirt it was.

# CHAPTER 3

It was rumored that the Writers' Union would formally protest Mandelstam's arrest. A meeting was scheduled, then postponed—once because of a newish and unexpected work holiday, then again when the acting chairman developed a head cold. Bulgakov had not returned to Mandelstam's apartment though he made inquiries around the Union. The exchange of information was generally the same. Most lamented the event. All secretly desired to know what Mandelstam had done to bring such disaster upon himself, though only a few asked, and then with varying degrees of delicacy. It was clear to Bulgakov that they'd not heard of the poem. Of course those who knew would not be asking questions. He heard that Nadya had met with Bukharin, but reports of this differed. His own play had been delayed by additional edits that Stanislawski had requested. The director seemed to be taking arguably random trips to Crimea, and with these and various other excuses Bulgakov worked on the changes alone and worried. Occasionally he walked past the DRAMALIT house. He counted the frames of glass that made up the third-floor windows, guessing at those which would be Mandelstam's. Generally it was at night and their panes were dark. He shrank from risking Nadya's vitriol. Several weeks later, an unsigned note appeared in his postal box; it gave only a date and a time. There was something about the script; he guessed it was a woman's. Was it Margarita's? It was written on the back of a line of verse that was in Mandelstam's hand. He could envision the masculine arm that had made those strokes; he could hear the words shaped by his voice. It was a reminder of his loss and an inducement to attend. He studied the other side of it as well. It was hope that she might be there too.

Bulgakov was modestly late and yet the second to arrive. The conference room was at the top of the stairs leading from the foyer of the Union's first floor. Sounds from the kitchen funneled up through the stairwell and into the room, lending an impression of greater activity and purpose than it deserved. Its only other occupant was the Chairman's assistant who sat mid-length along the oblong table, writing into what appeared to be a composition book. The room's window casements had been left open and were filled with the streetlight's amber color; drab and stained curtains hung through them and over the outside sills. Despite this, the temperature within was stifling.

"The Enhancement Committee meeting has been moved to Room 24," said the assistant. He gestured with his free hand, over his head.

"Has Berlioz returned?" said Bulgakov.

"He extended his holiday by a month." The assistant appeared neither dismayed nor surprised by this.

"And the Acting Chair?"

He repeated his earlier gesture, then went back to his writing. Bulgakov settled into a window ledge as a makeshift seat. It seemed safer somehow; his escape route, no matter how precarious, at his back.

Over the course of the next three quarters of an hour, a half dozen others joined them. Some took refuge in the window casings as he did; others sat somewhat uncomfortably around the table. One asked another the time, then, after receiving an answer, checked his own watch. Bulgakov was about to leave when Margarita came in. Her eyes flicked over him and he was left with the immediate impression that despite whatever secret they might share from that other morning, she was skeptical of his motives, perhaps wondering herself why she'd bothered to deliver the note.

The acting Chairman entered: Leonid Beskudnikov, an essayist who specialized in historical pieces. He directed his first question to the rightful Chairman's secretary, asking if there was yet any word of the other's return. The reply was the same as before and the essayist looked visibly uncomfortable. "What are you doing?" he asked sharply of the secretary, as he appeared to be writing with great energy.

"I am minuting your meeting," he said. Beskudnikov's discomfort went to the extreme. "I don't know if you can call it *my* meeting," he said. "This seems more of an informal gathering. Quite informal." He searched the room for agreement.

The novelist Poprikhen, an amply sized man, leaned back in his chair. He appeared neither unhappy nor frightened. "Do we know exactly what Mandelstam did?" he asked the general audience. Others leaned in, hopeful of gossip. "Maybe he deserved it," he said. "I think that should first be established."

"Seems like it's always the poets," sighed Natasha Lukinishna, a diminutive woman with round glasses, who wrote naval stories under the pen name Bosun George. "What else can they write about except how unhappy they are with the world?"

Poprikhen wagged his finger at the others around the table. "Not everyone is a saint and it's not always the wrong person who is detained. They must get it right sometimes." With this, several began to talk simultaneously. Beskudnikov held up his hands but was ignored.

All conversation stopped. Nadya entered, accompanied by the poetess Anna Ahkmatova. Both were in black. Anna's hands were clasped around Nadya's arm, but she looked to be the one in need of support. Nadya's posture, and in fact her entire demeanor was poker-like, while the otherwise stately

Akhmatova was as bedraggled as a refugee. Beskudnikov rose, followed by the others; the women sat near the head of the table and the rest resumed their seats. Their effect was funereal. Everyone avoided making eye contact and struggled to find something to look at besides the two women. After a few moments, however, no one could unfasten their eyes from them. Nadya seemed impervious, staring into some unseen world.

"Have you had any news of your husband?" Beskudnikov asked.

She took an inordinate amount of time to answer. "I've heard nothing specific," she said. Her fatigue was palpable. She told them she'd met with Bukharin three times. The third he'd asked what *she* knew, admitting he knew nothing more. The fourth he'd refused to see her. Someone with connections to the Secret Police asked her the rank of the agent who'd searched their apartment; evidently the higher the rank, the more serious the case. Another had made inquiries on her behalf, then was advised not to get involved. "I wait in line," she said. "I leave packages daily—I have no idea if they make it into his hands. I have no idea."

"Of course we want to do something," said Beskudnikov. He looked at the others, summoning a tone of chairman-like magnanimity. "We've discussed a collection—food, perhaps." He paused to judge her reaction to this. "Or prepared meals might be better. Someone suggested a collection of money." From a spot around the table came a noise of concern and he added, "Of course, for the needs of the household, et cetera; any monies from the Union couldn't be used—not that you would engage in illegal activities, but you understand, there can't be the perception that the Union has funded anything untoward—not that you would consider such things." He began to repeat himself, his tone weakening. Others in the room seemed to retreat from him as well.

Nadya readied herself to speak. Beskudnikov stared at her lips as though they were perilous things.

"Thank you," she said evenly.

He seemed to register her lack of loquaciousness as disappointment and his fearfulness shifted again. "Of course, we could do more," Beskudnikov went on. "We should do more. We could." He searched the room for agreement.

Clearly they knew nothing about the poem, Bulgakov thought. If they did, such a meeting would have never convened. He was annoyed; there should in fact be two Unions—one for those who were actually writers and another for people who simply placed words on a page. Mandelstam had stepped forward. He'd sacrificed in defense of all of them. Yet they would call it something else. They would assign it a different motivation—discontent, naïveté—to make their lack of action defensible.

"The Union could pen a letter to the editor," he suggested. "A formal protest—*Pravda* would be best. It's read by the world." Those with their backs to him swung around in their chairs. Beskudnikov appeared to be seized by terror.

"You, of course, would be its author," Bulgakov went on. "As the Union's Chair."

"Only the *acting* Chair, you understand. Something of this nature should really come from Berlioz, I believe." He'd gone pale.

"Who knows when he'll return—that could be too late."

*Too late for what?* The gathering seemed to register his words with a kind of belated understanding; several glanced at the door as though thinking to leave.

Poprikhen shook his head with grave significance. "I don't see how a letter can be fashioned if we don't know exactly what he's done. What are we to protest? This all seems quite ill-conceived." He glared at Bulgakov.

"He wrote poetry," said Margarita.

"Well, there it is," retorted Poprikhen nastily.

"I'm not certain your opinion matters here," Beskudnikov added faintly to Margarita. "It's not entirely clear why you are here, seeing as you are not a Union member."

Bulgakov had some vague recollection she wrote for one of the daily newspapers. They had their own union, of course. "She's with me," he said quickly.

Nadya's gaze shifted to him. Her face was impossible to read.

"Regardless," he went on. He stumbled for a moment. "Regardless—of whatever he did, do we allow even one of our members to be arrested for the act of self-expression? Otherwise we might as well invite monkeys to come in and do our job."

"I agree," interjected the dramatist Glukharyov from the corner. "So they don't like what he writes—they're allowed *not* to like it. Censure him, censor his work; but arrest? Are we now back to the practices of the Tsar and his thugs?"

There was a clamor of voices, then Poprikhen's rose above it. "You know what Mandelstam writes—we'd be fools to align ourselves under that banner."

"And if you were to be arrested," said Bulgakov. "The rest of us should sit back and collect canned fruit for your wife and family?"

Beskudnikov began to protest but Poprikhen's retort pushed him back. "There is precious little chance of my arrest," he growled. More than one Committee member considered himself the novelist's patron.

"Indeed, what a grand loss it would be for Soviet literature if you were," said Bulgakov.

Poprikhen gave a wordless roar and attempted to launch himself toward Bulgakov, though he became entangled with his chair. The din rose until Beskudnikov stretched himself over the beet-faced novelist, essentially sitting on him and preventing the match of words from becoming a fistfight. The secretary continued to write, madly flipping pages and wiping his sweating brow. "Stop it!" cried Beskudnikov, to no one in particular. Eventually the room quieted. Gingerly he dismounted from Poprikhen's lap and resumed his seat.

"Stop it," he repeated, though the room was now silent. He adjusted his suit jacket. "There will be a box, placed in the foyer downstairs for the collection of foodstuffs, for the Mandelstams. In the meantime," and he stretched his neck as though recovering from his recent gymnastics, "Comrade Bulgakov will draft a formal letter with some representative *suggestions*. This committee will review it in one week's time." With that, he stood and fled the room. The secretary remained at the table, still scribbling.

Others filed after him. Poprikhen extracted himself from his chair and slammed it under the table. "You are stupid to make enemies," he said to Bulgakov.

"Better that than to be plain stupid," said Bulgakov after him. The novelist seemed not to hear.

Nadya and Anna departed and the rest of the room emptied, except for Bulgakov and Margarita. He wondered what he'd been thinking. Perhaps he should follow Beskudnikov down the hall and beg off his assignment. He had edits to complete, a director to satisfy. Margarita considered him with what seemed to be the same skepticism as he felt. He thought to tell her that her suspicions were well founded

"You were right to say what you did earlier," she said. She appeared almost sympathetic to him. As though she understood his anxiety, his desire to retreat as the others had. As though she could forgive him for this and would offer a parcel of her own faith to feed his courage.

For the first time that evening, perhaps since the arrest, his furtive need to hide lessened.

She didn't move, studying him. "I'm not *with* you, though," she said, strangely gentle, almost amused in her correction of him. "On that point, you are wrong."

But she could be, he thought. She might be. And with this a different kind of fear overwhelmed him. He felt the night air at his back. The heat of her presence pressed against him like a hand to his chest.

"You'd probably survive the fall," she observed easily, as if aware of his impulse. Or perhaps at the spark of a thought to dart across her brain: that she herself might push him.

But she turned and left. And for the briefest moment, the evening became infinitely less satisfying because of his survival.

Mandelstam stood in a grey concrete cell in a shallow pool of water tinged with his blood and urine, his hands shackled to a rope that hung from the ceiling, his feet chained to the floor. He'd not slept for what he thought had been several days. A series of guards watching him from a slot in the wall saw to that. Behind him, beyond his view, the door to his cell opened. The chief interrogator, an assistant, and a smallish man carrying a pad and pencil entered. Typically, it was this last one, the stenographer, who would collect the confession; however, this was unnecessary. He was there to collect names; already he'd amassed a good number. Mandelstam waited. A rubber mallet sailed up between his legs. His knees buckled; his shoulders seared in pain. He heard screams. Slowly he found his feet again. Beating him had been easy for the interrogators; their fists rose on the updrafts of his words. He had been poetic in his venom for their beloved leader; they were now poetic in their rage.

Vomit and perspiration stained his shirt. The stenographer sat down in the only chair in the room and waited for the crying to subside.

Mandelstam heard a gentle scratching. He couldn't make

sense of the noise. It seemed the room rustled with insects. He wanted to listen, to decipher their language.

Pain exploded again in his genitals. The insects fled screaming.

Then: "Mikhail Bulgakov," said Mandelstam. The scratching returned.

# Chapter 4

One of the poems Margarita found at the Mandelstams' apartment had been written about her. She'd kept it apart from those she'd given to Bulgakov. She recognized the early draft, different from the published one. It was an early version of his love.

Reading it reminded her more sharply of its dissipation.

They'd taken risks in being together. She remembered a midsummer's party at Nadya's parents' farm. She hadn't planned to attend, but he'd insisted; even if they couldn't be together he wanted to be able to see her in that landscape. She remembered Nadya pretending not to know; or perhaps fortifying herself against it. And she, likewise pretending. She remembered their embrace, the pressure of the other woman's arm against the back of her neck. Their speaking of some childhood memory they shared as though they were actually talking about that. Osip approached them then, greeting her, slipping an arm around his wife's waist. Margarita blushed and he beamed, as though it was his doing. All seemed dangerously transparent. Later, when his visits to her apartment came less frequently, she sensed in him a recalculation of these risks.

She remembered him telling the story of a former lover who'd burned his belongings. He described looking down from his apartment one morning and seeing the clothes he'd left with her, the books, a notebook, a few gifts, aflame in the street. He smiled as one who was mildly perplexed, yet not sufficiently bothered by the mystery to give it more thought.

"I would never do such a thing," said Margarita.

His expression was of muted skepticism. How could either of them know of what she might be capable under these unexplored circumstances?

"Why did she hate you so much?" she asked.

"I have no idea." He responded as if the thought itself was exhausting.

How was it that this man who could not commit a lie to the page found it so easy to lie to her?

Several months later, she would ask why he didn't simply break it off with her. Why not say the words. Say that he didn't want her anymore.

He ran a finger up the length of her thigh. Of course he wanted her, he said. He looked amused at her misery. Who wouldn't want *this*, he said, trying to push his finger through the fabric of her undergarments.

She shoved him away and he got up to leave.

"What's wrong with you?" she said.

He'd rather invite her hatred; he'd rather she set fire to his possessions. Somehow it was easier this way. Somehow he could go on writing poems about love.

# CHAPTER 5

The child awoke in the night crying and out of the darkness his mother took him in her arms and chided him. They were only fireworks after all, she told him. She called them "sticks of fire" and he could make no sense of her words and the sounds from the street below their apartment. He breathed in her sour smell. She rocked him, shushing, saying *you are not a baby* over and over, but the rippling booms were muted by her arms and chest and he thought for that night perhaps he would be a baby and he clung to her and allowed himself to cry a little longer in order to keep her there. She seemed to know this and she kissed him on the head and promised him sweets to eat in the morning.

The next day, the table was set for a party and small cakes decorated with red sugar were distributed among the plates. He was told it was Comrade Stalin's birthday and he must make a special wish for their leader's health and happiness. He thought about this as he ate his cake while the grown-ups talked and he kicked the table leg absently until his mother told him to stop. He listened to her speak of his uncle who lived in a distant town called Magnitogorsk. He'd been recently promoted. A sprinkle of sugar fell on his arm and he licked it and his skin was smeared with red. He licked it again and the smear widened.

A photograph of Comrade Stalin hung between the bookcase and the doorway. After the meal, he stood below it and studied it carefully. Their leader's gaze extended over his head, surveying their room with an expression of concern. Behind him, his own father was telling a joke to some neighbors who'd joined them for their meal. The boy knew the ending well though he didn't understand its meaning. He pressed his hands together and concentrated on the face on the wall as if he could fix it there.

"I wish *you* health and happiness," he whispered, echoing his mother. But deeper, in thoughts he couldn't shape with words, he wished to be encompassed within the Great Man's expansive concerns; he wished to be included in his gaze, as his mother's arms had held him before, and remain therein his child forever.

Letter writing to their nation's leaders had become a bit of a pastime for the average Soviet citizen. They wrote when they'd been unfairly passed over for a promotion or when the goods store in their district was lacking in a certain item that was apparently in healthy supply in the town where the writer's cousin lived. They wrote about their lack of living space in comparison to a particular neighbor, usually a person of questionable background (the wife's brother had been a priest or a kulak or a count at one time), who they suspected was reporting more occupants than who actually lived there. They wrote about the hooligan youths that lived in the alleyway alongside their building and harassed their mother on her way to the markets—there must be a work farm for them somewhere, some canal that required digging. They wrote about the policies their government had most recently applied, providing their own opinions as to their potential workability and success, with suggestions for alternative methods that should be considered. The recipients of these letters varied from deputy heads of various ministries to committee members to the Secretary General himself, and despite the awesome bulk of these communications, citizens were encouraged to write them. It was a means for the government to determine the outlook of the people; and aside from the large and unwieldy network of informants that it used, it was its only means. Indeed, it wasn't uncommon for a new policy to be launched then shortly revoked following this kind of appraisal of the public sentiment. It was never clear with a new initiative who had been its author until it was found to be unpopular and summarily pulled back—in which case it was nearly always the idea of some mid-ranking bureaucrat who in short order was found to have some blemish on his record explaining his grotesque lack of affinity for the Soviet people and resulting in his disappearance from the political stage.

As for the letter writers themselves, one can only guess what particular satisfaction they took in penning their observations, complaints, concerns, and advisements. It is perhaps notable that the vast majority of the population had only a few years earlier been living in small towns and villages; indeed in the minds of most Soviets, despite massive translocations to urban areas, the world was still small and accessible, and because of that, malleable. They could imagine their leaders collecting their mail from their boxes just as they did; sorting through their letters, coming upon the one they'd penned and reading it straightaway with great interest. The fact that replies were rarely given didn't matter; they preferred their leaders stay occupied with the administration of the country, yet if a certain policy was dismantled, or a particular person disappeared in the night, our letter writer would pound his chest among his friends and say, yes—that was him, that was his doing.

Bulgakov began to think of it savagely as the Mandelstam letter. He had decided to take a dispassionate approach; cool intellect would have the greater appeal. By no means would he mention the poem. He thought to point out how poorly it served the government to place its writers under lock and key, how free thinking fed creativity, which fueled innovation which would be the engine of Soviet success on the world stage. Which all sounded well and good, he thought, but needed to circle back to the specifics of Mandelstam's detainment. He went through many drafts, and when he read them with the impassive eye of a Party Leader, the unspoken arguments for keeping the poet incarcerated seemed stronger. He referred to their greater humanity, to their superior compassion, to their modern outlook—old-world leaders might put their writers in front of firing squads; but *they*—champions of the new age, they would instead allow for dissent, even welcome the discussion, for they were beyond the need for bullets to enforce their way. Indeed, if their way was best, such things were unnecessary.

He'd lost count of the different drafts, holding his head in his hands. He added a final paragraph, in desperation it seemed—*Writers by their nature love their country but if their countrymen no longer have affection for them, then perhaps the better answer is to allow them to emigrate.*

He sensed the danger in those words—the suggestion of self-determination. Where the pen had come to rest, a blot of ink began to spread across the page. It would require rewriting again.

He'd not heard her enter. Margarita looked as though she'd wandered into a forgotten gallery of a museum near closing. When she saw him staring she blushed, caught in the act of her trespass. "It was open," she explained. She lifted a hand to a book on a bookshelf.

"You've become quite famous," she said. "Everyone is talking—did you know?"

He suddenly wished to discard all of the drafts. "Wonderful," he said. He tried to sound unaffected but she seemed to see the distress in his face.

"Everyone admires you," she said. "You stood on principle. Many agree with what you said."

"And someday they will be happy to donate a jar of jam on the behalf of whatever remains of my family," he said.

"No doubt," she said lightly. She refused to fuel his self-pity. "How is the letter coming?"

He gave it to her. She read it twice then handed it back. She'd resumed her expression of general encouragement.

"Well?" he asked.

She hesitated. "I'm sorry—I thought you were a better writer."

"I am a better writer." He scanned the page himself.

"It's not particularly convincing."

"I'm trying to appeal to their logic."

"Because it was their logic that led to his arrest in the first place?"

"Perhaps I'm not the one to write it," he said. He dropped it on the table, glaring at it where it lay.

"You are the one." This was a sad truth it seemed she was forced to explain. "You loved him. No one else will write it better."

Was it true—was he the best Mandelstam had? He should have left behind a better friend for this.

"Would you really leave?" she asked. "Those last lines."

"I wasn't writing about myself," he said.

Though perhaps he had been. He'd considered it before, in moments of frustration. He imagined himself in a Parisian cafe, scribbling on a roll of pages, foreign words darting over his head. Their country harbored many artists writing freely. Here was another with a strange accent. This one who pined for his Russian coffee. Who had to count out his coins so carefully.

Then what—he could write but would they read? Were his concerns too parochial, too Russian in their nature? Would they be relevant in another land? He could imagine his work being met with tacit interest, himself a passing phenom even. His audience would be curious about his world. They would then go home with glad relief that it was not theirs. In a foreign place, his words would fall on stone. They'd not last a fortnight.

But to write freely!

Her expression was of one who both questioned his motivations and easily understood them. He could see a kind of calculation taking place, a loss in some measure of trust.

"Leaving is complicated, isn't it?" he said.

She turned to go and he was taken by a sudden sense that the room would become difficult to bear once she'd left it.

"Please don't," he said. "You've just arrived. Would you like some tea?"

She hesitated over his books. "No." This was drawn out, as if she was making her decision as she spoke. "I should probably go."

"You don't have anywhere you need to be."

"You don't know that," she said with mild surprise.

"Some coffee then?"

"No, no thank you."

"Vodka?"

She smiled a little. "It's not about the beverage."

He got up and guided her to the chair. "Well, I'm certain it's not me," he said.

She took the offered seat, still amused. "Tea would be nice, I suppose."

He turned to a low metal cabinet where his wife had kept tea and various other utensils safe from mice. He hadn't opened it since she'd left. The door gave some resistance and he looked inside as one who might find something possibly unpleasant. He got on his knees and began to go through it. This could take some time.

"Margarita is an interesting name," he said. "It's uncommon." His voice echoed from within the cabinet.

"My grandmother's name. She was French."

"You could have been named for *Faust's* Marguerite." He turned back to her, his search paused. He wanted to tell her it was his favorite opera.

"Things did not end so well for her, I think," she said.

"I've always thought that the story should have been told from her perspective. She's the more interesting character. Who cares about the old man?" He looked over her face, her figure, much as an artist would. Inspecting its lines. Where it held light, where there was shadow. The story would begin once he'd divined its first sentence.

"You could be her," he said.

She seemed to grow self-conscious.

"Your story would end differently of course," he said. Why was it so difficult to have a conversation? What did normal people talk about?

He remembered from Mandelstam's apartment her scent, the darkness under her sleeve. The things she'd done.

She glanced at the door. He changed his tone.

"In truth," he said, "I find there are few writers who can comprehend the female spirit. Either on the page or off it."

He wanted to reassure her. She was quiet for a moment.

"I saw *The Days of the Turbins*," she said. "It was a number of years ago. I remember the sister, Elena. *Your* Elena. She was so real. Even today she could walk through that door— right now." She stared at it, her lips parted. "I'd be not at all surprised." She looked back at him; admiringly, he thought. And grateful. As if he'd created the character for her, and with this one creation he'd given her hope for the eventual understanding of all women. Or maybe just one woman; maybe just her.

Her gratitude, if it could be called that, seemed to shift then to embarrassment. Perhaps she'd gone on too long.

"Thank you," he said. He looked back at the cabinet,

uncertain if it would produce even a spoonful of tea. How else could he keep her there?

"Is this too much for you?" she said.

"I don't usually make tea for others," he confessed.

"I see."

"I do have friends—but they know not to come here for tea."

"I suppose it's encouraging you have friends."

He found a tea set and canister. He suspected it was empty. He smiled confidently at her.

"I managed to have two wives," he said.

"And this would be an appealing quality?"

He set the tray on the table in front of her. "I'm better at beginnings than endings."

She opened the canister then showed him its shining interior. "Is this part of your method?"

"Vodka is usually more effective."

She made to leave; not in an unpleasant way, not in the way of one who would not be willing to try again perhaps, but as one who'd lost their reason for staying on that particular evening. But he knew if she left she'd never come back. On her way home she'd ponder their few encounters and remember his behavior in Mandelstam's apartment. She'd remember their peculiar conversation about her name. If she saw him again perhaps the memories would be vague but she'd not be tempted to leave any current companion with the purpose to greet him. Later still, he'd become someone she'd met once before and if asked, she would answer no, she didn't remember much about that meeting. In the end, she'd say she thought he'd been a friend of Mandelstam's and it had all been so long ago.

He straightened as she stood. His only hope was to give her the truth.

"I have another confession," he said.

She might have thought he was admitting to other domestic shortcomings, but when she looked at him she became more serious.

"I've been wanting to meet you," he told her. "For quite some time actually."

He could see she was surprised by this. She blushed a little.

"Is it so difficult to meet someone?" she said.

Perhaps he blushed too. "As horrible as all of this is—and it is horrible—a small part of me is glad that it's brought you here."

As quickly as her face had warmed with his words, it cooled in consideration of their larger circumstances. Hurriedly, he asked her to dinner. He hoped she wouldn't think too hard on the specifics of their situation and consider being with him a disloyalty to Mandelstam or a belittling of his arrest. He hoped she'd say yes as a kind of reward for his own confession. Or perhaps feel sorry for him, as he was attracted to someone who did not yet feel the same way; he could see she had that capacity. Or perhaps—just perhaps—she was attracted as well. He didn't care which of these might be true; he only hoped there'd be one, and because of it, she'd answer yes.

She agreed to dinner. She made it clear this would only be a meal. There was the letter to discuss, and he had failed—miserably, in fact—on his promise of tea.

The restaurant was smoky and dim and seemed smaller than he'd remembered. The trio playing in the foyer was loud and poorly balanced. He asked if she'd ever been there but he didn't hear her answer. They were seated in the back near the kitchen; he'd requested a better table but the waiter raised his hands at this impossibility. Bulgakov ordered soup for them both. She thanked him. He knew this by watching her lips shape the words.

The song ended abruptly; it appeared that the bassist had

lost a string and was without its replacement. The instruments were put away and the musicians retreated into an alcove to argue with the manager.

The lack of noise seemed to fill his ears and at first when she spoke he couldn't hear. He leaned closer. He thought she smiled more easily than at his apartment. The candle between them was set in an ordinary dish; it illuminated her face in a way that was particularly agreeable. She repeated herself. She was going to order the sturgeon.

A muffled crash came from behind them, followed by a second, more distinctive shattering of china, and the swinging doors of the kitchen opened and roughly extruded a large man, a patron. He turned unsteadily and appeared at once to both gesture rudely and apologize profusely to those who'd just cast him out. All who were seated turned in curiosity. The doors swung inward then reflexively out again, and the man, who by any standard was inebriated, sprawled against a nearby table as if trying to escape their reach, upsetting a glass of wine on the blouse of the woman seated there. He stared at her bosom as he pushed himself up and muttered that he liked her dress. Her dinner partner threw his napkin to the floor in anger but did nothing else. The drunken man appeared not to notice and catching sight of Bulgakov's half-amused, half-concerned expression he stopped. His face was ruddy and shiny and loose as a child's, and he looked at the same time both belligerent and half-asleep. He leaned over Bulgakov and it seemed he might topple on their table as well. At the last moment he swayed back.

"The sturgeon," he said, nodding, as if he shared Bulgakov's concerns. He made a face. "It's inedible." He gestured toward the kitchen. "I warned them." He then noticed Margarita. She looked up at him pleasantly, then away.

The man muttered, "Perhaps your appetite lies elsewhere."

"We've not ordered," said Bulgakov. He kept his voice amicable and gave a conspiratorial air. "We'll be wary of the sturgeon, though."

The drunkard turned his attention back to Bulgakov as if trying to understand the meaning of his words, then burst into laughter, and Bulgakov was left with the impression that the man's amusement lay not in what he'd said but in the fact that he'd tried to converse at all. The man slapped him on the shoulder as he moved away. "You do that," he said, and he went back to his table. His companion, a younger woman sitting near the front of the room, appeared unaffected by his behavior. She leaned close as he spoke, then, seemingly on cue, looked at Bulgakov with interest, as if she'd just learned he was a test pilot or an amateur parachutist. Someone who might at any moment die an extraordinary death.

"Would you rather leave?" Bulgakov asked Margarita. He hoped she'd say yes. He felt their evening had been blemished in some way.

"What an astonishing person," she said, staring across the room.

He was surprised by her choice of words and followed her gaze to reassure himself that they were speaking of the same person.

"No—I want to stay," she added, "—and I have every intention of trying the sturgeon."

He thought to talk her out of it—bad fish was bad fish even though freely given advice might not always be the most reliable—but she ordered it. Midway through their meal a bottle of wine appeared; according to their waiter, it was given with the apologies of the man who'd earlier disturbed them. A solid vintage, he said, though Bulgakov suspected he knew little to nothing about wine. The cork broke, however, with half remaining lodged in the bottle's neck, and the waiter's efforts to retrieve it only resulted in it being pushed back down into the wine. Bulgakov watched it bobbing through the dark glass as the waiter poured.

Margarita held the bowl of the glass in her hand. The wine swirled red along its walls.

Bulgakov hesitated. "I'm thinking of a toast," he said, lying. He fingered the glass stem. He wanted to say something about her.

"There is only one," she said. "To Osip's release."

With that they drank.

The wine was slightly sour, threatening to turn. As he lowered his glass, the drunkard was standing between them.

"Thank you for accepting my apology," he said. "Most gracious. May I join you?" He pulled over a chair from the table vacated earlier by the doused woman and settled into it rather heavily. "With sobriety comes regret, I'm afraid." He seemed somewhat more articulate, though his face was as red as before and his eyes still as glassy. A glass was brought for him.

"Where is your friend?" said Bulgakov.

"Annuschka? She is my neighbor. She is a working girl," he said. "She must be off."

"Thank you for the wine," said Margarita. "It's wonderful."

Her assessment surprised Bulgakov. Perhaps she was only being kind. Bulgakov tapped his glass and nodded. "Wonderful, yes."

But it was clear the man heard only Margarita. Despite his size, he'd draped himself in the chair and over its arm, leaning toward her in a manner that could be considered almost graceful. Bulgakov decided perhaps he wasn't as large as he'd originally thought; that instead it was his raincoat, grey and unadorned, that provided the effect. For a moment, he had a fantastical imagining of what form the man might actually take beneath it.

Margarita's words drifted to him through the fog of his thoughts. She was going on at some length about modern poetry, respectfully though at a superficial level as one might adopt with those of a general education. He wondered how they'd come to that subject. He listened as though he had missed some critical connection that was unlikely to be revealed again.

Had the stranger overheard their toast of Osip?

She spoke of Gumilev and Akhmatova. She didn't appear to notice the man's stare. They were notorious dissidents, but the man reacted as though she had listed the ingredients for soup.

It was possible—he told himself—that the drunkard was no one in particular.

Margarita continued seemingly unrestrained by such worries and his nervousness increased. He made a noise, and she turned to him expectantly as if he'd disagreed with her.

"Wonderful, yes," he said again. His words came out weakly.

The man gave a vague smile. He shifted in his chair and attained equipoise between them both.

Perhaps he was no one.

"Is she still alive?" asked the man, referring to Akhmatova. She'd been popular for a time he remembered, then, it seemed she'd vanished—and with this he waved his hand—"like a fad." Margarita assured him that she was very much alive and still writing.

"Remarkable," he said. He didn't sound terribly impressed. Margarita glanced past him at Bulgakov. Her eyes had brightened with conversation. She seemed not to notice the flatness of the man's tone.

He looked at Bulgakov. "Are you likewise a poet?" He apparently had little admiration for this, the question asked in politeness.

"He is a playwright," she said.

The man's response showed a bit more enthusiasm. He

admitted he did enjoy a good play. Had he seen any of Bulgakov's? He was always reluctant to ask—there seemed to be a great many more plays being written than could ever be performed.

Bulgakov wanted to say that he suspected not, but Margarita answered for him.

"I should think so. He wrote *Days of the Turbins*."

It seemed for the first time that night, the man's reaction was genuine. "So that was you," he said, with both interest and incredulity. "You are younger than I would have guessed—but perhaps not." He seemed to appraise Bulgakov. "It struck me as a rather—and don't take this poorly—but as a *personal* piece. Well-constructed, though." He conceded it'd made for an enjoyable diversion. There was an evasiveness to his manner, in the movement of his hands across the table, the adjustment of his position in the chair; Bulgakov sensed a vague dislike or resentment. He was unable to guess its basis.

"Perhaps we have met before," suggested Bulgakov.

"No—I assure you—we have not," said the man.

Bulgakov was again struck by his sincerity, all the more startling for the earlier conversation he'd observed with Margarita that had seemed to lack it.

The man went on. "What are you working on now?" There was something about the tone of his question—as though he already knew the answer.

"The MAT is producing my newest play."

Margarita reached across the table and touched his arm. Her face filled with admiration. He wished they could be alone.

"What terrific news," he said. "I will look for it. What is it called?"

"*The Cabal of Hypocrites*," said Bulgakov. "It's about Molière, set in the French court of Louis XIV."

The man seemed mildly perplexed, as though Bulgakov had

said something wholly unexpected and what he'd next intended to say no longer applied. "I beg your pardon—what is a *cabal*?"

"A circle of intrigue—for lack of a better expression, I suppose. A group of conspirators."

Again, he seemed at a loss for words. "It's about Molière, you say? I vaguely remember learning something about him in school."

"He was a comedic playwright, highly satirical; he suffered from censorship; repression by the priests, the religious." The man's reaction was blank and Bulgakov hurried forward. "Of course there is also humor, a love story, betrayal—I suspect it may not appeal to everyone," he added.

"Are we to assume then that the hypocrites—a cabal of them, you say—are the authorities? The establishment? And the poor writer is a victim of the regime? There is an intriguing theme."

In the drunkard's words the plot sounded rather two-dimensional and Bulgakov began to question its structural integrity. "It's not a political piece, if that's what you mean—not at all. As I said, there is comedy, absurdity, romance." His voice trailed off, rethinking his opening scene.

The other man laughed aloud. "You can't be serious? How can it not be political?"

The implication of his words—and now he sounded anything but drunk—shifted Bulgakov's worry. "It's simply the historical backdrop," Bulgakov explained. "It was long ago—a different time—another country—it's not my intention to make some sort of political statement."

"Well—I'm certain there are those who will want to see it," said the man. Bulgakov registered the truth of his words, their warning. Indeed, while he might pray for its success, that would only intensify its scrutiny. He felt slightly queasy.

The man turned to Margarita. "You keep company with

one such as this?" He indicated with a nod toward Bulgakov that this could be a questionable enterprise. His tone was difficult to interpret. Was he trying to be funny? That seemed to be his desire only there was a heaviness to his words as though he lacked practice at this.

"I assure you it's not political," Bulgakov repeated.

The man appeared finished with that conversation.

"A girl has to eat," said Margarita lightly with a shrug. She smiled at Bulgakov, in case he might take offense. She seemed not to have noticed their darker exchange.

"Is that all that's required to gain your company?"

Her reaction to this was strange. She withdrew; the crease in her brow deepened and Bulgakov wondered if there'd been something in the man's words to which he'd been deaf. It had seemed he was only playing off of her humor. She acted as though something entirely different had been said.

"Of course not," she said, her manner turning cold.

The man responded immediately.

"I've upset you. Please forgive me." He leaned toward her. "That was not at all my intent. I have been clumsy. Please, my dear—"

"Perhaps you should go," Bulgakov suggested.

The drunkard ignored him. His words to her were soft and insistent. He was not simply apologizing, rather he was entreating. "I would never intentionally hurt you."

She hesitated. "Of course," she said. She smiled a little as evidence of this. "Of course you're forgiven."

Her words seemed to carry restorative powers. The man raised his glass first to her with gratitude, and then Bulgakov. When their eyes met, Bulgakov sensed in him a kind of admiration, though for what he wasn't certain; the man then looked away and in that Bulgakov detected something darker that lingered, a competitiveness possibly. He might have imagined it. The man took his first taste and immediately spat the wine across the table. Margarita and Bulgakov both recoiled. The man roared to the waiter and several new bottles were produced. Glasses were replaced and refilled. The man lifted his again. "To better wine," he said after a moment's thought. All three drank.

He told them his name was Ilya Ivanovich. They talked at length, and after several hours and equally more wine, they were the last of the patrons to leave. They parted at the door. Later, Margarita would wonder aloud if they'd ever see him again. They both would comment on how neither of them could remember what he'd said of his occupation. Margarita would suggest that perhaps it was the wine that had caused them to forget. She seemed to want to speculate further about the man, but she refrained. He wanted to ask about her exchange with him and the supposed offense. It was as though the specifics of that night would be irretrievable by morning. They stood at the door of her apartment.

"He was rather old," said Bulgakov. "For the girl he was with, I mean."

"I don't know," said Margarita. She seemed mildly distracted.

"Annuschka—that was her name."

"Hmm."

Her cheeks were flushed; she was clearly distressed.

"What is it, my dear?" He was alarmed by her reaction.

She shook her head, then covered her mouth with her hand, as if it would be impossible to explain.

She was sick, and for the rest of the night and into the morning hours he sat beside her on the floor of her apartment, wiping her face with a cool cloth, smoothing damp hair back from her forehead, from time to time rising to carry the bucket to the bathroom for disposal.

Not long before dawn she lay curled on the rug; her head rested on his lap. He thought she was sleeping. He'd turned off the overhead light. The sky outside her window was a steady grey; inside, darker forms took on unrecognizable shapes. He watched them in the way one would monitor large, slow-moving creatures in the wild. He'd guard them both against their bulk and the advent of their sudden and arbitrary disregard.

He thought of Ilya in his grey raincoat.

"How can one know?" she said. Her voice rose up from the floorboards.

"Know what, my dear?" He stroked her head.

"The fish—when it's starting to turn. How can one know that?"

He didn't have an answer for her.

"People can warn you—and they do," she said. "But how can they know? Yes, there is a risk, but I'm not giving up fish." She lay quietly for a moment, then added:

"I'll not live my life in fear of fish."

The gray in the window had lightened. The beasts surrounding them were once again a chair, a sofa, a table strewn in clothes.

"I thought we were talking about the sturgeon," he said quietly.

He could dream of their life together, in a small cottage by a stream. Writing with a quill pen; listening to Schubert every evening. And every evening the soft light from a green-shaded lamp reflecting inward from the night's dark window-glass. He could see her in that reflection; leaning over him, her hands resting lightly on his shoulders, urging him to come to supper; he could feel her warmth through his shirt. In the afternoons, they would sit at the water's edge. The weight of their bodies would crush cornflowers into silvery hollows. Turbulent currents fighting to break the surface would pass them unawares.

In his dream-vision she sat, her arms wrapped around her legs. The sun bore down on her like a spotlight in an already bright space; shadow still puddled behind her. She stared

intently at the rushing waters—he could not tell if with longing or dread. She seemed utterly alone—he wanted to move
toward her, place his arm about her shoulders. Something held
him back.

He awoke to her gently shaking him.

CHAPTER 6

Margarita sent him home that morning. She assured
him she was much improved, saying they both
needed sleep. She glanced at his cheek before closing the door, as if she had considered kissing it, then decided
otherwise. He waited for a moment, imagining her on the
other side. He imagined her scanning the empty room, the
loneliness of the space, then turning to call him back. He imagined her brow, creased with worry that he'd already departed.

Instead he heard the muffled harrumph of bedsprings
receive her.

Outside it was still early and pedestrians were rare. The
morning was cool and fresh and he paused at the apartment
building's entrance. The earlier foreboding had passed and he
considered with some pleasure how in so little as one evening
it could seem that all aspects of one's life had changed for the
better. He thought of the play. He tried to recall the drunkard's
words—what was his name? And what could he know of literature? Bulgakov was filled with a renewed confidence. Did not
Stanislawski himself select his play for production? The
esteemed director who'd first staged *The Cherry Orchard*? His
life *had* changed for the better, and he thought he would walk
rather than ride the tram so he might better enjoy the morning's loveliness.

Movement across the street caught his attention. Someone,
a man, stood in the verge of an alley between two buildings. He
lifted an arm as if to light a cigarette, then lowered it—perhaps

too quickly—it was this movement that seemed strangely aggressive. The man then, as if aware he'd been detected, retreated into the shadows.

Someone was watching her building. As quickly as it came to him, he discarded the thought; it was fatigue that made him paranoid, he was certain. He stared at the alley's entrance, and without effort the thought returned with greater vigor. Not only was someone watching but they were waiting for him to leave. He thought of Margarita, asleep and vulnerable, the bedsprings now silent beneath her.

He crossed the street and entered the alley. The sky above narrowed to a thread. It was empty and smelled lightly of refuse, ending in a small cul-de-sac made up of the back entrances of other buildings. He considered that it had simply been a tenant who'd wanted to escape his own family for a quick look at the day. A door opened and a babushka emerged with a heavy rug in her arms. She draped it over a railing and began to beat it with a broom. The dull, hollow sound seemed to linger in the closed-in space. She eyed him malevolently, then, unexpectedly, stepped aside and gestured with her thumb that he should enter the door behind her. *Who did she think he was?* The door was partially open. Dare he enter? He could go back to the street. The old woman's expression was unchanged; she wasn't helping him by this; as far as she was concerned, he and those like him could all go to the devil.

The hallway was narrow and poorly lighted. Several doors were open and their doorways were filled with their occupants, as though their morning had already been disturbed by an earlier trespasser. The smell of rubbish was stronger inside. Near him, a woman holding a small boy regarded him silently. In the room behind them, a table was set, their breakfast half-eaten. It appeared they were alone. Tacked to the wall was a paper icon flanked by brackets for candles. The woman looked away.

He wanted to reassure her. He wouldn't tell anyone—she could trust him—but she might have thought to hide it. Hang it in a closet. Or behind a landscape painting. Indeed, what did her husband think of such a display?

She looked at him as though he'd spoken aloud. As though she was challenging him. At least she hung hers on a wall, she could say. Where an icon belongs. What about his faith? What did he believe in? Was it buried in some play about a sixteenth-century playwright?

The boy in her arms sucked on two fingers and stared at him. He seemed curious rather than fearful, too old to be held in such a manner. The boy took his hand from his mouth and reached for him, catching hold of his cheek as though for the purpose of inspection. Bulgakov felt the stickiness of saliva on his skin. The boy's smile widened to reveal the gap of his missing upper teeth. A man's voice came from another doorway further down the hall.

"May we see your papers, Citizen?"

They thought him some kind of official.

"Did someone else come through here just now?" he asked. He avoided a presumptive tone. He tried to ask as though he was himself lost.

*"Intelligentsia."* The whispered sneer came from behind, from the walls. Were there others he could not see? Listening through the plaster? Apartments overflowing with the displaced and the poor? He'd heard Stanislawski speak of them; they filled his theater each night. They had come from the villages and farms at the height of the famine. They were wanting in the knowledge of the use of cutlery and soap. They were curious. Curious and distrustful.

The boy had removed his hand and now both arms were wrapped around his mother's neck. He pressed his head into her chest. He seemed childlike again. The woman stepped inside her door and closed it until only her face could be seen.

"Why should we tell you anything?" she said.

"He might be dangerous," said Bulgakov.

"Your papers?" the man repeated. "It's within our rights." He was likely the local Housing Chairman. The woman opened her door slightly. The boy was no longer in her arms.

The woman turned to speak to the boy; she told him to go into the other room.

Down the hall there was movement from others. Bulgakov's escape seemed less certain.

The woman opened her door further.

"Perhaps you are the dangerous one," she said. She sounded more confident. "Perhaps you should be reported. How can we know the difference?" She seemed to think she knew.

Bulgakov's skin prickled. "Just tell me if someone else came through here before me—tell me who they are?"

Someone tugged on his watch chain. An old man, hairless and pocked, had crept beside him.

"Nice," he said of it. He rubbed it between his fingers. He had no teeth.

"A gift from my mother," said Bulgakov.

The old man pouted, clutching the chain. "I didn't have a mother," he said.

Bulgakov was about to correct him: everyone has a mother. Something stopped him. Further down were others, invisible before, now creeping forward, growing bolder. Behind was the same, as though to block every exit.

Who were these people, all at once vain and pitiful, self-important and distrusting? Were these for whom he wrote? They seemed ready to rise up from the gallery and take the stage in their name as if it were a battlefield. To take it apart if they chose. It wasn't that they might fail to understand the subtleties of his metaphor or be lacking in interest. They understood. They were interested. They proclaimed themselves both judge and executioner.

*"He's a spoiler,"* said one.

He felt hands encircle his arm. *"Why don't you stay with us?"* said another. Someone snickered with this.

Bulgakov passed through them roughly and came to a short flight of stairs, then upwards to the outer doors that provided an exit to the front of the building. The sun was bright and momentarily everything was washed in white. The street was as before; no one showed any particular concern with him. A man passed on the sidewalk; then turned sharply and took him by the shoulders.

"You!" the man spoke with great enthusiasm. "You are Bulgakov! Are you from my neighborhood? I had no idea you were my neighbor!" He looked around as though there might be others to introduce him to, but the sidewalk was empty. The man was now pumping his hand. He said he was a writer as well. Bulgakov vaguely recognized him from the Union. He clasped Bulgakov's shoulders again; he seemed intent upon maintaining some kind of physical contact. Bulgakov was relieved and grateful; it felt as though he'd been plucked from the depths.

"I heard about what you said," said the writer, he lowered his voice a little. "At the Union. To Beskudnikov and the rest of those hens. It needed to be said. But come—" he resumed his former tone. "May I buy you a coffee? You've already had breakfast?—I see." He looked temporarily disappointed as Bulgakov shook his head.

"It's a terrible business about Mandelstam, terrible," said the man. "One of our greatest poets—the man should be treated like a treasure. I suspect they get a bit overzealous at times—who knows? Perhaps they have some quota they're required to fill—I've heard that. They just need to be made to see reason. Everyone one can be made to see reason."

The sidewalk around them was empty. This man's presence seemed uncomfortably convenient.

He went on. "Say, my mother lives just around the block.

She'd love to meet you. Do you suppose?" He grabbed his arm again, as though he might drag him there.

"I should get on," said Bulgakov, trying to pretend amicability. "You're very kind, though."

"Not at all!" He continued to hold onto Bulgakov's arm. "They act as if they're afraid of him," he said. "It's all quite nonsensical. They need to see reason."

Bulgakov pulled away. "I've held you up. I should let you go—you must have other matters—I'll let you go."

Bulgakov crossed the street without bothering to look. A car was required to brake and honked in protest.

The other man was still on the sidewalk, watching him. He called out cheerily, "It was wonderful to meet you."

Bulgakov studied him from the other side. He thought he'd recognized him from the Union, but had he? It was hard to tell from that distance and it was a nondescript face. "What is your name again?" shouted Bulgakov.

The writer waved, but didn't answer, and Bulgakov wondered if perhaps this was the man he'd been following in the first place.

Initially the agents knocked on the wrong door. The older neighbor averted his eyes and redirected them with a crooked finger. The agent leading the team was annoyed at their sloppy intelligence. When they knocked next on Bulgakov's door, they waited not at all before he gave the command to just open it. The one that first entered commented on the high ceilings. So hard to find in the newer buildings going up now in Moscow.

A criminal waste, growled their leader. He swept his foot along the skirt of the armchair. He took a book from the bookcase, opened it in his hand briefly, then tossed it aside. He waved the others further into the apartment, then swept the entire shelf clean. Books clattered into a heap. A packet of papers toppled forward to rest flat on the shelf. He took it and seated himself in the armchair; he crossed one leg over the other in a somewhat delicate manner and began to read through the pages. Across the room, the drawer from the bed-table rang out as it hit the floor.

Bulgakov lived on the top floor in the corner apartment of a repurposed nineteenth century house that had once belonged to the paramour of the Dutch Vice-Consulate to Russia. His particular space, at one time the modest spare dressingroom of its former occupant, was oblong in shape though still had good light and was of sufficient size to fit the Moscow code for the standard housing allowance without requiring some crude refashioning of partitions or walls. The room formed itself into two spaces by a decorative archway that spanned the narrower of the two dimensions. The larger space was beyond this division; here Bulgakov's bed fit into the far corner, next to it a small side table with a single drawer; its spindle legs were obscured by multiple stacks of books. On the wall a modern utilitarian sink had been added later and with remarkably poor workmanship. The newer plaster used to fill the oversized hole lacked the creamy texture of the original walls, and was perpetually collecting on the floor in irregular powdery piles. No effort had been made to repair the wall below it. Since Bulgakov had lived there, the spigots hadn't produced a drop and he suspected the pipes were never connected. A table with chairs sufficient for two, or in a pinch, three, if the third was willing to sit on the bed, was pressed against the wall. On the other side of the arch, nearer the door, a short sofa with an armchair made up a small sitting area with a squat table between. Bookcases stood on both sides of the chair. These were filled and double-layered, with yet more books in varying stacks on the floor in front, as if waiting in queue. Squeezed between a bookcase and the archway, a narrow wardrobe fought for space.

Few remnants of the room's previous Dutch life remained: the floorboards along its perimeter were finished with a row of

Delft tile; each square was slightly larger than a woman's hand, painted in shadowy blues and baked in the kilns of that famous factory town. Each was a quiet and singular scene of bucolic seventeenth century meditation without repeat. By some miracle of neglect or more likely ignorance, not a single tile was missing or damaged save one. As if with the thoughtlessness of a blind scalpel, the piece had been parted in two with a gentle curving swipe, leaving behind a young Dutch maiden, holding in her hands the strand of pearls she wore, extended upward, to show to her vanished partner. Another maiden? Her mother? Some young man who'd come to woo her? She was forever alone, her gaze held captive by those opalescent whorls now long divorced from their meaning.

When the agent had finished reading, he leaned forward in the chair; the collection of papers in his hand he'd rolled into a baton. The rest of the apartment was unrecognizable. His gaze came to light on the fragment of tile along the baseboards. A remnant of another time; so many clung to these kinds of things. He rubbed his eyes. What was the take, he asked of the others, as if tired of it all.

Numerous manuscripts. Poems from the poet Mandelstam. A few letters. In truth, little of interest.

"Good," he said. He stood and slipped the roll of pages into the side pocket of his raincoat. One of the agents asked if he'd like to keep the poems. "No thank you," he said, his hand loosely touching his coat pocket.

He told them to wait for the writer's return.

Bulgakov's first impression when he entered was that his apartment had been quite suddenly enlarged. The walls were bare and open and very white. Then he saw the books were gone from their shelves, the prints from the walls. They lay thick on the floor, like ancient tiles pushing up and sliding over a shifted landscape. Two agents waited, dressed in dark suits, one sitting in his armchair, another on the sofa. It was impossible to tell for how long. First one stood, then the other.

Bulgakov asked if he might leave behind a note, a possible explanation. But he stopped there; he didn't want to suggest that someone in particular might be looking for him.

The agents told him no and for a moment he was relieved by their answer.

They nodded toward the door and his relief disappeared.

# CHAPTER 7

In the fall of 1917 Nadezhda was pretty and slender, with large dark eyes and good skin on which she prided herself. She worked as one of the typists on Stalin's armored train. She'd bully him when he came back to their car with his revisions and corrections. She called him the Great Man; she'd complain of his handwriting, his atrocious grammar, the things she had to put up with. The other girls would giggle and watch them together. She'd smile and lean toward him. They were old family friends; she'd known him since childhood when her parents had sheltered him during one of his escapes from Siberian exile. He gave his work only to her. "Perhaps you can teach me," he'd say, and wag her chin between his fingers. She was sixteen and living away from her mother, filled with purpose and unafraid. She saw how the men feared him; her fearlessness placed her above them.

At night, however, when they worked alone on his speeches or his party communications, she was all business. "You alone I trust," he told her. One night he tried to kiss her. He'd come for the latest revision of a memorandum; she rose from her chair and handed it to him. The last several changes had simply been the rephrasing of a single sentence; he'd gone back and forth with it. She'd made the changes without complaint; *the preponderance of evidence of their crimes against the people calls for the execution of these four men.* In the alternative version, there were four men and a woman. The tapping of her keys took a life then gave it back. She watched him read over the words. The car was dark except for her desk light; he held the page under it. The train lurched and she swayed. He commented on the hour, how she must be so terribly tired. He brushed his hand over her head, her hair, seemingly with absentminded affection. She told him she was fine. It pleased her to be a help. To him with his important work. With her words, he turned to her, lifted her face, searching for her lips with his. She stepped back with surprise and his groping became awkward. He stepped toward her. Her legs pressed against the desk behind her. The lamp clattered against the typewriter, shining light across the room. She panicked and turned her face away and he kissed her cheek. He stepped back and wagged his finger at her.

"I'll tell your mother on you," he said, smiling.

"I'll tell my mother on you," she said. Her words carried a breathy seriousness and with them he changed; his face stilled and she was sorry for having said them. He stepped back further and thanked her for her efforts. She didn't want his thanks. He told her to get some sleep now. She didn't want sleep. He took the page with him. The woman would die.

In the weeks that followed, she sensed his affection for her had cooled. She no longer teased him as she had before. He gave his work to other girls of the typing cadre. They did not complain as she once had. She felt herself sinking into a pool filled with the others.

One night, weeks later, they were celebrating the Red Army's victory over Kiev. In the dining car of their train there was liquor and dancing. Stalin sang a Georgian lament. Nadezhda watched from across the car, unable to catch his eye. Later that evening, he flirted with a communications officer, a tall Tatar girl. The girl sat somewhat rigidly on the edge of one of the booth seats; he leaned over her, one hand against the top of her seat, the other on his thigh, as though waiting for its occasion. Nadezhda put off the advances of a young lieutenant. She waited until Stalin had retreated to the back of the car to replenish his drink and she followed him there.

In the near darkness of the corridor, she plucked his sleeve. He smiled at her easily, she thought, as if she'd slipped his mind and now that he remembered it was the same as before. His eyes were glassy with liquor. She took his hand and led him into the lavatory. She locked the door, undid his belt and lifted her skirt for him. She wasn't wearing her undergarments. The cool of the air against her skin was surprising. She was a virgin. She watched somewhat distantly as his square hands reached for her bare hips. This was what she'd wanted.

Later, shortly before they married and after one of the rows for which they would become famous, she sat on his lap and touched his face, smoothed his hair back from his forehead, and kissed him on the cheek where the redness from one of her earlier slaps still remained. She laughed lightly. "I told Pavel, if anything happens to me, anything, you know. It would be you."

His waxen face never moved with her words. The moustache lifted slightly; it was almost imperceptible.

She knew in that moment she'd condemned her brother and his family as well as herself.

One agent drove. The other sat in the back beside Bulgakov; this one stared out the side window as if bored. Flattened cigarette butts littered the floor around his feet; the agent shifted occasionally in the cramped space. The air had a dusty odor. Neither gave any indication of their destination. The car seemed to be of its own mind as they negotiated the grid of streets. With each turn Bulgakov hoped to detect some reaction from the agents. By all appearances, for all their concern, they could have been transporting livestock or corn.

A horizontal crack extended through the side window,

transecting trees and buildings and pedestrians. They passed a woman with a perambulator; a lone man in a suit sitting on a bench, his arms crossed over his chest. A breeze lifted and threatened to dislodge the man's hat. They disappeared beyond the edge of his window with their smallish worries. He did not figure among them. On the seat in front of him there was a smear of something—possibly blood. They did not care.

They passed the Moscow Arts Theater. A single workman on a ladder was using a long pole to dislodge the lettered tiles from the theater's marquis. The word *Cabal* had already been removed. He, like his play, could easily disappear. Beside the ladder the box of tiles waited, bearing the scrambled hopes of some other writer.

The car slowed. They drove through the gates of the Kremlin. His escorts straightened, then; they faced ahead, alert, as if aware of the possibilities.

They drove past the Cathedral of the Annunciation and the Cathedral of the Assumption to a small, more modern building. They parked and entered. There, his papers were reviewed and he was searched, thoroughly though not impolitely, then conducted on foot to an annex of the Armory. From within, the low long building appeared to be a motor pool, with twenty or more sedans parked at a slant along the interior perimeter, a variety of models, all modern and expensive. In the center of the garage stood a particularly beautiful vehicle, a convertible; it crouched, golden brown, on low haunches. Bulgakov did not know its maker. Its hood was propped open and a mechanic was bent over it. His escorts stopped inside the door; they gave no further instruction. One remained expressionless. The other, the driver, regarded Bulgakov with what seemed respectful curiosity. Across the room, the would-be mechanic straightened and called to him, and the driver looked ahead.

"Bulgakov—lend a hand, man. What? Afraid of a bit of grease?"

It was Josef Vissarionovich Stalin, General Secretary of the Central Committee of the Communist Party, Chairman of the Council of Ministers, People's Commissar for the Defense of the Soviet Union, the "Coryphaeus of Science," the "Father of Nations," the "Brilliant Genius of Humanity," the "Great Architect of Communism," and the "Gardener of Human Happiness."

The Great Man laughed and waved him closer.

Bulgakov recognized him, of course, then thought—absurdly, really—he was thinner than his pictures portrayed. A measurable breadth of time seemed to pass before he understood that he needed to approach. Stalin waited, motionless, and—it appeared to Bulgakov—with a manner of tolerance that the powerful will extend toward their supplicants. A sympathy toward those more fragile beings.

Of course he was nervous; even Stalin could understand this.

His sleeves were rolled past his elbows like a workman's. His hands were streaked in grease. Bulgakov stopped beside the car; its open body lay between them like a bathtub.

Stalin leaned toward him. "Do you know anything about cars, Playwright?"

He shook his head.

Stalin lowered his chin. "Neither do I." He smiled. "Much to the sorrow of my chief mechanic."

He wiped his hands with a cloth and closed the hood. He opened the driver's-side door and extended his hand to Bulgakov to join him. Bulgakov got in. Stalin took the place behind the wheel.

"Perhaps we'll tinker another day," he said. He no longer smiled, only started the engine. His words seemed to mean something else.

A strip of light appeared down the center of the far wall; the large garage doors moved apart as if compelled by his fancy, and they drove into the sunny midday. The brightness was momentarily dazzling. They went past palaces and gold-domed cathedrals. Stalin was talking about the car.

It used the Hotchkiss drive, unlike the Phantom I that used the torque tube. He held the steering wheel firmly as he drove. It was a matter of how to propel the car forward. The torque tube carried the force from the traction of the rear wheels turning against the road, to the transmission, and then through the engine mounts to the frame of the car. The Hotchkiss drive transmitted the force directly to the car frame through leaf springs. The Hotchkiss also used two universal joints instead of the one, providing a smoother drive. "You getting this, Playwright? It's a matter of how we push the earth away." He nodded. It was he who moved the world; he liked that idea. "You know nothing of cars, do you? You've heard of Piaquin? The painter? No? Well you won't now, either, I suppose. Piaquin was like you."

Bulgakov had heard of Piaquin.

Stalin turned from the wide boulevard onto a smaller road, tree-lined, driving away from the buildings. Loose rocks from the roadway twanged against the mounts of the body work. The engine droned in a continuous metallic yawn. The road was empty of pedestrians and other vehicles, and the car accelerated; the wind roared in their ears. Stalin raised his voice to be heard.

"Had him under the hood. God knows what the fool thought he was doing." Stalin released the wheel and held up his hands to Bulgakov, knuckles forward, his fingers folded into his palms. "Chopped off his own fingers in the fan blade." Stalin laughed, incredulous. He dropped his hands back down to the wheel. "Every single one. Blood everywhere. A damned mess. And the sobs. I told him he could hold the damned brush between his teeth." He fingered the leather for a moment. "Hold the brush in your teeth, I told him. Should've worked. I think it should've worked. Sound advice. It would've worked." He glanced at his side mirror. "He managed to tie the noose with his teeth."

A bird flew low across the road in front of them. There was a muffled slap as it hit the grille. Bulgakov scanned the passing trees; there was no one else around.

"Why does my favorite playwright wish to leave his homeland?" Stalin looked ahead as if the question was for the road. Or the world beyond it. He seemed to wait for the world to answer.

Already he'd seen the letters, or perhaps just that last draft with its final words.

He went on. "'*If a writer cannot publish, perhaps he should go somewhere his work will be accepted.*' Or some such nonsense." Rather melodramatic, didn't he think? Self-indulgent as well. This was not a time for self-indulgence.

Bulgakov waited until he was finished. Later, he'd consider that he should have simply agreed with whatever Stalin had said. He'd wonder why he thought he could converse with the Man. By all appearances they were two men. Did they not ride in a car together as two men would? He would wonder if somehow he'd been deceived; that the humanlike appearance of Stalin had duped him somehow.

Instead, he tried to explain. "My work does not pass the censors."

"Then write what can." Stalin's words were stiff. Bulgakov sensed disappointment rather than displeasure.

"I am a satirist," he said. Strangely, he very nearly added, "Father."

"I have no use for satirists."

If Stalin had affection for him, he sensed it in that moment, in those words. There was no apology in them, yet they were more than simply matter-of-fact. They were words of caution from a man who provided no warnings. Even to a recalcitrant wife who'd become a political liability. She'd been found one sunny day like this one, in a pool of old blood, a gun near her hand. The medical examiners were tortured until they agreed to list the cause of death as appendicitis. Afterward they were executed anyway.

Stalin slowed the car and pulled to the side of the road. The sound of the wind stopped.

"Get out," Stalin said then, cheerfully, and he motioned for Bulgakov to go around to the other side. "Do you know how to drive? I will teach you." He maneuvered into the passenger seat. Bulgakov hesitated at the door's lever, but could think of nothing to say and got in.

The steering wheel extended towards him, over his lap, yet seemed uncertain of this arrangement as well.

The road ahead glowed. Trees rose up on both sides. The sky paved blue overhead.

"Are you nervous, Playwright?" said Stalin.

The world stood with mute alertness; it was nervous for him.

He instructed Bulgakov on the placement of his feet. The engine roared momentarily, then stalled. He went through the pedals once more, and again started the engine. This time the car lurched forward.

"Easy, easy, there you go." The engine purred. Bulgakov looked up at a sizeable tree as Stalin grabbed the wheel sharply. "You have to steer as well," he said. Bulgakov took his foot off the accelerator and the engine stalled. Stalin restarted it.

After several tries, they were driving along the straightaway in second gear. Bulgakov rehearsed the rhythm of the pedals in his head as they drove. Before them, the road turned abruptly to the right; the wall of the fortress lay in their path. Stalin was talking; Bulgakov wasn't listening; he was anxious to slow the car without inadvertently heading into the stone.

"You should seek work as a librettist and a translator," said Stalin. He seemed unconcerned about the barrier in their path. He said he would make the arrangements.

"Should I—" Bulgakov's feet wobbled over the pedals; the car groaned.

"Well, of course. I imagine the Theatre Director will wish to meet with you. I can't comment on the specifics of how these arrangements come about. I imagine you will need to ring them up." He sounded annoyed.

Bulgakov's world was losing air. The wall ahead grew in size, seeming to taunt. Would he try to run through it? Did he think he could? He'd better stop short, play it safe, live a bit longer. Go home and write a catchy score.

Though, if he wanted to, go ahead—try to break through.

He touched the accelerator and the engine squealed in protest.

"Damn it, man. The brake—"

Bulgakov stamped down. The car shuddered—with uncertainty or relief—and the engine died. Bulgakov stared at the wall.

Stalin gestured toward the door. "Lesson's over," he said. Bulgakov went around to the other side as he slid into the driver's seat. He drove them back toward the garage. The breeze hummed over their heads. He rested one hand on the steering wheel, the other out the open window.

"I like you, Bulgakov. Do you know why?" He smiled, waiting for an answer. The foliage rushed past behind him. Bulgakov found himself staring at his mouth. He could not dream of a reply.

"You make me feel smart." He seemed triumphant in this pronouncement, as if providing the solution to a troublesome puzzle. His smile turned slightly. "You may be the most brilliant writer alive today. Some say that. Some say I should trust none of you. Yet *somehow* you make me feel smarter." Stalin's gaze moved past him, into the woods alongside them. He grew more serious. "Perhaps that's why you're still here." With the writer's expression, he laughed aloud. The road opened into the larger Ivanovskaya Square. Pedestrians raised their heads as though they'd heard his laughter too.

"You are like the rabbit," said Stalin. "Happy in your burrow, fearful of the sky with its owl." He seemed pleased with himself for conceiving of this. He looked at Bulgakov again as if to verify his hypothesis, then nodded. Yes, the rabbit.

The car approached the low building; the doors opened. Stalin stopped outside and turned off the engine. "You have a wife?" Bulgakov shook his head. Stalin smiled. "But there is a woman," he said. He tapped his finger on the side of his brow. "That is all a Bolshevik needs. A good woman. Good purpose. This you have." He stopped smiling. Again he stared off to the side, beyond Bulgakov. "Perhaps if you got smarter, things would change." He turned to the writer directly. His eyes trembled slightly beneath the thick brows. "Don't try to be smarter than me." Then, the skin around the eyes broke into scores of tiny lines. He smiled again and leaned toward him slightly. "I might miss you."

Bulgakov felt flattered and alarmed; beloved and yet perfectly disposable. How did one measure that kind of standing? Was Piaquin beloved? Were similar endearments bestowed on Mayakowsky and Gorky before they disappeared? How did he rank among his peers in this?

"What about Mandelstam?"

The sound of his voice first startled, then frightened him. It sounded a thin bravado; an outlay of currency he could ill afford. There was no other sound, no bird, no passing motorcar. Nothing else in the world dared to speak or offer a needed distraction.

Stalin got out. He moved slowly, as if he'd aged. A driver

appeared, but Stalin waved him back. He turned and leaned on the door. He stared at the floorboards near Bulgakov's feet.

"What about him?" said Stalin.

"Will you miss him?" Again, his words were wildly disengaged from his better sense. They seemed determined to sound out the space of that affection, as though by such he could measure his own worthiness.

Stalin shook his head. "No. I won't." He studied Bulgakov.

His was an honest answer. Mandelstam did not make him feel smart.

"Truth is," he confessed. "I don't understand most poetry."

First the thought came, *Mandelstam is lost.* Then, with growing despair, *We are lost.* The value of each of them, their loves and desires, their efforts and failures, would be measured by this one. *The one with the cockroach on his lip.*

"Will you miss him?" Stalin asked.

Here was his opportunity.

From above came the rhythmic chirping of a bird; a single note, a relentless pinging against his brain like the rapping of his door. They were here for him. Just on the other side. They waited for his reply. He needed to answer.

Stalin seemed curious now, his eyes bright.

What was there to say? *Of course! Yes!* Such words should be shouted. Osip was his friend—his mentor—his champion. He loved him. Of course he would miss him. He would miss all of the particulars about him. The world would miss him too, though that would be a vaguer thing, distant and sadly diplomatic.

He imagined speaking the words aloud. How that face before him would change—the eyes would cloud. Earlier declarations would be reconsidered; affection that had been professed would be reassigned to another. Something within him quietly reasoned—Osip had created his own future. He didn't share his beliefs. He didn't care to share his fate.

*Would he miss him?* A small place in the world would be vacant; a beautiful and loving mind blotted out. Every day, such things go unnoticed.

*If he said it*—he imagined the scene—agents would come in the night, deliver him to a prison. There would be a fabricated charge. Torture and a mock trial. Then eight years in a penal colony. Sentences were often doubled for inscrutable reasons. Hard labor underground scraping nickel from the earth; his skin turning white like paper. There would be no pen, no ink. Only chalklike flesh.

Arrests were made for far lesser things.

The breeze lifted for only a moment. The day was absurdly beautiful.

*If he answered*—what difference would it make? It wasn't by his word that locks would be undone. That Stalin would exclaim *I'm sorry—I didn't know. You'll miss him? Then of course I shall free him. Immediately—come—we'll make the call together.*

And if he was silent. The sounds of the world would continue. The bird. The car. They would fill the stillness. It would go unnoticed.

He remembered Osip's shining head. Could he leave him again—here—when his voice might actually matter? His shoulders drew in. They were his words to say.

"Will you?" Stalin repeated. His voice seemed to fill his military tunic. The very flesh of his face, his cheeks, seemed to grow. Every whisker became defined. Every pore to be counted. There was room for only him.

*Would he miss him?* Oh God. *Oh God.* He could have spoken those words.

Instead, irrevocably, he pressed his lips shut.

Stalin smiled; but before this, there was a flicker of something akin to sympathy. A knowing. For a moment they were not ruler and ruled. For the first and last time that afternoon—

perhaps for a lifetime—they were two men understanding one another.

His cowardice, the most horrible of vices. For this, Stalin forgave him.

As if Stalin knew fear as well as any man and he could forgive Bulgakov for it.

For this Bulgakov's mortal life was made safe.

There would be no cottage, no green-shaded lamp, no Schubert softly playing. The cornflowers along the river would stand unharmed in unending sunlight. There would be no Margarita beside him on a riverbank. There could be no Margarita.

There could be no peace.

Again, Stalin tapped his finger against the side of his head. "Marry your woman and live quietly," he commanded. He pushed back from the car. Once again he was the smart one. He glanced at Bulgakov as though he'd spoken. Or perhaps, to make certain he hadn't.

*You can't hear our words.*

Bulgakov saw it in his face; it was barely perceptible. This was what Stalin feared. This was what would have him eliminated.

Faced with this, Piaquin had cut off his own fingers.

Stalin then smiled; whatever Bulgakov had thought he'd seen was gone.

"I like you, Bulgakov," he repeated. His gaze wandered past him. It seemed his declaration had surprised even him a little. He gave a small shrug as if to say, *So be it.*

Stalin left him in the car and went into the building. The two escorts returned and walked him to the sedan. They drove just beyond the Kremlin's gates and left him to find his way from there. Storm clouds seemed to appear from nowhere. It began to rain. The wind intensified; falling drops sped toward him with certain intent. His clothes became weighted by them;

his skin cooled then chilled. His head bowed; his apparent path was paved of wet and variously broken cement walkways.

Somehow he was expected to find his way from there.

*It was getting darker and darker. The storm cloud rushing toward Yershalaim already filled half the sky. Turbulent white clouds swept by in front of the thundercloud, which was bursting with black water and fire. Lightning flashed and thunder clapped right above the hill. The executioner removed the sponge from the spear.*

## CHAPTER 8

S
he was there when he opened the door of his apartment. For some reason, he wasn't surprised by this. Her presence had the same inevitability as the earlier rain.

Despite this, he wasn't prepared to see her.

She was refilling the bookcase. Around her, the small tables and dining chairs lay as if tossed; clothes and books were everywhere. He hadn't remembered the extreme wreckage. In that midst, she seemed unduly tidy: a simple skirt and sweater. Buttercup-yellow, he thought. It was becoming. Outside the rain had passed. Through the window, rectangles of sunlight stretched across the floor to her feet. He found he was still momentarily startled by the loveliness of her face.

Her expression was of disbelief at the sight of him.

Had she thought he'd disappeared too? He wanted to tell her, No. He wasn't another Mandelstam, it was clear. He was something else entirely. Something they were willing to let go.

"I thought you'd been taken—I thought it was happening all over again," she said.

"Clearly I wasn't."

She seemed disarmed by his manner, uncertain how to proceed. "But your things—this place—"

"I was looking for something."

His tone was dismissive and she didn't deserve that. She continued to hold the book in her hand. She looked perplexed, uncertain if she should place it on the shelf, or put it back on the floor. Or perhaps throw it at him. Yet she held it.

"I wanted to thank you—for last night. For taking care of me." She added this part, as though conscious of other possible interpretations. "It was kind of you."

Behind her hurt, an infatuation was revealed. He hadn't anticipated this; and she looked away quickly, not wanting to show that this was the real reason for her being there. "I hadn't expected that." She sounded embarrassed. Perhaps she was surprised as well. She put the book on the shelf.

He felt badly about his behavior. Her concern for him was genuine and well-meaning. "You're feeling better then?" he asked. She nodded.

"When I saw this place," she said, "you can imagine what I thought." Then her tone changed. "You're completely soaked through."

He took off his jacket and hung it on the doorknob. "I had a driving lesson," he said.

"A driving lesson? I might believe a swimming lesson. It's as if you took a bath fully clothed."

"It was raining."

"In the car?"

The afternoon light had set her aglow. Her hands rested on her hips. She was radiant and undeniable. She believed none of it.

He sank into the chair. "I'm sorry." He rubbed his face. "I'm sorry, I'm exhausted. Forgive me."

As quickly as she had challenged him, she softened again. She pressed his shoulder briefly; fatigue required no forgiveness. Explanations could wait. "May I fix you some tea?" she said.

He shook his head. "No, it's all right." He looked at her hand, wishing to hold it. Wishing for the possibility of a different life.

"Vodka, then?"

He smiled at their reflected conversation. "What—no coffee?" He took her hand then. He rubbed his thumb over her fingers. Their texture was that of a child's.

"I find vodka more effective for my purposes," she said.

She had hope for them, and in that, he could see the trajectory of their future. Their potential was real and if followed carried the certainty of affection and love and lovemaking. Only the man who'd left her that morning was not the same as the one with her now. She did not know this yet.

Her fingers interlaced with his, willingly.

Perhaps they need not speak of Osip; perhaps they could set aside that part of their lives, move on from it together. Perhaps he could be allowed to forget certain things.

He brought her hand to his cheek.

They could go away. Together—perhaps even emigrate. With time and distance they would both forget. Someday he would tell her what he'd done. She would understand. She would say it'd been so long ago. It'd been a different time. A dangerous time. At such a distance who could recall the missteps of youth?

"I have news," she said. "They are allowing Nadya to see Osip. Not alone, of course, but nevertheless."

Mandelstam would have no knowledge of his betrayal. Bulgakov need not dread their brief reunion, as though through it his shame might be revealed. No one need know.

He looked at their hands clasped—so many fingers, he thought.

"When did she hear this?" he asked.

"Not long ago. She's beside herself with happiness."

What did it mean? "I'm surprised they're allowing it," he said.

"Nadya believes Bukharin arranged it."

Was it really a happy coincidence? Or had his meeting with Stalin determined some other outcome? If the poet's dearest friend was not willing to speak for him, why should Stalin believe that others might? Was it now easier to execute the troublesome poet?

"Do you wish it was you?" he said. "Instead of her?" He wanted to ask if she was still in love with him. Not out of jealousy, but somehow it seemed necessary to pace out the dimensions of his own offense. Did it include her?

Her reaction was unexpected. She looked embarrassed.

"What you saw at the Union restaurant," she paused, as though still searching. "It wasn't what it seemed, I think. We'd been apart for some time. Both of us—neither of us had been particularly satisfied. Not for a long time."

She wanted to allay his concerns that should Mandelstam be released, she'd go back to him. That her heart wasn't being honest with his. She thought this was what he was asking.

He remembered the restaurant at the Writers' Union and Mandelstam's exceeding generosity and he felt a sudden rise of emotion. The eve of his arrest, possibly his last night of freedom in this world, and he'd chosen to spend it with him.

"Do you think he'll be released?" he asked her. This now seemed so unlikely as to be impossible and his asking of it all the more desperate, as though he had been the one who'd doomed Mandelstam. As though her optimism could save him. And in saving Mandelstam, save him as well.

She noticed none of this. She was coldly analytical in her reply.

"I don't know. A lesser writer would be exiled, I think. But he is well known. It's hard to predict if this will save him or— quite the opposite."

He remembered the recitation in the street. If it'd been written on a building, they'd knock it down to destroy such words. They'd decide it wasn't such a wonderful building. They'd build a lesser one in its place and proclaim it a palace.

"You don't think they'll let him go?"

"Why should they? Why would they risk whatever else he might say?"

"But if he promised—not to write?"

"Is that any different than locking him up?"

*And if he promised not to speak?* Bulgakov could hear Mandelstam's voice recite the lines. No one would be saved.

He had released her hand; he wasn't certain when he'd done this, at what point during her speech. The sensation of her fingers remained. How long before that would pass?

She crouched beside the chair and cocooned his hand within her own. As if he needed to be made still in order to listen. "Please understand—I think what you're doing is—well, it's brave. You're not pretending that there wasn't a crime committed here." She paused. "I'm proud of you."

She was thinking about the letter he was to write; believing this was his concern. He wanted to tell her that the letter had already been delivered; that its work was done.

"Don't say that," he said.

"But I am proud."

He remembered the empty slate of the theater's white marquee. What if he were never to publish again? He could tell her everything; confess his fears, his transgressions. She could redeem him. She had that power. If she could love him as a lesser man, perhaps he could tolerate himself.

"I'm certain whatever I do makes little difference," he said. He tried to sound as though he believed this. He tried to sound weary of it all. As though he'd pushed against the world and the world was resolute. *Tell me*, he silently begged. *Say there was nothing I could have done.*

"It makes all the difference." She took his face in her hands. "You know this."

And even if she loved him, even if she forgave him, she'd never be dissuaded from that bedrock of faith. And he could never survive on that shore.

"I think—I'm tired," he said. Her fingers slipped away.

"Of course." She patted him on the shoulder, then kissed

him lightly on the head. She said something about buying some food for them, preparing dinner.

He didn't know what to tell her. Then he thought of a lie.

"I will be out later," he said.

"That's fine," she said. "Whenever you return."

"I don't know when I'll be back."

He didn't know what she'd registered from this. He couldn't bring himself to look at her. The room was quiet. Then, after a moment, as though she'd come to some greater understanding, her words took on more certainty. "That's fine."

She made some excuse for her departure. He didn't press her. He suspected whatever her reasons, they were truthful; she would not leave with even the smallest lie between them.

He nodded and closed his eyes.

The latch clicked softly. He listened to her steps on the stairs; to the outer door close. The building seemed abandoned.

He was free to do whatever he liked. He was free to do nothing.

He opened his eyes. A sunny room awaited him.

# CHAPTER 9

O                utside Bulgakov's apartment, she turned left rather
                 than right, which would have taken her toward the
                 streetcars on Tverskaya Street. This seemed a kind of
act of defiance, though of what or who seemed vague. After
several blocks she came upon Patriarch's Ponds. Any other
day, she'd have continued past, not being one to sit idly in a
park. She ignored the path and cut across the damp grass; she
took an empty bench. The afternoon was already hot again
despite the recent rain. The sun, low over her shoulder,
seemed directed solely upon her. The water before her occasionally rippled; from the random fish, she guessed; there was
no wind. The seat was uncomfortable. No one else was
around.

An orange beetle crawled near her thigh. She offered the tip
of her finger and it climbed onto it. As she lifted it, it raised its
capelike wings and took to the air.

*Why writers*, she thought. Why did she think they might be
actual human beings?

A man came from behind and sat on the end of the bench.
She straightened a little; the slats of the seat were uneven and
pressed anew. She recognized him as the man from the restaurant. What was his name? She wished he would go away. If she
had wanted to cry, and she wasn't certain she did, she couldn't
now.

If he noticed her displeasure, he said nothing of it.

She remembered: Ilya Ivanovich.

"Your poet, Anna Akhmatova, her son was arrested today," he said.

She'd met him once—Lev Gumilev; he'd seemed a teenager at the time. That was several years ago. First Osip, then Bulgakov—there was the wreckage of his apartment—something had happened to him, she was certain. Now this. All seemed to be circling. "Why—what did he do?"

He leaned forward, his hands clasped. He stared at the water.

"Nothing." He turned his head slightly. "He's her son. That is his misfortune."

Before she could say anything, he continued.

"They will exile him." As if anticipating her question. "They will keep him alive. It should keep her in line."

She imagined Anna—the mother's reaction. My son—*my boy!* She remembered her from the Writers' Union. She would do whatever was necessary to maintain him. Everything that was necessary. There would be no question.

She thought of Osip. Should he be released, there would be the need to keep him in line.

She thought to ask how he knew. Of course there were only a few ways he could know.

There seemed then a growing acuity for her surroundings—the sunlight that glittered on the water became crystalline; from somewhere came the sound of its trickling; leaves which had hung limply from the tree branches now seemed cut with the precision of knives. The air itself nudged her skin into alertness; the hair on her arms rose. She was sitting next to someone dangerous. Dangerous in a way that was particular to her. She was afraid to look at him in case she might reveal this knowledge; she stared at the pond until her eyes began to water.

She wondered—was this a warning or a confession? She took care in the words she chose. "Why are you telling me this?"

"I don't know," he said. There was a mild incredulity in his voice, as if something unexpected had broken the pond's surface.

In the water, near its far edge, several feet from shore, the heat of the afternoon seemed to give shape to a figure. It blurred, then drew clear again. There were arms, a head; it floundered then sank. She started to stand.

"It's a child," she said. "There's a child, drowning! There!" She hurried around the pond's perimeter, vaguely aware he was following her. She watched the spot where she'd seen him. A boy, she thought. Playing too close to the edge. He'd gone in after a toy. The muck of the bottom had trapped his feet; he'd lost his balance and the water closed over him. Where was his parent? She came up and stared into it. The water was still. It reflected only sky. Ilya came beside her.

"He was here," she said, pointing. "Here. I saw him. He's gone."

"No one's here, Margarita," he said.

"He was here! I saw him!" She started in and he held her arm. He waded into the water and crouched low, spreading his arms below the surface as he went, searching. Water splashed noisily.

From a nearby kiosk, a woman's voice called over.

"There is no swimming in the pond, Citizen. Remove yourself immediately!"

He turned slowly, toward the voice. The woman stood a little ways from her stand and pointed at one of the many small signs placed around the water's edge.

"Do I look like I'm swimming?" he said to the woman.

"There was a boy," said Margarita. "A boy in the water."

The woman looked at her strangely. "There's been no boy. There's been no one. I've been here alone."

Ilya stood, the water came to mid-thigh, and he made his way to the edge. The top of his coat from the neck up was still dry, the rest below was flattened against his torso and a much darker grey. He seemed younger than before. Younger and more vulnerable.

The woman returned to her stand.

"I thought there was a boy," said Margarita. Ilya stood dripping next to her.

She tried to recall her vision of him but it was gone too, as if her memory had allied itself with Ilya and the woman. The water was silent, ripples from Ilya's movements reflected back from its edge and moved unhindered toward the center.

"When is the last time you ate something?" he asked her. When she didn't answer, he took her arm and led her to the stand. The woman stood waiting with an annoyed expression. All she could offer was apricot juice and it was warm. Ilya insisted she drink it. It was overly sweet like a child's medicine and she felt queasy, but he appeared quite earnest. Its frothy surface clung to her lips and when she wiped them, it stained her hand. He seemed pleased with her efforts. It gave her the hiccups.

Bulgakov rose and went to the table. He took a clean page from his folder and wrote a sentence:

*Early in the morning on the fourteenth day of the spring month of Nisan, along the roofed colonnade that connected to two wings of the palace of Herod the Great, walked the procurator of Judea, Pontius Pilate.*

His thoughts went to Margarita. Perhaps she had returned to her apartment; perhaps to the market first and then home. In his vision she had discounted him already. He'd done little damage. He saw her as she waited in a queue; behind her someone asked a question. It was a younger man, someone her own age. Something about directions—she gestured as she described the route. Bulgakov knew the man wasn't listening to her; the man watched her speak and was thinking instead of something else to ask her, something to keep her talking. As she spoke he moved a little closer; she would notice this, she'd suspect his interest, but his smile was warm and she didn't move away. This was how people talked to one another. They would keep speaking and around them common ground would form. This was how it was done.

Bulgakov placed his face down on the desk, his forehead against the page. As if he could take the words directly from his cranium and impart them there. As if he could be spared the need to think any of it through.

They were on a different bench than before. Ilya laid his raincoat over the back of it to dry. Each seemed lost in thought. She could provide no reason for why they'd stayed. Perhaps he was still concerned about her; the juice had helped. Soon his clothes would be dry. Soon they would leave, each in their own direction; they would part ways forever and she'd carry her knowledge of him with her.

"Why writers?" he asked her.

At first she was uncertain of what he was asking; then she understood this was about her romantic involvements. She wanted to say there was no particular reason. She stared at the water.

She wanted to correct him by saying Bulgakov hadn't been a romantic involvement.

Perhaps his question was a caution. She was reminded of the danger she'd felt before; the sensation was now a memory. She no longer felt any particular threat. She looked at his hand where it rested on his thigh. It was large and angular. It seemed itself a self-aware organ. She could envision it nesting a fledging bird; in her imagining his fingers curved around it, protectively. The bird's eyes in its downy face were black beads. It looked about, uncertain, yet not altogether protesting. Then, as though without reflection on their intent, the fingers closed in and broke the creature's neck.

He moved his hand to the bench between them and she jumped a little. He didn't appear to notice.

This was a man who represented everything she detested. Yet here they sat together. The sun showed no preference toward one over the other. The universe itself seemed ambivalent of them: one might survive, one might not; it was all the same. She'd not given thought to the concept of God in many years, yet He seemed at that moment to be utterly remote—not even a pinprick in the sky. It was easy to believe that He didn't have a preference either.

This was a man who *was* everything she detested. She didn't know the specifics of his involvement in the arrests of Mandelstam or Lev Gumilev—or others—but she could assume the worst. Yet she remained; she shared this bench with him. This planking, this park, this sun, this sky. Was he only an emptiness that was capable of intolerable deeds? What was missing in her that she didn't immediately leave?

Perhaps God was there, only silent. Silent and curious.

Ilya seemed to be waiting. She was about to answer as she'd first thought: there was no particular reason. But he spoke again.

"It makes it harder for the rest of us, you know."

His question hadn't been a caution.

His hand remained, resting against the plank. She watched it as one might a wild animal; something not inherently dangerous or with malice, but nevertheless unpredictable. She could be drawn to it, she thought, and she was surprised by this. Perhaps it gave some license for her own wildness.

Would she risk the touch of his hand on her neck just to feel it there?

It would be the heat and lack of food that turned her thoughts so strangely. When she looked down again, his hand was in his pocket and she was given over to the sense of something being forgotten or mislaid. Or something imagined; yet wholly unobtainable, just the same.

She expected never to see him again after that afternoon.

# PART II
## NEVER TALK TO STRANGERS

# CHAPTER 10

In the early years, the artists and intelligentsia were eager to remake the world in their leaders' vision. It was the dawn of a new century; the climax of a millennium. They weren't just Bolsheviks; they were Modernists, Futurists, Constructionists. The *Ivan Ilychs* of their past with their caged canaries and dusty rubber plants were to be plowed under in the building of a steel-girded utopia. The writer and poet Vladimir Mayakovsky believed the Revolution had quickened their future. His play, *Mystery Bouffe*, produced in 1918, dramatized the conquest of the clean and proper bourgeois by the grimy, stubble-faced proletariat. At its climax, the audience joined the cast onstage and with them destroyed the theatre curtain that had been painted with symbols of the old world. Spoke Diaghilev in 1905, "We are witnesses of the greatest moment of summing up in history, in the name of a new and unknown culture, which will be created by us, and which will also sweep us away. That is why, with fear or misgiving, I raise my glass to the ruined walls of the beautiful palaces, as well as to the new commandments of a new aesthetic."

In early spring of 1930 Mayakovsky was found in his apartment with a gunshot wound to his head. His death was labeled a suicide. In the previous year, he'd published a dazzling satire on Soviet behavior and bureaucracy, and was immediately damned by the authorities. His detractors concluded he'd be neither relevant nor even circulated in twenty years' time.

In his apartment that morning, the agent in attendance pressed the revolver's barrel against the writer's temple, then angled it slightly back, toward the opposite ear, to assure the kill. The writer's eyes bulged forward; his pupils darted repeatedly as if he needed to see the thing. He no longer made sense. Most pleaded until the end. This one instead over and over repeated, until there was only a mutter of words:

*What did it matter?*

The agent disliked poets in particular. Pick something, he told him. He thumped the table; it was strewn with handwritten pages.

The writer looked down, then seemed to understand. His suicide note.

*What did it matter?* The words softened to a chant. His hand touched a page, then moved to another, as if trying to recall something forgotten. He picked up his pen and added a line. He held it for a moment longer as he read over the words.

Mayakovsky looked at the agent and mouthed the question one final time. Only the question had changed. There was the smell of gunpowder and burnt skin. Eyes turned skyward. He fell from the gun's barrel as if indeed it'd been holding him up all along.

The poet's final question had been genuine. It was the one they all asked.

*When did he stop loving me?*

Stalin kept the poet's original note in the side drawer of his personal desk until his death in 1953.

Years later it was revealed that the apartment where Mayakovsky had been found had had a secret entrance within a closet. His lover Lily Brik had been an informant for Stalin's political police. The poet's death tolled throughout literary Russia with an unmistakable voice: there was no place in Soviet literature for the individualist. The land that had borne

Pushkin and Gogol, Tolstoy and Dostoevsky, Chekhov and Pasternak, fell silent.

It was Bulgakov's third banquet in as many months; these were Party affairs and though he was not a Party member it would be ill-conceived to decline the invitation. He had drunk too much at the last one and his suit jacket had disappeared from the back of his chair. He cursed himself for this; it'd been his second best, so when the invitation for the next banquet came on its heels and his other jacket was still with the laundry woman, he was left with his third, which, upon inspection, could hardly be called a jacket but perhaps the ghost of one, the fabric along its back seam so threadbare as to rip with the slightest pressure. He decided to wear his overcoat instead. The room would be dark, he determined, and once the liquor was flowing no one would notice or care.

This one was in honor of the novelist Poprikhen. Some newly-hatched award for his most recent effort. Bulgakov had written a letter to the editor of *Crocodile* in praise of it. He'd written many such letters, opining on the works of his various contemporaries and was surprised at the ease with which they made their way into print. He was also surprised by his colleagues' reactions. At the Writers' Union, he had become someone to know. Introductions and invitations flew about—"Gregor, Gregor! You must meet Mikhail Bulgakov—Come! Oh wait, you've missed him, but here he comes again from the bar, and this time you will have your chance." "Bulgakov—my man, next summer when we open up the dacha you will join us—now don't shake your head! Irini—my dear, didn't he promise? See—you've promised; my wife has the memory of an elephant. We have the best chef in the district—you will be as fat as a bathtub when you return—I promise you!"

Despite his frequent attendance at the Writers' Union, he

never saw her there. From time to time he would scan the room, registering each figure anew as though it was possible his memory might misrepresent her. He wondered if she was avoiding him. He could have gone to her apartment and he reasoned that he'd been busy with the novel and the play, yet in truth, he was anxious of her response. He could imagine her under his arm; he looked about at the women near him who wished they occupied that spot, and he remembered her face from the vestibule of Mandelstam's apartment. Her careful apportionment of hope and distrust. Would it now be entirely distrust? When it was determined that his play would be reinstated at the MAT, he sent her tickets to its opening. It was months away, but he liked to imagine her there in the seat he'd chosen, her face illuminated by the lights of the stage. He could wish she might come alone, but he doubted it, and had sent her a pair of them as a way of demonstrating this kind of understanding. He didn't allow himself the hope of her coming to find him backstage afterward, pressing her hand upon his arm, revealing in her eyes the wonder at what genius he'd achieved. He imagined theirs was a different kind of communion. It existed on a higher dimension.

He would then berate himself for these dreams; how pathetic they were! This was no way to live. He looked around at the swell of conversation and laughter—this was not how others lived. Already someone had drawn their arm around him—he joined their conversation, laughing as they did, at the expense of something he knew not what.

He arrived at Poprikhen's banquet late; the room at the Dynamo Club was already filled with people; tables were set in expectation of multiple courses; silver and glassware glittered under low chandeliers—yet, to Bulgakov's dismay, not even a single hors d'oeuvre had been passed. It all seemed a sad trick of luring together a room of hungry writers. Poprikhen appeared at his elbow; quickly he led him to a seat marked with a name card; it was next to his—the guest of honor. Poprikhen touched his breast pocket. Bulgakov wondered if he was yet beefier than before and if this could be possible without him actually exploding.

"It was my request," said Poprikhen, his hand to the back of Bulgakov's chair. "I know we've had differences in the past, but I credit you—" It seemed he might mint a tear from between his thick lids. "You, my friend." He would not try to finish. "Thank you!" he added huskily.

Bulgakov mimicked the other man, waving his hand in the general vicinity of his breast pocket. His fingers brushed the coarse fabric of the overcoat and he quickly stopped, not wanting to call attention to its oddity; nor did he want to prolong any false gesture of affection. He scanned the table; it wanted for no treasure other than food. Poprikhen seemed to anticipate his question.

"We're waiting," he said. "It is rumored *he* might attend." He could not suppress the joy from his words.

At that moment the heavy double doors of the club were opened. Half a dozen men firmly but politely pushed aside those standing near; on their heels several committee members entered. There was a whoop from the crowd, then loud applause. Bulgakov struggled to see—there between milling bodies; it was Stalin himself. *Oh dear god*, he thought.

Every exit was maintained by some semblance of guards or police. He could make an excuse that he was ill. They'd not deny him departure with that pretext. Poprikhen's hand closed around his forearm. His face was even redder than before; bursting with emotion he was nearly apoplectic. "This will be remembered as the greatest day of my life," he sputtered. Tears ran down his cheeks. The central committee members made their way to the head table. The room had quieted; only happy expectant twitterings could be heard. Bulgakov edged backward slightly, hoping to be lost in the novelist's tremendous silhouette. Everyone waited for Stalin to take his seat. No one moved.

"Bulgakov—man, is that you?" Stalin's voice thundered down the table. There was a horrible pause; everyone in the room waited—Bulgakov leaned forward and looked to where Stalin stood.

"So what is it, then—are you coming or going?" said Stalin.

Bulgakov could not imagine what he meant. "I beg your pardon," he said.

"Your coat—take it off! Join us for this sumptuous meal!"

Oh dear god, he thought again. He started to remove it, then stopped. "I'm sorry—my suit jacket—I haven't one." He stammered, embarrassed and frightened. The room as well seemed to inflate with these same emotions, faces up and down the table, as though his confession spoke poorly for all there, all of them waiting for Stalin's reaction.

"What! No suit jacket!" Stalin's roar seemed laced with amusement.

"It was stolen, I'm afraid."

"My writer without a jacket—that cannot be! Ordzhonikidze, give him yours then," said Stalin to the man on his left.

"What?" said the Commissar.

"We can't have our favorite writer without a suit jacket!" Stalin rubbed his hands together as though in pleasure of having solved the meddlesome problem. Bulgakov could only think of Mandelstam's words—ten thick worms were his fingers. When Ordzhonikidze didn't immediately disrobe, Stalin stopped rubbing and glared at him. Did the Commissar of Soviet Heavy Industry value a suit jacket more richly than his leader's pleasure? Ordzhonikidze looked terrified—the entire room reflected their terror for him. He handed his jacket to a waiter who flew like the devil to Bulgakov's chair. Bulgakov put it on. It hung poorly, but Stalin appeared satisfied. He took his seat, and immediately, food and drink seemed to appear from nowhere.

Toasts were given. Stalin was first, saluting poor Poprikhen; however, he gave the wrong patronym and his error was perpetuated in all other toasts of the evening. Bulgakov sensed Poprikhen's efforts to not let this blemish the event. At one point he leaned heavily against Bulgakov's shoulder. "I may not be his favorite writer," he said, drunkenly. "But I have my seat next to his." With every toast his tears had flowed and now his face was spotted with their tracks. As soon as they were finished and the Party leaders left, Bulgakov got up to find other company. The music had begun. Poprikhen was singing with a few others, crying again, and appeared not to notice.

Bulgakov wanted a fresh drink and while it had seemed the waiters were as populous as the guests, now that he required one, they were not to be found. He felt somewhat abandoned and for a moment, despite the crowded room, his orbit was a lonely one. Being Stalin's favorite writer appeared not to ensure one's popularity. Indeed, he sensed a vague inquisitiveness in those near him, and in equal measure, their desire to maintain a certain distance. He noticed a woman's stare; their eyes met then parted and she turned back to her conversation laughing suddenly, as though she'd never left it. Others in her small group laughed too. They were wondering what he'd done to claim that title, he thought. Though they would not offer it aloud, they were each in secret giving harbor to their own suspicions. Another, the man at her side, glanced at Bulgakov's suit jacket—or rather Ordzhonikidze's, then blankly looked elsewhere as though like Bulgakov he was in fact in search of a waiter. He shook his glass slightly as a kind of testament to this. He leaned into the woman's ear as he spoke briefly. To his query, she shook her head.

Bulgakov imagined wedging himself between them. *Perhaps this Bulgakov is an old family friend*, he'd offer. Perhaps he'd shown some valor in battle. Or medical care for some unsavory condition and, of course, all confidences would be maintained.

Such favoritism wasn't necessarily the result of intrigue or cowardice. Such affection was not obviously the reward of a betrayal.

"Have you been to these parties before?" At his side was the drunkard from the restaurant some months ago. Ilya Ivanovich reintroduced himself. "I remember," said Bulgakov. There was no hint of drunkenness; he looked in fact as though he'd not taken a drink since. A waiter appeared. Ilya repeated his question.

"This is my first," said Bulgakov. He spoke to the waiter as though he'd asked. He couldn't explain why he lied so easily over the trivial fact. Anything to extract himself from a prolonged conversation, though why such should be avoided, he likewise couldn't explain.

"If this is your first, then you should have some fun with it," said Ilya. "Order anything—the most exotic thing you can imagine. They will produce it."

Bulgakov was surprised by his suggestion. "Persian Vodka," Ilya said to the waiter, deciding then for the both of them. "Bring the bottle, so we can see it." Bulgakov would not have guessed that Persians manufactured vodka. The waiter registered the request with a slightly glazed expression, as though imagining the trek he was to undertake. This could take a while.

"I understand the MAT will produce your play," said Ilya. "My congratulations." He touched the breast pocket of his jacket over his heart. His gesture was similar to Poprikhen's, only Ilya seemed more to be searching for his.

"So they say," said Bulgakov with brisk cheerfulness.

"Tell me again, its name? I'd like to see it."

"Oh, I shouldn't think so," said Bulgakov quickly.

"Why not?"

*A Cabal of Hypocrites.*

"You must be delighted," said Ilya. "Many will want to see it."

His words reminded Bulgakov of their other conversation. The memory of his earlier anxiety returned. "Would you like to meet the guest of honor?" Bulgakov hoped to pass him along to someone else. He nodded toward Poprikhen.

Ilya leaned in to speak though this was unnecessary. There was no one nearby who might hear them. His breath was unpleasant on his cheek. "I believe I'm speaking with him now," he said.

Bulgakov was sufficiently vain to have at one point desired such admiration. Suddenly he wished he might disappear.

"I apologize," said Bulgakov. "Why I should fail to remember is rather embarrassing—what is your interest in literature?"

"I suppose I am a critic of sorts." Ilya smiled.

"Still," said Bulgakov, his unease growing. "I feel I should ask for your papers."

"Then you should be disappointed. I carry none."

His anxiety was transformed into something more certain. Yet why was this Ilya Ivanovich interested in him? He wasn't political. He wasn't another Mandelstam. What had he done to attract such attention? He sensed a kind of chase and felt the need to escape, to hide, more strongly than ever.

"I wonder," said Ilya. "How does one become the General Secretary's favorite writer?"

"I imagine one would have to be a good writer," said Bulgakov without much conviction.

Ilya seemed amused. "There are a lot of good writers," he said. "But why not—let's say that might have something to do with it." There was a savageness in the way he put this last part.

The vodka arrived and was poured into two glasses. Alborz vodka, it was indeed Persian; the waiter looked only slightly fatigued. Ilya raised his to give the toast. Bulgakov remembered this same gesture from before and he felt a sudden and sharp longing for Margarita as though he'd just overheard the mention of her name.

Ilya paused. "I'm sorry," he said, his glass hanging in midair. "I'm at a loss."

"To better writing," said Bulgakov. He surprised himself a little with this.

Ilya's lips curled slightly. He then drank.

"This stuff is wretched, isn't it?" Ilya set his glass on a nearby table as he turned to leave. His words were an indictment—not of the vodka, but of the gathering itself, its pretense of opulence; perhaps it was a condemnation of their times.

Bulgakov watched him disappear into the crowd. Strangely, he felt less endangered, as though the drink had been an antidote. Was he not wearing Ordzhonikidze's jacket? Ilya had wondered why he was Stalin's favorite writer. *Because I'm a damn good writer*, he thought with a fierceness that matched Ilya's.

On the other side of the banquet hall, Poprikhen had been dancing, but was now splayed across several chairs. Another dancer fanned a napkin over his face ineffectually. Bulgakov suspected he was the only one in attendance with any medical training. Poprikhen greeted him with a drunken sputter. Bulgakov found a pulse in the man's meaty wrist and told him to rest for a while.

"Will he be all right?" A woman's voice came from behind.

Bulgakov turned. It was Margarita.

How did she look? Not more aged; nor more youthful. She'd neither gained nor lost weight. There was a change, but not in her appearance—perhaps it was the distance she maintained. As well there was a set to her features. A calculation to what she might reveal. He couldn't blame her for this. She kept herself at a difficult reach so he simply held his hands out to her, palms upward as if he was checking for rain, and asked how she was.

She didn't answer his question.

"Congratulations on your play." Her smile was warm and

genuine. "I'd heard—then I received your tickets. It was very generous. I'm not sure why you sent them but thank you."

He was vaguely aware of the room around them, the shifts of light, of bodies. Couples were dancing. She alone seemed fixed.

"I didn't expect to see you tonight," he said. "You look—wonderful." He wondered who she was with.

A dancer nearly careened into her; Bulgakov lifted his arm to shield her.

"We should either dance or leave," he said. She shook her head beautifully.

Instead, she told him Mandelstam had been released. He and his wife were to be relocated to Cherdyn. There would be an opportunity to see him if he liked, to say good-bye; tomorrow, just after noon. If he liked, she repeated. She seemed to step around this possibility with caution. He wondered if she'd heard Stalin's pronouncement. He could not imagine what she thought of it.

"Yes, of course," he said quickly. He'd not anticipated having to face Mandelstam again; at least not this soon. He wondered how she'd come to hear of his release. "This is amazing news," he added, trying to fuel his words with some enthusiasm. "Thank you for thinking of me," he said.

"It was Nadya's idea," she said.

"But you took the trouble."

Still, it was Nadya. She would take no credit.

He wondered if she was seeing someone else and this depressed him.

They agreed to meet near her apartment. He thought to suggest his place instead, but didn't. He didn't want her to refuse again something he might offer, as though this could form a habit that would be difficult to overcome.

She hesitated. "You were speaking with someone," she said. Her manner had changed; she seemed uncertain, almost shy.

"You remember," he said. "The man from the restaurant. The drunk—the sturgeon." He hesitated in giving Ilya's name, as though this would summon his form. He repeated instead. "The drunk."

She nodded. "I noticed you were talking." She seemed to want to say more, but looked uncomfortable, possibly even worried for him.

Was her discomfort wrapped up in her memories of that night, with their later encounter that she longed to set aside? Or had she observed something from across the room; something vague yet troubling. Perhaps it was her concern that gave him more courage.

"We talked of the play," he said.

"We thought we'd never see him again," she said. He decided she seemed more shy than worried.

"Do you remember that terrible wine?"

"The entire evening was strange."

Not disagreeable, though. Not regrettable, only strange. He wished he could go back to it; he wished that he would have stayed and not left her that morning. There would have been no trip to the Kremlin. He imagined finding their way under her blankets, feeling the warmth of her shift against him as she moved. The world would have stopped there.

He thought to reach for her but she stepped back as though she'd sensed it. Time had indeed moved onward. Yet she could not be heartless. She placed her hand on his jacket sleeve.

"It is exciting—your play," she said. Her eyes were shining. He didn't try to understand her misgivings any further. He wondered what else he could do to make her happy. What more he could promise her?

"It will be good to see Osip," he said. He hoped his eagerness would sound credible.

"Do you think so?" she said. "I expect he will be quite changed. Physically, I mean, of course. I'm a bit nervous."

Briefly he imagined not appearing at the appointed time. He imagined Margarita waiting, scanning the streets for him before going on alone. For some reason, an arbitrary universe had afforded him a second chance. Perhaps it was not so arbitrary.

# CHAPTER 11

They met just before midday and walked to Patriarch's Ponds together. Her step was slightly ahead of his. As they crossed the street, her arm shot into the air. A figure rose from a small table set among others near an open kiosk, an overhang of aged trees shading it; beside him, a second figure, a woman, remained seated.

Mandelstam was barely recognizable.

Bulgakov was suddenly flooded with guilt; his recollection of the Writers' Union, the apartment vestibule, his meeting with Stalin; as if these actions were responsible for the transformation before him. He slowed. She moved ahead and they walked the last few paces obliquely.

The once dark fringe of hair was grey and shaved close. His rotund form had withered; he'd become a whisket of limbs and torso such that he appeared taller than before. She lifted her arms in an expectant embrace. Bulgakov marveled at her fearlessness of this specter.

Mandelstam raised an arm; a bony thing emerging from what seemed to be the cavernous opening in his short-sleeved shirt. The other leaned heavily on a cane. As she hugged him, he leaned forward, to steady himself against her. Bulgakov and Nadya watched this, yet made no move to acknowledge each other. Bulgakov then clasped him about the shoulders; the circle of his arms that closed in around the poet was pitifully small.

"This is wonderful," said Bulgakov, trying to manufacture enthusiasm.

Mandelstam turned to his wife, proposing that she and Bulgakov might enjoy a short walk, with a smile that suggested the plan had been previously discussed and at least tacitly agreed upon. Bulgakov offered his arm to her. Margarita was already seated; she held the poet's hands, or rather, maintained hers like small tents pitched over his that rested loosely on the table. Nadya pointed out the pond where two swans passed serenely. They followed the walk that circled the water.

"I saw Tatiana last week," she said. "She asked after you. She looks good." She didn't say what she'd told his ex-wife. "She cut her hair. It's quite stylish."

"She's a pretty girl," he said.

"She said something about some dishes of hers."

He knew the ones of which she spoke. A wedding gift from friends of hers. They'd had a special place. She'd left them behind and because of them, for a time, he was certain she'd return. "I don't know," he said slowly. He couldn't recall when he'd last seen them. It was possible they'd been broken in the search.

Nadya seemed to assume something else had happened. "She said it didn't really matter. I said I would ask, but she said not to bother. She said they weren't particularly important to her." This last bit seemed more of a pronouncement. As though nothing from his wife's time with him could have held any lasting importance.

He'd never thought of the two women as friends. Both had married writers. Both had been hurt by them, though in different ways. Yet it seemed one was willing to wound for the other, on the other's behalf.

"I told her," she went on. "I said, 'How does one lose dishes? He must still have them somewhere.' 'Oh, you know Bulgakov,' she said. 'He'd have used them for an ashtray if I'd let him. Or to wedge under a table leg. You know Bulgakov.'" Nadya laughed at this. It wasn't clear if the laughter was recreated for him, like the conversation, or simply her own.

"I know the ones," he said. "She'd want them." He felt self-conscious in correcting her, in defending his relevance in his ex-wife's memory.

One of the swans lifted up from the water briefly; its tremendous wingspan extended over its mate; the sound of its wings against the air was like distant thunder; others walking nearby turned. Nadya studied the fowl as though it carried a message that was particular to her.

"She said it wasn't important." This time the bite was gone. She sounded only tired. They were dishes after all; not lives broken and swept aside. The swan settled again.

"We leave tonight," she went on. "We can bring our clothes. No books." A list of suggested items had been provided. Like a children's camp, she mused.

"I've heard Cherdyn can be pleasant in the summer," he said.

They were over halfway around the pond. She removed her arm from his and crossed them over her chest.

"I'm not entirely sorry to be leaving this place," she said. He could see she was watching Osip and Margarita on the other side. "I won't miss this."

"Will he be able to write?" he asked.

She didn't know. He hadn't slept since his release.

That wasn't what he'd meant but he let it alone.

"Has he talked about what they did to him?"

She said nothing for a moment, only hugged her arms around her torso. "No—perhaps we can hope that he will forget. We should hope for something." As though it was the act of hoping—not the thing itself, not the granting of it—which made it possible to continue.

He sensed her manner change with this. Impart a new sympathy. But perhaps in larger dimension there was a growing acknowledgment of endings. Their walk would soon be through. The time of bitterness and reproach was over. It was a time for amends. She took his arm again.

"I remember when he first brought you to our apartment. You couldn't have been in Moscow very long. Do you remember? You were so reserved. And shy. Every time I stood, you leapt to your feet as well and Osip laughed at you. I thought—here is this physician. What must he think of our bohemian life? Emptying our pockets to their very lint just to gather enough to buy a couple of eggs or a bottle to share. Who would want this, I thought? Why would he want this? Osip said—I think he can write—and I thought, 'So what. Why would he want to?'"

"You were kind to befriend me," he said.

Nadya smiled a little. "That was Osip," she said.

"No, that was you as well, Nadyusha." She didn't argue with him.

"His poems aren't lost, you know," she said. She touched a finger against her temple. "I memorized them all. You needn't have worried."

With this, they both looked toward Mandelstam and Margarita.

Margarita sat erect, her hands in her lap. Mandelstam drew his hands along the sides of his scalp; it seemed he'd forgotten how little remained there. Bulgakov recognized this gesture. He wondered what she'd asked that he could not fulfill.

"Osip is lucky to have you," he told her. He said this absently, still thinking about Margarita. Nadya seemed grateful and he smiled to reinforce his words. He thought them both supremely unlucky. He thought it was possible that she was the least lucky of all.

Both Margarita and Mandelstam looked up at their approach as though their time allotted had been overestimated. Margarita had been crying. She got up and moved away from the table. She stared at the water. She seemed not to notice the swans.

Mandelstam nodded to his wife; again this appeared to be

expected and Nadya went to sit on a bench a short distance away. She took a cigarette from her purse and lit it. Bulgakov took off his suit jacket and sat in the seat Margarita had vacated. It was warm; he pushed up his sleeves. Mandelstam watched his wife for a moment.

"You look well," said Bulgakov. "All things considered." He stopped, feeling clumsy.

Mandelstam turned back; he appeared not to have heard him. "Do you remember when we first met?" he said.

Bulgakov remembered. It had been after a coffeehouse reading, one of Bulgakov's first, not long after he'd moved to Moscow. There'd been many amateur writers that night, reading from their work. He remembered the soft flesh of the poet's handshake. Somehow it'd made him less fearful of him, his ability to crush all hope, until the other man smiled, his lips parting to speak, then all fear rushed back.

"Do you remember what I said to you?"

Mandelstam had said that someday he would come back to this same coffeehouse to listen to this same man, only the line would go around the building, perhaps even the block, for they would stand for hours, happily, to hear the voice of a great writer. Of course Bulgakov remembered. He'd gone home that night and written it down.

"You were very generous to me," said Bulgakov.

"Was I? I couldn't remember. Did it matter?"

"Of course." A small twinge of that fear returned.

"If I had told you to go back to medicine, would you have?"

Mandelstam patted the front pockets of his shirt. He removed a silver case, opened it, and placed its last remaining cigarette between his lips. Bulgakov lit it for him.

"It's too late for that," said Bulgakov. "Your words did their damage."

The poet sat back. He worked the cigarette between his lips, then removed it.

Between them lay a green worm, a moth larva. It had fallen from an overhanging branch to the table's surface. Some unlucky turn of a leaf, a wisp of breeze, and a misstep had sent it from its universe of green. Neither of them spoke; it was something to brush aside. For a moment, its legs moved helplessly; then it curled inward to right itself. Immediately two black ants set upon it as if waiting for that opportunity. In their arms, the larva contracted reflexively, then ceased to struggle, paralyzed from their bites of formic acid. The ants hesitated at the table's edge, burdened with their prize, then disappeared over the rim. Mandelstam maintained his gaze on that spot. His frown deepened.

The larva would not know a life of wings and air; it would not grieve that loss. To this larva, the meaning of its life was to provide food for ants.

"I've done things—will you take an old man's confession?" Mandelstam looked away again. "God—it's beautiful today." Despite his words, his expression was of one who mistrusted what he saw.

"You have nothing to confess," said Bulgakov. He tried to sound assured of this.

"I'd always considered the possibility of arrest," said Mandelstam. "I had believed it was only a matter of time." He inhaled from his cigarette. His hand visibly trembled and he lowered it quickly.

"I'm not sure what you want to hear. The physical details aren't important, I suppose. At first you live for your release. That is the composition of your hours. When you will see the sky again—the trees, the sun. Your wife. You live for things you never gave thought to. You believe if you can be strong, you can withstand them. You believe such strength is possible."

"You are strong," murmured Bulgakov. "The strongest man I know." This part he felt truly.

Mandelstam lowered his voice; he seemed anxious to continue.

"I don't know if it's the beatings. Or the isolation. Maybe something else. At some point you stop living for your release. You stop thinking of your wife, of your future. You stop thinking." He paused. "You only live. Questions are asked and you answer them. There is food and you eat. There is pain and you cry openly. If your life were to suddenly end; you think this is how life is; this is how it ends." He seemed to search Bulgakov's face for comprehension. "You have no regret, no sense of loss. No care for those you leave behind. You do not consider that it could have happened another way."

The loveliness of the afternoon grew deceptive. "Those are terrible circumstances," said Bulgakov.

Mandelstam sat back a little. A piece of ash fell from his cigarette. He flattened it against the table with his thumb. "Questions were asked and I answered them." He looked out over the pond. "Many questions. About a lot of people." It seemed he was counting their number among those enjoying the afternoon as though it was this reckoning for which he was accountable.

"Who did they ask about?" said Bulgakov. His apprehension grew. What could they want to know?

"Among other things—the names of those who'd heard the poem."

His poem—as though it was a contagion. For some diseases, the afflicted couldn't be saved.

Mandelstam's face remained impassive, unapologetic. Harsh experience had stripped all comfort. Truth would no longer be urged gently forward, to steal upon one as in the verse of a song. Truth would be delivered bare-boned. He had no desire for Bulgakov's sympathy. He would dare Bulgakov to look away from his actions, to layer himself in kindness and pity and self-deception; he himself could do it no longer as though he lacked the appendages for it.

Mandelstam continued. "Then one morning a different door

opens. You are pushed through it and there is sun, sky. Arms wrap around you. Slowly it comes back; names first: this is sun; this is sky. Slowly you understand whose arms are around you. Explanations are given for questions you haven't asked. You've been released." He seemed to struggle to continue. "Then the rest returns: your past, your future. You don't know what burdens they are until you assume them again." He looked at his arms, his hands, as if those things were visible to him. He studied his hands. "By them, you know what you've done."

He leaned forward. "Do you know the moment I was most happy? Do you? Standing in the sun. Without pain. Without names. Without knowledge. That is death. A man should never know how pleasant death will be. A man should never learn this."

Bulgakov recoiled. "Why are you telling me this?" The skin over the other man's arm was thin, mottled; dark ecchymoses ran its length. He'd not perceived these before. From shackles? Beatings? Mandelstam's fingernails were yellowed and overly long; Bulgakov noticed then that several were missing entirely.

Mandelstam folded his fingers into his palms.

"Perhaps," he went on. As though this was what he'd intended all along. "You should consider that you would have done the same."

Mandelstam's words found him as easily as if the poet had touched his shoulder. Had he known of Bulgakov's meeting with Stalin? Had he listened for Bulgakov's pleas on his behalf and heard only silence? Would he point out Bulgakov's nails, his teeth: they were whole, unbroken. Instruments of torture hadn't been required. Bulgakov wished he would never have to see Mandelstam again, as if in this manner such memories could be rooted out; at the same time he wanted to cry out for that loss.

Mandelstam looked toward his wife. "There is my heart,"

he said. He lifted the cigarette to his lips. His tremor had lessened. "She believes I'll be better someday."

Margarita remained a short distance away. A group of children came upon her, kicking a faded ball. They swarmed her, then maneuvered the ball along the path away from her. With them gone, she looked more vulnerable. He could blame Mandelstam for this, but in some anticipatory way, he already blamed himself.

"Nadya has us packed," Mandelstam went on. "I think she is happy to go." He was signaling the end of their time together. He met Bulgakov's eyes only once more. There was no regret with this. Like Bulgakov, he had no wish to see him again.

Mandelstam stood, holding the edge of the table until he took the cane. He passed Margarita as he moved off to join his wife. The two clasped hands and set off on the path together. Neither of them looked back.

Bulgakov imagined them walking the landscape of Cherdyn. It was a new town, utilitarian and bold, rising from the dark and freshly turned tracts of bulldozers. A glowing city on the steppe, the sun shattered and amplified by glass and steel. It would be hard to see in the continuous glare.

Mandelstam would only need to see the spot of land before him, that place where he would next set his foot. He would pray for no greater vision than this. They could all pray for blessed shortsightedness.

Margarita sat down next to him. Her face had warmed in the afternoon heat; it glowed with the faint sheen of perspiration. She seemed as young as the children who'd crowded her. She touched his arm and asked if he was all right. Her hand remained there, hopeful. "He said you'd be like this," she said.

She should know better then.

She looked out over the pond; the swans were well-behaved under her watch. She still held his arm, but it seemed different now. The sense of her fingers was weightless. He could easily escape her, but he was reluctant.

"I didn't think you'd come today," she said.

But he had.

The skin she touched seemed more human than before, as if she had applied this quality with her fingertips. She believed that someday he'd be better, too.

He kissed her hand. Then he laid his cheek against it. He could try to keep her there.

Though perhaps then things would not end well for her.

There came again the slow beat of the swan's wings from across the pond; it seemed a pulse in the air, better felt than heard.

He could pull his head back into Stalin's rabbit hole. He glanced at the sky.

# CHAPTER 12

First Margarita had a deadline to complete. Then there were plans with someone else. A girlfriend, she added, as though she could sense the panic in his silence. The following evening she had a head cold. "It feels like I'm carrying a ball on my neck." She sounded annoyed that this required explanation but perhaps it was just the cold. Bulgakov wanted to know how this could come upon her so fast, but how could that be asked? "I hope it leaves as quickly as it came," he said, trying to sound confident. The line went dead and he reasoned she needed her rest. Shortly thereafter he went to her apartment anyway. He would say it was to check on her. He would bring something, a gift. Isn't that what a friend would do? He looked around his apartment, then slipped the empty saltcellar from his table into his pocket.

He knocked twice before the door opened. She was in a bathrobe and looked disheveled from sleep. She didn't question his appearance, though neither did she welcome him and instead returned to her bed. He came in and closed the door.

"This looks worse than a head cold," he said, as if to provide good purpose for himself. She only hugged the pillow and rolled toward the wall. He sat down; first on the saltcellar, then removed it from his pocket. "I brought you something."

She rolled back; she tried to focus on the object in his hand, then reached for it. He was at once sorry; he could have gone without this further embarrassment. She seemed to find the gift no odder than his appearance at her door. She put it on the table beside her and rolled back again. Shortly she was sleeping.

He had dozed off in the chair because he awoke to her voice. She was on her side, her head propped on her arm. He couldn't tell how much time had passed. She seemed in better shape than him. "I'm not sure this makes sense," she said. His head cleared immediately; what had come before this pronouncement? What didn't make sense?

"I'm not blaming you," she said. She picked up the salt-cellar and fidgeted with it. "Perhaps I'm skeptical of love in general."

He wanted to tell her she was young for such an attitude, but thought it would sound judgmental. When instead he wanted to touch her.

She laid her head back on her pillow, and stared at the glass piece as she turned it over. "Love is no different than any other relationship. At its core, it seems to be more about power."

Was it not obvious that she had all the power? "I couldn't disagree with you more," he said.

She turned toward him. Again with her hand under her head. She was utterly divine for all of her disarray. "At the very moment I fall in love with you, you will cease to be captivated by me."

She could imagine loving him! He should be overjoyed by this. But she had been hurt before. Perhaps by Mandelstam. Possibly himself. There were lesser men who'd be enthralled with her until their dying breaths. Let her find one of that species, she seemed to be saying. Let her be with one for whom she was never intended.

She smiled then, and it was as if to break his heart. "Isn't this the way it tends to work for you?" With other women, she meant. She'd added this last part carefully, not wanting to hurt him.

"Come to my reading tomorrow," he said.

She looked surprised. He put his hand to his heart. He could feel it knocking.

Her face seemed to empty of all expression. She asked how she could say no. Later he would wonder if she'd actually expected an answer to her question.

Bulgakov arrived at the apartment of the playwright, Alexei Glukharyov, early the following evening. Glukharyov met him at the door, half-dressed and apologizing that there were no spirits to be had. He insisted he'd forgotten though Bulgakov guessed that it was his wife who was not completely approving of these get-togethers and had scotched the idea, who'd wisely predicted that hosting an evening of liquored-up writers would end at a much later hour. Bulgakov told him he'd invited someone. He then sat on the sofa and waited for others to arrive. He had one cigarette remaining. It would calm his nerves, but he feared smoking it too soon. Perhaps someone would think to bring a bottle and he stared at the door as though he could will this to happen. A roll of pages was pressed between his shirt and suit pocket. He'd been unable to decide what to read, uncertain of what she might like, and he vacillated between telling himself it mattered not at all and that his future happiness depended on this choice. Glukharyov had disappeared behind the curtain that hid the bedroom; he was arguing with his wife. At some point in their past they'd found sufficient interest in one another to register their union, to sign the required documents. Was love an elusive thing or this banality? Was it as Margarita had predicted? More writers arrived; one had brought wine and glasses were passed. Perhaps she wouldn't come; then he could read anything.

Chairs, cushions, an ottoman, and the sofa were arranged in a rough circle. When these were filled, the rest sat on the floor. Lights were dimmed save one and it was beside this that each writer would stand, the illuminated page drawing all eyes like a

torch. Four had brought pieces that evening. The press of bodies, the room made smaller by its dark corners, provided the
gathering with a sense of propitiousness. Theirs was art; each
had a special duty to listen. Glukharyov provided a short introduction for each reader, fanciful and humorous, and the air
stirred with short bouts of laughter and applause, as
Glukharyov revealed (then demonstrated) how the first, a poet,
had been a former actor who'd been forced to give up the stage
because of narcolepsy. Another had been a member of the first
expedition to the South Pole. Tragically, the Norwegian herring
had given him terrible gas and the Vikings sent him home
before achieving their destination. In such ways, these lucky
ones had escaped the grip of fame. Bulgakov watched
Glukharyov's wife in the shadows. She laughed as the others
did, and he imagined how she might see her husband anew and
remember the initial spark of faith that had caused her to slip
her hand in his. It would feel like taking another breath.

Bulgakov was the final reader. As the applause for the one
preceding diminished, Glukharyov stood to give his preamble,
only Bulgakov wasn't listening. Margarita had not come and it
seemed a well of disappointment had closed around him. He
tried to imagine any number of reasons. His instructions had
been poor; her illness had worsened; yet he felt it was none of
these. She was alone in her apartment. She was aware of the
time and the place. She had found some way to say no.

Glukharyov's introduction was different from the others.
He took up a volume of Gogol and began to read. It was the
opening paragraphs from *Dead Souls* and the arrival of
Chichikov, Seliphan, and Petrushka to the provincial town of
N—. He was an excellent reader and took his time over the
winding passages. Bulgakov knew these words well and it
seemed as though Glukharyov and perhaps all in attendance
knew of his disappointment, and it was in this way that they
sought to arouse him from it.

Gogol himself would speak to Bulgakov, his voice reaching across the decades. *Do these words sound familiar,* he went. *Like a coat one might don? Dare you—dare you?*

Indeed! In his later years Gogol had become convinced that God had abandoned him. Tortured, half-crazed, he burnt his remaining manuscripts only days before he died. As though the promise of man's redemption must perish with him. He claimed the Devil had tricked him into doing so. He'd been only forty-one.

Glukharyov closed the book and, extending his hand toward Bulgakov, welcomed him forward. "Follow that!" he said. The command was spoken with admiration. The expectation of the room seemed to lift him to his feet.

Under the light, Bulgakov unfolded his pages. From the darkness, one laughed. "Bulgakov will keep us until breakfast." He shook his head—no, no. He was still uncertain what to read. His opening chapter was likely of the best quality. Further, there was the scene of his burgeoning romance with the Margarita of his story. Of this he was less certain; he might have read this had she come, but even then questioned this strategy. Now in her absence, he could set this aside.

The door opened and Margarita appeared. She slipped past the others and took the empty seat on the sofa. She struggled to remove her light jacket; the woman beside her helped, and she folded it across her lap and clasped her hands on top of it. Another voice called from the shadows. "Are you going to read something tonight or are we only to appreciate the spectacle of your dumbfounded wonder?" Even Margarita smiled in the warm room, dropping her eyes a little.

She'd come! He rifled through his pages again. He could impress her with the wit of his satire, his knifelike caricature. The idiocy of entrenched Moscow; the amusements of the Devil's entourage. She would be dazzled for his genius. She was watching him, waiting with the others, her eyes shining.

In 1931 when Gogol's body was exhumed he was discovered to be facing downward. The writer had had a terrible fear of being buried alive, so much so that he'd willed his casket be fitted with a breathing tube as well as a rope by which to sound some external bell if needed. Sadly, such wishes were viewed as the paranoia of a madman and were not implemented.

Gogol's voice came back to him. *Did you know I had a terrible infatuation of Pushkin? I called him my mentor but I wished he was otherwise. He had a most beautiful chin. I dreamt of taking it into my mouth. Alas, his life's purpose was to catch a bullet with his spleen. I only wanted love. Is it possible that is all any of us desire?*

Bulgakov began to read.

"One hot spring evening, just as the sun was going down, two men appeared at Patriarch's Ponds . . . "

At its conclusion, his audience sprang from their seats, the applause was explosive. Margarita seemed to have been swallowed in their midst. He searched for her even as he was repeatedly thumped on the back, congratulations pummeling his ears. Where was she? Then he saw her! Glukharyov had pulled her to the side and was speaking intently. Bulgakov studied his lips but the voices around him were overwhelming. Yet she was there, watching Bulgakov as she listened, as though he was the only person in the room.

What was Glukaryov saying? He seemed overly serious, his hand on her arm, unwilling to spare her his prognostication. Would he convey some warning? Persuade her to look askance at writers? She looked anxious and Bulgakov parted the crowd, stepping over furniture, trying to make his way toward her. Only then did Glukharyov's words find him—*dangerous writing*. Not so, Bulgakov wanted to protest. Then, so much worse—*foolish risk*. It was too late. He came up to them ready to drive Glukaryov into the wall.

"Well?" said Bulgakov, breathless for his emotions.

Glukharyov shook his hand; he seemed not to register Bulgakov's acute dismay. "Great work, great work." He leaned in. "My friend, you realize it's not publishable." His face was gathered in concern and apology.

Bulgakov's exhilaration crested with this. Should he believe that Glukaryov was expert in such things? Should she believe him? Did she think she might be better off with a lesser writer? She could not! What was the point of all of this if it didn't matter?

What did she want? She looked worried for him, but she could not retreat. She would believe whatever he wanted to believe.

But what if it was true? Bulgakov couldn't think it!

"I'll let you take those words back when you have a signed copy in your hands," said Bulgakov.

Glukharyov drew up for a moment, then bowed, and the room opened before them. Bulgakov took her hand. She didn't resist. They would step into that abyss together.

# CHAPTER 13

*The play was ruined.* Bulgakov returned home in the middle of the afternoon, too angry to remain at the theater, this thought repeating itself like some evil chorus. In the streetcar that ran the length of Tverskaya Street, the gentleman on the bench beside him only perused his newspaper. When he then nearly missed his stop, jumping up from his seat, the paper fell to the floor and Bulgakov handed it to him, adding with empathic gravity that he understood how easy it was to become distracted when they, with both great arbitration and little thought, destroyed one's art. The man could only thank him as the tram was starting to move again.

He opened the door to his apartment. Margarita was kneeling on the table that she'd pushed against the window; various tools were laid out around her. The room was sweltering and though she wore her hair off her neck, some had escaped and lay in damp tendrils along her skin. When the window latch had failed and the window would not stay open, she'd found a neighbor willing to lend her the required tools and spent the evening and then this next day taking the mechanism apart and rebuilding it, replacing the broken bit with one she took from a basement window. Similarly when the toilet would not work she'd enlisted a plumber to repair it in exchange for tutoring sessions with his son who was sitting for university entrance examinations. Bulgakov told her how grateful he was for her, for her resourcefulness. She let him kiss her as he said these things.

The afternoon light through the dirty glass was particularly

generous to her. She frowned at some part of the metal workings in her hand that would not cooperate.

Her friend Lydia sat in the armchair, her legs dangling over
its side. She was an attractive girl, though she spurned all makeup and dressed severely in only trousers and shirts. As though
the world need not make any excuses for her. He didn't like her
very much. It had occurred to him that Margarita might take on
some of her tendencies and he was vaguely watchful for this,
though what he might do if this were to happen he had no idea.
Lydia fanned herself slowly with one of his magazines.

"Lydia," he said.

"Bulgakov." She mirrored back his cool acknowledgment.
Only the magazine moved.

"Are you pretending to supervise?" he asked her. "Or do
you actually know something useful to contribute?"

Margarita seemed amused by their sparring.

"I know many things," said Lydia. "Alas, my dear friend
doesn't listen to me."

"Lydia," said Margarita; it was a low growl of warning.

"But I must fly now," she added airily and pushed up from
the chair.

"Care to borrow our broom?"

She ignored him and kissed Margarita. "Think about
Tuesday night," she said. She held her chin for a moment.

"I'll think about it," she said.

She waved a hand at Bulgakov as she passed as though bat-
ting an insect. The door closed behind her. "What's Tuesday?"
he asked.

Margarita was back at work. "Some meeting."

"She doesn't like me," he said.

"I can't imagine why not."

But he was serious. "Are you going?" He wanted to say,
*You're not going, are you?* Lydia's meetings seemed dubious
things, though in truth he knew little about them.

"Do I have a better offer?" She had lowered her head before he could think of one. The window latch needed her.

"You've said her meetings are tedious."

"They can be."

"She seems to associate with questionable individuals."

The frown returned. He changed the subject.

"Is there something I can do to help?" he said.

She seemed to give consideration to his question. "Do you have a welder's torch?" she asked.

He shook his head.

Her hands were streaked with grime. The gadget seemed to respond and slid obediently into place.

"I think it will work now." She rubbed her brow and it became soiled as well.

"Everything works for you," he said.

She turned to fasten it to the window frame. She was wearing a pair of his trousers, rolled up to the knees. He liked it when she wore his clothes, her smaller form disappearing into them. She wasn't skilled in the use of the tools, yet even they seemed to cooperate. "What happened today?" she asked.

He didn't want to speak of the play. She would no doubt have some series of practical suggestions and he didn't wish to argue why none of them would work.

"What makes you think something happened?" he said.

"You're trying to pick a fight."

"No I'm not."

She pushed the window open; the latch grasped at the passing metal spikes, then, as she let it go, it held one fast. Abruptly, she put her head and shoulders through the opening as though she needed to be immersed in this other air, and for a moment he thought she might actually fly from it, revealing herself to be an entirely different creature than the one he knew. He was startled and excited by this thought.

She pulled her head back inside. "All right," she said.

"What have they done to it today?" The strain was gone; there was only concern. She sat on the edge of the table, waiting for him to speak. She seemed available to any question. He wanted to know why she stayed with him.

He kissed her neck. It was slick with sweat.

"You need a bath," he said.

She slipped her hand between his thighs. "What happened?" she asked again.

Nothing, he thought, until this very moment. "I'd be lost if you left me," he said.

She unbuttoned his shirt and began kissing his chest.

"Do you know that?" he said.

She muttered something he couldn't understand.

He slid her across the table and she fell onto the adjacent bed. She let out a sharp noise, like the start of laughter. He toppled over beside her. She was already shimmying out of his pants. Within moments, her hands were cradling his erection as though it was some sort of religious totem.

"Do you know that?" he repeated. He held himself over her, waiting for her answer.

She smiled, her hair splayed across the pillow. "I know you'd still have a broken window," she said.

He lowered himself over her, kissing her gently. She tightened her hold and he felt as though he could bring about the end of the world and be without blame.

Later, as she showered, he waited, lying on his back, listening to the creak of the water pipes hidden in the walls. He'd promised to take her to supper. The light in the room had shifted, deepened slightly. His thoughts unfastened themselves from the complications of the day. A small but unwieldy problem in the novel presented its solution. It slipped into place like the window latch in her hands, as though the mechanism had been there all along; it'd only required the correct pressure to be applied. He listened—the water still flowed. He got up and took the manuscript from the drawer and spread it over the table. He found the part—would this new stratagem work? He needed to know and he sat down to write.

When he raised his head, she was dressed and sitting on the bed watching him. Her expression was inscrutable. It occurred to him, as his eyes went back to the page, that its mysteries could be revealed to the person who stared long enough. Only there was a phrase he wanted to assign to the page before it eluded him. She offered to bring him something to eat.

He said something about their going out and she said it was all right.

He asked her to go by the theater and retrieve some papers he'd left behind. If it wasn't too much trouble.

"No trouble." Already she was at the door.

He'd let her down. He wondered how much she minded. "Marry me," he said.

"I'll bring you supper." As though this was a reasonable compromise.

CHAPTER 14

The evening was unusually quiet, as though all of
Moscow had spent the afternoon as they had and were
now relaxing in their lovers' arms. When she got into
the streetcar that would take her to the theater, there were few
other passengers and she wondered about their situations as
she did her own. What was the state of their love affairs? Why
were they each out in this night alone? Who loved whom
more, for this was never a balanced equation.

Outside, the streets and cars and buildings glowed in the
evening light, yet the windows reflected the interior of the tram
and in them she could see both worlds juxtaposed. Their bodies were altered, elongated in the curved glass. They were
lovelorn ghosts floating through the city. They stared from the
windows as she did, searching.

Lydia had told her she was too generous. She had asked,
*Why him?*

He worried about the play. The principal actor had quit
suddenly for no apparent reason. Then one of the secondaries
had become pregnant with complications that confined her to
bed. The director found replacements yet every problem
seemed magnified in Bulgakov's vision. Issues so small, yet she
would awaken in the night to find him on the edge of their
bed, his head in his hands. He would mutter, *No one wants me
to do this, you know.* He had told her of his past: a series of the-
atrical failures, novels written that then were refused. Yet she
sensed his lament was more personal and she felt compelled to

answer. *Of course she wanted him to do this.* His return each day from the theater had begun to evoke in her some vague anxiety. What fabrication would she need to dispel, what problem to resolve? Night after night it seemed it was she who coaxed him back in from the ledge. What if one night she wasn't there? Would he climb in through the window on his own? And if he didn't? She could think it no further.

The tram passed one of her favorite restaurants. She had lost weight these past weeks and had taken to pinning in the waistbands of her clothes every morning. Her friends brought in plates of bitki and kundumes and excuses that once again too much had been made for their own families. Some they ate, some went bad by sitting in the cooler for too long and had to be thrown away. Those who knew her a little suggested she take a vacation; or even better, they urged: go home and spend time with her mother.

She imagined Bulgakov at his table, his head bent over the page. Or more likely staring away at something she couldn't see.

There were simpler men who would have loved her better.

How could she explain this to Lydia? She just needed to get used to the task. Who were those created to love the writers of the world if not the ones with a nature too generous?

The streetlamps were burning when she arrived and she was relieved to find someone still in the theater office. Margarita recognized the woman; she told her she needed an updated version of the script, then waited, sitting on one of the low, plush-covered sofas that lined the marble lobby. The lights had been dimmed. No one else was around. A series of double doors led to the empty theater. Quite suddenly, her skin prickled; to the far right, along the distant wall, she caught the movement of an animal, a large rat, making its way along the silvery floor. Its snakelike tail hovered over the tiles as it moved. She lifted her feet and tucked them beside her on the sofa. It then shot back across the room, behind a potted palm.

There were voices from within the theater and a side door opened. The director Stanislawski appeared; he was speaking with great animation to another man. By his manner, the director seemed to be anxious to assist in his guest's departure. Both were walking toward the exit; neither had noticed her. The other man turned as though vigilant of his surroundings; something the director said then distracted him from this—it was Ilya Ivanovich. She froze.

She hadn't spoken to him since Patriarch's Ponds. It was in his demeanor, she thought; he was there about Bulgakov. Stanislawski held open one of the heavy gilded doors so that Ilya might pass. His coat floated back across the threshold. She strained to hear their words. She thought, desperately it seemed—perhaps he was there about another writer, another play; this had nothing to do with Bulgakov. Ilya passed the line of windows. Did Bulgakov know? Was that the cause of his earlier disquiet? Ilya looked in through the glass, obliquely as though at the last moment he'd sensed her presence. He turned further and she felt a small burst of panic; then he disappeared, out of her sight. If he'd seen her, it was only for a slip of time. She waited, unable to move, expecting him to reappear, to search more carefully. Stanislawski stepped in front of her.

"My dear, you look like you've seen a ghost," he said. "They say that an empty stage is never silent. Oh, what I wouldn't give to hear again the great Nikolai Khmelev."

She nodded as though she knew that name.

Ilya—over the last few months he'd not been entirely absent from her thoughts. There was a moment when he had entered the lobby that it seemed he'd stepped from that other shared landscape. She'd never told Bulgakov of their encounter at the Ponds. Though she'd had some sense of what he was, she told herself it had been a chance meeting. And now he'd been here as though he'd slipped past her pitiful guard.

She remembered that afternoon at Patriarch's Ponds. It'd been overly warm; others had retreated to fanned interiors or shaded spots leaving them alone in that sun-filled place; even the woman who'd sold them the juice had kept to her kiosk. Nothing in particular had been said. Nothing had been promised; there was only the sense of occupying the same space, sharing the same sky and air. Looking back on it, as she'd done over the months, it seemed to contrast in a particular way with the loneliness she otherwise felt. As in the way one might reach into the past to reimagine the tactile quality of some childhood comfort; even if it no longer existed, it gave hope for some future comfort.

She now felt pathetic and small for its keeping.

The office worker had returned with the script and handed it to the director. He stared at it for a moment. He seemed reluctant about something.

"Tell me, my dear. Has our Bulgakov engaged in any new projects? Something perhaps," he hesitated. "Controversial?"

She thought of Bulgakov's reading; Glukharyov's words to her. She shook her head.

He glanced toward the doorway. "Every production comes with a certain number of queries." He handed her the script. "'It's just a play,' I tell them." His smile seemed strained. As though these times required one to say things one didn't completely believe. "It's only a play. No one should live or die over it."

When she returned to the apartment, Bulgakov showed her a piece of paper. It was a telegram telling him to report to Lubyanka in the morning for an interview with the Deputy Director of the Literary Division. It had arrived after she'd left.

He collapsed into the chair. "It is Ilya Ivanovich. I'm certain of that."

That name given aloud seemed itself to be an entity in the room. How could he have known?

"He was there tonight," she said. "Talking to Stanislawski."

She thought more might tumble forth and she closed her mouth.

"That's it," he said. He got up then sat down again as though there was no place to go. "They are going to pull the play."

He worried about the play? She could think of other possible outcomes, more dire ones. How was it that none of these had occurred to him? Did he not know who Ilya was? She touched the table as though it would steady her.

"Stanislawski said nothing of that," she said.

"Well, he wouldn't tell you, would he?" His tone was dismissive. He took the manuscript and began to search through it. When he came to a certain page, he stopped. Much of the text had already been scratched through. He turned it; nearly an entire scene had been redacted. A strange calm seemed to gather within him. "It doesn't even make sense now."

Oh dear God, who was this man? He was at once so vulnerable, so beautiful. Her next thought overwhelmed this—she *loved* him! She could let nothing happen to him. "It will be all right," she whispered. It had to be all right. He needed to believe her.

He slid the telegram toward her. He was neither kind nor unkind. "You didn't receive this."

CHAPTER 15

The building had been commissioned by the All-Russia Insurance Company and built in 1897 in the neo-baroque style. It rose nine stories and filled a city block. Within, its floors were laid with individually polished light and dark woods; scallop-shaped alcoves were molded into its high walls to house statuettes of alternating bronze and marble. This was the new face of Russia, commented the company's president as he toured the structure nearing completion. He meant that a building such as this could easily be found in Berlin, or London, or even New York City, yet here it stood in this city of Tsars. He meant that a place of business could look like a palace. That no longer would the palaces belong only to the Tsars. He touched a wall as he passed, almost instinctively; then pounded the plaster with his fist. He smiled to the architect as he did this. It would stand forever, he told him. Those in his entourage laughed when he laughed.

In 1917, the secret police of the Bolshevik regime took over the building on Lubyanka Square, later renamed Dzerzhinsky, not far from Red Square, as its headquarters and prison. Forty thousand political prisoners would pass through its doors on their way to execution or exile. Citizens joked that it was the tallest building in Moscow: from its basement one could see Siberia.

When Bulgakov awoke, it was dark outside. She still slept. He lay thinking about his father's death, the particulars of those last days. Bulgakov had been twenty-one.

It had taken the better part of a week from the time his father was last coherent. When his last words were to stop feeding him. Bulgakov had been adamant that his father was not to pass from life while unattended and his siblings and mother accepted his schedule of watches without a word. Perhaps they read into his controlling nature something akin to guilt or regret, and not wanting to interfere with those demons they did as he asked. He himself almost never left the room for those days. He wondered if his father knew he was there.

A few months before, his father had confessed to him in private about his fear. "I'm afraid," he said simply. "I don't want to die." He stared into the empty hearth of his study as though some flame might appear. "There's too much left I want to do."

Bulgakov had been in the third year of his medical training. His visits home were short. He made excuses about the inflexibility of the hospital schedule. With each he sensed his father's growing resentment of him, the resentment of the abandoned.

"You're not going to die," said Bulgakov. He shook his head in emphasis. "Your health has improved these last few months. It's clear the condition is waning." Bulgakov wanted to believe this. He looked to his father for affirmation. He feared his argument; he would fight any he made. He would tell him he'd live forever.

His father said nothing; his expression was introspective. Perhaps he had only wanted to confide in another person. Bulgakov had let him down yet again.

"Have you spoken with Alyosha—about this?" said Bulgakov. His father shook his head.

"My concerns are not of a spiritual nature," he said. He regarded his son with what seemed like brief forgiveness. For not being more than the child in their relationship. "I see more of myself in you than in your brother." As if this was some excuse for his choice.

All his father had desired was the company of his son for a few hours, conversation that might fill the drink of time with something other than his own meditations. Not long, he might have thought to say, though he didn't.

"I wonder what your mother has planned for supper," said his father, preparing to rise.

"I have to go back to the University," said Bulgakov.

"Of course you do," he said. His voice had deepened, the resentment returned.

*Margarita had awakened.* She pulled the sheet across her and sat on the edge of the bed. In the dim light, undressed as she was, she was stunningly vibrant.

"I'm afraid," he said. "I'm afraid of dying."

There was no helping it. Would she answer as he had, so many years before? Would she deny their truth, as he had done? Was it not enough that he had been so unable to bear it in his father that he avoided him entirely? Even when his father had said it plainly. Even then he had denied him altogether.

She still hadn't moved.

"I'm afraid of disappearing," he whispered.

"You won't disappear." As if by the force of her will she would maintain him.

"You can't say that."

She looked away and he was suddenly afraid that she'd never look at him again.

She turned back. "You'll not disappear." She seemed to possess new resolve.

He felt her warmth close in, skin to skin, and he thought he could never be parted from her. That would be unbearable, unthinkable. He wouldn't think it.

He pressed her closer. She could say the words and he would believe them every time.

Like a child, he asked her to say them again.

Bulgakov arrived early at Lubyanka that morning. The foyer of the former insurance company, though several stories high and paneled in rose-colored marble, had been repurposed for office space and was a maze of desks and cabinets of various vintages that were sorely at odds with the drama of the room's architecture. Those few who were at their desks at that hour looked at him with something between curiosity and concern. Only Committee members or their entourage used that entrance. When it was determined he was none of these he was directed to an empty row of folding chairs along the foyer's side wall and told to wait. He sat down. A dead moth lay in the corner near his foot. He kicked it under the chair where he couldn't see it.

On the distant wall, below the room's peak, a large clock hung. He watched its second hand catch itself at the top of each turn about the dial, taking four to five tries, sometimes more, to achieve its apex. Bulgakov waited nearly an hour by its time then went back to the woman who'd directed him to his seat and asked if she knew her clock was broken. She requested his name and again pointed to the same row of chairs. He told her he'd already seen that view.

"Most who visit are not so eager for another," she said with a tilt to her head. She seemed to understand that people fell into one of two categories; however, she was still uncertain to which Bulgakov might be assigned. She appeared agnostic to this; no doubt such determinations were made without error. It was her indifference which sapped what little confidence he had and he did as he was told.

The moth lay near his foot again as though it'd moved. He reasoned he could leave. He could say he was going out for a breath of air and never return. He rubbed his palms across the tops of his knees. The cloth felt damp. Perhaps this was a mistake.

A uniformed figure appeared. Bulgakov was uncertain of

the insignia. The officer seemed exceedingly enthusiastic and indicated Bulgakov was to follow him. Bulgakov hesitated and the man looked confused.

"You are Playwright Bulgakov?" said the officer. When he nodded the man's enthusiasm returned. As they passed the woman's desk, she was preoccupied with a co-worker, smiling at the younger man who leaned against her desk. Bulgakov wanted to point out his escort to her: evidence that he was a respected guest. As they entered the adjacent corridor, she broke into laughter. It sounded incredulous. It seemed to follow him down the hall, as if to say:

*You think there are mistakes? Even coincidences? Do you not choose with care every word you lay down, dear Playwright? The moth, the clock, even myself—all have been placed with the same consideration, I assure you. Take nothing for granted.*

Her laughter disappeared. The air was chillier than before.

They continued for what seemed to be the width of the block. They passed doors spaced intermittently; some opened into offices. Telephones jangled; the wavering buzz of an intercom punctuated the voices of clerks and secretaries working within. They turned down a second, then, midway, took another turn down a third corridor. Immediately, the atmosphere quieted; the ceiling heightened; the doors, slightly larger, were made of polished wood with carved cornices. The nameplates on each were brass; the names etched in script. After passing several, they came to a painting, hung between two doors, and here the officer stopped. He held out his arm like a docent. This was a Vereshchagin. Truly, he said. He smiled. In this place.

The officer waited patiently, as if inviting Bulgakov to admire the work.

The painting was dominated by the outstretched wings of vultures swarming over the ground. Long shadows of evening stretched from the bottom of the frame. Further in, in the rosy twilight of a secluded glen, a majestic tiger reclined. Between the animal's arms lay the corpse of a man. Its head and shoulders were in the tiger's embrace; the creature's open mouth was poised above him. To the side, other vultures waited; some beat their wings; their eagerness at odds with the languorous gestures of the beast.

"Many of his works were barred from exhibitions," said the officer. "The romantics of his day had little stomach for his brutality. We Russians," he smiled. "We always have something to say about our Art."

The plate under the frame named the piece: *Cannibal*. The officer went on. "He gives a strange nobility to the victim; don't you think? There is honor in one's life culminating in the provision of sustenance to the beast. And even as we recognize the victim, we struggle to see him. In death we are so changed."

Bulgakov disagreed. The man was not a victim; in his repose, he looked more the willing lover giving himself over to the creature. There was no protest, no scuffle or thrashing of limbs. The man had willingly accompanied the creature into the glen; he'd lain down with it. He had allowed for their differing concepts of love.

The officer told him the painting had once hung in the Summer Palace of Prince Orlov. Now it belonged to the people. He didn't seem to consider the irony of this. The officer opened the door on the other side. This one had no nameplate.

It was a small antechamber to another office. There was a table with an ashtray and several chairs. The walls were bare. The inner door was closed. The officer sat down and brought out a cigarette case from his breast pocket. He motioned to Bulgakov to sit, then offered him one. The officer lit it for him and they smoked in silence. They were clearly waiting for someone. Bulgakov thought back to the painting in the corridor. The objects in the room, the few that were there, also seemed anticipatory. *Like the moth and the clock.* He was grateful for the cigarette; it gave him something to do with his hands.

The officer spoke. "I am a fan of yours." His manner was as a friendly conspirator. "How many times did I see *Days*?" He took a quick drag, as though this was needed for courage. "I write," he confessed. He seemed slightly embarrassed. "I keep a journal. Write stories. If you could read one for me, tell me what you think—I'd be quite grateful."

Bulgakov told him he'd be happy to read his work. Typically this wouldn't be true, however, in his asking, it seemed that the officer had made up his own mind as to Bulgakov's innocence and Bulgakov was suddenly and wholly grateful for this and willing to read even the most pedestrian of offerings. The officer was at odds with everything else there. Bulgakov glanced at the inner door.

"I could send it to you," the officer said.

There was movement from the adjacent room—the closing of an outer door, the sliding of a chair. The officer put out his cigarette; Bulgakov did the same and they stood.

A clerk entered, pushing a small metal cart that held a stenotype; he was followed by Ilya.

Ilya told the officer to leave them and he departed, the details of his manuscript review left unsettled. Ilya took the seat that had been unoccupied. The clerk, a smallish, older man, pulled the remaining chair against the wall, where he then sat. No one spoke as he guided the cart into position in front of him. Bulgakov cautiously took his seat. The clerk began to type. Ilya held his brow in his hand, between his thumb and his forefinger. His eyes were closed.

"State your name," said the clerk. His voice was nasal as one with a chronic sinus condition.

Bulgakov hesitated. Ilya opened his eyes.

"He knows my name. He's talking to you." Ilya had already closed them again. Bulgakov complied. The stenotype rattled anxiously over his words.

*What had caused* the man in the painting to enter the jungle that afternoon, the declared realm of the tiger? There was no weapon in sight. Bulgakov imagined him empty-handed, sun-dappled leaves brushing his shoulders as he left the well-trod path.

"The address of your domicile?"

What of his planned course? Were those goals yet worthy? Or had he garnered a new faith? One that called to him from the shadows. One that promised a different reward; that exacted a more certain tribute.

The clerk repeated the question. Ilya raised his head. The clerk appeared to recognize this motion and ceased his questioning. The room was quiet for several moments.

"My apologies," said Ilya. "My head is splitting." It wasn't clear to whom this was intended. "Vasily is here simply to take notes. This isn't a formal inquiry. Call it a conversation. You don't mind?"

Beneath the table, Bulgakov pressed his hands together. His arms were lost under its sharp edge; he saw the braided scar it'd made across the chair's arm. He tried to sound unconcerned. "I'm still not certain why I'm here," he said.

From the darker shades of the jungle, a pair of yellow eyes glowed. The creature drew him in with its sympathy, its desire. It understood him, loved him for what he really was. It was the tiger after all. *We hunt what we love, wouldn't you agree?*

He could hear the predator's breathing before he saw it, more rapid than a human's. Its life force exceeded that of a dozen men. Nearby the call of an invisible bird plucked the evening air. Other concerns seemed difficult to recall. He no longer wished to deny the tiger. Desire and fear had melded into one. He stepped in further.

Such pain would be brief. Most were the fodder of worms. He could be a tiger's feast.

"Is this about an overdue library book?" said Bulgakov. The stenotype's clatter paved over his attempted joviality and he stopped speaking. Ilya waved his hand at Vasily and the secretary left through the same door.

Ilya produced a cigarette case. He offered one to Bulgakov and took one for himself. He lit them both then leaned back in his chair. He studied Bulgakov through a thin coil of smoke, then manufactured a smile.

"I admire you," said Ilya. "These are challenging times—for writers in particular. This business with Osip Mandelstam for example." Bulgakov tried to speak and Ilya waved his words away. "You were friends though I would imagine?"

"More acquaintances," said Bulgakov.

"But you knew him."

Everyone knew him. Would they arrest them all?

"It must seem what you do is a dangerous enterprise," said Ilya.

There was an audible ticking from the other room. "I have no particular politics," said Bulgakov.

"Everyone has their politics."

Bulgakov threw himself onto the one truth he couldn't abandon. "I simply want to write."

"Of course. And why shouldn't you? Are you working on something now?" It sounded innocent. A question of polite interest.

The room felt warm.

"Something new?" Ilya suggested.

"No—the play consumes all of my time."

"That's too bad." Ilya's smile changed slightly. Bulgakov couldn't tell if it was triumphant or sympathetic. "As I said, these are challenging times. I have to wonder what is keeping you here. In this country, I mean."

He remembered his conversation with Stalin. He could say he'd asked to leave but had been denied, though that seemed a trap. The better answer was to want to stay.

"There's a lot to leave behind," said Bulgakov.

"You have a sister with whom you've not spoken in several

years. A mediocre career—and that is perhaps generous." He didn't wait for his assent. "Few friends. There is no disputing these things."

Bulgakov felt suddenly depressed. "Where would I go?"

"The world is larger than Moscow. Though perhaps you believe there would be difficulties publishing abroad. Or even worse. Your work may be published but no one will understand it. No one, except perhaps another Russian."

The rapidity of Ilya's diagnosis seemed to extract air from the room. "I have considered that possibility," said Bulgakov.

"Do you lack faith in your own greatness? Or in the ability of a foreign audience to recognize it?" His expression appeared to sour a little, as though a bad taste had entered his mouth. "Particularly if it comes to them so heavily accented."

Bulgakov sensed in the bureaucrat a pointed dislike for him. It went beyond that which might be directed toward his profession; it was something else—something personal. It seemed a slip of a kind. Once again Ilya appeared sympathetic; any trace of a more ominous sentiment was gone.

"I would miss my homeland," said Bulgakov.

"Nonsense." Ilya's voice boomed slightly in the small room. "Expatriates abound. You would have no difficulties. You might even find those willing to read your work." He seemed momentarily distracted by a page left on top of Vasily's stenotype. He picked it up; his brow furrowed as he read. "At one point you petitioned to leave," he reminded him.

"Perhaps I've changed my mind," said Bulgakov.

"Perhaps?" Ilya sounded mildly incredulous. He then changed his tone. "Perhaps. People change their minds all the time. About their politics, their philosophies. Even their gods. This building is particularly adept at helping people to change their minds."

"I have a play about to open," said Bulgakov.

"You do," said Ilya. His tone was neutral, and Bulgakov wondered what he might know about its fate.

"I have—" Bulgakov was suddenly reluctant to continue. "I have—someone."

Ilya did not answer immediately. "You do." His skepticism was gone, as though he'd been momentarily disarmed by the words. "In some ways, it would be easier for me if you were to leave."

Bulgakov was uncertain of what he meant. He remembered the night in the restaurant when they'd met Ilya. He'd had an inhuman quality, and perhaps that was the nature of one in his occupation. Only now there was a sense of regret, a reluctant acceptance of personal loss that was very human. Not all desires were going to be pursued in this lifetime. Did he have a woman? There was no way such a question could be posed.

"I'm not trying to make things difficult for you," said Bulgakov.

With that, Ilya seemed restored. "Perhaps you believe that only in this country writing is respected," he said.

There was an echo of Mandelstam. Bulgakov spoke carefully. "Respected or not, it is my home."

Ilya then seemed to change the subject. "I've always wondered: what is the writer's inspiration? How do you choose which imaginative peak to scale on any given day?"

Again, Bulgakov was surprised by this turn of conversation. "I can't speak for everyone," he said. "I suppose it's an observation of some incongruity in life. Some paradox that I want to explore. The answer to *what would happen if . . .* " Ilya's expression was unreadable. "Perhaps it has to do with my scientific training," he added weakly.

"Of course," said Ilya. "You were first a physician. A venereologist—your specialty in syphilis? Your practice in Kiev. Given up, because—why?"

"I suppose I lost my ambition for it." He'd done nothing to prepare for these questions.

Ilya seemed ready to ask another, then appeared to change his mind. "I feel we have this in common," he said. "I too pose such questions to the world—questions of *what if*. For example, what if a passably successful playwright met with such censorship that none of his plays could be produced?"

Bulgakov felt his chest contract slightly. "I should have no idea of that outcome," he said.

"No? Then here's another—what if a physician of comfortable means, *bourgeoisie* means, was faced with the loss of these luxuries at the hands of an invading proletariat army? What then—would he enlist in a failing Nationalist cause in order to protect the old ways? Would he betray his country's destiny? That should be a fine plot for a story."

Bulgakov's mouth went dry. "It sounds rather flat, actually."

Ilya went on. "And what if this physician, this traitor, seeking to hide from his past, left his home, and turning to another career, found himself still frustrated and pining for the old life—his petitions to emigrate refused again and again. *What if* he then took every opportunity to infuse his writings with seditious ideas, cloaking them in some guise of literature?" He leaned forward slightly, and now, for the first time, seemed agitated. The ash from his neglected cigarette fell to the table's surface and noiselessly shattered.

Bulgakov grew strangely calm, even as the waves of accusation became stronger. They had nothing. Otherwise there would have been not a telegram, but agents at his door. This would be not an interview but an interrogation.

The ruddiness of Ilya's face had deepened. "And what if—*Writer*—what if the leader of this great country was so taken in that even he failed to see these obvious sentiments, even he was blind to the treachery in the words. What if he protected this writer because he found him entertaining, unknowing of the real damage this spoiler caused? What would happen if this was revealed to him? What then—"

The room seemed to collapse, losing air, until there was space for only the two of them, their faces inches apart. Bulgakov gathered his breath. "Perhaps you should be the fiction writer," he said.

"You think it fiction?"

"I love my country," said Bulgakov.

"You love yourself," said Ilya. His voice dripped with disgust.

# CHAPTER 16

Ilya got up abruptly and left the room, jostling the table with the force of his departure. The unseen door from the other office closed in succession. Bulgakov was alone.

No instruction had been given; was he to wait and for who? Would the officer who'd brought him come to fetch him? The one who wanted to write? Or the secretary from the foyer who'd thought him a criminal? Or were there others at that moment being summoned to imprison him? Had Ilya been so angered that he'd gone to procure some contingent of guards? Could Bulgakov find his way on his own? Would it be labeled an escape attempt when he'd come in the first place of his own choice?

The door opened and Vasily appeared. He sat down, positioned the cart, lifted its side arms which provided a broader table, and removed a thick folder from the shelf below. In a manner that appeared well practiced, he placed the ream of pages to the left and the folder to the right. He fed the first page into the machine's roll, then rubbed his hands together. He was there to take his confession, Bulgakov thought.

Vasily began. "Name?"

"I told you already," said Bulgakov. Then he gave his name again.

"Place of domicile," said Vasily.

"What is this for?" Bulgakov would have asked if he'd been arrested, but the words were too terrible to speak.

"We need to update your file," said Vasily.

He had a file? For what purpose, he thought miserably.

Vasily seemed preoccupied with adjusting the paper on the stenotype's roll.

"May I smoke?" said Bulgakov, feeling depressed.

"Do I look like a Committee member?" said Vasily.

The questions began with his parents; the concrete statistics of their existence—their place of birth and death, their education, the condition of their health, their travels and occupation; as well as their interests, their beliefs, their politics, and their prejudices. Had anyone in his family been a priest? A teacher? A writer? An artist? What views did they maintain about the Tsar? The West? The East? Karl Marx? The war? One by one, they went through his siblings as well. At first, Bulgakov had been somewhat lengthy in his responses, but it seemed Vasily was incapable of paraphrasing and progressively his answers shortened.

The pages to his left seemed not to diminish. After several hours, and with the alignment of a fresh form, Vasily smiled at Bulgakov. "Now we may commence with you," he said. Bulgakov felt sickened; this wasn't an interview, but a slow and meticulous evisceration.

When Bulgakov left Lubyanka, it was late in the afternoon. Vasily had asked about Mandelstam and Stanislawski, Poprikhen and Likovoyev. He'd asked about his current and former neighbors. About their wives, their lovers, their parents, and their children. He'd asked about Tatiana. Then, about Margarita. In the fading light, Lubyanka seemed no longer a building; Bulgakov had been given a pinhole's view of the machinations of the universe. He could not get away fast enough.

*He only wanted to write.* Such was his desperate truth, he thought. Had that as well been left behind?

Despite the hour he went to the theater.

The marquee was dark, yet his name remained, side-by-side with *Molière*'s. He recognized the cashier in the ticket office; she gestured from her slotted window as he passed through the lobby as though to dissuade him from going further. Of the series of doors along the far wall he knew the one on the end would be unlocked. It was late; he wanted only to see the set; *his set*. She called out his name as the door closed behind him.

The stage provided the only illumination with an irregular smattering of footlights and one misdirected Fresnel lamp. The set was partially assembled. Fresh beams rose in the backlight—a vaulted gallery with the French monarch's throne; adjacent, the playwright's seventeenth-century apartment. The varnished floor was marked in chalk with stage directions.

Two figures, presumably actors in street clothes, stood near its edge holding scripts. One gestured; the other held his hand against his head as though it ached. Otherwise the theater was empty. Bulgakov took a seat midway through the orchestra section. If the actors noticed, they gave no indication. The one with the headache dropped his script to his side and paused from his speech, looking about as though in search of some responsible party. When none was apparent, he resumed.

Bulgakov sensed that something was wrong—it was odd for actors to be rehearsing this late despite the proximity of opening night. He couldn't place the scene. Had Stanislawski made yet another change?

The actors were discussing the religious implications of burying the victim of a drowning in blessed ground should the death have been the result of suicide. One pretended to dig a grave. He appeared to be doing a particularly poor job of it even as he moved air.

This made no sense—there was no graveyard in *Molière*— then there came a new and terrible certainty: the scene was from *Hamlet*. These after-hours rehearsals were a contingency against *Molière*'s cancelation. This was a blow he'd not anticipated and it seemed now that he was the one scrambling through loose dirt. How could this be! Then—what could be done?

Stanislawski appeared in the aisle and sat next to him. The light from the stage set his face in sharp relief. Bulgakov expected to feel anger toward him, the swell of betrayal. Instead, Stanislawski looked surprisingly old, surprisingly vulnerable.

*Vasily had asked: "Are you acquainted with Constantin Stanislawski?"*

*Bulgakov: "It is a professional relationship."*

This wasn't entirely true—despite their working relationship, they were friends. It seemed unwise though to intimate any further association. Vasily did not challenge his answer.

*Vasily: "To your knowledge, does he carry significant personal debt?"*

*Bulgakov: "I would have no information about that."*

*Vasily: "Is he faithful to his wife?"*

*Bulgakov: "Of course."*

*Vasily: "Is he a habitual user of laudanum, opium, or heroin?"*

*Bulgakov: "I'm certain I don't know but I consider it highly unlikely."*

*Vasily: "Is it your impression that his selection of plays for production is an accurate reflection of his anti-Bolshevik views?"*

It was his particular phrasing which had alarmed Bulgakov. He'd hesitated and this, in turn, seemed to heighten Vasily's interest. He'd wanted to say no, but the question had been twisted such that any answer could indict.

*Bulgakov answered: "I don't understand the question."*

*Vasily typed.*

Evidently not all questions were expected to be clear.

Somewhere offstage, pounding could be heard. One of the actors spoke: "What is he that builds stronger than the mason, the shipwright, or the carpenter?"

The other answered: "The gallows-maker, for that frame outlives a thousand tenants."

The first stuttered through his next line and the other whacked him with his script. Stanislawski watched without reaction, as though the words were without meaning to him.

"When were you going to tell me?" said Bulgakov, his voice low.

"If there is something to tell, I imagine you will know before me," said Stanislawski.

"What have you heard?"

"One hears everything if one talks to enough people." Stanislawski spoke matter-of-factly, and the actors paused. One shielded his eyes with the script and searched the orchestra for its source. The other looked behind, as though nervous of what other voices might leap from the darkness.

"Do you intend to stage *Molière*?" said Bulgakov.

"I intend to stage something. *Molière* was already pulled once."

"And reinstated."

"And reinstated." Stanislawski parroted his words but not his conviction. "Someday you must tell me how you managed that."

Did the director think him an informer? "You know me better than that," said Bulgakov. He tried to muster some confidence in his voice.

Stanislawski turned to him. Half of his face disappeared into shadow. What remained was etched with sadness. A sympathy extended to all of them. "I've known you a long time," he said.

As though he could know all of Bulgakov's struggles, his disappointments. His other failures that, if examined each alone, were small and of only passing importance. Yet these together would gather as ballast for this newest one. If this play was canceled, no one would ever stage another of his. There would be no more to follow. He couldn't fail. This was all he had.

*Vasily paused from his typing; his fingers rested lightly on the keys. "Tell me about Margarita Nikoveyena."*

When Bulgakov returned that night, she rejoiced with the news that his play was still in production. But he could see that she waited to hear something else. She asked about his meeting with Ilya. Was there mention of Mandelstam? His manuscript? Did his earlier fears hold true? He told her the People's Commission for Internal Affairs had little concern about his association with Mandelstam or anything else. Still she waited, her eyes bright.

He lay down on the bed. He said something about being exhausted. He listened to her movements as she undressed.

Stanislawski had told him that he'd been advised by the Deputy Director of the Literary Division to commence rehearsals for an alternative production. *Hamlet* had been Ilya's suggestion. One of his favorites, he'd indicated. One he was certain would be well attended, should some misfortune befall Bulgakov's *Molière*.

She turned off the lamp. The mattress shifted. He sensed the discontent in her breathing; it persisted against his back even as he rolled away, pretending to sleep.

*"Tell me about Margarita Nikoveyena," said Vasily.*

*"I believe she is a copyeditor for the Moskovskaya pravda."*

*"And her affair with the poet Osip Mandelstam?"*

*Bulgakov paused. "I'm not aware of a relationship. Seems unlikely, if you want my opinion."*

*Bulgakov listened to the keys set ink upon the page. If only such were sufficient to imprint the past with new truths.*

*"There was a child, you know," said Vasily. He shared this news as though it were casual gossip.*

*The air in the room seemed altered by this. "I didn't know." Was that his voice? No effort had gone into fabricating that answer. Here was one slim truth in a sea of lies. "What happened to it?"*

*Vasily glanced over the stenotype. "It died after birth," he said.*

*How was it possible he'd not known this? Volumes of secrets seemed to be packed behind this one. A vision of Margarita came to him; volumes of secrets hidden by that tiny frame. All of their intimate moments seemed to flood him. The memory of each now darkened by this.*

*Vasily appeared to be waiting.*

*Bulgakov thought to say that he'd misspoken. That, yes, he'd been aware of their relationship—their love affair, to be precise. Of course, he'd known. No different than anyone else in their circle. He'd been privy to much information. He'd been important in that way. But the words that emerged spoke only of some strange sense of loss, a particular kind of betrayal, an examination of his own diminishment. "How is it that I didn't know?" said Bulgakov.*

*As though Vasily might have some consoling words. He only typed.*

# CHAPTER 17

He was finding it difficult to write.

Each night was the same, as though his dreams traveled the same rails every time he closed his eyes. He was following her. At some point, she'd pause and turn—had she heard his footsteps? But every night, her gaze passed through him as though he was a ghost in her landscape. That was when he would lose her, in twisting alleys, in a maze of hallways. In the high grasses of some foreign plain. He would call to her, but as happens in dreams, his voice froze in his throat. Then he would awaken.

"You act like there's something you want to say to me." She said this more than once. He would find that he'd been staring at her, unaware of the weight of his gaze. Then, as in his dreams, his voice failed him and he shook his head.

He made excuses for her. It'd happened long ago. Before they'd known each other. Of course she was allowed to maintain the privacy of those earlier years. They weren't necessarily secrets. No doubt she didn't consider it a secret. He imagined asking her about it, the bloom of remembrance across her face. Sadness and loss reassembling there, for certainly there had been sadness. He'd regret then having reminded her of it. He liked to believe that it was this final thought which stilled his voice. His consideration of her happiness.

When she would return from her errands he'd ask where she'd been. He tried to ask in a way that wasn't asking.

"Were you able to find that ink by Sheaffer?" He was at the table, writing.

She put the package by his arm and kissed the top of his head.

"I knew the GUM would have it," he said.

"I had to go to Mostorg to get it." Her back was turned as she unloaded her shopping bag.

"That was out of your way."

"I didn't mind," she said over her shoulder. "It's fine outside."

"You must be hungry. You haven't eaten since breakfast."

"I ate at Grendal's." She folded the empty bags and put them behind the metal cabinet. She kissed him again. "Stop talking," she said. "You need to write." As if it were that simple.

He didn't tell her about Ilya and Stanislawski and *Hamlet*, so she was perplexed by his renewed efforts to attend Party events. He didn't tell her that maintaining high visibility at such functions might protect his *Molière*. He didn't want her to think it required his protection, as though that might diminish it in some way. She teased him that his primary interest was in the cuisine that was offered and he didn't disagree. In the beginning, he invited her, but she always had an excuse, and he stopped.

He would ask about her plans for such evenings and at first she answered as though he was inquiring only out of politeness. He'd press for more detail and she'd ask why he was curious.

"What is interesting to you interests me," he said.

"It's a kind of women's club," she told him.

"A club for women?"

"Men can come. It's in support of working women." Women such as her. "You'd be surprised how many have been demoted, replaced even."

"Will Lydia be there?"

She seemed to make light of his question, knowing his dislike for the other woman. "I'll tell her you asked after her," she said.

He wanted to be supportive. "It sounds like a good cause."

"It is. She's done an excellent job of organizing it. We have a mission statement, a charter, club officers."

He grew somewhat uneasy. "Perhaps I'll join," he said.

She shook her head. "No, you won't. But that's all right."

He suspected Lydia associated with undesirable types. Those more pointedly antigovernment. She'd voiced a complaint once in his presence regarding the apportionment of luxury items between those of the Party and regular citizens, and he felt defensive. "Do I live like a Party member?" he said. She didn't answer. It occurred to him that if it happened again, he'd say nothing. He'd let her complain. He might even make notes of it. He wondered, vaguely, distantly, if he actually would. He wondered what then would follow.

"Maybe Lydia isn't such a good person for you to associate with," he said.

Margarita said nothing at first. The book she was reading clapped shut. She opened then closed a cabinet more firmly than needed, then seemed to stomp her feet into her shoes as she readied to leave.

"Perhaps you should come and see for yourself before assuming the worst in everyone," she said.

"I don't want you caught up in something that could be misinterpreted," he said. "I'm thinking of you."

When the door had shut and the silence returned, it was as if to remind him of what his life had been like before her.

Too often it seemed he said too much.


The evening was spent—or perhaps *misspent*—at the third and final lecture of a series sponsored by an organization which had named itself *Wives for the People's Advancement of Literacy*. Bulgakov had missed the first two and was sorry not to have missed this final installment; he daydreamed through most of the two hour-long ramblings. The auditorium was overflowing. The speaker was a high-school principal and Soviet success story who'd nearly tripled the literacy rate in his rural district. He read directly and without pause from a loose collection of dog-eared pages, not lifting his head once, despite his effusive flattery of the regime. Margarita had said she was going to a movie with a friend and while Bulgakov at the time had silently praised himself for not pressing for the friend's name, he wondered about it while the man rambled. Why wouldn't she tell him? Was it Lydia? What if the friend were another man? Was her thoughtless ambiguity a real evasion? He reminded himself that he had no reason to be suspicious, yet continued to ruminate on this after the final applause.

His efforts to increase his visibility appeared to be having a positive effect. The week before he'd seen Stanislawski at the theater and for the first time in a very long while, the director had appeared relaxed, even jovial, embracing Bulgakov as though the previous burden had been lifted. Even on this night many had stopped him, speaking warmly and with anticipation about his upcoming production. There was a general buzz in the air, a shared sense of confidence about him and his work. Stanislawski no longer held late-night rehearsals of *Hamlet*. There were no further telegrams from Lubyanka.

Afterward, on the street, he looked about for the next streetcar. The exiting crowd jostled him. A voice at his side asked if he would consider sharing the fare of a cab.

He turned and it was Ilya. He'd not seen him earlier in the lecture hall. Bulgakov tried to appear pleased by his suggestion. He shook his head and explained that he didn't have enough money even to share in that kind of luxury.

Inexplicably, a cab appeared and Ilya directed him into it.

"I'll see it as my happy duty to assure you get home safely," he said. He gave the driver Bulgakov's address. Of course he would have known this. Ilya settled back. "What did you think of the speaker?" he said.

"Passionate," said Bulgakov. It seemed a safe answer. He wished acutely that he could be anywhere but in that car. The driver swerved suddenly and Bulgakov's head knocked against the window.

Ilya didn't appear to notice. "Really? I must confess—I wasn't listening," he said.

Bulgakov rubbed his temple.

"Headache?" said Ilya. He smiled sympathetically. It seemed artificial and Bulgakov felt a swell of distress and anger for being forced to ride in this car with him, for the urgency of attending these insipid meetings in order to protect his work. His grievances spread—there was the new wariness he felt toward Margarita. He tried to suppress this yet he glanced at the passing sidewalk as though he might see her there with someone else. It seemed his entire world was off-balance; there was not a stable plank upon which he could set his foot.

"The French have a cure for a headache," said Ilya.

"Yes?"

"They call it the guillotine."

That would be relief from this ride! Who was this man? What was lacking in his life which drove such singularity of purpose? Why had he chosen Bulgakov as the target of his efforts? Bulgakov tried to imagine him as someone's son or a brother. He tried to imagine a wife or a friend. Ilya had never given any indication that such things didn't exist, yet somehow Bulgakov felt certain that they couldn't. If Ilya sensed any of this, he appeared unconcerned. He stared out the side window, his poor joke forgotten, as though the purpose of this shared ride had little to do with Bulgakov.

Across the back of Ilya's coat was a single blonde hair. Long, like a woman's. An innocent hanger-on, deposited in the crush of strangers. It glinted in the regular pulse of passing streetlights, disappearing in the intervening darkness as though its existence could never be proven.

"They don't even see us," said Ilya. He spoke to the glass. He seemed to marvel at the people outside. He half-turned to Bulgakov. "But we make certain they know of us, don't we? We have our own particular ways of making ourselves relevant to them."

The car pulled to the side of the street opposite Bulgakov's apartment. Above, he could see the light in his window. Margarita passed; she stopped. He saw her face in the window's frame. Her hair was pinned up; she wore it thus when she was cleaning. She moved off again.

He was relieved she was home; more so than what he knew to be rational. He thought of the questions he would ask her, how he might phrase them. He'd ask about the film first, then about her friend's opinion of it. Had he met this friend before? Someone she worked with? He would express interest, he hoped, rather than probing curiosity. His questions seemed a temporary solution, lines thrown to her, transient entanglements to keep her near until he could think of a better remedy.

Ilya stared at the window above. "So she stays with you," he said.

"Some nights." Nearly every night, he thought, though he was uncertain how that would seem.

"You didn't bring her to the lecture."

"She's generally not interested."

Ilya's face was hidden in shadow. "She's comfortable with you?" The question didn't concern itself with Margarita so much as it did with Bulgakov, as though his integrity of character made this conclusion questionable. Ilya wanted to know if he was taking care of her. Was he mindful of her welfare? Was being with Bulgakov a good thing for her?

"I'm not keeping her hostage, if that's what you mean."

Ilya didn't react to his indignation. He looked up at the window again as though even the briefest view of her could confirm or refute such a statement.

Ilya had wanted to see her. That had been the reason for the suggested ride. Of course he could have come alone. Sat in front of their building for hours. Perhaps he'd done this already. Perhaps every night. Only tonight, for some reason, he'd wanted Bulgakov to know.

That he desired Margarita?—he probably cared little if Bulgakov knew. Rather, that regardless of how he might feel about it, they were not so dissimilar.

Bulgakov got out of the car and crossed the street. At the building's door he thought to turn back. To tell him that in fact, yes, she loved him.

He pulled open the door instead and went upstairs. He needed to know if she did.

# CHAPTER 18

She was removing the curtains from the windows. Panels of material lay on the floor in untidy piles and the night sky, grey-orange from the city's light, now hung on their walls like uncertain art. She was on a chair beside the third and final window; she unpinned the fabric from the cord which served as a curtain rod.

"I'm surprised you're home so early," said Bulgakov. He shut the door behind him.

Margarita pushed a stray lock of hair from her eyes; it immediately fell back. "The film broke," she said.

"I'm sorry."

She put the pins in her mouth as she worked her way across the window.

"Can't they normally fix that?" he said. "I mean, restart the rest of the film?"

She took the pins from her mouth. "I meant the projector broke. The bulb." The curtain fell to the floor. She put the pins on the sill then started on the last panel.

"They didn't have another?"

"I guess not."

"So the film is O.K."

"I guess so." She sounded tired.

He really wanted to stop. "Do you need some help?" he asked.

The curtain dropped next to the other one. He offered his hand as she climbed down from the chair.

She asked nothing of his evening, of the lecture, its atten-
dees; of those he might have conversed with, flirted with, longed
for, as though she was indifferent—and, he thought, stubbornly
indifferent, sticking to this stance as if she would teach him
indifference—and in this she seemed even more guilty of some
concealment. He was closer than he'd ever been to achieving
his dream—the play catapulting upward to some new and better orbit, yet at the same time and seemingly in some strange
and cruel reciprocation, it felt as though she was quickly
falling away and there was nothing he could do to stop her.

"What's your plan with this?" he asked, gently touching a
crumpled pile with his shoe. He wanted her to answer a different question. He wanted to know what her plan was for him.

"Laundry." She sat on the bed and began to unclasp her
stockings from their garters.

The windows seemed to harbor a curious gaze into their
lives. "And until then?" he asked

"Until what?"

He changed the subject. "I'm sorry the film didn't work
out," he said.

"You said that already." One stocking snaked translucent
and docile from her hand. She laid it over the chair in front of
her.

"You used to like to wear my trousers when you worked,"
he said.

"Are you complaining about me?"

"No—I'm just noticing." He sat on the bed beside her. "I
like looking at your legs too." He wanted to stroke his finger
along the curve of her knee, to where it disappeared under her
skirt. She stared at her leg as well, as though expecting this too.
She seemed ambivalent about it and when he didn't she went
to work on the other stocking.

It was then that he decided to lie.

"I saw Stanislawski tonight." His mind raced ahead. "I wasn't going to say anything—I didn't want you to worry. Perhaps it's nothing." He glanced away. "He seems concerned."

She slowed her movements. "What is it?"

"The censors want another viewing." He wondered how to modulate the tone of his words. Fearful? Resigned? He maintained a flatness instead; she seemed not to notice.

"It's already passed. Why another?"

"I don't know. He didn't know. Of course he can't refuse them." He wondered how she might discover his lie. On the rare chance the director attended a Party event, she was never there.

"This is just muscle-flexing," she said. "Some bureaucrat trying to show how important he is." She patted his leg and went back to her stocking.

"There's something else," he said. He thought quickly. "There've been other visitors from Lubyanka."

Her seriousness returned. "Ilya Ivanovich?"

"No, not him," he said.

"He's been there before. Remember?"

He'd forgotten. They'd seen each other there—or she'd seen him.

"It wasn't him," he repeated. "Someone else. I don't know who."

"Maybe it's nothing," she offered. "Maybe they are no one."

He was conscious of his own breathing. "Stanislawski doesn't think so. He's started rehearsing *Hamlet*. He's talking of it as a replacement."

"Oh, my dear," she said. Her stockings were forgotten. She touched his hand.

He thought, first, not of the pleasure of her touch. He thought of his betrayal of Stanislawski, who'd stopped all rehearsals weeks before; who'd embraced him warmly. Here he'd delivered an image of the director's cowardice, of his expediency. He'd besmirched his name in the necessity of a lie. To seduce a woman.

"Perhaps I'm overthinking this," he said. If he sounded miserable, he thought, this was an honest thing.

She kissed him. He was conscious of the texture of her lips in a way he hadn't noticed before. As though this was their first kiss—or, he thought then, their very last.

She eased back on the bed, urging him back with her. For a time they simply lay next to each other, still clothed. She kissed him purposefully, as though she could expunge his sad and fearful thoughts. When she went to unbutton his shirt, he started a little.

"I'm sorry," he said.

"Whatever for?"

*What was he sorry for?* Her head was bent slightly against the pillow as she worked. He was sorry that somehow she needed to feel pity in order to find love for him.

"I'm sorry you have to worry," he said.

She brought her face close to his, her expression resolute, and for a moment he was uncertain of what she intended. Her lips touched his and she filled his mouth with her tongue, as though to fill it with something other than words. It seemed, then, gloriously full. He began to pull her clothes from her. Flesh-to-flesh—he couldn't be close enough. Somewhere below, he heard what sounded like the distant tattling of fireworks; the fabric of clothes ripping. It grew louder.

Later, they lay together, her cheek against his shoulder. He touched the smoothness of her stomach; he spread his hand, his fingers wide, over it.

He could push away these last few weeks. There had been the pressures of the play. The worry of secrets kept; barriers between them. He could imagine these things gone, the whole of Moscow laid flat for their pleasure. There would remain only the two of them.

Would she want that? She seemed so still. Perhaps there was less love on her part and more pity; itself not an antidote, but a poison to love.

"Maybe you're right," he said. "About the play. Stanislawski is overreacting."

"I'm certain I'm right." She patted his chest, then sat up, her legs over the edge of the bed. She seemed suddenly tired. She scratched a patch of skin just above her elbow. He bent forward and kissed it. When he was done, she rubbed it absently, as though wondering how exactly he thought that would be helpful.

"We can hope that the actors won't confuse the Danish for the French."

"Hmm?" she said.

"Those rehearsing *Hamlet*."

"Yes. Of course. They won't." She didn't react to his humor. They were words to quiet him. She stared at one of the bare windows. It reflected the interior of the room. As though a chorus hovered invisible on the other side, some congregation to whom she must answer.

"Are you missing the curtains?" he asked.

"No."

The skin of his chest where her hand had been felt strangely alive, strangely empty.

"It's funny—when you think I'm not doing well, you seem to find it easier to love me," he said.

She turned—her expression was inscrutable. "What do you mean by that?"

"Maybe I'm wondering if you just feel sorry for me."

"You're picking a fight again," she said, as though making a casual observation.

He stroked the back of her arm, then he kissed it. She let him.

She got up and crossed the room, naked as she was, and turned off the light. The window became immediately translucent, revealing the exterior night. Any watchers, be they angels or demons, vanished in that moment. She came back to the bed in shadows.

He wondered if Ilya had been outside, witness to it all.

He decided, in the morning, he would ask her to marry him.

# CHAPTER 19

She feigned a headache at work and was told to go home for the rest of the day. At Lubyanka she gave her name to the clerk at its entrance. She admitted she didn't have an appointment and was directed to a row of chairs. Once there, she decided it was ridiculous that she'd come, though where she would go now in the middle of the day in the middle of the work week she couldn't imagine as though the world outside was transformed during those hours and she in its midst would be lost. Ilya appeared from a side corridor and she stood; he took her by the arm and walked with her out the door. They crossed the street and continued down the sidewalk.

"Next time," he began. It seemed he would say something else, but he finished differently. "There are better ways to meet."

A block beyond Lubyanka he slowed his pace; the grip on her arm relaxed as well. He glanced at her. She expected him to make a comment about her appearance but he said nothing. He directed her to an outdoor café, to a small table set back from the street; it was late morning and there were no other diners. The waiter came up; he wiped his hands on the towel around his waist and looked ill-prepared for customers. Ilya ordered for both of them: two café au laits and for her a large serving of their okroshka.

"I'm not hungry," she said.

Ilya nodded to the waiter and he withdrew.

He offered her a cigarette; she declined and he lit one for himself. She watched the pedestrians pass on the sidewalk nearby. She looked back and found he was watching her.

"You must stop that," she said quietly. He looked away.

Sitting together as they were she was reminded of their last meeting in the park. She glanced at his hand where it rested on the table.

The waiter appeared with their coffee. He apologized for the delay; the okroshka was not yet ready. He told them it would be provided shortly, then retreated.

"This is a surprise," said Ilya, as if explaining his behavior. She didn't say anything.

"You are a surprise," he said.

"Not really."

She'd rehearsed what she would say to him.

A breeze lifted for a moment, it was cool on her skin. Morning's condensation beaded on the table; she drew her cup toward her, holding it for warmth. The drops coalesced around its base into a crescent-shaped puddle.

"Did Bulgakov tell you I gave him a ride home last night?" he said.

She retraced their conversation. Why wouldn't he have mentioned it? For a moment she felt confused, uncertain why she was there.

"You must stop harassing him," she said suddenly.

"I paid for the cab."

"I saw you at the theater," she said. "Talking with Stanislawski."

He fingered his cup but didn't drink. "I saw you there, too," he said.

She thought to tell him that that hadn't been her intention.

"How is our writer?" said Ilya.

"He wants us to marry."

Ilya drank from his coffee.

The waiter appeared with the okroshka and set it in front of her. She felt strangely hemmed in by it.

"He's made all of the changes requested by the review board," she said.

"Then my additional scrutiny should pose no problem."

"Why him?"

He hooked his arm over the back of his chair. "You should try it," he said, indicating the stew. "It's quite wonderful here." He seemed distracted, bothered in some way, and she wondered if she'd touched on some hidden discomfort. Or was it something else, and she was given to the sense that she'd endangered herself, and somehow this was what distressed him.

"It's only a play. No one should live or die over it." She echoed Stanislawski's words.

He pressed the cigarette to his lips, then quickly pushed it away again. His hand was shaking. She was startled by this.

"It's true," she insisted.

"Please stop talking," he cut her off.

What else could she say? She felt desperate to undo any damage she might have caused. "Can you not leave him alone?"

"Was this his idea? Your—meeting me?" He looked off, shaking his head, as though amused by the morning sky. "You're not going to marry him," he said to it, as though the real absurdity was in the sky thinking itself capable of marrying anyone.

She got up but his hand was already around her wrist, holding her there. She stared at it, at his arm. Strangely, she didn't mind it. It worked to infuse her with calm and she didn't pull away. "It was my idea," she said. "And now I'm sorry for it." She could see he believed her; that he was perhaps even hurt by it, and he released her. He stared where his fingers had been. She crossed her arms over her chest. He smiled a little at her then, as one who acknowledged her power.

"Please stay," he said. "I don't wish us to part under these circumstances. Please. I'll ask nothing else of you."

It was only with his request that she then wondered where she would otherwise go. The sun hung at an unnatural angle; the rhythm of the street was unfamiliar. The world at this hour appeared uncharted and uncertain for her such that even going to a store or a movie house would require extraordinary physicality. Where would she go—*home?* She imagined Bulgakov at their apartment, at the table, his head bent over it; the sound of his pen against the paper. She imagined him rising at her appearance, concerned. Beside her now: this table, its chair, both were solid. The stew waited. The breeze came again; it'd warmed slightly as though in service to Ilya's request, to provide encouragement. To suggest she needed a small reprieve from the other thing. To tell her the apartment would still be waiting; she would return to it soon enough. Had her friends not told her to get away for a little while? Was this not better? To do this small thing for herself was not a betrayal. Such a word made no sense. It was a table, a chair; someone had ordered a bowl of stew. All for her.

She sat down.

Ilya showed obvious pleasure and seemed determined to direct the conversation toward more agreeable topics. He encouraged her again to try the stew. She drew her spoon through it; steam rose from the seam she'd created.

"You are considering marriage? I think that will be a good state for you," he said. "I think that for most women. I suppose I'm old-fashioned in that way."

He confessed to his traditionalist view in the manner of one who was comfortable with this in himself. But was marriage a good state for him? Men such as Ilya were capable of setting aside love for their own interests. If this was the case, he hid it well. His gaze seemed to harbor true interest and concern. She didn't doubt he could be at times unyielding. Yet she remembered in the restaurant, the night of the sturgeon, when he'd begged her pardon for the most minor of slights. There had been a vulnerability he'd revealed as though offering it for her to examine. She'd sensed her power then. She wondered now if it was a flimsy thing, an infatuation that could quickly disperse. It seemed as though she was tapping forward on ice, staring hard at its surface; coming to realize that it would be impossible to gauge its thickness without applying her full weight.

"Do you feel women are the weaker sex and should be cared for?" she asked. He looked as though she should already know this answer.

"I'm not a romantic," he said. "You shouldn't confuse me with one."

She wanted to say that she hadn't, but found it uncomfortable to confess that she'd given any thought to it at all.

"I don't believe women, as individuals, are fully realized until they marry. Men too, for that matter. Too many these days—and I believe men are more guilty of this than women—remain in an extended childhood. They focus on their particular needs and wants—they react instinctually like children. Marriage insists that one grow up. That one think of someone beyond oneself. I believe this comes more naturally for women." He shrugged then, as if he'd gone on too long. "I believe it is a more natural state for them. A good state." He paused as if conscious of what he might next say. "A good state for you in particular." He seemed not at all embarrassed to admit that he'd given this quite a bit of thought.

She looked at her stew. "I think I'd like to know someday why you never married," she said.

"Perhaps someday I'll tell you."

Something in her middle moved as though whatever she'd been ignoring those many weeks and months had now aroused itself, opened up, and yawned with sudden ferociousness to be filled. The aroma seemed to want her to faint from it. Her appetite raged at her. Her stomach ached. She drew her spoon through the stew again, almost fearful of its power. She felt like a child, she thought; she desired as a child desires. She only wanted to be filled.

*It's obvious—you've been starving, my dear.*

Had he spoken? It was his voice, but it could not have been him; he looked only about to speak.

"Please eat," he urged her.

"Do you need to leave?" She thought she would immediately follow, as soon as he was out of sight. She'd leave the stew behind if she could manage to lift herself from the chair. She had hardly accomplished what she'd hoped. She would return to Bulgakov. She'd confess it to him.

"I feel compelled to watch you finish this," he said.

"I can't."

"I believe you can," he said. Not in the fashion of insisting on his way, but rather as an expression of a kind of faith in her. "I'm in no hurry, Margarita. You may take your time."

Was it hunger she felt? Why had she come?

Was she not complicit in everything that had befallen her? In her future, as well? Knowing this, would she have come anyway?

"You've done terrible things," she said.

"I have." She was uncertain if he sounded apologetic or not.

She thought of Bulgakov, home, writing. She studied the stew; then she tasted it.

She returned the spoon to the bowl and stared out at the street. It had brightened from before, its edges softened.

He didn't ask what was wrong or why she was crying. It didn't seem to trouble him, as if he had expected it.

She'd never tasted anything so wonderful before. And briefly she thought she would never be satisfied again.

She had decided to accept Bulgakov's proposal. She wouldn't tell him about Ilya. She told herself there was no point to it.

When she opened the door, Bulgakov was at the table, pages in disorderly piles around him. He didn't seem as surprised as she'd expected. He reached for his pocket watch and she turned to put her satchel away.

"They called from the paper," he said. "They asked if you were feeling better. I was worried." His words seemed to have been crafted earlier when the call was taken. His tone no longer agreed with their meaning.

She felt sudden remorse for her lie to her colleagues. She thought of their concern for her over the past months.

"I had a headache," she said.

He looked helpless at her words. "Are you better then?" he asked.

She nodded. "But tired."

He said something about how headaches could do that. She noticed how he stared at her.

"I may lie down for a while," she said.

She didn't make a move for the bed, nor did he return to his work.

"It was your editor who called," he said. "We talked for some time. He's worried about you. I felt like a young boy again, being called to task by the headmaster."

"It was only a headache," she said, trying to press truth into her words.

"Have you lost weight?" There was an echo of self-reproach in his question.

"Do you know if we have any powders?" She pulled open a cabinet door and began moving things around.

"I thought you said it was gone."

"It may be coming back." As though he was causing it. That was what he would think she had meant. She closed the cabinet and sat on the sofa.

"It took you a long time to come home," he said. He sounded nervous.

"I walked for a while. It seemed to help and I kept walking."

Again he was quiet. Then—"Where did you walk?"

"Does it matter?" She immediately regretted her answer. His nervousness visibly grew.

"You walked for two hours?" he said.

Had it been that long? "I stopped for a time. Then came home." She tried to manufacture fatigue in her voice. Perhaps he'd give up.

"Were you alone?"

"Of course," she said. This time instead of fatigue, she tried to invent credibility.

His nervousness seemed to change into quiet panic. What was she saying, what was she doing that he didn't believe her?

"Who were you with?"

"I told you. No one."

He got up from the table and sat down next to her. He took her hand, stroking it.

"You can tell me," he said. "You can trust me."

"I am telling you," she said. But she felt her own hope fading. Somehow he would know. Somehow she would tell him.

The tips of his fingers moved over the slight mounds of her knuckles, as though these were precious things. As though they might at any moment be taken from him, and in his longing for them, he was already anticipating their loss. She no longer wanted to lie to him.

"There's nothing to tell," she said.

"Tell me." His pain had transformed itself into despair.

"I met with Ilya."

She didn't know what his reaction might be. He seemed to be trying to understand it as well. She rushed ahead.

"I asked to meet with him," she said. "I wanted him to stop harassing you. To leave the play alone."

He set her hand down. "Why would you think that would help?"

"I couldn't think of anything else."

"He's a Deputy Director in the NKVD. Why would you think he would do this for you?" He was no longer questioning. His voice was cold. "For all we know he was responsible for Mandelstam." As though now she was somehow, in some way, responsible too.

"I was trying to help."

"He thinks he has feelings for you. Did he tell you this?" he said. "He's not capable of love. He would destroy what you love."

"I know."

His next words seemed to come out of nowhere. "Did you sleep with him?" He said this as though the thought had suddenly presented itself. He made no effort to censor it.

"God—no. No. Why would you say that? We talked."

"Who can say what he might have asked for in return?" He paused. "Or what you were prepared to offer in exchange."

"This is all your imagining! We only talked."

"Where—in his office?"

She could see he was trying to envision this. "Outside. At a restaurant. Not far from the prison. I don't know the name."

"Did you eat?" he said.

"We had coffee." She suddenly resented his need for these small details. She tried to appear transparent, even remorseful of the coffee, and he seemed satisfied.

"Did you convince him to leave the play alone?" He sounded strangely wistful, as though this was no longer a real concern and he might wish it still were.

"If anything, he was surprised by the accusation. He mentioned something—he'd given you a ride last night. He'd paid for the cab."

He didn't answer her. The constancy of the room around them—the piles of books on the floor, the morning's teacups on the low table, last week's paper wedged against the sofa leg—all appeared to intend normalcy when all was now changed. He seemed to see this too; he seemed to react to this. He got up and began to circle the room. He glanced at the window as if someone was outside waiting.

"He's not out there," she said.

"Do you know that?" His tone was neutral—no longer accusatory, yet not forgiving. Wondering if she had special knowledge of this. If she knew when Ilya wasn't there, then of course she would know when he was.

*Let me go*, she thought. She could leave him. There was the door. He seemed a wisp of a man. He'd be unable to stop her.

He continued to study the window. It wasn't just Ilya, she knew; it was the world beyond. He believed it conspired against him. He believed she was now one of them.

She'd done this to him. His fear, his uncertainty, they were her fault.

"He's not out there," she said. "I promise you."

Her confidence had a strange effect on him; grief seemed to overwhelm him, as though he was certain he'd lost her as well. "Are you going to see him again?"

She told him Ilya had wanted to take her to dinner. She told him she had no intention of meeting him, of course. That had never been her intention.

She told Bulgakov that she wanted to marry him.

Here was the currency of devotion. He suddenly seemed so poor as to be threadbare.

"I love you," she told him.

As though she could fill his pockets with it.

# CHAPTER 20

Bulgakov didn't tell her where he was going when he left that evening and he wondered that she didn't ask. Perhaps she knew. She'd showered and remained in his robe, a towel around her head like a turban. He'd prepared supper: rounds of sausages and cucumbers dipped in yogurt sauce. She commented favorably on it when she emerged from the bathroom.

He told her she looked wonderfully exotic.

She thanked him for the meal more than once.

Their conversation seemed a cautious enterprise.

Later, as he was leaving, she was curled in the chair. The towel had given way and her hair lay coiled against the robe's collar, dark-gold and slick. She was reading a book under the lamp's soft light. For the first time he noticed how thin she'd become. He could stay with her instead; he could prepare more for her to eat, some hearty dish to urge her appetite along.

When he said he was going out, she raised her head; he thought she nodded but he wasn't certain. Perhaps she was providing her allowance for it as though she understood it was something he needed to do. Perhaps she wanted to be left alone.

He touched her cheek. Unexpectedly she took his hand in hers. She smiled, perhaps surprised, as if her fingers had acted on their own accord.

"I won't be long, my dear," he said.

She kissed his hand. She covered it with her other one as well.

He must stay with her—how could he leave—yet he kissed her cheek as though he only understood her gesture to be a sweet thing and she released him. He promised himself, on the landing, then again outside their building: he would make this up to her when he returned.

Ilya had wanted to meet her in the bar at the Metropol. Bulgakov saw him through the window from the sidewalk outside. The bar was dimly lit; small alcohol lamps at each table. Ilya sat alone, leaning over a white tablecloth, his face washed in a flickering glow. His eyes were trained on the restaurant's foyer. He was waiting for her.

In profile, his face seemed younger. Perhaps he'd never expected to find one such as her; perhaps he'd given up on that hope many years ago. What thoughts would come to him when it was Bulgakov and not Margarita who appeared? How would disappointment and certainty dress that face?

As Bulgakov entered, he saw the rapid recalculation. By the time he'd reached the table even this was complete. Ilya looked up with careful surprise; his hands rested lightly on the table on either side of his glass. They seemed poised for anything.

Bulgakov sat down without invitation. "This is all right? I saw you from the street. You're not expecting someone?"

Ilya smiled in what seemed acquiescence, for a moment wordless. There was a second recalculation. "I wasn't expecting you," he said.

"This is a nice place," said Bulgakov.

Ilya hesitated. "The salmon is excellent."

Bulgakov pretended to be impressed by such knowledge. "Then I shall have some." Bulgakov motioned to a waiter. A quartet in the shadows played a languorous piece. He leaned in toward Ilya.

"I feel like I'm going to see someone important here," he said. "What fun!"

Ilya gave no indication that he shared Bulgakov's enthusiasm.

The waiter came and Bulgakov placed his order. Ilya asked him the time.

"You need to be somewhere?" said Bulgakov.

"Perhaps—a hazard of the job."

"That's too bad. I have been thinking of you though," said Bulgakov.

Ilya seemed distracted. "I'll assume not romantically."

"You've inspired my next novel. A young man of uncertain means rises to the position of—well, whatever your position is. These stories are popular right now. Their success lies in getting the details right."

Ilya was gazing past him, again toward the foyer. He wasn't paying attention. If he'd been concerned about Bulgakov's play or his writing in general, it seemed now of little interest. His cares had shifted to something else.

Bulgakov should have felt relief for this, but there was a certain pique that was difficult to assign. He had been, after all, Ilya's foremost interest at the start; he'd been the relevant one. Not the girl—must Ilya be reminded of this?

Of course it worked in his favor for Ilya to believe that Margarita might still appear—either tonight or in some indefinite future. But again he felt a queer contradiction in this. He wanted Ilya to know that she'd chosen him. He lightly considered that it was Margarita's story to tell, that in telling it himself, there was a kind of betrayal of her. But he didn't care. As he stared at the older man's hopeful face, it came on him more sharply. He wanted to cause that face to change.

Bulgakov tapped the tablecloth lightly. "She's not coming," he said. "She told me of your plans to meet."

Ilya's reaction was unexpected. "May I hope that she has decided instead to meet another friend? Perhaps take in a film? Attend a lecture?"

"She is at home. With a good book," he said. He wanted to add that she was waiting for his return, but something stopped him.

Ilya said nothing for a moment. "You are certain." His expression was difficult to read. There wasn't the disappointment that Bulgakov had expected.

The quartet's music sounded dissonant, as though a critical instrument begged to be tuned. Somewhere in the kitchen there was a muffled crash. Nearby, a passing man had jostled a seated customer. Words were exchanged and now their conversation had become heated. The second man stood. Bulgakov wanted to tell them it was all for naught. Indeed they must stop—it would only come to blows. All of these elements he recognized separately, yet here they'd assembled as though by providence, as though through them providence might deliver its terrible message.

"What would you do without her?" said Ilya. He asked as if this was an outcome that deserved appraisal. But his expression was not what Bulgakov had come to know. He looked frightened.

"What have you done?" said Bulgakov. His voice faded to a whisper. He turned the question upon himself—*what had he done?*

Ilya sat back and looked into his empty glass. He was frowning deeply, sorrowfully, in a way Bulgakov had not seen before.

"Indeed, she took your place," said Ilya. He rubbed his eyes, then over the top of his crown, roughly, as if he could unroof his scalp. His hair stood on end and when he lowered his hand, he seemed a different person.

A person capable of something terrible. He'd caught the wrong prey.

A plate of coral-colored salmon was placed between them, its edges crisp and gleaming. They both stared at it.

"I must go to her," said Bulgakov, rising.

"She's no longer at your apartment," said Ilya.

The outer door to the street had opened to admit a stylishly dressed couple. The lamp's flame flickered.

Ilya set a ruble note beside his glass and abruptly left the table; Bulgakov followed. The waiter collected the uneaten salmon; the plate was knocked and its skin fell open along its midline.

The salmon was rotten; its putrescence filled the room. The odor detected, the couple looked at each other and left.

Bulgakov opened the apartment door. A waltz was playing on the radio even as it lay on the floor behind the sofa.

It wasn't difficult to imagine the events that had transpired:

*The lamp on the table softly illuminated the page. She stretched. Above her head and unbeknownst to her, a spider had lowered itself on a thin strand. It paused. She turned the page, then rested her cheek against her hand again. The spider scurried upwards, moments before the knocking, its needle legs working the air.*

*She started to rise as the door opened.*

*Two agents entered without introducing themselves. One was a woman. She told Margarita to dress. The other agent proceeded to take apart the room. Margarita put on a skirt, then buttoned her shirt. Books toppled to the floor as shelves were emptied. The lamp on the side table—the one she'd never cared for—dove from its stand. The pillows were slashed and the mattress upturned; feathers rose and fell like snow, onto her hair, her sleeve. A third agent, another man, entered. He seemed not to notice the wreckage. He went to the wardrobe and took the manuscript from its drawer. Margarita moved toward him; perhaps she was going to explain that it was nothing, perhaps she thought to take it from him. He hit her. She fell against the corner of the table then to the floor. Warm, thick liquid rolled around her tongue. She pushed up with her arms and he kicked her behind the ear. There was a silent explosion of light, then greyness, then nothing. The floor came up and met her in a downy embrace.*

Bulgakov touched the floor. Goose down had clumped on a patch of blood.

The manuscript lay on the table, glowing in the dim light as the lone survivor. As though it was so terribly important.

There were many ways she could have left him. In this particular way she'd established her relevance.

# Part III
## What to Fear

# CHAPTER 21

A t that hour, the office light shone in a bar below the door. Ilya first touched the knob, then knocked. The voice within summoned him.

Pyotr Pyotrovich was a diminutive man and didn't much care for Ilya.

Ilya would need to make it seem like releasing her was his idea.

Pyotr was at his desk, writing. He raised his head. He didn't look at Ilya, or at least no further than the collar of his coat; his eyes then lingered on the knob as if it'd committed some minor betrayal. He resumed writing.

"You're here late," said Pyotr. "Or is it early now?" Pyotr would consider such comments pleasantries.

Ilya shut the door. "It's early."

Pyotr smiled a little at the page. "This is why my marriage ended in divorce."

He would consider this a moment of camaraderie.

Ilya sat in the chair opposite the desk.

A portrait of Stalin hung on the wall between them. Its gaze passed over their heads to the other side of the room.

Pyotr waited a moment, then lifted his head with a stiff smile. He held his pencil between both hands, rotating it like a slow-moving turbine.

"I fear I've been miserly in my compliments to you, Ilya. My apologies. Your recommendation for this evening's adventure was an excellent one."

Pyotr appeared truly pleased. Moreover, he was pleased with Ilya. This was unanticipated.

"I was ready to apologize for wasting their time," said Ilya. "Did they find the manuscript at least?"

"We did." Pyotr stopped turning the pencil and jotted a note on the page. He gripped it at its nub as if it might attempt some aberrant mark.

"I suppose it makes sense to hold the woman for the time being. Then he can be arrested." Ilya tried to sound mildly skeptical as though already anticipating someone's complaint about the extra paperwork.

"That would be one approach."

The pencil scratched. "Who is she?" said Ilya.

"No one," said Pyotr. "At least not to you or me." He raised his eyes to Ilya's face as if hoping to catch his expression. "But she's someone to him."

So this was it—she was in terrible danger. "I would think it better to take the writer himself," said Ilya. He tried to sound as though it mattered little to him.

Pyotr made a face. "That business with Mandelstam was bad."

What if he could do nothing for her? "Perhaps he doesn't care about her."

Pyotr bobbed his head. "He'll care. We can make certain of that."

Ilya was well aware of their capabilities.

"I'm having Yuri Mikhaylov question her," said Pyotr. "She may be useful in other ways too."

Mikhaylov was a sadist. This evening, this interview had quickly worsened to disastrous proportions.

"I should leave you to your good work," said Ilya. Another misstep. He could see Pyotr's new interest: *why was he so eager to leave?* Ilya glanced at his own hands; they seemed overly large and awkward. He felt so new.

Pyotr set down his pencil and leaned back in his chair. He regarded Ilya with what might be considered a mixture of concern and affection. His fingers tented over his midsection. Pyotr wasn't ready to let him go.

"I've always thought your obsession was an interesting one," he said.

"I might take exception to 'obsession,'" said Ilya.

"With certain writers, I mean."

"You're not much of a reader, are you?"

Pyotr's expression didn't change. His fingers parted briefly.

"It seems just as much a personal crusade." Pyotr leaned forward as if to emphasize his concern. "I wonder if it may be hampering your advancement, quite honestly."

Pyotr was finding too much enjoyment in this.

"Mandelstam, to be certain," he went on. "Mayakovsky, of course. Others, though, you seem to approach without the discriminating hand. This is not typical for my friend, Ilya Ivanovich, whose deeds are legendary."

Pyotr had risen through the hierarchy, past other capable men for a reason. His methods had been gathered into textbooks. The remembered cadence of his voice could rob sleep from both guard and victim years later. "My friend"—the words seemed to tag one; the victim upon hearing them felt their menace as a spotlight. "My friend" who was not. "My friend" who would come to learn the meaning of atrocity. Words that were a preamble to indecencies that would be enacted.

"Have you a wife? A girlfriend." Pyotr said it as if he'd answered his own question.

Ilya had read these textbooks; Pyotr looked not for the truth but the reaction to the falsehood.

"I am committed to my work," said Ilya.

"Family? A sister."

Ilya's lips felt dry.

"A brother," he answered.

"You are close?"

Ilya chose a random word.

"Very."

Pyotr smiled as though the prisoner had capitulated. "Family is so important to keeping one grounded."

Ilya stood. Pyotr's gaze followed him. A disinterested Stalin looked away. Ilya touched the door.

"You may go," said Pyotr, a pointed command. Its belatedness mattered not at all.

"I'm glad I was able to play some small role in this evening's success," said Ilya with a bow.

"Of course you are," said Pyotr.

She was somewhere in that complex. Somewhere beyond his reach.

Ilya wouldn't recall leaving Pyotr's office. He wouldn't remember the maze of passages he took as he fled. Or if he'd closed Pyotr's door behind him. But if he hadn't, if the interrogator-turned-Director had listened to the anxious cascade of footsteps in his retreat, he'd have understood as well as if Ilya had barked forth his confession.

He loved her. *Dear God*—he loved her.

# CHAPTER 22

Margarita was processed then taken to a large room of grey painted cinderblock, occupied by a dozen or so women. It was early morning. Those who were awake looked at her, pale ovals turning toward the light from the hallway. They looked away again as though what they saw was simply a reflection of themselves. She brought no answers to their particular concerns. The door shut loudly behind her. The sound of its locking mechanism lingered. One of the guards who had escorted her laughed in response to something another guard had said.

She sat down on a bunk board. There was a woman on the other end.

"You're bleeding," said the woman.

Margarita touched her ear. It was sticky. "It's stopped," she said.

"You were beaten," said the woman. She sounded alarmed. Margarita sensed others around them turn with curiosity. She felt them withdraw as if she among them was the true criminal, the one they should fear.

Margarita lay down, first toward the wall; however, this pressed the injured ear against the wood, so she rolled over and faced outward. She heard snoring; and perhaps also weeping, though it was faint and could have been the breathiness of dreaming. Strangely, the grey, boxlike room seemed more real to her than the other world. As if the former could be easily dismissed, and in her dreamlike meditations she thought that the world had been turned inside out: all that had been external: the buildings, streets, landscape, sky, was now squeezed down inside her, perhaps as a memory or as a miniaturized version of creation for her to keep as a souvenir. And those things internal, her secrets and fears, were real and manifest in the shadowy space, available for all to touch and comment upon.

When she opened her eyes the lights had been turned on. The clock on the wall indicated it was close to eight. It was covered by a metal cage.

She sat up. The room tipped for a moment.

On the edge of her sleeve was something—a piece of goose down from one of their pillows. She touched it, then held it between her fingers; it was so light she couldn't feel it. She remembered the snow of it falling in the dim room—she needed to keep it—she hadn't a pocket—where? She closed her hand around it. She opened it to ensure it was there, then closed it again.

A woman sat down beside her. Different from the woman earlier. Margarita guessed they were of similar age. She seemed of lesser means with a roughness that came of less education. Margarita had the sense she'd been waiting for her to awaken. She touched Margarita's hair where it was matted to the blood by her ear.

"Does it hurt?" she asked. She didn't ask who'd done this to her.

Margarita lied and said no.

"Look at them," said the woman, indicating the others who sat in groups of twos and threes. "You'd think they were at some kind of newcomers' tea party."

Others were chatting in lowered tones. Exchanging information about their families and children, their jobs and their circumstances. Two had just discovered they had been neighbors as children; they spoke warmly of the grocer that had once lived on their block. Their voices rose for a moment over the memory of the man's son who'd been a few years older than them; a memory once dull that was now precious in their current situation. They clasped hands briefly in what they shared.

"They act like bosom friends," said the woman with scorn.

"You've been here before?" said Margarita.

The woman seemed not to hear. "Like this is all some silly mistake," she said. "Like they'll get to go home."

Some of the others stared at them. Margarita felt their fear, and, more particularly, their dread of her. She touched her ear. She was what they feared they might be.

There were footsteps. All faces turned to the door. It opened but no one entered. A man's voice rang through the cell.

"Margarita Nikoveyena Sergeyev."

Margarita stood and felt at once dizzy and slightly nauseous. She didn't want to leave; who could say where they might take her. Hands from behind shoved her forward.

The woman who'd engaged her in conversation now pushed her. She hissed. "Go!"

Margarita started toward the door. Its opening seemed to dip. She grabbed at its frame to steady herself. The other woman rose and spoke out.

"I'm not supposed to be here," she said. "There's been a mistake. Check your records. I'm not supposed to be here."

Margarita passed through and fell against the chest of the guard. He grabbed her arm to right her. No response had been given to the other woman. Her voice was lost in the shutting of the door.

They descended stairs then sloping passages. Walls were in places rough-hewn as though of a medieval dungeon. Her questions wrapped themselves in the pounding of her head and her growing nausea. Lights came and went overhead. She stumbled again and they hauled her upright. She wanted to tell them to take her back. She'd feel better tomorrow if they gave her more time. She'd speak nicely with the other women, share stories, express sympathy. She thought she had said that, but she heard her own voice, ragged and begging, utter different thoughts.

"Just tell me," she said. Just say what was coming; tell her what she needed to fear.

They didn't answer.

# CHAPTER 23

M*olière* opened despite Margarita not being there to see it. This was the case with many things in those first weeks. Streetcars kept to their schedules. Newspapers continued to print. The world had changed—yet passersby appeared to give no notice to it. They bent their hats against the weather, they walked back and forth from work as before. The world had changed—yet it seemed to maintain some stubborn indifference to this, and if Bulgakov mistrusted it; if he resented it in fact, it was for this disregard.

The play's reviews were generally positive. Stanislawski was pleased, and, perhaps more so, he was relieved. He arranged interviews for Bulgakov with major literary magazines and with *Pravda*. When Bulgakov missed his appointment for this, not once, but twice, Stanislawski first called, then came to his apartment to harangue him in person. This was important, the director told him. Actually, it was more than important—Bulgakov needed to earn the privilege of keeping *Molière* on the stage. He told him he would reschedule the interview once more—and that there would be others to follow. Now was the time to become a true literary figure. After everything he'd invested, that they both had invested. Bulgakov said he'd do better in order to get him to leave and Stanislawski slammed the door behind him.

Bulgakov cleaned up the mess from the night she was taken. He'd acquired a new kind of pragmatism with this. Rather than repair a tear, he turned the cushion over. Shattered picture glass was swept and prints were rehung on the wall without its protection. As if his anticipation of the agents' return and further mischief was protection against it. Her blouses and skirts he hung in the wardrobe. Sweaters and slacks he returned to their drawers. Her boots near the door where they waited for her. Their belief in her release seemed alternately reassuring and absurdly naïve.

The novel itself remained on the table where they'd left it. One early morning when sleep gave no reprieve, he returned to his chair and laid his hand on the first page. It was as impenetrable as a grave. He put it back in the drawer of the wardrobe then lay down again. Still he sensed it as though that part of the room had settled under its weight.

He debated what to do about the curtains and one night he rehung them. They were rumpled from having sat in piles for too long. Most of the pins she'd used still lay on the sills; some had been scattered and, with the hanging of the final panel, he found himself on the floor, on his knees searching the seams between the floor's planks for the last remaining ones. What looked like a pin was a grain in the wood, a stray thread, a strand of hair. He would go to pick it up and his fingers grasped air. The world had done this to him. Ilya had done it. Then one small part of his brain went past this to think absurdly, selfishly, childishly, perhaps she'd had some hand in it. How could he blame himself and go on? *Did he know how hard it was to lay one's hands on pins?* He pressed his forehead against the wood. How could he have known?

Bulgakov posted letters to Stalin nearly every day. There was never any indication that they were read. He went to Lubyanka looking for Ilya but was turned away. He stood in long queues with the families of other prisoners. He thought they all looked the same—pale, shell-shocked. They spoke not at all to each other, as though this would acknowledge some terrible commonality. As though it would unduly test their faith that their particular case—their husband, their wife, their child—was different from the rest. They waited for the opportunity to plead with a guard whose lips were hidden behind a small metal slit in a wall. Ten-second conversations that were unvaried. The guard would review several lists for the given name. A rattle of paper might be heard but not always. Sometimes there was the odor of onions and animal fat.

Bulgakov wished he could talk to Nadya. He wondered how she had managed those weeks waiting for some bit of information, yet dreading it too. What would she have thought of this turn of events? Once again, her husband and his lover were aligned in ways that excluded her. Would she feel vindicated or would this be a different kind of loss? Or had all feelings been wrung dry?

"Margarita Nikoveyena Sergeyev." The sound of it fled quickly and made for Bulgakov a renewed loneliness.

The voice paused. "I have no information available."

How was that possible? "Every week I hear the same thing—do you know if she is even in there?" said Bulgakov.

There was another pause, and for a moment Bulgakov wondered whether if by deviating from the typical dialogue, he'd actually broken some internal mechanism. The voice returned.

"Is she out there with you?" it said.

"Of course not."

"Then she is here."

A woman behind him pressed against his coat. "You've had your turn," she said. "Give it to another." Bulgakov didn't move.

"And if you were to have new information, what might that be?" said Bulgakov.

Another pause, then Bulgakov sensed a kind of sympathy to the words. "That she is no longer here, either."

Bulgakov stood at the tram stop outside of Lubyanka, watching those who converged upon that spot waiting for their own particular route. He wasn't certain whom he was looking for. There were office workers—men and women, older women, perhaps mothers in their own right, and younger, attractive ones. There were guards in uniform. Many read newspapers. Some smoked and kept watch down the avenue. Some stared into space. Several trams stopped and filled with passengers. Bulgakov continued to wait. The afternoon shadows began to lengthen. A women with a perambulator appeared. The baby was crying and the woman bobbed the handles, cooing into its cover, trying to soothe it. A youngish guard standing nearby glanced toward the child. Bulgakov could guess that from his angle he had some view of the carriage's interior. Bulgakov surmised he was of lower rank given the few stripes across his sleeve. Perhaps the guard was only bored. Perhaps he was reminded of some younger brother or sister, some past time. He smiled slightly, and then, and Bulgakov's heart rose with this, the guard's expression shifted. There was a moment of understanding—the day was chilled, the wind stung, the afternoon had been long already and one could simply be hungry. Or bored and with only a child's sensibility there would be no anticipation of what would certainly be relief once Mother could get it home. Yet unlike others nearby who either ignored or were irritated by the noise, unlike even the Mother who seemed to think jostling the buggy might provide some comfort, the guard seemed to understand the world of these things; he seemed to feel them all at once. It was there—one instant that said, *Yes. I can imagine what you are feeling right now.*

The tram arrived and the guard climbed in. Bulgakov followed.

His interview with *Pravda*, rescheduled now for the third time, was that evening. The tram was headed in a different direction.

# CHAPTER 24

A clock hung on the wall inside her cell. For sixteen minutes each day, sunlight passed through a single, high window and painted a rhombus of light on the cement floor. For those sixteen minutes, she sat in the light, feeling the coolness seep through the fabric of her skirt. For those minutes the rest of the cell seemed darker.

Each day she followed the guards down two flights of stairs to a room that was painted white on the top and blue-grey on the bottom. Here her interrogators waited. There were three of them. She did not know their names. She called them Matthew, Mark and John. Matthew was handsome and in some ways her favorite. He wasn't interested in learning of her anti-Bolshevik sentiments, if indeed she had any. He had imagination.

Their first session, he held her hand at the beginning as if they'd been formally introduced. He seemed to linger over it, admiring its structure, and for a moment she was self-conscious of his attention. He then let go.

"Take off your underwear," he told her.

"What? No!"

There was an explosion of light, then pain. She fell to her hands and knees. No one in the room said anything or moved to help her. She touched the inside of her cheek with her tongue where it'd been torn by her own teeth. She got up, for a moment unsteady, then lifted her skirt, slid her underwear down to her ankles, and stepped out of them. She held them in her hands, her arms crossed over her torso. Tears came and rolled down her cheeks. Matthew nodded to one of the men behind her and her arms were lifted and extended over her head. Loops of rope were tied around her wrists and then to a hook that hung from the ceiling. The hook was raised until she was standing on her toes.

"Oh! Oh! Please! I can't—please!" Her voice sounded muffled, her arms pressed against her ears. She wanted to cross her legs but couldn't maintain her footing. Matthew didn't respond. He walked around her slowly, slipping from her sight. She quieted, listening, breathing in short airy gasps. After a few moments he reappeared. He sat on a stool in front of her. He now carried a policeman's baton. He stroked the hem of her skirt with it.

"I'll bet you can do lots of things," he said. "I thought we'd start slowly, being your first time." He pushed the tip of the baton between her knees. "You were Mandelstam's whore. Tell me about him."

She couldn't speak or think, only wisps of air came from her. He pushed the baton upward a little.

"We don't have to start slowly, whore."

"I—I don't know—I mean, what do you want to know?"

He removed the baton and sat back.

"What was it like—your first time with him?"

She struggled to find words. He looked bored, then he wagged the baton in her face.

"I think you can do better."

She started again; her vocabulary became more eloquent as she went on. He brightened at first, then seemed to grow agitated as he listened. She stopped, uncertain that she might be upsetting him. He growled at her to go on.

"Tell me what it felt like the first time you put that bastard's cock in your mouth."

Her voice seemed to come from a hole behind her head.

She went on, feeding him words, words she never used, and his breathing deepened and he started to grimace. He stopped her again and had her repeat herself. Finally, he sprung from the stool and struck her with the bat across her cheek. The walls flickered with pinpoints of light. She had satisfied him.

Each day he questioned her then beat her; afterwards he'd sit awhile until the red of his cheeks faded, until his breathing steadied, until the trembling of his hands subsided. Then Mark would have his turn. Mark was interested in other things.

It was Mark she could imagine as her lover. Shorter and more compact than the sprawling and emotional Matthew, he maintained a stillness in his features during their exchanges. It was only when he would step away, remove his wire-framed glasses, and wipe them carefully with his handkerchief that the silent and muscular John would step forward with a short leather-sheathed bat. Then she knew she'd touched him in some way. She heard her voice exclaim in short beats as John laid into her; each slap against her thighs and buttocks followed by a bright burst in her brain. Eventually he would tire and the cadence would slow and her exclamations would crescendo into round moans. When the beating was finished Mark would fold and return the white cloth to his pocket, slip the glasses back behind his ears, and raise his eyes to her again. He was patient with her; he forgave her these interruptions. She imagined him dressing in the morning, thinking of her as he took each button through its hole, as he looked in his mirror.

Most of the accusations were fabricated. Associations with people she'd never known, conversations that had never taken place, meetings impossible for her to attend as she'd lived somewhere else at the time. She commented to Mark once that his fiction was compelling.

She was told her attitude did not help her. When she returned to her cell, a metal shutter had been screwed over the window. Where the clock had hung there were only wires.

When alone she tried to imagine all they could do to her, the worst they could invent. And when they did something new, she'd return and examine her limbs, press on the bruises, and recall the memory of their specific tools. In the places she couldn't see, she'd trace the swellings with her fingers.

At night the guards woke the prisoners repeatedly. It was difficult to estimate the passage of time. One morning Mark happened to mention she'd been there for twenty-one days. She'd counted over twice more and with this she cried. For one strange moment he looked apologetic. Puzzled and pained and perhaps in some way embarrassed. As if he had inflicted a wound he'd not intended. The room was silent. Tears took random paths down her cheeks and lips.

Later, after her escorts had returned her to her cell, she imagined the other interrogators ridiculing him for ending the session early that day. She knew the same as he knew: he'd given up a temporary advantage for reasons he didn't understand. She imagined he'd complain of a headache then retreat to the infirmary for an aspirin.

Usually they talked about Mandelstam. One day, he wanted to talk about Bulgakov. He suggested the topic as if he were suggesting an outing on a fine day. Matthew was home with a mild fever and they'd not yet tied her up. Mark offered her the extra chair. She sat down. Its padding was thin and the underlying curve of its metal support pressed into her tailbone that'd been bruised during their last session. She shifted. She rested her arm on the table. He sat facing her, his arm resting like hers in a mirror image. John stood near the door. She allowed her feet to lie flat on the floor.

Since her arrest, she had wondered if Bulgakov had been taken the same night. She feared for him, that she might implicate him in some way. Sometimes she envisioned him in a nearby cell, staring at the same colored walls, eating the same watery soups and old bread. At night lying on her bedboard she imagined them reunited in sleep, his arm around her waist. Other times, but not at all times, she grieved for his lost work. It was easiest first thing in the morning, after she was awakened. Later, when her interrogators were finished, she cared less for his words. They flitted about her like moths, thoughtless of the difficulties they had caused her. By the next morning though, she felt guilty for this betrayal. As if in the night they had fought their way to the light and by morning their carcasses were scattered on the cell floor, upturned and motionless. She was regretful for such an end to their short lives.

—*Let's talk about Bulgakov*
—*I've heard of him.*
—*You were found in his apartment.*
—*I've been found in many people's apartments.*
—*Do you like his work?*
—*I've never seen it.*

She wondered why she aligned herself with writers. Surely men such as her interrogator had come through the doors of the stores where she shopped, the cafes she frequented. She could have smiled at their attempts to tease her name from her; she could have let them take her to the movie theater and buy her flavored drinks. In the flickering darkness she could have let their fingers wander over the seam at her shoulder, move to the curve of her neck. Afterwards, they'd have talked about the movie, the news in the papers, the latest feats of their local Stakhovite. Later they'd have gossiped about their neighbors and friends. The shape of their lives together would form about such things. If she picked up a book to read, she'd give no thought to the writer who'd penned it for her. It might be nice to think nothing of him.

Mark drummed his fingers lightly against the table. During their time together, he seemed always to have formed an opinion as to whether, with any particular exchange, she was lying. For the first time, he seemed uncertain. He motioned to John and when he came over, he spoke in his ear. She stiffened; she dreaded being beaten again. She didn't think she could take it; not after sitting in a real chair for so long.

John left the room. Mark went on. His fingers quieted.

"I saw the play, *The Day of the Turbins*."

"I wouldn't know."

"Nothing else he's done has amounted to much."

He looked away. He was embarrassed, she thought. As if she was a pretty girl he wanted to get to know. She felt a strange sympathy for him for that.

"Are you done with me?" she said.

There were plenty of ordinary men to love. Ordinary monsters. Monster love. No different than extraordinary love. Her mind was wandering. Perhaps it had wandered away. She shifted in her seat. Her tailbone ached.


Fedir Andreivich sat outside the office of the deputy director. The appointment had been at the deputy director's request, a note found on Fedir's desk after returning from lunch. He'd have worn better clothes had he known. He scratched at an old stain on his trousers; a dried fleck of gravy or soup that had gone unnoticed until that moment. He had hoped for a promotion and a move into his organization. He no longer wanted to be an interrogator. The Deputy Director was said to be fair and even-tempered. Fedir would remember to cross his legs in such a way as to hide the spot. He crossed them then to see if this solution would work.

The door opened and Ilya Ivanovich appeared. Fedir stood. Ivanovich appeared surprised to see him.

"You're not Yuri Mikhaylov?"

"I'm sorry," said Fedir. "I thought you wanted to speak with me."

"Don't apologize." Ivanovich barked with nearly the same harshness as his initial demand. "You didn't misplace him. I thought he was leading the interrogation proceedings. Am I wrong?"

"Yes," said Fedir. He was surprised with the directness of his own response. He softened his tone. "You are mistaken."

Ivanovich seemed momentarily amused, and Fedir wondered if it was his boldness that had satisfied him. Ivanovich turned and gestured for Fedir to follow.

The inner office was the larger of the two rooms and dominated by an ornately carved desk. Two upholstered chairs were positioned in front of it. Ivanovich sat in one of these and motioned for Fedir to take the other. It seemed as though they were occupying a borrowed office, as if the meeting itself was surreptitious, and could end at any moment once the true occupant returned. Ivanovich leaned across the desk and opened a cigarette case. Again, it seemed an act of delinquency. He took one for himself and offered the box to Fedir. Fedir felt compelled to take one. After lighting them both, Ivanovich sat back and crossed one leg over the other.

Fedir inhaled; the tobacco was of high quality and he was a little sorry he couldn't take his time and enjoy it without the distraction of this interview. He was now fully convinced he wanted to move into the Deputy Director's organization. Any other outcome would result in a decrement in the satisfaction he enjoyed in his job. He sat up straighter. He remembered the stain but did nothing to hide it.

Ivanovich asked his name and he told him.

"That's Ukrainian, is it not?"

"My mother was Ukrainian."

"I see." His tone was neutral. Fedir interpreted his response to be less than neutral. But before he could apologize for his bloodline, the subject shifted again.

"What do you think of Margarita Nikoveyena?"

Fedir was unaccustomed to the use of her name. It was irregular for Ivanovich to go to him for information regarding the prisoner. Fedir hesitated, uncomfortable that this might be perceived as circumventing his own supervisor. This could be some sort of loyalty test. The door to the outer office was still open.

"Wouldn't you do better to review this with Deputy Director Petrenko?"

Ivanovich's expression stiffened slightly. Fedir hastened to answer the original question. This man was still a superior.

"She's had significant associations with known enemies." He ticked off a short list. Ivanovich looked impressed. Fedir hoped with him.

"And a longer list of persons of interest," Fedir went on. "I'm surprised that her case didn't fall under your purview." He wanted to say that it would have been his honor to investigate such a case, or any case, within the auspices of his organization. He crossed his leg over the stained fabric.

"What of the playwright Bulgakov?" said Ivanovich. "Have you discussed him?"

"I don't think there is much there."

Ivanovich seemed surprised. "She was found in his apartment."

"But your people have investigated him, and found little, is my understanding." He wanted to show his diligence to the larger picture.

Ivanovich smiled. "You're correct. Are you enjoying the cigarette? You may have another if you like, for later." He opened the case for him.

"Yes, I will," said Fedir. "Thank you. These are wonderful. Where did you get them?"

Ivanovich didn't answer his question.

"On the other hand, if interrogators such as yourself don't pursue these answers, then we will never know."

"I can question her again," said Fedir. He was eager to please him.

"Only as you see fit." His tone was mildly obsequious.

Fedir's cigarette had acquired a subtle bitterness. He considered setting it aside.

Ivanovich went on. "What do you think Director Pyotrovich has in mind for your prisoner?"

"I don't know." He said this, even though he did. His supervisor, Pyotrovich's subordinate, guarded such information closely, yet nevertheless had trusted him with it.

Ivanovich said nothing as though waiting for a different answer. At the start of their interview, Fedir had felt a bond growing between them. This seemed to have dissipated.

"I suspect he's going to recommend exile," said Fedir.

"Really? She'd make an excellent informant. Why lose that advantage?"

"Director Pyotrovich believes there are already too many informants of the literary ilk." As soon as he said it, he realized that this could be an unpleasant revelation for Ivanovich. "He said he'd rather make an example of this one."

Ivanovich's demeanor shifted. "How interesting."

Fedir felt obliged to provide some defense for these sentiments. Or perhaps simply soften their blow. "Truthfully, I'm not certain she'd make an effective informant." It was difficult to articulate why. Perhaps she lacked sufficient fear of them. Or failed to show a desire for something they could threaten to take away. It seemed they had little to work with. "Occasionally the process of interrogation reduces the prisoner's value as an informant."

He was confused by the Deputy Director's reaction to his words. He thought he saw a sudden admiration for his effectiveness as an interrogator. But there was something else as well—Ivanovich had retracted slightly into his chair. Behind his admiration, there was what could be described as a detached sense of horror, as one who was observing at some distance the antics of a grossly disfigured creature.

"We'll continue to work on her, of course," said Fedir. "Perhaps she can produce." He tried to sound hopeful of this plan, despite his growing disquiet. The space had become warm. He started to lift the cigarette to his lips, then stopped. He wanted only to escape the room.

"Do you think she is actually an enemy of the people?" said Ivanovich. It seemed the first honest question he'd asked of him; the first question for which he didn't already know the answer. He asked as if it was a question Fedir needed to consider himself.

The room seemed false. The interview as well. As though the furnishings, the bookcases, the portrait of Stalin had been hastily moved in and put up; that the walls themselves were temporary dressings tacked over the standard blue and white paint of the interrogation cell. If he had looked up, he believed he would see a lightbulb dangling; he'd see the single hook.

He had thought of them together, as a couple. He'd thought of coming home to her at night after work. Bringing her flowers and groceries. He'd thought other such ridiculous things.

"I find everyone is an enemy, if I look hard enough," said Fedir.

Ivanovich seemed not at all surprised nor angered by the impertinence.

Fedir tamped out the remainder of his cigarette. He bowed and left the office. He left the building. He didn't return to work the next morning, complaining of a head cold. Several months later, he passed away suddenly. The NKVD reported it as a mishap with an electrical appliance.

# CHAPTER 25

T he appointed time of their meeting had passed for the third straight day yet Bulgakov continued to wait at the small white-clothed table which abutted the front window of a tearoom located several blocks from Lubyanka. For the third straight day he ordered only a Narzan water and a lime, sliced. The server was an attractive young woman whose face had been disfigured by a well-healed scar that ran the width of her forehead, Bulgakov thought, as if someone, in Shelleyian fashion, had attempted to remove her brain through the top of her skull. She never looked at his face as he gave his request, a pencil held over a wad of paper in her hand, and when she heard it, neither did she write it down. Yet, for the hours he waited, his glass never emptied and each plate of rolled and wasted rinds was quickly replaced by another with more jewellike fruit. She seemed a crude experiment of the State's, one of engineered industriousness that had ended surprisingly well. He had joked with her that first day: the limes were necessary since he feared scurvy. He could see she did not know what that meant and she did not ask. Who jokes about their fears, he thought and he considered her flat affect and scar as only a doctor would. Afterwards, he asked simply for the fruit and the water.

The street between the tearoom and the prison was crowded with people; streetcars ran according to routine. He watched as pedestrians hurried across the tracks before each passing tram; this could be any city in any country; there was little which particularized the scene to their time and place. Yet he could pick any one of these figures, follow them home, or to their workplace, and craft a story that examined the particulars of that life. Each was specific, personal, important. Each deserved notice in some way.

Another streetcar approached; he saw Ilya's friend, Annuschka, from the restaurant so long ago. She was driving; she wore the driver's hat and jacket. He caught the flash of her face; her youthfulness seemed to challenge the authority of the uniform's gold trim and epaulets. Sunlight flared white across the line of windows; then it passed.

Ilya had called her "a working girl," a neighbor. Was there more to that relationship? Could it be counted as coincidence that she had appeared, on this street, on this particular day, as though she was only doing her job, following arbitrary rails set into the road, as though there was nothing to witness, to ponder, to report upon?

Bulgakov rubbed his eyes. He was losing his mind. Yet he studied the street again. Strangers' faces seemed both familiar and foreign. He watched for any that might linger in his direction.

Two hours after the appointed time, that third day, a man crossed the square and entered the tearoom. The bell nailed to the top of the door jangled anxiously.

He went to the counter directly, scaned the display case, and ordered several teacakes. He answered the girl, Bulgakov's server, that yes, he needed them packaged, then casually inquired of directions to Pokrovskiye Gate. He waited, glancing at the specimens under the glass while she went to fetch the manager. The customer was tall and slim with youthful features, yet his brownish hair seemed to be graying prematurely. Bulgakov pretended disinterest, touching one of the empty rinds on his plate.

The manager appeared from a back room, wiping flour

from his hands with a towel tucked into his waistband, and Bulgakov stood and motioned to the server to indicate he was leaving. The manager was marking the top of the display case with a still floury finger as if he were pointing to a road on a map. Bulgakov opened the door and their words were lost in the bell's sound. Outside the light was curious. A thin layer of midafternoon sunlight was sandwiched between the earth and a low-lying bank of gray clouds. Large spots of rain began to darken the sidewalk. Bulgakov headed toward Patriarch's Ponds. He dared not take a cab. Drops pelted his shoulders and back as he went.

The details of his arrangement with the guard from Lubyanka seemed laughably transparent. Bulgakov knew it could be anyone who might act as an informer. It was the girl server whose gaze now followed him from the tearoom's window, down and across Teatralny toward Tverskaya Street. Who glanced then at the man at the counter then back to the glass and suddenly understood that she would never see her customer again. It was the man's co-worker, a fellow guard in the D-block of Lubyanka, who observed aloud that for the second day in a row the man had been late for his afternoon cigarette break. Who noticed that his words were ignored, that the other simply lit his cigarette then spoke as if something entirely different had been said. It was the man at Patriarch's Ponds who would sell them two bottles of ginger beer and pocket the extra change he'd held back from the one who seemed nervous. It was the housing commissioner of the guard's apartment building who'd been annoyed by the late hours he kept and simply wanted his room in order to house her recently divorced sister and her sister's children.

With the rain, Patriarch's Ponds had been abandoned and the kiosk shutters closed and Bulgakov sat alone on an empty bench under a linden tree. To the west, the sky was clearing and the light swelled even in the declining hour as if someone had peeled back a corner of its stormy roof. The rain had stopped.

A screech of steel against steel sounded and the kiosk window rolled open. The guard from Lubyanka sat down on the other end of Bulgakov's bench. The kiosk seller poked his face through the opening and looked at them. His head disappeared.

The guard opened the bag of teacakes and offered it to Bulgakov. Bulgakov shook his head. The guard removed a cake and inspected it briefly. He confessed that he ate constantly and he took a bite. He always had and yet he looked like this. He gestured to himself. He said the cakes weren't half bad. Perhaps a little stale.

Bulgakov asked about Margarita. The guard finished chewing, then looked away, down the sidewalk that ran in front of them toward the distant street.

"I brought payment," said Bulgakov.

The guard told him she was being interrogated.

Bulgakov paused before his next question. What did that mean exactly?

The puddles in the walk caught the light of the sky. The air smelled wet and moldy.

The guard had heard of her interrogators. Their reputations. She could have done worse. He took another bite of the teacake.

Had she been tortured?

Not that he could see.

"It took me a bit to find her," he said. He removed another teacake from the bag.

Bulgakov took a roll of bills from his pocket and placed them on the bench between them.

"Were you able to give her my message?" asked Bulgakov.

"Do you suppose they sell anything worth drinking?" said the guard. He covered the bills with his fingers, then slid them into his trouser pocket.

The price was just over a hundred rubles.
Bulgakov went to see.

It'd been about the money. The guard was certain that the
man would pay whatever was asked. The man had worn a suit
when they'd first met, old but not frayed; the chain of a watch
fob was visible though he never saw the watch. He'd become
good at sizing people up and gave the price. The man had hesitated, but when he made to leave, he quickly assented. He
was good at sizing up. It came from observing a multitude of
prisoners, the rich and the formerly rich and the poor and the
penniless, flowing past him every day. People were base creatures. They only valued that which was painful to acquire.
Once the price was set, the man was quiet. A hundred rubles
was steep for information. The guard added then that simply
finding one prisoner among the thousands held there would
be no small trick. The man nodded. Perhaps that had made
him feel better.

Finding her was not simple. He asked questions he'd not
normally ask; took interest in conversations he'd typically
ignore. He knew his change in habit was noticed and he
ignored this as well. He saw her only twice. The first time no
words were exchanged. She had no idea she'd been the subject
of such scrutiny. He suspected she was being held for interrogation. He listened in on the conversations of guards assigned
to those wings. After several false leads, he fabricated an
errand to one of the midlevel blocks. He saw her as she was
being escorted back to her cell. It was simply a moment; for
some reason she turned as she passed through the riveted door,
for some reason her gaze rested not upon those who'd brought
her back but rather on the corridor beyond, on the one unfamiliar face. She did not look away from him, even as the door
between them closed. She was the kind of woman who was
accustomed to the stares of others, both men and women, he

knew. But she'd know in this exchange that his chance appearance was not chance. He was certain of this even before their second meeting. She would be waiting for him.

He had only a sister who worked on the sly as a seamstress, sliding the extra kopeks gleaned from her guilty customers into little pockets she had fashioned in the hem of her skirt to hide them from the Kolkhoz inspectors. Their mother had left them in 1905 and she had raised him even though she was barely older and certainly no bigger. He'd only seen her once since coming to Moscow. She sent frequent letters. He had the sense that she wrote them thinking she was writing to the world. That they would be opened and read and collected and filed was not her concern. She complained that he rarely wrote and when he did, he said nothing. She gave no warning of her visit. The evening he'd found her waiting in his apartment was one of record snowfall in the city. She was sitting in his armchair with her bare feet propped up on the seat of another. The snow that had dusted his shoulders began to melt and he felt the cool dampness sink through the wool. She said she'd brought the storm with her. Her small frame was enveloped by the chair. He took off his overcoat. She refused to be extricated from his life. He kissed her on the forehead. She waved her hand about his apartment. What was it about the two of them, she said, that they should both live their lives as a solitary endeavor. He told her he preferred it that way.

He saw the prisoner for the last time several weeks after the first.

It was a chance meeting and he was ill-prepared for it. She'd been moved to his cell block in order to repair a broken pipe that was flooding her cell. He'd not given a thought to what he might say to her. Despite the arrangement and the agreed-upon sum, he never really thought the opportunity would arise.

When he arrived for his shift that morning he was told to escort the prisoner in D-242A for her quarter-hour breather. There was a light rain and his clothes were still damp from it, yet it was a better alternative than making the rounds and collecting food tins. D-block guards unbolted the stenciled door. He joked with one of them, some reference to a woman he'd seen him with at a bar the night before. A woman well above his pay-grade, he suggested. The door swung open and he saw her. He saw her and saw his own surprise and uncertainty reflected in her face and could think only of the implausibility of their meeting being random. They—the unknowable, unnamable *they*—knew and had decided to allow for this happenstance. They would be watching. He didn't hear the other guard's response. Someone else nearby laughed at something that had been said.

He directed her along the corridors with single-word commands until they reached a series of doors. He unlocked one with a key on his belt and revealed a small outdoor alcove. Its grey light glowed in contrast to the dark inside. The outdoor space was boxlike; three meters square with two-meter-high concrete walls. The ground was dirt. The earlier rain had changed to a low mist. She entered and turned around in it. Her posture was slightly stooped.

"How much time do I have?" she said. She seemed both in awe of this freedom and reluctant of it.

He told her a quarter hour. He realized then that she'd not been let out before; typical prisoners were given time for exercise each week. This made it likely she was a political and at once she became a much greater danger to him. The likelihood of their situation being chance was even more remote. He lit a cigarette and leaned against the wall. They could watch all they liked, he decided. They could listen to silence fill their ears. He had no intention of talking to her.

"It's funny; you look like someone I know," she said.

He looked at her hard, and, he hoped, discouragingly, and continued smoking. Did she have any idea of how stupid she was being?

"Like the younger brother of someone I know."

"I don't look like anyone," he said. *That's how they pick us*, he wanted to add. *We are the ones with forgettable faces.*

"Well, he is a nice man and you look like him." She spoke as if she'd held her words for so long that now she'd begun, they were beyond her control.

"We can make this a three-minute breather instead of fifteen." He wasn't willing to take these risks.

She pressed her lips into a thin line.

Small puddles had collected on the uneven ground near one of the enclosure's corners. From one she rescued a drowning earthworm. She showed it to him before depositing it on moist soil. It arched up from her palm then fell back against it, its mass in the air too much to support. She placed it on higher ground then stood and rubbed her hands together. As if she could find more things to save. He thought—here she stands, for the moment vast and almighty; the low and mindless at her feet. Did she not feel some urge to squash it into the dirt? To stand square with those who still moved freely in the world? To wield the same power as those who would crush her? Did her toe not turn, its compulsion growing, held back only by her initial horror of the imagined act?

She stood over the worm. Even the whitest soul could not stay forever unsullied. He could imagine she was not so white. From beyond the wall came the muted and intermittent blare of a car horn.

She turned to him. "I'd forgotten," she said. The horn sounded again. Her expression changed. Even a world of car horns was something to long for.

Her ease with him unnerved him. As if something was missing from his uniform or his demeanor, and he was less recognizable as a guard. He pushed the remainder of his cigarette into the wall.

Or worse, she had read a different politic on his face.

The door opened. Another guard with a prisoner appeared. He said he'd thought the enclosure was empty. He looked carefully at Margarita. "That one doesn't get a breather, mate," he said. "People's Enemy. They should have told you." He left with his prisoner to find another enclosure.

They were watching. They were wondering if he still recognized himself.

"Let's go," he said.

He saw her disappointment and he looked away; she passed before him through the door.

She reminded him of his sister. His mood sank further when he realized this. She would have been similarly transformed. The same stooped walk. The same held face. She'd have saved the fragile worm without envy of its salvation. He imagined her expression, the gentle smudge of her quizzical forehead, should he have suggested otherwise. He thought of her skirt, fiercely embroidered, weighted along its hem like a fisherman's line.

At D-block he was told her cell had been repaired and he should escort her back. Someone offered to take her if he wanted a break—he said no, of course. A break wouldn't make sense; he'd only just started his shift.

As they ascended the stairs they passed one of the interrogators coming down. His reputation was well known. The guard took her arm and maneuvered her along, placing himself between them. The interrogator stopped just as they passed, on the same step.

"We missed you today, whore." He grinned at her and wagged his head in mock concern. "I guess we can't let a prisoner's feet get soggy. We'll have to double our time tomorrow."

She swayed slightly. He wondered if she might faint.

"Excuse me, friend," said the guard. "I must get her back to her cell."

The interrogator ignored him. "Perhaps I'll request an extra session today," he said to her.

Whatever he saw in her expression caused him to laugh.

"I'd be forced to work late, you know, but if you beg me, I will."

The guard placed his foot on the next step. The interrogator didn't move.

"Beg me," he ordered her.

"Comrade Interrogator," the guard began.

"Shut up," said the interrogator. "Beg me, whore."

"They are expecting her back," said the guard.

"What's your name?"

He told him.

"Well, Miklosh," the interrogator immediately applied the diminutive form. "You should make it your job to care about what I care about and not worry about other wormlike guards like yourself."

"I beg you," she said.

They both looked at her.

"What's that, whore?"

"You heard me."

"I want to hear it again."

"You'll have to tie me up first," she said. Her words were matter-of-fact, as if she was reminding him of a familiar practice; one they'd agreed upon long ago.

The interrogator laughed and set off down the stairs. "And I will," he said. His words rang from the cement walls. They heard him then shout to someone below and hurry his descent. A lower door opened then shut.

She leaned against the wall. He urged her forward. "Come along. We're almost there," he said. Words that might be a comfort under other circumstances clearly were not here. He thought to give some apology for this blunder.

"Listen," he said. His grip on her arm tightened to the point he thought might be painful; he needed to wake her up. "The writer wants to know of you."

She was silent at first, as if she couldn't make sense of his words. "You've talked to him? Where is he? Is he here?"

"No—he's outside. Don't say anything more."

She obeyed him. He was surprised by this and almost regretted the command. At her cell block he turned her over to the guards. He could see she was careful not to look at him.

On his way back to D-block, he stepped into the alcove they'd occupied earlier and lit another cigarette. The mist overhead had lifted revealing an empty sky. His hands shook for a few moments, then calmed. A car horn sounded. This calmed him further.

He went to the place where she'd released the earthworm and squatted. He stroked the dirt. It was nowhere to be seen. He heard wings and a blackbird landed on the top of the wall. It eyed him, then toggled its head back and forth.

He removed his hand and stood back from the spot.

The guard learned in subsequent days that she'd been put on the list for deportation to a Siberian camp. Again, his gain of such knowledge appeared serendipitous: a glance at some documents he'd been asked to deliver to another unit. He wouldn't tell Bulgakov this news. That would've been an additional hundred rubles, he reasoned. Besides, what difference would it have made? He'd do better to keep his money.

Bulgakov returned with the beer.

The guard was gone and Ilya sat in his place. Ilya took one of the bottles.

Bulgakov sat down. He wondered what—if anything—had transpired between the two. Or if perhaps the guard had transmogrified in some way. The evening light seemed tricky.

"It's not that warm," observed Ilya. It wasn't clear if he was referring to the drink, or the weather; a reference to the waning year. He tipped his head back and drank. The bottle was half empty when he lowered it again. He delivered his news without preamble.

"She's been sentenced to eight years. The penal camp of Oserlag. The best I can do is have her processed as a common criminal."

The bell of a distant streetcar announced its approach.

"That information," said Ilya, with a touch of sarcasm. "Cost you little to procure." He indicated the beer.

Ilya got up, leaving the bottle on the bench between them, and took the path toward Bronnaya Street. He crossed; the streetcar passed between them.

Along the street, one after another, the gas lamps were being ignited. Restaurants were opening; people still wandered there. The kiosk which had sold him the beer was closed and dark. The park was empty except for him. It was beyond twilight; darkness filled the spaces between the benches, along the paths, as easily as did the light during daylight hours, yet there was the sense it harbored other things. Those who required their eyes to navigate the world had no business there.

# CHAPTER 26

I lya wanted to tell her himself.

He stood in his office and stared at the photograph of Stalin on the wall. His was different than Pyotr's: the Great Man's gaze was slightly lower. One could imagine his domain was more personal; perhaps one's own particular cares figured there. Ilya looked at his watch. Momentarily they would arrive, the prisoner and her guard, and through the wall he would hear the movement of chairs, muffled words, some fidgeting, then silence. They were always silent while they waited for him. He hadn't seen her since the day of her arrest and he realized he was anxious. Anxious of her changed appearance. Anxious she would blame him. Did Comrade Stalin have insight to share? Could Father Chairman provide counsel? How did one woo a woman whose sentence one had enacted? Ilya stamped his cigarette into the ashtray.

The reports of her interrogations had been transcribed on papers as thin as onionskin. They lay on his desk in a dainty stack. Young Fedir was fastidious, his language nearly clinical in its descriptions. In the typing, his machine had dropped every "r" to the level of subscript, and it was easy to become distracted from the prose by the undulating waves of print. But then a phrase would find him—*the prisoner seemed frailer than usual today; will consult with the infirmary regarding iron supplements.* He reread those lines. Did he, he wondered? Had the medics acted on this concern? There was no further mention in subsequent reports. Was there a *usual* level of frailty that required no action? A subtle shift in the hanging of her dress? Bluish shadows under her eyes that told of malnutrition and sleeplessness? The young interrogator had come to know such specifics and Ilya disliked him for this.

Overlaying the reports was a single page with the recommended disposition. It was the standard text. The prisoner was an excellent candidate for rehabilitation, so it read. She would derive great benefit from Siberia's robust frontier and the opportunity to make a dedicated contribution toward the strengthening of the Soviet infrastructure. She would learn firsthand of the joy in communal living and the satisfaction of working with others toward the larger purpose.

Ilya traced his fingers downward. Below Pyotr's signature was a place for his.

He signed such documents every day.

The outer door in the adjacent room opened. Two people entered but there was only the voice of the guard. He'd typically wait as long as a quarter hour, but he could not help but think: *She is here.* He opened the door. They had just settled into their chairs and immediately they rose.

She was thinner than before. She appeared surprised to see him and this unsettled him. He looked away, not wanting to know more until they could be alone. He'd carried the stack of reports with him. He grumbled of being too harried and pressed for time. He put them on the table; the pen beside them, and took a seat.

"You may leave now," he told the guard. If the guard felt this was irregular, he gave no indication. He departed and the door closed. Ilya pretended to focus on the reports. He heard the other chair shift as she took her seat.

He turned the pages one by one as if they required some careful inspection. The text rippled across the page; he read none of it. She was silent; not even the wisp of her breath could be heard. There was only the sound of moving paper. He sniffed, then rubbed his brow as though something he read had pained him. He cleared his throat but still said nothing. All seemed staged, only he'd been given no dialogue. He was at a loss as to how to begin. The reports offered nothing. He reached the end and started to page through them again.

Her hand rested on the table. Her skin seemed translucent.

A phrase on the page caught him: *The prisoner smells of lavender today, the source of which is inexplicable.*

He knew then. She'd not survive that first year in prison. As though she already carried her contagion dormant in her chest, biding its time. Across the steppe, then into the Urals, as roads became trails, then paths, it would awaken. As food and supplies dwindled, as the cold took its turn, the entity would grow. It would break down her tissues and rebuild them to its own specifications. After a time, after much suffering, whatever remained would stiffen in an unmarked grave.

Even in the stale, overwarmed air of his office, this future was as real as if it'd already occurred. Behind her shining eyes, he saw dead ones staring back at him. As if there were two of her, the second in the background, waiting, certainty giving it patience; its turn would come. The hopelessness of the moment rose in him.

"You're to be sentenced tomorrow," he said quickly, his voice deepened. "It's more of a formality, in truth. The decision's been made." He pushed the disposition letter forward. He watched her read it. Her expression didn't change from the start of it to the finish, as if she'd expected it.

She placed her hands in her lap. He had the sense she'd withdrawn not in anger or regret, but rather so as not to taint him. He could not see what she was doing below the tabletop; if she was praying, or wringing her hands in despair. He wanted to take one hand back in his, he wanted to separate it from the other as if apart they'd be easier to persuade.

"How long?" she said. It was the only sound in the room, yet it seemed he strained to hear her.

"Eight years."

She lifted her hands to the tabletop as the drowning might, as if to steady herself on a piece of flotsam.

He weighed the expanse of this for her. His words were soft. "This is exile."

All things she knew and loved, all freedoms both cursed and enjoyed, would disappear. The tips of her fingers whitened where they pressed down.

Those hands would look different after a few months.

"Why wasn't he arrested?" She asked this without rancor. It was the most natural question.

How could he answer? His frustration with her dissipated a little into a more general disquiet with the rest of the world. Her arrest made his unnecessary.

He tapped the paper. "This doesn't have to happen. If you give them something, something to indicate you're willing to work with them, they will make an arrangement instead."

"An arrangement?"

"Something that happens here every day. Many times a day. For many, such as yourself." He was given to a vision of Muscovites, thousands of them, walking the streets, looking over their fellow citizens in the stores, in the parks, on street-cars, evaluating their deeds, their words, their hearts. Listening. Always listening. Knowing better than to speak themselves.

"I'd make a terrible informant," she told him.

It seemed like a small thing, in exchange for her life. "Do you think that you are protecting him?" he said.

Her face held not an answer to this, but a different question. If she took this offering, how was she to return to Bulgakov? Now with the ability to destroy him? With the expectation to do so? Perhaps she'd already envisioned this darker future. Perhaps she thought she was saving herself.

He wanted to tell her that no one escapes these kinds of choices.

She took the disposition letter and reread it. "You can sign this," she said, as though it was her permission to give.

He didn't want her permission. He certainly didn't need it.

"I don't want to sign it, but I will," he said. "When you leave this room, when this meeting has ended, I promise you." His words had become threatening; he wanted her to feel threatened. He got up and paced. Behind her chair, then back again. "This is real," he went on. He couldn't see her expression. It was easier this way. "They will load you on a train like livestock. Worse than livestock. Livestock they care about, you they won't." There would be typhus. Disease. He would never see her. Did she care about such things? "I won't be able to help you. Do you understand?" He picked up the pen and threw it across the room. It hit the wall and scuttled to the floor leaving a mark.

"Don't do this to me," he said.

He thought he was prepared for this outcome.

Something he'd said had set her in motion. She seemed at a loss over what to do with her hands. She slid them high under her arms, trapping them; her arms pressed tight into her sides. As if she was trying to hold herself together.

"I'd like to go now," she said. She glanced around the room as if to escape.

"Give me something. Any bit of information. You don't know what will happen to you." He stopped there. It was difficult to continue.

Her shoulders were square; her hair hung past her shoulders, no different than before. Not a strand moved. She would not be moved. It was no use.

"I'm so very angry with you," he said quietly.

He picked up the pen and signed the letter. He dropped it against the table as if it'd done this thing on its own. He pushed the page away.

242 · JULIE LEKSTROM HIMES

"Goddamn you," he said.

He suddenly felt old and filled with regret for impossible things. Their impossible situation. Was he flattering himself to even call it a *situation*? He would never see her again. He combed his fingers through his hair. "I'm old enough to be your father," he said. Where had those words come from? Those were the last he'd intended. How did she cause him to reveal himself? Did she think of him in that way? What could those unfathomable eyes see? In truth he was afraid of them. He was afraid he'd see only a tepid sympathy for an old man's unrequited affection. He was afraid he'd see nothing.

From behind, her head seemed immutable. Perhaps she had no feelings for him. Perhaps all had been imagined.

He sat down, weary. His hands rested loosely on the table near hers. They were so unlike his own.

She touched a finger to his. Then drew it lightly over his skin. He sensed her gaze. Was this only sad kindness? He looked up from her hand.

She'd heard his confession for what it was. He saw her understanding, perhaps even her reluctant acceptance of it. It seemed on her to be a kind of miracle.

Love was a wholly selfish thing. He would not give this up.

He turned over the ashtray onto the table and spread out the ash. A thin mist of grey hovered above. He traced words as he spoke.

"Your sentencing is scheduled for tomorrow. It would have been easier for you, Comrade, had you chosen to help us root out these enemies." He paused, intent on his writing. "But you did not."

In the ash, he'd traced *They are listening*.

Her head tilted as she read it. He wiped the ash back through the words and continued.

"Our actions may seem capricious to you, but I assure you, they are not. There are those who would thwart our efforts to build a sound and worthy nation. They are cowards: selfish and lazy and morally destitute." His last word was drawn out, as he scrawled through the ash again. There was an awkward pause for any listener beyond their room. When he was finished he drew his finger across the table under his words.

She read his words and nodded. He passed his hand over them and began to write again.

"I am no different than you," she said. She watched his finger work across the table. "I want a healthy and productive country, like all good citizens. I love my country. Of those few you mention, if I knew any, I would certainly hand them over to you."

He smiled at her words. They sounded like a terribly written radio play. She leaned her head toward him and tried to read as he wrote.

"Then it is a shame you were less than convincing for your interrogators." He moved his hand away so she could read. His fingers were thick with the dust. "You will be an example to others. May you spend your years in Siberia hoping that other citizens will learn from your error."

He saw in her face a fresh despair. He went to wipe the words away as if they were the cause, but she held his hand back. He felt immobilized.

*I will find you*

*Hold this close*

Then, at the bottom, in the faintest layer of ash, he'd added:

*Believe in me*

Her fingers tightened around his hand.

# PART IV
## MIRACLE, MYSTERY, AND AUTHORITY

# CHAPTER 27

T icket sales for *Molière* had tapered off. Bulgakov attended one night; he guessed that a third of the seats were empty. Those who were there, however, appeared engaged, and their applause was sincere. He said this to Stanislawski backstage after the performance. The director looked grim. Bulgakov gave an interview for *Crocodile* and sales showed a nice bump. Stanislawski hosted a lavish after-party at the Writers' Union. Several committee members attended. Rumors were started, no doubt by Stanislawski, that the lead actor and his co-star were having an affair. The following week, *Pravda* ran an article, and afterward reservations could only be made months in advance.

Bulgakov received a telegram from Stalin, congratulating him on its opening as well as offering a dacha for his temporary use. When he returned, the telegram read, they would discuss a new project for the writer. One that would cement his name in history. There was no mention of Margarita.

It seemed to suggest that he might consider forgetting her too. Come back in three months as fat as a whale. He wanted to talk to Ilya; he would know more of her fate. He took a chance that Annuschka's route had not changed, that she'd not been dismissed from her position, that she would be working that night; indeed, that they were still neighbors; and he walked to the stand near Lubyanka and waited. Several trams passed before he saw her. She didn't notice him amongst the crowd and he sat in the back of her car until another driver took over at the end of her shift. He followed her to a run-down apartment building.

The outside was hemmed in by toppled trashcans and loose trash. Foodstuffs hung in tattered cloth bags from every window though this was expressly forbidden by law. It seemed an unlikely residence for the agent. The mailboxes in the entry-way gave little indication of the occupants. He wandered down the first-floor hallway. He paused, listening for Ilya.

A door opened and Annuschka appeared. Her hopeful face immediately soured at the sight of him. Her head disappeared but her door remained ajar. The light from the room shone into the hall and he went toward it, mothlike.

The number eleven was drawn in nail polish on the door; a scarlet drop trailed from the first digit and ended in a small bubble. Bulgakov imagined her forming the numbers with an irreverent brush, its tip burning with the same red found on her still-damp nails. If the housing officer couldn't take care of this small task, she'd manage it herself. From within, her dis-embodied voice called to him. "I suppose you're going to want some supper," she said. Despite the resignation in her words, she sounded pleased.

He went in.

She was a pretty girl. She had dressed in a short kimono robe and was reclined on a dilapidated couch, curled hair piled atop her head, her legs extended across the cushions—like a Venus, he thought. There were only a few pieces of furniture, mismatched and worn to the point of disrepair. The small table before her was set with a cup and a pot and a single plate with toast spread with goat cheese. Beside the plate, a glass acted as a vase for a clutch of dying daisies, their petals floating in the greenish water and dotting the table. She reached into another small table beside her and pulled from it a second cup. She blew into it then put it next to the other. She appeared to have no interest in serving.

It wasn't clear where he was supposed to sit. There were no other chairs.

"When Ilya Ivanovich is here, I sit on his lap," she said.

Bulgakov squatted on the floor in front of the table and sat heavily. "In case he returns, then. You wouldn't happen to know where he is, would you."

"No—do you?"

The floor was gritty under his hands and he brushed them together before pouring the coffee. He poured her a cup as well. She rubbed her thumbnail with her finger, then frowned. Suddenly she looked at him.

"I remember you," she said. "You were with that woman that night."

"Yes—I think you went home early," he said.

"He sent me home." She went back to her nails. "She is your girlfriend, your wife?"

It was strange to hear her talk of Margarita. Mention of her in this place, by this woman, seemed irreverent. "We're engaged," he said.

She made a small face as though he'd chosen an odd word. "He'd asked me what I thought of her," she said. "I didn't think much of her shoes." She'd picked a piece of lint from the fabric of her robe and she dropped it off the edge of the sofa.

"I was hoping to see him tonight," he said.

"I can tell when he's home." She tilted her head toward the wall behind her with an authoritative smile. *Thin walls.*

"Perhaps I should check just in case."

She leaned forward. "I saw a ghost last night."

"Really?" He was amused by her announcement but didn't want to offend her. Perhaps she knew more about the mysterious Ilya Ivanovich that could be helpful.

"A girl killed herself in this building." She let her eyes get big, then gestured to the ceiling. "They found her—*dangling.*" Annuschka shivered. "It was the building officer's fault—

everyone thinks that. The witch ordered the poor girl out without a thought. And she spies on us—all of us girls. Reports on us to the police, no doubt." She giggled. "I probably have a file that thick." She held up her finger and thumb spaced apart.

"You? What could you have done? You're still a youngster."

She seemed to like that. She turned onto her knees and reached into the space between the sofa and the wall. She produced a brightly colored fan which she opened and extended to him. A gift from a friend, she said. After he had complimented the thing, she fanned herself slowly with it.

"You won't tell him," she said.

He supposed she meant Ilya. He promised he wouldn't.

The coffee was terrible. Perhaps Ilya was back, he said. She shook her head. He'd have come to her apartment first. That's what he usually did.

"Has he ever brought a woman back with him?"

She frowned. Perhaps the walls weren't so thin. "How would I know?" she said.

"He doesn't have a girlfriend?"

"Ask him yourself," she said, feigning disinterest. She then brightened again.

"I'll show you something, only you must promise never to tell. Do you swear?" She didn't wait for his answer. Her lips parted as if she would continue to speak and what appeared to be the roof of her mouth dropped down; she cupped her hand at her chin and expelled a dental plate into it. It carried two teeth, lined along its rim like pearl beads. She closed her lips, still smiling, and extended her hand to show him. Her expression danced as if she'd demonstrated a magic trick.

Bulgakov focused on her hand and its plate, trying to control his surprise and mild revulsion at the abrupt extraction. She was watching him, expecting his admiration and perhaps a certain awe of her resourcefulness. Who did he know in

Moscow who wore a plate, she'd want to know. Not a one, she might wager. He sat back and did his best.

"Well!" he said.

It was clear she'd expected a more exuberant reaction. She pretended not to care and slipped the plate into her mouth. He felt he'd disappointed her; he could see she was determined not to show it.

"I have a friend who's a dentist," she said casually, as if anyone could say such a thing.

"But a plate—I don't believe I've ever seen one."

She eyed him, as though suspicious of the compliment, then decided to accept it. "Well, now you have."

"I'm very impressed."

She believed him; after all, who wouldn't be.

"So—your girlfriend," she said. "Are you going to marry her?" She picked up a piece of toast, broke off a bit, and popped it into her mouth. Crumbs scattered over the silk of her robe.

"She's been arrested," he said. The newness of the words made him pause for a moment. "She's been sent east—to a camp."

"I know lots of people who've been arrested," she said airily. "They do come back." Not necessarily to give him comfort, but rather to demonstrate her expert knowledge of such matters. When he didn't say anything, she added:

"You can marry her then." It seemed simple.

"I can," he agreed.

"Or perhaps you will meet someone else."

The guileless cruelty of her words seemed to take his breath. She broke off another piece and stared at him, chewing. He could see her thoughts turning. She put the unfinished toast back on the table, then brought her hand to her hair.

"Tell me what you do," she said. "No, I'll guess."

"I'm a writer."

She pouted only a moment, then smiled. "I'd have guessed an engineer. Someone who builds things." She eyed him hopefully as though he would at any moment turn into such a person.

"Alas, I am a mere writer."

"Writers are necessary too, I suppose. Someone has to fill the papers with words each day." She seemed to warm to the idea. "I know a place—it's just around the corner. They know me. I never have to pay full—we can get something better than this." She waved to the half-eaten bread.

"I feel I need to wait for Ilya."

"He'll still be here."

"He's here now?"

She gestured vaguely at the wall behind her. "Maybe—I thought it was him but it was you instead."

"I should check then."

She was disappointed in him; perhaps it was in his determination, but that seemed imprecise. As though she was accustomed to being wrongly discounted; as though he was no better than the others who underestimated her. "He's going on a trip somewhere—I don't know where—not that I particularly care," she added. "He asked to borrow some women's clothes. Don't you think that's odd?"

A trip? Bulgakov rose to his feet, waiting for her to continue. Her gaze followed him upwards.

"And not just one piece, but several changes, blouses, skirts, and they had to be just so."

"Just what?" His thoughts raced ahead. *Just her size?*

"I don't know. Boring." She made a face. "As if I'm running some sort of boutique. I asked who they were for and he wouldn't say. You don't suppose he's married, do you? And giving her my clothes? No, that's too strange, even for him. And why not buy them himself?"

She suddenly seemed tired, as if all of this speculation was too much. She leaned against the cushion and went back to frowning at her nails. Supper with him had been forgotten. "It makes no difference to me," she said to herself.

"I don't know any of that," he said softly, glancing at the shared wall between them. He knew so little as to fill the head of a pin.

"Now it's you who's seen a ghost," she said, musing. She appeared to make little else of his surprise. The light in the room seemed to have grown in intensity and in it she looked even younger than before. A child's face could be seen through the wash of day-old makeup. She looked desperately hopeful for so many things.

"Tell him I'm expecting my fruit," she said. She seemed to be trying once again to sound casual and upbeat. "He promised."

He told her he'd tell him.

"If she doesn't come back—your fiancée—I can be your friend," she said. Her offer seemed a vague thing—after all, he couldn't be expected to produce fans or teeth. Still, one could keep an open mind.

He didn't know what else to do but to thank her.

He entered Ilya's apartment without knocking. Ilya appeared to be neither surprised nor bothered by this. A suitcase was spread wide on a low table. Beside him on the sofa was a pile of clothes. On the chair were travel documents. Bulgakov moved the papers and sat down.

"Annuschka said you are taking a trip," said Bulgakov.

"Don't worry about Nushka." His voice was gentler than Bulgakov would have expected. "She has a gift for finding someone to take care of her."

Ilya turned the case sideways; then, as if this was a most natural thing, he lifted the lining from the lid's interior and released a panel that hid an upper compartment. He went to the bureau and returned with a second pile; this was of women's clothing. He began again, only this time, there seemed to be a kind of reverence to his motions. He smoothed a blouse of filmy cloth then laid it in the curve of the case. The loose threads caught on his coarse skin and the fabric lifted as if it was unwilling to let him go. He as well seemed reluctant to retreat; his hands hovered as if to coax it to stay.

"There's a strange parcel," said Bulgakov. He felt helpless and angry for it.

Ilya picked up a grey skirt and folded it lengthwise. He placed it in the suitcase, but its hem and waistband seemed uncooperative and hung over the lid. He pushed down its edges, then, unsatisfied, lifted it out again; this piece would require another strategy. His concern seemed excessive, as if it was more than a skirt.

"This is unlike you," said Bulgakov; he wanted to sound skeptical.

Ilya continued to work. Writ on his face was an unexpected vulnerability; a combination of hope and nervousness and measured anticipation. By it he seemed a much younger man, as though he'd been freed of the burdens of wisdom and experience. He could believe in something that was close to impossible. He would give himself the luxury of that faith.

"When are you leaving?" asked Bulgakov. The question itself depressed him further.

"At the end of the week. Though I've been delayed once already."

A small pile remained beside him. A cluster of women's undergarments, and he hesitated above their silken glory, his hands paused in a kind of nervous devotion.

"What are you planning?" said Bulgakov.

"I don't know." Ilya seemed to answer to their daintiness, as though made helpless by it. Finally he took them, en masse, and pressed them into a corner of the case. They would have to suffer a certain amount of boorishness. They would have to forgive him this.

"Then—after—where will you go?" This was the danger-ous question. If Ilya was successful he would be with Margarita.

"It's a big country," said Ilya. He was willing to point out the obvious.

Bulgakov would never see her again.

Ilya closed the lid. He set it on the floor then went to pour himself a drink. He worked over a small sink that hung from the wall, similar to that in Bulgakov's apartment.

Perhaps he'd asked Ilya for one—he couldn't remember, yet Ilya handed him a drink. The glass was crystal though badly chipped; some remnant of old, discarded wealth. Bulgakov held it in his fist. Its wounded surface bit into his skin.

Ilya stood near the sink, empty-handed, studying him. "I can take care of her," he said.

He was neither apologetic nor boastful. He'd perused maps and collected false papers. He'd made provision for travel. He could appear at the camp under the guise of authority and communicate some plan to her. She could act on that plan. He was her best chance.

"I can make her happy," said Ilya.

"No."

Ilya didn't argue with him. Perhaps he questioned himself. "I can take care of her," he repeated.

Bulgakov gripped the glass. "Were you at least going to tell me?" he asked.

Ilya's expression was surprising. He seemed of all things embarrassed.

Did he think he would follow him to Siberia? He could imagine only the emptiness of that space. Its tundra a frozen ocean. A quiet so profound one's ears rang from it.

Did he think he would stop him? Report him to the authorities? Relegate her to years in prison, perhaps worse, just to keep him from her?

Or would he stay and get on with his life? Enjoy his literary fame. This was his moment. There would be parties, glittering honors. Lesser writers would vie for his attention; great ones would usher him into their midst. There would be people to fill rooms. Rooms upon rooms. He would not be alone.

There would be Annuschkas aplenty.

Bulgakov downed his drink and set the glass aside. His hand was bleeding from scores of tiny cuts. Blooms of red appeared in a fresh and unexpected crop.

He wondered, momentarily, if she would have been surprised by his decision.

# CHAPTER 28

B ulgakov obtained travel papers from a man whose name
Stanislawski provided. For as illegal as the transaction
was, it seemed oddly cordial. They met at the man's
apartment in the middle of the afternoon; the man had been late
arriving and apologized as he opened the door. He offered tea
and seemed genuinely disappointed when Bulgakov declined.
He drew some official-appearing pages from a desk, then
asked about his destination. He scratched in the name of the
town with a quill pen. He appeared to add other particulars of
his own invention; Bulgakov tried to decipher the movements
of the pen. When he was finished, the man took what appeared
to be a block of wood from the lowest drawer. The block separated into two halves and he placed the paper between them.
Here, he got up from his chair to leverage his weight and with
both hands pressed down on the seal. He stared at Bulgakov as
he did this. His gaze seemed vaguely inquisitive. Then suddenly he smiled. "This is it, isn't it?" he said. It was this for
which he'd paid his money. He separated the blocks and
handed him the page. The seal was crude, blurred, it seemed
clearly fraudulent. "They don't look very carefully," he said, as
if anticipating the complaint, and took the page back and
folded it. "Most of them can't read." He found an envelope.
He seemed to interpret Bulgakov's hesitation as disappointment. "It'll do the trick," he said. "Haven't lost one yet."

Lost—to where? Prison?

Bulgakov then asked about acquiring a gun. He felt sheepish, as though the asking made him already guilty of some crime. The man pulled a large metal box from under his bed. A variety of firearms were within. He squatted, his fingers on his lips; he glanced once at Bulgakov then back at the box, as if he was fitting a suit to a man. Finally he selected one. He sat on the bed as he explained its parts, then passed it to Bulgakov.

The piece was heavier than he'd expected.

"It's a Nagant," said the man.

Bulgakov didn't know what that meant. "I see," he said.

"It was standard issue before the TT became popular."

He wondered if he shouldn't ask for the TT instead.

"It'll do the trick," said the man.

"I hear it can be a wild place," said Bulgakov.

The man gave no reaction. He'd participated in scores of illicit transactions; he was beyond any need for understanding the particulars of these things.

Bulgakov offered it back. "I'll think about it."

The man didn't move to take it. "Best to think before you need it," he said. "It won't take down the People's army but it might slow down a wolf."

Bulgakov hadn't thought of wolves. What other dangers had he not considered? He tried to accustom himself to the weight.

The man sold him a partially filled box of ammunition and showed him how to load it. Finally he found a paper bag from a closet, so Bulgakov might carry it discreetly.

Bulgakov went to the station in central Moscow. Timetables were not to be trusted and despite the hour the platform trembled with the crowd of huddled bodies. In their midst a locomotive towered. The air was dry and bitterly cold. Half a dozen darkly rusted metal casks were scattered throughout the crowds; therein small fires provided some warmth to those waiting. Working men called to one another and cursed. Trestles groaned, pallets of goods were loaded and unloaded. Whistles and horns floated in from the street. A garbled, indecipherable announcement came from a loudspeaker. All of this made for the moment of departure: when the familiar lost its claim on one. With this the blood moved faster, looser, limbs warmed. Even the discomfort and inconvenience of travel could not dissuade. Bulgakov needed to find one who would be willing to give this up. He was willing to pay.

Nearby a small convoy of women prisoners sat together, distinguishable not by their clothes, but by their posture and the unnatural closeness they maintained with one another. Their guards appeared only vaguely troubled by their duty, their rifles slung over their backs; several were smoking. That small section of platform did not hold the same anticipation as the rest, as though it was part of an old and more tired country. Bulgakov searched the faces of these prisoners. From that distance the details of loss and trepidation could only be imagined. He didn't expect to see Margarita, but perhaps some semblance of her, and he wondered if that would be comforting. He wanted so badly to see her.

"They never look like criminals, do they?" An older gentleman in a suit and an overcoat of above-average construction appeared to be observing them as well. He looked at Bulgakov as though grateful for one of his kind. It was unlikely this one would give up his ticket.

"Perhaps they're not," said Bulgakov. Such a sentiment he would not have expressed openly before.

The man gave no reply. He gestured as if he'd spotted an acquaintance and moved away without explanation.

The prisoners began to jostle each other, rising to their feet. The train whistled. Those waiting on the platform then stood and the prisoners disappeared from view.

Another man, closer to his age and of lesser means, in a cap and factory-produced clothes appeared to be traveling alone. Bulgakov sidled up to him.

"Quite some crowd," said Bulgakov.

"When is it not like this?" said the man.

"How far are you going?"

The man held out his ticket. Ulan Ude. Bulgakov shook his head as though the man had pulled a losing ticket from the lottery. The man reexamined it then shrugged. His mother was sick; such was his luck.

"That's a tedious trip," said Bulgakov. The man reacted little; perhaps he didn't know the word.

"Boring," said Bulgakov. The man agreed. He'd brought an extra bit, he said. One could usually find a game if one knew where to look. Several of his teeth were missing, his gums grey above the gaps.

Bulgakov offered to buy his ticket; he told him it was for his brother whose application had been mishandled. The man looked around for the unlucky person and Bulgakov waved generally toward the far end of the platform. This one always pulled the short stick, he added, shaking his head as though it was some unfortunate inborn trait.

"How much are you offering?" asked the man. He seemed both skeptical and greedy.

"Fifty rubles."

Bulgakov could see he'd miscalculated. The amount was too much and the man relaxed; he sensed Bulgakov's need and was ready to wheedle. One who would offer fifty could go higher. The crowds around them had thinned a bit. The man scratched his head under his cap. Time was his friend.

"She's pretty sick," he said. "What kind of a son would I be?"

"You could send her the money," said Bulgakov.

"Mail is chancy."

"Then bring it to her later." The clusters around each carriage were shrinking. "Come now, fifty is more than fair," said

Bulgakov. The man seemed rooted to the platform. The train called again.

"Where is your brother?" the man asked.

"I have no idea," said Bulgakov, annoyed. "Come now."

"Who has a ticket and who doesn't?" The man wagged his head. Who was the smart one, he would say? This man in a suit and overcoat? *I think not!*

"Maybe your brother has more?" said the man.

"The ticket is for me," said Bulgakov. "This is what I have." He would turn out his pockets if necessary.

The man seemed unaffected by the sudden contraction of opportunity. He kicked lightly at Bulgakov's shoe. "Those are nice," he said.

"What would I wear?"

"We could trade." He pulled up on his trousers to reveal his well-worn pair. Bulgakov accepted and put on the other man's shoes. The toes of his left foot curled against the stiff leather upper; they were of unequal size.

"Why do you want a ticket so badly?" asked the man. For a moment, his question seemed less about gauging its value. He rubbed the paper between his thumb and middle finger.

On the other side of the platform, the prisoners were being loaded into a boxcar. Two of the guards stood in its opening. One by one, they grasped each woman by the arms and hauled her up. Midair only for a moment, each kicked her legs slightly then struggled to gain the step; some stumbled and caught themselves, others landed on their knees then hands, and Bulgakov was given to the thought of mythical creatures being pulled from the sea into a waiting boat of fishermen; these creatures were trusting of the men, their legs new and strange to them. They would never go back.

"There's a woman," said Bulgakov, half under his breath. His brain seemed incapable of producing lies.

The man asked the time and Bulgakov checked his pocket

watch. The glint of the timepiece disappeared under the man's fingers. Bulgakov winced.

"I hope your trip is a tedious one," said the man. He sounded uncomfortably sophisticated. He departed for the street as though he'd never had any intention of boarding a train. The watch chain dangled from his trouser pocket.

Almost immediately an official appeared, asking to see Bulgakov's ticket. Then his travel papers. "These are an obvious fraud," he said indignantly. "Follow me." He led him to a squat building at the far end of the platform that housed several rooms, only one of which maintained a warming stove. Bulgakov was told he would be dealt with shortly. The official took his papers with him.

The room was empty save a few chairs around the perimeter. The stove had an unpleasantly pitched hum. Bulgakov sat down. Lithographs had been tacked to the walls; they carried familiar slogans: *Don't be a big mouth—even the walls have ears!* Another was a quiet scene of Stalin writing at a desk: *Stalin in the Kremlin cares about each one of us.*

Perhaps Margarita had spent time in a room such as this, waiting, uncertain of her future. He felt calmer for that, as though this room, and his anticipated journey, might be a kind of pilgrimage. He leaned his head against the wall and listened for the train's departure.

The door opened and a short, diminutively built man entered, dressed in a manner not dissimilar from Bulgakov and carrying a leather valise. He pulled one of the other chairs around and sat opposite him. He had a trace of a smile, one of confidence, as though he'd already predicted his next meal to be a pleasant one. It was clear who was being detained and who was not.

He wet his lips before he spoke. "My name is Pyotr Pyotrovich," said the man. "I understand you desire to travel to Ulan Ude today. This has become a problem, yes?"

Pyotrovich brought his case to sit on his lap. He withdrew

a photograph the size of a standard sheet of paper and showed it to Bulgakov. Its features were made grainy and indistinct in its enlargement. "Do you know this man?"

It was Ilya. Bulgakov nodded.

Pyotrovich produced another. This one was Margarita. It was of better quality. Pyotrovich let him take it.

She'd been beaten. The right side of her jaw was swollen, discolored. Darker matter was near her ear—what else could it be but blood? Her lips were parted as though she would speak to this. But it was her eyes: they stared straight through him. They harbored an expression he'd never seen in her before. He was wholly responsible for this.

"It was taken after her arrest," said Pyotrovich. He sounded almost apologetic for her appearance. "It was handled poorly," he added. He took the photograph and Bulgakov's hands fell lightly to his lap.

Pyotrovich sat back. "We have reason to believe that Ilya Ivanovich is planning to effect her escape." He paused slightly, perhaps hoping for a reaction, but then continued. "If you help us apprehend him, we will release her."

Could he believe this? Could such a promise be true?

"Given the dimension of his crime," said Pyotrovich. "Other things—using fabricated travel documents, securing a train ticket by illegal means—such would be forgivable, of course."

What did this agent think he could do? Did it matter?

"May I see her once more?" He reached for the photograph.

Pyotrovich seemed to hesitate at first.

Bulgakov studied its shadows, the points of light in her eyes that had captured the flash of the photographer's bulb. The flatness of the page belied the curves of her face, its texture, in a way that seemed deliberate. Would she describe the ache of bruised flesh? Invite him to touch it himself? Tell of other humiliations suffered? Would she teach him what was worthy of fear? He was willing to learn.

"It is imperative we secure Ilya Ivanovich. He is a traitor."

It seemed like a gift, only she appeared skeptical. Did he trust this man with the moist lips, the close-set eyes? This one responsible for her battered face?

"All other matters are secondary, in fact," said Pyotrovich.

Bulgakov perceived the faint sense of opportunity. Not unlike the man who'd sold him his ticket. Someone savvier would negotiate.

He studied her eyes. She wasn't thinking about him. She might never again. "I'll do anything," he said.

Pyotrovich seemed pleased with Bulgakov's answer. He returned the pictures to the valise. He provided Bulgakov with new papers and a second-class ticket and a story. He was traveling to Irkutsk for the Arts Theater. A fledging provincial theater there required some stewardship; this was as a favor to Stanislawski and wholly sanctioned by the authorities. It was actually plausible. Pyotrovich told him he would be contacted when he arrived.

Pyotrovich reached into his valise one last time and produced Bulgakov's pocket watch. The gold shimmered white for a moment. "It can be calming to mark the passing of time while traveling across the steppe," he advised. Bulgakov returned it to his pocket.

It seemed to fill the same space as before, as if nothing about its workings had been changed by its passage through these other hands. It still looked like a watch. It could still provide time.

# CHAPTER 29

Margarita arrived at the Oserlag camp in Irkutsk Oblast, near the town of Tayshet, six weeks after leaving Moscow. No one spoke to her for the first day and a half other than to tell her to move along or that she was taking too much time in the latrine. On the third morning her clothes were stolen. She was one of the first to rise with the buzzer, still only sleeping fitfully. The back of her head ached continuously. At that hour, all within the barracks seemed grey: a fine crystalline snow had blown all night and the small, square-paned windows set high under the eaves perfused the room with a steely light. The box which had held her things at the end of her bed board was empty. She closed its lid, confused, then opened it again. Around her, others were getting up, sighing, groaning in the damp chill. She went to open the one assigned to the woman who slept below her but stopped as realization set in. Again she opened her own. She touched its bottom. There was only sawdust in its corners. The other women seemed quieter than the mornings before, as if they were watching, waiting for her response to the deed. But perhaps she imagined this. A sudden gust of wind outside lifted. Soon the second buzzer would sound, instructing them to assemble in lines to go to the dining hall. She wrapped her arms around her torso. All she had was the one thin shirt she wore. She would certainly die here. The wind rose again as if in agreement. On the other side of the barracks came a woman's laughter. It disappeared, then more whispers. That was what they all wanted. Margarita pulled the thin blanket from her bed and wrapped it around her shoulders. A few bunks away, a woman stopped and looked at her. In the dim light she could make out only her long thin face, her dark eyes, her collected disinterest.

The woman on the bed board below groaned loudly and sat up.

"Who are you?" she asked.

Margarita touched the upper board. It seemed strange she'd gone unnoticed but in truth, Margarita had only the vaguest recollection of those preceding days.

The woman looked at the underside of the board over her head. "Well, you certainly smell better than the last one." She stood up. She was about Margarita's age, stocky in build, measurably shorter, with a round face and small eyes. Her skin was pale and chapped from the cold. Her light brown hair had a boyish cut. She squinted at Margarita.

"What's wrong—goddammit, you're crying." She swung her arm as if she intended to hit something but it veered through the air and stopped awkwardly. Her arm was a stump, amputated below the elbow.

"I'm not crying." Margarita stared at her arm in a way she would not have done in her other life. The woman continued to rant.

"If you cry, you might as well dig a hole and lie down in it."

"They stole my clothes," said Margarita.

"Who stole them?"

"I don't know."

The woman shook her head strangely, then turned and walked up the central aisle of the barracks. As she passed each bunk, she opened other boxes, pulling out garments and gathering them over her arms. Cries of protest followed her and women went rushing to their boxes. Halfway down, she turned around, and headed back toward Margarita. Several women tried to grab back their clothes but she pushed them off. She stood in front of Margarita again, her arms overflowing. A thin, fortyish woman appeared at her elbow. She handed Margarita's cardigan back to her, then plucked a blouse from the amputee's arms.

"It was ugly, anyway," she sniffed at Margarita. A handful of other women came forward for similar exchanges. The amputee dropped the rest on the floor and others reclaimed them.

"I'm a problem-solver," she said, grinning.

"You're a cow," said one of the women, shaking the dust from her slacks as she retrieved them from the floor.

The amputee's name was Anyuta. She sat across from Margarita at the long benches of the dining hall during breakfast. Women jostled on either side of her, but she refused to budge. She talked while she ate, fixing her gaze on Margarita. It was difficult to focus on what she was saying.

"You've got great eyes," said Anyuta, the way one might compliment something they'd like to borrow. Anyuta dropped her fork on her plate and covered her own eye with a fist. Her other arm moved in tandem as if wanting to mimic its mate. "I've got BBs for eyes," she said. A woman passing behind Anyuta stopped and looked at Margarita.

"Anyuta has a new girlfriend," she announced. Her tone was mocking yet there was something else about her expression. The woman raised her eyebrows, then left. Anyuta didn't say anything but continued eating. A buzzer sounded. She reached across the table for Margarita's plate.

"I'll take that." She stacked it on her own without waiting for an answer and carried both dishes away.

After their meal, the prisoners boarded a bus. The exterior of the windows had been painted in whitewash. Anyuta moved in behind Margarita in line. As they came down the aisle, she grabbed Margarita's arm, propelled her into an empty seat, and sat down beside her. Margarita studied the window. In places, she could see the blur of dark objects. A car, the building beside them, the vague movements of people. Bubbles in the wash had flaked away leaving scattered pinholes. She leaned closer to peer through them but saw only crisp fragments. Ahead, the windows around the driver were clear. She lifted up to look but was suddenly blocked by the head of a woman who sat down in front of her.

"There's not much to see," said Anyuta, almost apologetically. "Just a chickenshit town."

Were they going to the town?

Anyuta shook her head. To the factories beyond. They were building dormitories for the workers.

The bus began to move. Shadows passed across the white blur.

"What'd you do?" Anyuta's voice was close to her ear.

At first Margarita thought she was asking of her occupation.

"My sister's husband died," said Margarita. "I tried to sell his clothes on the black market." She'd made up this story before arriving at the camp. "We needed the money."

Through the window dark shapes flickered across the paint followed by stretches of only white. Forests and fields? She began to feel queasy and closed her eyes.

"I'm sorry about your sister's husband," said Anyuta.

Margarita turned back to her. Anyuta had been staring at her hair; she averted her eyes. In the white light cast by the wash, she seemed more acutely weathered than before.

Margarita asked why she was there.

Anyuta made a face.

"My father was a kulak," she said. She smiled suddenly. "Do I look like a kulak's daughter?" She studied the window as if watching a scene unfold. The empty sleeve of Anyuta's jacket was partially collapsed; its end was folded over and fas-

tened with a straight pin. It rested against her trouser leg opposite its fuller mate as if unaware.

She made a sound like a small sigh.

"He'd take me fishing," she said. "I was small and afraid of
their teeth." She shook the empty sleeve. "He'd pull the hooks
from their mouths, then he'd string them on a pole and carry
them to the village. He'd call on everyone to admire 'Anyuta's
catch.' As if he was proud." She glanced at Margarita. "I was
bothersome for my mother. I talked too much." She smiled. "I
still mind their teeth, you know."

The bus slowed and the forms through the window took on
angular shapes. Buildings. A car. This was the town. Moisture
from the breath and perspiration of so many bodies had con-
densed on the inner surfaces and with the slowing of the bus,
voices from the prisoners behind and in front of them began to
lift in protest to the stifling air. On both sides, arms went up
and windowpanes were dropped down. Crisp snowy images of
brick and planking and glass darted past. A brief chorus of
gladness rose up as the cold whiffled through the bus. The
guard who sat next to the driver came down the aisle waving a
baton from side to side and ordered the windows shut.

"No one's supposed to see us," said Anyuta.

In his wake, from the front to the back, the windows rose
up again. Margarita half-stood and watched as the world slid
away. Once they were closed, she sat down. Rivulets of water
now streaked across the glass. The air was cold and damp.

She'd heard of prisoner jobs in the towns, outside the
camps and the typical work sites. Jobs with less supervision.
She would have to get one. She would have to be seen as trust-
worthy. She studied the empty sleeve beside her. Perhaps
Anyuta could help her. Anyuta the problem-solver.

"Is it hard to get a job in the town?" she wondered aloud.

There were always such jobs, Anyuta told her. The people
who took them would try to escape and get caught. She held

up her hands as if firing a machine gun. "Ch-ch-ch-ch-ch," she said, sweeping it at the seat in front of them.

The woman across the aisle looked at Anyuta then away as quickly.

"They always get caught," Anyuta repeated. She touched Margarita's sleeve. "Don't get caught," her BB eyes pinned her back. "Ch-ch-ch-ch-ch," she warned.

# CHAPTER 30

In the summer of 1826, Prince Sergei Volkonsky and the other Decembrists walked six thousand kilometers from St. Petersburg to the silver mines of Nerchinsk, a penal colony near the Russian-Chinese border. One foot of each man was shackled to the same-such foot of the prisoner preceding; the alternate foot was chained to one in the rear of him. Thusly, in lockstep, they came to know each weedy hillock, each crusted rut of the road that was Levitan's *Vladimirka*. The Russian steppe extended an indecipherable distance in all directions until it met with the towering sky. There it formed an encircling seam of which they were forever captive, low and at its center. After the second week, they rarely looked beyond the edge of the road and when they did, it only served to renew their utter despair for the years that remained of their still young lives. *There could be no better prison*, said Volkonsky to his friend, Prince Sergei Trubetskoy, chained to his rear. No stone wall could so completely extract all hope from a man's breast. Trubetskoy did not respond. The failure of their revolt, their failure to wrest from the Tsar even those most modest concessions for representational governance no longer caused him to wonder. Indeed, how could the Tsar, no different from any Russian, understand freedom, trapped in a land that went on forever yet never changed?

Ilya said nothing when Bulgakov first opened the door of their shared compartment. He'd been reading the paper; it came to rest in his lap as Bulgakov struggled to enter with his luggage. It seemed to Bulgakov that he himself was the more surprised. He consulted his ticket. He was in the correct berth. How was he to explain this cosmic alignment?

"This isn't entirely coincidental," said Bulgakov. He shut the compartment door. "When you told me of her destination, I immediately requested relocation to a nearby town."

"Have you been to Irkutsk in January? You may rethink your fortune." Ilya resumed his reading. He seemed too accepting of this happenstance and while he may have found Bulgakov's explanation absurdly thin, he did not appear to consider him a threat.

The compartment was small and clean, though there was a musty odor. Its walls were paneled in honey-colored wood. Two benches faced each other with a short table between. The longer of the two would serve as a bed; above it, a narrow door concealed a second berth which could be prepared as well. The window was hung in velvet drapes; beyond, a wintry Moscow rushed by. The train jerked suddenly and Bulgakov reached for the wall beside him.

If Pyotrovich could detain Bulgakov on the platform, why would he let Ilya proceed? "Aren't you afraid of being caught?" Bulgakov asked. He'd lowered his voice.

Ilya paused before answering. "There is no crime in riding a train."

Pyotrovich would want to catch him in the act, convict him of the greater crime.

"I'm visiting my brother," said Ilya.

"I wouldn't have guessed you had a brother."

"He would likewise be surprised." Ilya shook his head at the page as though amused. "It seems a company of workers, led by an up-and-coming Stakhanovite, worked for days on end to surpass all timelines for the laying of pipes between a reservoir and their town's cisterns. Unfortunately, they connected the lines to a sewage tank. Thousands were sickened."

"There may be opportunities to visit her," said Bulgakov. "I've heard such can be true."

"I'm surprised this was published," said Ilya, frowning at the byline. "Stupidity is not generally a problem here. Ah—*of course*—he was revealed as an enemy of the People. Wreckers we have by the thousands, idiots nary a one."

"I'm willing to wait for her," said Bulgakov.

With this declaration, Ilya reassessed him. His expression seemed something akin to sympathy. He raised the page again, as though to hide it.

"I can ask the porter about moving to a different compartment," said Bulgakov.

"There is no need," said Ilya.

Bulgakov recognized the suitcase on the rack above; the one with the hidden compartment. It seemed then there were three of them traveling together: two men and their shared purpose. The newspaper fluttered slightly. After a while, there came the sound of snoring.

Beyond the outskirts of Moscow there were provincial towns. Beyond these were villages strung along the rails, some with only a handful of unpainted huts. Occasionally and in a seemingly arbitrary manner, the train would stop and allow its passengers to disembark. Older folk, women mainly, clad in layers of shapeless black cloth, waited on the platform with baskets of prepared foods at their feet. Bulgakov tried to engage them with simple questions, of their livelihood, their families. They answered by indicating with their fingers the number of coins required for a sampling of food. As if it was inconceivable they might share the same language of the travelers. Bulgakov wondered of the content of their days when the rails were quiet. They wouldn't wonder of him, he knew, as though, like his language, his life was impossible to comprehend. After a day even such scraps of civilization were gone and there was only hour after hour of empty steppe.

It was difficult to focus one's thoughts in this landscape. Bulgakov tried to imagine the future with no more ambition than to conceive of an upcoming meal and found this nearly impossible. Thoughts drifted into the undergrowth of the past. He ruminated on his first clinical appointment in the year following medical university, assigned to a village that offered little more than those they'd passed. He could remember none of his successes, only those who had succumbed in spite of his efforts. He might say their spirits visited him, but in truth, he was the ghost who went to their bedsides, interrogating those moments of indecision and exhaustion, of gross ignorance and utter inexperience. He was young then. He knew better now of grief. He was sorry then, but perhaps not sorrowful. That was his sin and he returned to it again and again.

The drone of the rails was unending. Vibrations from the churning wheels gave even fixtures of steel and wood the look of animation. Beyond their window, the interminable expanse of crumpled earth took the form of the multitudes who had perished there: centuries of dead entombed, from insect and fire, disease and famine, from tyrant and infidel, layer upon layer, bones thinly veiled by the grassy sod. This vastness was their monument.

"You do this to yourself," Ilya groaned. "I thank God I lack an imagination."

Indeed, even as Bulgakov's moods deepened, Ilya seemed freer, more buoyant than before. As though in their travels from Moscow, an unraveling was taking place. Bulgakov felt himself coming undone, his mooring lost; whereas for Ilya, there seemed a loosening of a burden. There were times he appeared almost joyous.

Ilya was useful in his pragmatism. He insisted on routine. They ate their meals; they used the sink as a washbasin and shaved regularly. They walked up and down the aisles for their circulation then ate again. With such activity, Bulgakov's despondency would lift for a spell.

Bulgakov spoke of his time in Smolensk. "I was prepared for nothing I saw," he said in wonderment. "There was no one to consult, no other doctors, only the textbooks left by the last medic, and fifty or more patients each day waiting and me sprinting from the examination rooms to the books and back again." He became quiet after a while, listening to the memories that had returned to him. Ilya seemed to detect their intrusion as well.

"This was long ago," said Ilya. "I'm certain you were a good doctor. Come." It was time to walk again. Afterward, he would prepare their tea.

On the whole, thought Bulgakov, it was true; he'd been a good doctor. He followed Ilya along the narrow corridors that ran between the compartments of the train's carriages. The breadth of the older man's back filled his vision. Yes; he'd tried hard; he'd meant well. His patients with few exceptions had been the better for his intervention. He stared at the cloth across those shoulders. An imagined bullet wound suddenly expanded in a dark and silent stain. There had been a young man brought to his hospital on a sledge; the father who drove had accidentally shot him while hunting. The young man's clothes were heavy with blood as if they'd wicked it from him. On the examining table they peeled this away, his blood staining their hands, their clothes, the surgical linens; enough to fuel a dozen hearts, he'd thought at the time. When it was clear he would not be saved, Bulgakov instructed the feldsher to retrieve the gun in case in the shock of the news the father would turn it on himself. He appeared not to notice their intervention; once the papers had been completed he loaded his son's remains onto the sledge. Bulgakov remembered the way he'd handled the cooling flesh, securing the ankles and wrists as if they were cut saplings that might tumble from a swaying sled.

The rifle was returned to him to fend off the wolves that would take up the scent and he set out across the icy plain, presumably to his village. It was a rare winter day when the sky, though overcast, held back the snow. Between subsequent patients, Bulgakov would look and from the window or door would see the retreating figures, dark against the lighter bands of land and sky. Later, when the landscape was empty of them, he stared longer, as if he was the one who'd gone off course. He didn't understand at the time his sense of loss. Looking at Ilya and reminded again, he wished he could speak to the father. Not about the discharge itself, but of that moment when he knew the shot had taken hold, when the body had collapsed around that button of metal, before disbelief and horror had registered. What else was in that moment? What else did he know?

Ilya reached the end of the carriage and turned to face him, and it struck Bulgakov that there could be complexities to his dying; that somehow Ilya was singular from other men and inherent differences in his physiology would need to be anticipated. Bulgakov turned and they headed toward the front of the train. Ilya's footsteps sounded behind him.

In their compartment, the porter had laid the table for tea. Ilya measured the leaves and placed the pot into the samovar. He sat down heavily across from Bulgakov. The afternoon sun passed through the glass and into the carriage. Outside, gold stubbles of grass poked through rivulets of new snow. The sky to the east was darker, sullen; twilight was advancing, perhaps bringing more snow. It ran counter to the fields that glowed with unnatural light. It was toward this darkness that Ilya now looked, as though anticipating future difficulties.

Bulgakov didn't believe he could kill him outright, raise a gun against an unprotected man. He imagined them faced-off, as in a duel. Writers tended to fare badly in those contests. Perhaps they indulged in some final moment of introspection, searching the distant face, struggling to taste the grit of the killing emotion. Perhaps they waited to hear the other's shot as if none of it was to be believed until they did; then of course it was too late. The bullet would be felt before its sound reached the ears.

He wondered if Ilya was thinking of her. Perhaps he envisioned these routine gestures in her presence. Hopeful for something as simple as this. The chance to prepare her tea. The possibility of a different life. Ilya looked up as though Bulgakov had spoken. He seemed self-conscious. Perhaps he felt some guilt for such thoughts. Perhaps he had reason for guilt.

"You saw her," said Bulgakov. "After she was arrested. Before she was sent away." He considered hating him for that.

Ilya appeared surprised by the question. "Once," he said. "To see her more might have drawn scrutiny."

"How was she?"

"Physically?" Ilya hesitated, as though it was necessary to conjure her image. "No different than expected. Thinner. She appeared unharmed, if that's what you're wondering."

Was that what he was wondering?

"She's rather delicate, isn't she?" said Ilya. He touched the empty cup before him, smoothed his thumb across its porcelain surface, along the spine of its handle. As though marveling at its ability to exist when any careless movement could break it. "I worry about her. Contagion can decimate these camps in the winter."

Bulgakov could hate him for his concern.

Ilya took the cup in his palm. "She's stubborn though. Infuriating. I tried to convince her to save herself, but she would not."

Soon, Ilya would get to save her. Until then, he could talk about her. He wanted so badly to talk about her. The same as any person in love. To touch a cup and imagine her skin. To stare at the horizon and imagine their future.

Bulgakov got up suddenly, his hand to his lips. Nausea rose through his chest. Saliva pooled in his mouth.

Ilya said nothing as he left for the lavatory. His lingering gaze might have been sympathetic. Even after days of travel, sickness from the continual motion could appear without warning.

Even a creature such as he was allowed to dream, was he not?

The second half of their journey was punctuated by a series of mysterious stops, including one that went on for several days, such that nearly two weeks passed before they arrived in Irkutsk. Conversations between the two men dwindled to nothing. To Bulgakov, it felt as if the landscape had taken not only their fortitude but other bits of memory as well. The morning of their arrival, Ilya did not return from the lavatory; then Bulgakov realized the suitcase with the compartment was gone. The Bulgakov of Moscow would have felt some anxiety over this.

He remembered a conversation from earlier in their trip. He could not recall the context for it. Ilya had been describing an interview he had conducted with a suspected dissident. He'd seemed careful to omit the person's name and Bulgakov had wondered about it and about any concern he should have felt. Ilya had described a particular gesture the man had made, and how, with that one motion, all had been made plain, namely, whatever truth the man had been trying to hide had now been fully revealed. It was always that way, Ilya had said. His voice had trailed off—it often did in those days as though the purpose of any particular conversation had been forgotten before it'd reached its conclusion—then he'd shrugged and looked to the window. They were passing through the Urals. The bulk of any one of that range rose and filled the breadth of their compartment window for such a span of time that it seemed the dimensions of space were altered. His words had left Bulgakov with the lingering impression of anticipated loss. Perhaps not loss; sacrifice was the better word: here was a man traveling to a new place, a new life, where an interrogator's talents offered no particular advantage.

Later Bulgakov realized that the gesture described had been his own; one he'd made within moments of entering their train carriage at the start of their journey. It seemed then that to have once believed that Ilya would not have discerned his true purpose was itself naïve to the point of laughable. Theirs was a nation of informants; Ilya understood this landscape. In this he was like the physician towards the diseased: he could have compassion for them, yet remain untroubled. How else might one disfigure the flesh in order to remove the tumor?

# CHAPTER 31

For weeks Margarita watched for some opportunity. She flirted with their guards, though they seemed oafish in their capacity and of little use. Anyuta expressed disapproval of her behavior, but how could simple Anyuta understand? Should she pretend some illness? One of the women complained incessantly of stomach pains yet this was ignored. If she caught some contagion would she be quarantined? If she broke a leg would she be taken out and shot like livestock?

They arrived at the work site where they had been painting dormitory interiors the day before. Margarita had gone without water or tea since the preceding evening. She squatted beside the oblong pan on the floor as the other women returned to their workstations and loaded it with grey-green paint. She inhaled the vapors; they gave her a little jolt, a "painter's high," and she almost giggled. She stood quickly and, now dizzy, she willed her legs to weaken further. She fought the instinct to right herself and collapsed at Anyuta's feet. She thought for a moment to say something, but her head went back and banged dully on the cement floor. The pain was real. Anyuta called for the guard. She squatted next to Margarita and picked up her hand. "Tremble more," she coached her quietly. "No—not like an epileptic, that's too much—oh, never mind. Here they come."

Margarita was first taken to the small clinic on-site at the factory, where a doctor conducted a careful neurological exam which he pronounced normal. He asked her to follow his fingers with her eyes. She studied his face instead. He was young for a physician, perhaps a year or two older than her, and sad looking. He noticed her stare. "What did she do?" he asked the guard offhandedly, *to find her way into a labor camp*, but got no reply. He took her pulse a second time and leaned in. "Is there a chance you might be pregnant?" he whispered. She shook her head. She was touched by his concern. He wanted to keep her for more testing, but the prison guard said it was unnecessary, she would be transferred to the prison infirmary. He seemed gloomier than before as he signed her discharge papers, and she was escorted from the clinic.

At the infirmary she was given a bed in a room filled with empty cots. She stared at the ceiling. The prisoner who'd painted it years earlier had left swirls in the shapes of birds in flight. *Flight!* Where was this prisoner now? What was the penalty for such fancies? The room was cold and she pulled the sheet over her shoulders. The prison physician read the paperwork from the factory doctor and discussed her case with the medic at her bedside using words such as "paint fumes" and "poor ventilation" and "obvious malnutrition." These were the words of the factory doctor and it was decided that her paperwork would be given to the local authorities to determine if there was need for further investigation of him. The physician and the medic looked to her as if she might have an opinion. Margarita pretended not to listen. Birds, words, any of them could lead one astray. They left her alone. Later, Anyuta came to visit.

A new woman had been assigned to their block, she told Margarita. She sat on the edge of the bed. The newcomer had tried to take Margarita's bed board. "I told her you had lice," said Anyuta gleefully. She played with the bedsheet.

"I need a job in town," said Margarita.

"Her name is Klavdia Lenkaevna," said Anyuta. "She's from Moscow. Like you."

"Moscow is a big place."

Anyuta went back to the sheet.

"I did know a Klavdia Lenkaevna," Margarita said. "I think that was her name."

"Were you friends?"

"Not really. No."

Anyuta pressed her hand against the mattress. "I haven't slept on a bed in years." She said this as if it surprised her as well.

"What happened to her?" To Klavdia.

"Nothing." Anyuta made a face. "They took her clothes, of course. Or most of them. The nicer ones. I didn't help her, though."

Margarita slid over and Anyuta lay down next to her. They both stared at the ceiling.

"I don't want you to work in town," said Anyuta.

Her pretended spell was meant to convince them she was too frail for manual labor. But perhaps her act had been a poor one; perhaps they were still unconvinced. She was leaving too much to chance. It was her own fault if this opportunity passed. "It's what I want. Will you help me?"

"I'd forgotten how it feels to sink into a mattress," Anyuta marveled. "This must be how death feels. Or at least the first part—the dying part." She shifted, as if trying to settle in further.

Margarita pressed her fists against her forehead. This was not helpful.

"Raisa Sergeyna works in town," said Anyuta. She was an accountant. It was a special arrangement.

"How does that work?"

"The Super keeps her wages. I told you: a special arrangement."

Margarita lowered her fists. "I mean, how did she get that job? How was she picked? I really want this."

Anyuta was quiet for a moment. "I don't remember," she said. She sounded small and miserable. "Lucky, I guess."

The birds in the ceiling went in circles, nowhere. What could Anyuta do? "Don't talk about dying anymore," said Margarita. It was bad luck.

Anyuta laughed suddenly. "This bed is amazing."

They kept Margarita in the infirmary for another day. Anyuta didn't return. The next morning, Raisa was carried in on a stretcher. Margarita had just finished eating, sitting up in bed, her tray on her lap. The medics deposited the woman on the first cot along the wall; one remained. No effort was made to pull the sheet over her. Margarita went to the end of the bed. The woman's eyes were half open, her breathing irregular; several times a minute she gasped long and hard. It became a matter of waiting to see if that breath was her last or if there would be another to follow. The medic seemed to be waiting too.

"We think she ate rat poison," he said. He hung the stretcher from some hooks in the wall. It was a shame, he said. She was to be released in the summer. He didn't sound particularly mournful.

Margarita asked how poison came to be in her food.

He didn't speculate. As if this was a reasonable hazard in their everyday lives.

Raisa convulsed a little, her pale lips parted.

The medic told Margarita she was to be discharged that morning. She waited as Raisa intermittently gasped; he delivered her discharge papers to her in a sealed envelope. There was nothing to do but to return to the barracks. Midway across the prison yard she stopped and undid the still damp seal. It was late morning and the grounds were empty. The clouds were high and thin with the sun a hard dim circle over her shoulder. The physician had deemed her fit to return to usual labor. The slanted strokes from his hand had betrayed her. She glanced at the snow-covered yard as if she might light upon a pencil with which to alter them. Stray bits of old straw caught her eye but each time disappointed. She'd not tried hard enough. The reflected sun from the icy path burned her eyes.

She returned to the infirmary and knocked on the door of what she thought was the physician's office. With her second knock a woman answered; she was pinning some stray hair back into her bun as she scanned Margarita with mild suspicion. She told her the doctor was not available as if to imply that even if he was, he'd be disinclined to see her.

"There's an error on my discharge papers," said Margarita. She held the doorframe as though she could not be so easily dislodged.

"What error?" The woman looked personally offended.

"I'm not trying to get anyone into trouble," she said, as if it was all the same to her. "I should think he'd be grateful I checked before turning them in. But if he's not available." She turned to leave.

The woman paused with indecision. "Wait here." She disappeared into the room, leaving the door ajar. There were voices and movement; the door opened again revealing the physician. He was a large man though somewhat gangly, she thought; fair and in need of a haircut. He studied her as if uncertain she was the same person, now upright and dressed, as the woman he'd evaluated briefly in the infirmary the day before.

"There is a problem?"

He asked in an honest manner, unsullied by mistrust. He, like the factory physician, was a noticeable transplant from a different world. She hesitated, uncertain if she should deceive him or risk his confidence.

His nurse stood behind him, her arms crossed; she'd recovered her composure and maintained a wary if not protective manner.

"I must speak to you alone," said Margarita. She tried to

sound ambiguous: it wasn't clear if she was concerned for herself or for him. He nodded, and opened the door further.

Margarita waited for the nurse to leave then followed him into the office and shut the door. "I'll catch hell for this," he said under his breath. He sat on his desk, irrespective of the scattered papers. "Yes?" He spoke not unkindly but as though she'd better make this worth the interruption.

She held out the envelope and he took it from her. "I believe there is an error." She'd not thought through what else she might say. She watched him scan the pages, her panic growing.

"I don't think I should be sent back to the labor teams," she said. "I'm not yet well enough. I'm not ready."

"Really?" he said, still seeming to read. "What are you ready for, then?" He looked at her. "What can you do?"

His expression was flat, unperturbed; it wasn't possible to tell what he was thinking.

She'd heard of female prisoners making particular arrangements with their prison commanders or physicians or other personnel of note. Certain protections could be had for a price. The room was warm. He didn't appear to be bothered or embarrassed. "I can do other things," she said. Her voice seemed to come from far away. She repeated her words, trying to sound stronger, perhaps more enthusiastic for such a situation.

For a moment she thought he would accept her offer. Then he smiled.

"You're one of the healthiest women here," he said. He handed the papers back. "Look, I'm not political. I realize you may be wrongly imprisoned, but that isn't my concern. I'm sorry."

He didn't want her. And he didn't care about her. For the first time, this felt deeply personal. She felt sorry for herself in a way she'd not felt since her arrest. Tears came. He made no move to console her; nor did he hurry her. He repeated the words, *I'm sorry*, at regular intervals. It was all he would offer. She had no handkerchief; she rubbed her face, smearing her cheeks.

He'd been well schooled in the manner of delivering bad news, she thought ungraciously. In the next moment though, she took this back. Why should he take responsibility for a world not of his making? Why should he pretend more regret than he felt?

She returned to the barracks and gave the pages to the guard inside. She went to her bed board and lay down. She was more a prisoner now than she had ever been. She would become one of those who steals clothes. She wondered if Raisa's box still held hers; she could go through them before the others returned. A dead woman's sweater would keep her warm. She would wear it and watch others freeze. A guard came and ordered her into the dining hall for the noon meal.

The hall was nearly empty; one other woman was there: the new prisoner. Margarita sat at her usual place, across from where Anyuta would sit. The woman was somewhere behind her. Margarita listened to the sounds of her eating. A glass was picked up then set down. Then picked up again. Margarita stared at her plate. She remembered the rat poison. She drew her fork through her food; such was a reasonable hazard. Something crashed behind her and she looked around. The woman was staring in her direction, her face both apologetic and frightened. The floor around her bench glittered with pieces of glass. Margarita went to her.

As she crossed the room, Margarita recognized her as the passing acquaintance she'd known in Moscow. An older woman, fifty or so, she'd been a bookkeeper at the first paper where Margarita had worked. Perhaps they'd spoken to each other. Perhaps not. She was changed now; a prisoner version of the former Muscovite. Fleetingly, Margarita wondered about her own appearance; a prisoner version of the old

Margarita, of someone's daughter, someone's lover. She knelt and began to pick up the glass.

"Don't," the woman exclaimed. She sat and watched.

Each piece had its own particular shape: a fragment of the base, a curved wall, a wedge of rim. A slender point penetrated her palm, painless at first, then there was the button of red and the needlelike burn. As she watched, a second shard entered her finger near its base.

"You're bleeding," said the woman.

"I didn't mean to," said Margarita, then wondered what she'd meant. She took a napkin from the table and wrapped it around her palm. Briefly pale as her skin, the cloth bled as well, spreading dark along its fibers. With a second napkin, Margarita gathered the pieces into a pile. It occurred to her that the woman had dropped the glass on purpose. As if in some cosmic equilibrium, harm to one meted out protection to another.

"You should go to the infirmary," said the woman.

Margarita shook her head. She closed her hand and opened it again. The red crept across the cloth like a secret language revealed.

"I'm so afraid," said the woman softly. Of the glass. The blood. The pain. Of all things.

Margarita finished cleaning the mess for her. Somehow this meant that she was less afraid.

Klavdia had had the misfortune of falling in love with revolutionaries. This she confided to Margarita and counseled her against. In 1905, at the age of twenty, she met and eloped with her first revolutionary husband and her middle-class Muscovite family disowned her. A year later when the Tsar responded with a provisional constitution and their forbidden love had cooled, they separated and divorced. In 1917, she had married her second, a Trotskyite, who was subsequently arrested. Life had been hard for her, she told them. She preferred to speak in generalities. She would press Margarita for information about her liaisons then shake her head. She linked her own sad fortunes to men, and by extension, the sad fortunes of all women. Anyuta observed that she asked a lot of questions.

That evening when the others returned from the work site, Raisa's bed board had been cleared and her belongings removed. A guard volunteered that she'd been taken to the infirmary. Speculation circulated about a possible contagion. Later, during dinner, another guard reported that she'd died in the afternoon and conversations were reduced to whispers. Klavdia sat next to Margarita. At the news, she set down her fork and stared at her food with new dismay. This seemed an aspect to her sentence she'd not anticipated. She leaned in toward Margarita and whispered.

"Did you know her?"

Anyuta watched from across the table. "What does that matter?" she said.

Klavdia sat back.

"Did you ever find your sweaters?" asked Anyuta sweetly. Others along the bench looked over.

Klavdia shook her head.

"That's too bad," said Anyuta. "It gets cold when they run out of fuel." She banged her teeth together in an exaggerated chatter.

Someone suggested they hold a short service for the dead woman. Others agreed. Anyuta went on eating.

Margarita watched her and her misery grew. Oh Raisa! Poor Raisa.

"How has it been at the work site?" Margarita asked her.

"Why? Did you miss us?" Anyuta laughed harshly then stabbed at something on her plate.

The next morning the bus stopped across the street from

the Party Headquarters and idled. Margarita was beside Anyuta as always. Klavdia was across the aisle. This morning Anyuta had been as chatty as ever. A story about a dog and a rabbit. Her hand and empty sleeve moved in unison as she animated some provincial barnyard stand-down. The guard spoke briefly with the driver, then turned to face the prisoners. Margarita put her hand on the sleeve. She felt the stump beneath the cloth. Anyuta stopped talking.

The guard announced that an accountant was needed. A replacement for Raisa, though this was not explicit. He made eye contact with no one. Was there one among them with adequate experience? Nearly everyone raised their hands. He started down the aisle. Anyuta grabbed his coat and he stopped.

"Pick me, Comrade," she said gaily. "You need a 'counter?' I can make it to a hundred on most days."

His empty face filled with humor. "You?" he began. "We all know your talents." He glanced at Margarita as though suddenly embarrassed and remembered his mission.

"You," he said to her. "You have sufficient training?"

Margarita sensed calculation in her every move. She could not appear too eager, too intelligent, too conniving, too fearful. Too memorable. She watched him measure her. Perhaps he recalled the fainting episode a few days earlier. Perhaps not entirely, but somehow, choosing her would make sense to him. Perhaps because she was close to the front of the bus; because she could save him a few steps, a few more encounters; those simple truths were in her favor.

She shrugged a little. "Yes, Comrade. I have some experience." She tried to keep all expression from her face.

From the other side of the aisle, Klavdia spoke. "It should be me," she said, her voice rising as she saw opportunity slip from her. "It was my job, my work, before—I should be the one." The guard ignored her. She was too new.

He stood back to let Margarita pass from the seat. Audible protests echoed from the back of the bus.

Margarita felt a light push against the small of her back. It was the stump. She turned and saw Anyuta's shining face. Margarita touched the sleeve again, then followed the guard.

As she descended the stairs she caught Klavdia's expression: fear and disappointment, and a modest measure of resentment. Margarita would later speak to Anyuta. She'd ask her to look after the older woman at the work sites, help her navigate the prison world. Anyuta wouldn't want to. Why her, she'd say. Because she's new, Margarita would tell her. Because she needs your help. Finally, *Just do it for me.* Anyuta would make a face in the older woman's direction. She smells funny, she'd say. Margarita would laugh at this. *No different from the rest of us.*

Margarita followed the guard across the slushy roadway. There was a broad square of yard covered evenly with snow in front of a flat-faced building. The sign indicated that within were produced the materials for shoes for the betterment of Soviet women.

She took this as a message from the universe to her specifically.

# CHAPTER 32

Pyotrovich arrived in Irkutsk several weeks after Bulgakov. He seemed annoyed that Bulgakov had learned nothing of Ilya's plans. When Bulgakov demanded to see Margarita, Pyotrovich suggested he make the request through typical channels.

"That will take too long," said Bulgakov.

"In the provinces, people find they are happy with time," said Pyotrovich.

Bulgakov did as he suggested; his letters went unanswered as did Pyotrovich's promises to investigate the matter.

Pyotrovich had made the arrangements for Bulgakov's apartment. It was the larger part of the ground floor of a house; in the rear there was a small garden with a metal bench and a koi pond, though at the present it lay snowy and undisturbed. His neighbors were notable for their friendliness and lack of curiosity about him. One evening he was invited to supper by the couple who lived upstairs; he'd knocked, inquiring about the location of the library in town, and had commented favorably on the aroma of the stew the wife had prepared. Conversation was warm, though limited to the weather and local current events. She had the hint of a foreign accent. Bulgakov told them he was a writer; there was a fleeting expression of concern on the man's face but it quickly disappeared, and the subsequent conversation was about the latest upgrades that had been approved and initiated on the town's supply of drinking water. After he'd departed, he heard their voices for hours through the ceiling of his bedroom. From the next morning onward, though, it was so quiet he might have been the only occupant of the building.

He had brought the novel manuscript with him; it'd been neglected for months and at first it seemed to resist his revisiting of its scenes. He approached it with great discipline; the isolation allowed for this. He wrote from midmorning each day until the waning light of afternoon at which time he would prepare tea and a light meal. The rest of the evening he would read. Saturday mornings and Wednesday afternoons he would visit the library as well as replenish his supplies. Occasionally he would knock on the door of the couple above to inquire if they needed anything but there was never a response and he was given to imagining that they'd been spirited away in the night by demons or the secret police, though the truth was more likely that they'd decided to finish the winter in warmer climes. Whatever the reason, his present aloneness transformed itself into loneliness and he found that he would watch the meanderings of falling snow from his window, attributing its varying uplifts and descents with vague notions of hope and despair.

One Saturday morning after nearly a month, he heard the faint tapping of footsteps above him. It was past the time he would have typically left on his errands. Could it be mice? The sounds, though soft, were discrete and he rose from his chair to go to the door. Was it an intruder? The sounds immediately stopped and he waited. Had he imagined it? He went upstairs and tapped on the door.

The hallway was dim and chilled and he pulled his jacket across his chest. There was no answer. He tapped again, then turned to leave. The door opened slightly. He saw only part of the woman's face before it started to close again.

"Wait," he said. He put up his hand to keep the door from closing. "I thought you'd gone. Both of you."

She opened the door more fully. Her hair was covered in a large kerchief. A momentary expression of guilt crossed her face, then she recovered. "My husband says writers need quiet. We were hoping not to disturb you."

"May I come in?" said Bulgakov. He looked past her hopefully.

The door did not move. "Saturday mornings I clean," she said. She held a cloth in her hand.

"No doubt this is why I thought you were traveling," said Bulgakov. "I'm typically out, otherwise I would have heard you."

She smiled slightly at his conclusion.

"Oh—I have something for you," he said. "I'll be right back—don't go." He laughed aloud at the absurdity of his speech; did he think she would vanish the moment he turned his back? He returned with a small stack of letters. She was waiting as promised.

"These were delivered to me in error," he said.

She took the mail. "It was at one time our apartment," she said. It was her enunciation of "our" that caught him. The door had opened wider; the light from the interior showed the careworn lines of her face; she was quite a bit older than he'd thought.

"You're not Russian, are you?"

She hesitated. "I'm Scottish," she said.

"You have only the faintest accent." He wanted to ask how she'd come to live in Irkutsk. One might wonder that of any of them.

"This place is a long way from Moscow, I have to say," he said. "I guess even further from Scotland."

Her expression shifted a little. Perhaps, like him, she'd come here for love. Perhaps she'd been traveling through the region and had stopped, expecting to move on, yet still had not. The place itself seemed a midway of sorts; a point of pause in one's journey, one's life; not somewhere one would intend to stay. It struck him that despite the years which had passed, she was still quite homesick.

A curl of hair had escaped her cloth; what he'd thought was chestnut-colored from their evening together was nearly grey.

"I'm here because of my fiancée," he said. "I told you of her—she's innocent, of course. I'm hoping that I may see her."

The woman nodded politely.

"Perhaps there is a story as to why you are here as well," he said.

Behind her, a figure, her husband, passed between rooms. She gave no reaction to this. She gazed pointedly at Bulgakov as though challenging him in some way. As if to say that not all stories end well; some end poorly in fact. *Was this something he wished to know*, and he felt a strange chill, as though he'd just witnessed the passing of a ghost.

"My husband is planning to varnish the stairs," she said. She nodded to the space behind him. "If you don't mind; it can take some time to dry. We wouldn't want shoe prints in the treatment." He heard the lilt in her speaking of these words.

"I suppose next time I can simply slide your mail under your door," he said. "Now that I know you are home."

"That would be kind," she said.

"Once the floors have dried."

She had already closed the door.

The next morning Bulgakov noticed a dark sedan in front of the house. Moments later there was a knock at his door. The driver indicated that Bulgakov was to pack a small bag and accompany him. Pyotrovich was in the backseat. As he got in next to him, Bulgakov recognized the leather valise upright on his lap.

Bulgakov was to visit Margarita. "Here?" he asked. The driver was negotiating the smaller side streets. Had they brought her to Irkutsk? Was she with Ilya?

No; Pyotrovich indicated he was to travel to the camp. He wiped his nose with a handkerchief repeatedly. It was swollen and chapped. Each time he returned the cloth to his pocket as though determined to maintain some tangible hope for wellness.

It would take three days to get there. Possibly longer depending on the weather and conditions. This was an important opportunity, Pyotrovich emphasized, as though any amount of time or distance should not dissuade.

"We are certain now that Ilya intends to help her escape. Convince her to give herself up. Once she has escaped, of course. To give them both up. There will be any number of opportunities. Convince her that such cooperation will be rewarded. Previous offenses pardoned." He waved his hand as though he would say more, but instead retrieved the cloth from his pocket and hurried it to his nose.

"Then she will be released," said Bulgakov.

"Of course." Pyotrovich nodded. The cloth fluttered as it moved. "He's the one we want." Pyotrovich glanced at him, then away as though he did not care to remember his face. "Promise whatever you feel is necessary. Tell her we are capable of such." The cloth went into his pocket again. "Then you may be together." He spoke cheerily at the street before them; he had no interest in knowing what those words might actually mean.

"What if I can't convince her?" said Bulgakov.

"Of course you can," he said, and Bulgakov sensed some vague annoyance with the suggestion. Pyotrovich then added, perhaps more to himself, "We'll get them regardless." His tone now carried a cold assuredness. He studied the sooty snowbanks with a general expression of disapproval and it struck Bulgakov that he might wish for all of them, the snow, the driver, Bulgakov as well, to be eliminated, if for no better reason than the tidiness of it.

Ilya had said that she'd refused to save herself before. What did she know about that kind of bargain that he'd not considered? Why did he think she would make it now? What rationalization might he have her practice?

"I do hate traveling during this time of year," said Pyotrovich. As though even he could be demoralized by the continuous winter. He sniffed.

"I'll convince her," said Bulgakov.

Pyotrovich's car took him only to the outskirts of the town. There a troika waited. Its driver, a burly man of forty possessing a full and reddish beard, was accompanied by a thin teenage girl who giggled more than she spoke. They sat close together, high in the front with Bulgakov alone in the back. Beneath the layers of fur a coal foot warmer radiated faint heat. The driver did not give his own name but introduced her as Delilah. Bulgakov suspected this was made-up, a lusty joke between the two of them, and he avoided speaking to her so that he wouldn't have the need to use it. Indeed, her interest seemed fixed on the driver; Bulgakov could as well have been a sack of feed.

There was no discernible road and the drifting snow lent to the landscape the quality of a frothing sea. The city behind them melted into the grey horizon. Hills rose in the distance. The troika bells jangled anxiously as they went. The driver was an enthusiastic Marxist who desired to discuss politics; however, his words were lost in the bells and the wind and the perpetual high-pitched hum of the runners and he soon gave up his attempts to converse. Bulgakov suspected the girl was distracting in her own way beneath the fur robes; he watched the two of them, their backs to him.

Soon he would be with Margarita—soon he would hold her in his arms. His thoughts wandered past their more recent troubles to pause on a distant morning. Had it been midsummer?

They had resisted the call to rise, lying in bed together. He tried to remember what was particular about that day from all of the others.

Could he convince her to give up Ilya to the authorities? And if he could not—there was the certainty of Pyotrovich's words—what price would be exacted from an escaped prisoner, from an uncooperative one? He might never see her again. The thought itself was unbearable.

And if he could not convince her—would she be willing to forego escape? He would wait for her—eight short years. That was nothing to him. Could he ask that of her? Did time move the same for her as it did for him?

*The early light that morning had seemed liquid* as though passing through a shallow pool. Her silky head against his cheek; her warm skin pressed to his. Would that he could go back to those hours. He would tell her of their life together; his dream for them: writing each day, sunlight washing the page. Walks together in the afternoons around the town, his arm about her waist for all to see. Listening to Schubert in the evenings. The music of crickets and frogs from the garden, the splash of a koi. The soft light from a green-shaded lamp reflecting inward from the night's dark window-glass. Her figure in that reflection; leaning over him, her hands on his shoulders, her lips near his cheek, urging him to bed; he could feel her warmth through his shirt.

The girl's laughter rose above the bells. They were approaching a small hut, dark against the white expanse. A thread of smoke rose from its chimney. Bulgakov's feet tingled within his shoes. When they stopped the driver helped him down from the sleigh; supporting him across the snowy yard, until finally he carried him inside.

Bulgakov was vaguely aware of others in the room. He was placed on a bench before a tub of water. Delilah removed his shoes and socks and rolled up his trouser legs. His feet were angry red. Gently, with a hand to the calf and the other to his ankle, she took them one at a time and set them into the warm water. Her scarves removed, he could see her delicate features, the cap of red curls. He could not feel her touch.

# CHAPTER 33

It was a state-run factory that produced the uppers for ladies' dress pumps. Before the Revolution it was a family-owned business. After the dismantling of the NEP, its owner and family patriarch, a Turkestan, resisted the relinquishing of his business to the Commissat. He was taken from his office and brought to the building's front lawn one morning as his workers were arriving. By order of the district party leader, provided on newly printed letterhead, he was shot. It was late spring. His blood spattered across the blooms of annuals his wife had planted earlier that month to give color to the grassy border. She and some of his adult children were arrested; the remainder disappeared by other means. The running of the factory was given over to a part-time machinist until he was arrested for selling materials on the black market. He was replaced by the whistle-blower, a second-line manager who had been marshaling the machinist's shady transactions for a cut, who was shortly thereafter replaced by an illiterate bobbin spinner. The current manager was considered an excellent choice though he was not a Party member. He took the time to visit the homes of his workers after hours. He knew who drank to excess or beat their wives and counseled them against those behaviors. He was literate though had difficulty with figures. He was occasionally offered kickbacks which he refused and then reported. He never questioned the Party's legitimacy.

His wife was unhappy with the arrangement with the labor camp. She said the girls they provided were dirty. Ill-fed.

Lice-ridden. With that, her husband would look at her. Well, they were filthy, she said, and that was enough for her. They were criminals, for god's sake. Occasionally she'd follow him into his office and he'd wave her away with one hand, the other carrying a cup of milky, tepid tea. This was how things worked, he would tell her as if he was prepared to give her an actual explanation of how the world operated but he'd have already lowered himself into his chair while lifting some page of ledger in order to give it a closer review. When he heard the click of the door shut, he'd look up.

With Margarita's arrival, however, she was particularly unhappy. This time she shut the office door and faced him. He sensed her resolve, but his tea slopped over the edge of the cup and formed grey-brown puddles on the ledger page. "What is it?" he said, meaning, *What is it now that is different from every other day?*

"This one is worse than the others," she pronounced.

He intended to say something that would end the conversation quickly, then noticed the expanding circles of tea. More spilled. He groaned, wondering if she understood the spoiled pages were her fault, as well as the delay to the start of his day since his pithy rebuttal had now been forgotten. He used his handkerchief and began to blot up the liquid.

"She must be sent back."

"Why?"

"Besides, what happened to the other? She was at least all right."

He inspected a page. It would require reprinting. He dreaded this and hoped the new girl would be capable.

"I was told she took ill," he said.

"Was she infectious?" Her displeasure turned to fear.

"How would I know?" he said. "I need an assistant—they provide one."

"Send her back."

He was tired of her voice. "Fine," he said.

He watched her turn, smooth and victorious. "But not until tonight," he added. "These need to be redone," he jabbed the pages with the cloth. "And there are other tasks." She wouldn't have it her way entirely.

"Tonight," she said, still satisfied.

The front office with its dozen or so hourly workers was assembled of partitions and desks of various sizes and shapes. The perimeter of this space was a walkway raised above the main floor that allowed the manager to identify a needed clerk or typist. On the other side was a vestibule with a receptionist who had only a sorry-looking rubber plant for company, and adjacent to that, the manager's office.

About half of the office workers had arrived that morning when the manager showed Margarita to her desk. He stepped on one clerk's purse and stumbled into another's chair. Margarita caught sight of one of the women mimicking the slack jaws of a baboon after he'd passed. He left her with some vague instructions for the morning's tasks. From the perimeter's walkway, an older woman dressed in an apron watched. Margarita guessed her to be the manager's wife.

Margarita ignored the gossipy stories that came and went around her. At one point, someone asked her name. She gave it and the woman who'd asked nodded politely, then glanced to another woman sitting nearby. Neither offered their names and Margarita returned to her work. When she looked up again, the manager's wife had moved to another part of the walkway.

About midmorning, Margarita sensed a presence. The wife was beside her desk and holding a machine-made cardigan. "Here, Comrade," she said. Her face was thin and unattractive; her large nose and chin made it horselike. "You look cold," she said, as if her chilliness was an inconvenience she imposed on the rest. "Did you bring lunch?" she asked.

Margarita shook her head. Another inconvenience. "You will share mine." She turned before Margarita could thank her. She stopped in front of another desk. "This work space needs to be tidied," she announced. Her tone suggested this crime was of the same dimension as being cold and hungry. The other woman promised to resolve the matter. The wife swept past and disappeared behind the manager's office door. No one offered an imitation of her behavior. The woman with the untidy desk leaned over. "That is the warmest cardigan you've ever worn and it will be the best borscht you've ever tasted." Her laughing eyes softened then. "I don't think she likes you, though. I'm sorry. It was nice knowing you." The office door opened and the wife exited, heading around the perimeter and disappearing into the back of the building. Inexplicably, the office door slowly shut, as though of its own volition.

At half past noon, the atmosphere in the office lightened; someone laughed out loud. Books closed, pages were removed from typewriters and covers replaced, and the other women with their lunch boxes and pails headed to a door leading into the back of the building. The receptionist called to them and waved. She was to wait for a delivery and would join them shortly. Margarita, uncertain, followed the group. The wife waited for her along the walkway, her arms crossed.

"Have you already forgotten my invitation?" she asked. "I hope you like borscht." She spoke as if she fully expected Margarita would not.

"It's my favorite."

The wife's name was Vera. She led her through a series of doors to the back of the factory, then across a short snow-covered lawn to another, older building, following a path of packed footsteps. "This was the residence of the original owners," she said as they entered. "Of course, now others live here as well." They climbed the central staircase two flights, then passed through an ill-fitted doorframe that had been intended to provide an interior entrance where none had existed before. Margarita sensed a stiffness in her host, as if on their journey she'd thought to apologize for any number of flaws; the stained rug in the entry, the peeling paint of the upstairs hall, but thought better of it. Margarita was a prisoner after all. Once inside, she closed the door and pulled a curtain across its frame.

"Drafts," she said without thinking. She closed her mouth over the word as if she'd regretted it. She directed Margarita to a table already set with bowls and plates and flatware. She served the soup then sat down. As it happened, it was delicious. Margarita found it difficult to answer her questions; the soup was distracting.

The conversation was one-sided. Vera wanted to know Margarita's name. Her parentage. Her region of birth. The questions stopped short of her arrest. Margarita interspersed her answers with compliments on the lunch. With her third and most sincere, "You have no idea how wonderful this is," Vera seemed to relax slightly. She tasted the soup and agreed. She glanced at Margarita's bodice. "I don't think they feed you well at that camp of yours," she said and took another bite.

Margarita felt strangely self-conscious. "I'm naturally thin," she said.

Vera looked at her as if there was a shared complicity in this admission. It disappeared with her next question.

"What happened to the other one? To Raisa?"

As though the outcome to a prisoner's disappearance might be a benign one. Margarita looked down at her soup. "I really didn't know her."

Vera spooned through the liquid. "They say she's ill."

"We were told the same."

"And is she feeling better? Perhaps we should save her job for her. For when she returns. It would seem only fair, don't you agree?"

What if she told her of Raisa? Vera went on.

"My husband has an arrangement with the camp—but we've known Raisa for such a long time. Though I'm certain you are nice too," she said without much conviction. "You probably miss your friends—the other—prisoners," she added, unable to come up with a better word.

"I became sick at our last work site," said Margarita. "I fainted from paint fumes."

She frowned. "That's terrible."

Margarita considered her next spoonful. Perhaps she was being careless. Who was this wife? A clever woman trapped in muddy Siberia. Perhaps not so clever but smart enough. Fearful and frustrated. She was as much a prisoner as any of them. Her influence over the office workers imagined. She was the tyrant of nothing.

Margarita needed an accomplice. Willing—or not. Knowing—perhaps not. But she needed this woman to want to help her. She released the spoon and let it slide into the soup. She dropped her hands to her lap.

"Raisa's dead." Margarita said this much like a confession.

Vera shifted in her chair. "I really didn't know her very well," she said after a moment. "I knew nothing of her background—of her—" She didn't say the last part. *Of her crime.*

Of course it made sense to distance oneself.

Vera continued to eat. On the sideboard, a clock ticked. Her eyes had widened; she rolled them upward as she pulled the spoon from her mouth. Fear seemed to bloom within her. The spoon made a faint ring against the bottom of the bowl.

"Was she—" Vera didn't finish the question. What kinds of things cause death in a prison camp?

Margarita watched the woman tussle between curiosity and trepidation.

"She *was* a nice person," said Vera. She lifted the side of the bowl and scraped its walls vigorously. She repeated these motions again with her next bite. With the third time she slowed. Purpose seemed to calm her. The bowl's ceramic gleamed dully. When she caught sight of Margarita's gaze, she'd recovered herself; she gave Margarita a slight wondering smile as if questioning her interest. It was only a dead prisoner, after all. What cause for alarm? The soup should by all means be finished. She licked the spoon front and back then dropped it into the empty bowl. It rang out as if she'd thrown it against the china. The clock chimed the hour.

"Are you married?" she asked. The subject was changed. She seemed more cheerful.

Margarita told her no.

"Boyfriend, then." This wasn't a question. "He won't wait. If that's what you're thinking. They never do. Perhaps you'll meet someone here. It happens."

"Perhaps," said Margarita. She tried to sound somewhat forlorn. The woman patted the table between them.

"It happens," she said. "Not hungry? Oh well. I guess that's understandable." She carried the dishes to the sideboard. "Don't forget to leave the sweater when you go tonight. Chances are good you won't be back." With those words, she was positively giddy. Raisa was gone. This girl would be gone too. Margarita had miscalculated. The wife now had the ammunition she needed. Her husband could make no argument. She would consider the lunch a win.

Margarita returned to the factory alone. Vera was cleaning her windows. Margarita glanced along the corridors she passed, at the closed doors, a shallow alcove here and there. Places to hide when the guards came for her. At her desk the pile of ledgers requiring her notation had grown. Others around her worked quietly. There was under the desk. They would look there first.

She went back to the apartment. She stood outside the door for a moment. The interior hall was quiet; the midafternoon light was uneven through the windows at either end. She heard a dull movement from within, a piece of furniture across the floor. She took off the sweater and folded it over her arm. She'd failed with the camp doctor but she wouldn't with the wife. Fear was a better motivator. She knocked, then opened the door.

Vera had stepped down from a chair; one foot was still perched on the seat, the skirt of her dress bunched around her thigh. She reached to cover her bare leg as she lowered her foot. Her first reaction was alarm, even as she recognized Margarita. Margarita shut the door.

"I lied," Margarita began. "I knew Raisa. I knew her well. She told me things." She touched the table. "I don't intend to keep those secrets as she did. Look what happened to her."

Vera stared at her. "I don't know what you're talking about."

"You have a beautiful apartment," said Margarita.

The clock ticked.

"We've done nothing," said Vera.

Margarita considered her next words. Nothing terribly specific. She may indeed have done nothing. Her fear would have kept her in check. Not that it mattered. Plenty of people had done nothing.

"How on earth did you come to acquire such lovely things?" Margarita picked up the figurine of a ballerina from the sideboard and inspected it. She set it down in a different spot.

"We've done nothing," Vera repeated, her voice stronger. Partially restored. "I don't know what you think you know."

"You're a clever woman," said Margarita. She inspected the walls. There was a portion of wallpaper that did not align in pattern with the rest. A poorly rendered repair or something hiding beneath. Margarita smiled and touched the spot. "Prison is filled with clever women." She became serious again. "Well, one less now, I suppose."

Vera sat down.

"Raisa—I watched her die. Did you know this?" As if she had a power to be reckoned with. But this was truthful and Margarita envisioned those last struggled breaths. She remembered her own careless words to Anyuta. The way she'd come to have this job. Some would live and some would die. She could try to be unmoved by this.

Vera began to protest but Margarita cut her off. Enough had been said.

"Just beautiful." Margarita laid the sweater on the table. She smoothed its threads with a gesture of possession. "Thank you for lending this." She pressed down on the fabric. "I will see you tomorrow." She took another careful look about the apartment, then departed, the door standing open behind her, and returned to her desk.

At the end of the day, the manager seemed regretful of the pile of remaining ledgers on her desk. She told him she'd take care of them in the morning. He scratched the back of his head, but said nothing other than all right. It'd been her first day, after all. It would be as she said.

Across the room, Vera stood, watching her. Once again, Margarita felt calculation in her every movement. Her desk, in slight disarray, she did not tidy. Her chair, she did not push in. She left them both as she intended to find them. The other woman did not move to object, her expression indiscernible.

On the bus that evening, Anyuta and Klavdia were sitting together. Klavdia was speaking, staring down at her open hand while she pointed to it with her other. Neither Anyuta nor Margarita spoke as she passed; the bus started forward and Margarita grabbed the seatback next to Anyuta's shoulder. She took an empty seat several rows behind them. Anyuta turned and followed her movements. Only then did Klavdia look around.

That night in the barracks after Klavdia had departed for

her side of the room, they lay on their bed boards and Anyuta broke loose with detailed stories from the day. They'd painted ceilings and floors on the factory's fifth and sixth levels. A dead rat had been discovered in a can of paint where it'd drowned itself. After lunch, Nika and Svetlana had managed to paint themselves into a corner. Her papery voice rose up from beneath and Margarita imagined the factory rooms now haunted forever by their ghostly footprints. But quickly, the stories became about Klavdia. Did she know Klavdia had once been a dancer? She'd even auditioned for the Bolshoi. She'd gone to the University in Moscow for a year but had been expelled for protesting the monarchy. Despite the fact her marks had put her at the head of her class. Even before the men. Her great-grandfather had been part of the plot responsible for the assassination of Tsar Nicholas I. Her birthday was next month. If they could find some thread, she'd promised to teach Anyuta to tat.

Margarita rolled onto her side and whispered into the air. "Does she know as much about you?"

The voice ceased. After a time, Anyuta fell asleep.

The next morning the bus stopped beside the factory. Anyuta, who had sat with Klavdia as before, was asleep, her cheek resting against the older woman's shoulder. As Margarita passed, Klavdia looked up as though to speak. Her lips parted; Margarita saw the pink of her tongue flicker between her teeth, but then she was silent, her mind changed, and her lips stretched thin into a weak smile. Anyuta snored suddenly, but Klavdia did not move, and Margarita sensed that she herself had lost something and this woman had retrieved it, pocketed it, and refused to give it up to her. As she crossed the walk into the building, the closing of the bus door sounded distant behind her. The snow on either side of the path seemed dirtier than before.

Inside, at Margarita's desk, the cardigan lay on the arm of

the chair. Margarita set it aside and began to work. By the end of the morning, about half of her coworkers had introduced themselves and she had an invitation to join them at lunch in the break room. She met the rest during lunch. There was still no sign of the wife. When she returned to her desk, a red-pink peony in a slender bud vase sat on the corner of her blotter. She touched its petals, wondering where on earth one would lay hands on such a bloom in winter, then saw it was artificial. A metal coil wedged it in the vase. Perhaps pulled from an old hat. Fleetingly, it occurred to her to bring it back for Anyuta— she'd like it. She touched the flower again, with less care this time, then went back to her books. A few hours later she looked up. Vera was standing beside her desk and smiling. Her hands were pressed against her midsection, one atop the other, as if she was trying to hold something in.

"Did you like your flower?" she asked.

Margarita nodded, her words swallowed up in a yawn.

"Did you sleep poorly last night?" she said, her smile melting into concern. She lowered her voice. "Is it hard to sleep?"

"I'm all right," said Margarita.

"Well, you look nice today anyway." Vera eyed her hair, then her face. "Very attractive." She bent closer to her ear and whispered. "I have a surprise for you."

"I don't understand," said Margarita. She patted the pile of ledgers.

Vera motioned with her hand and Margarita followed her to the factory's vestibule.

The receptionist was speaking with a man. She went then to knock on the manager's office door. The man turned. It was Ilya. He smiled, as if confused.

"You're the manager?" he said to Margarita.

*It was Ilya.*

Vera giggled, covering her mouth with her hand. This was one of their assistants, she explained, a hand behind

Margarita's back. A newcomer to their little family. Ilya nodded and smiled as if he'd never seen her before.

The receptionist returned. The manager would see him
now.

Ilya bowed to the women and followed her.

"Handsome, isn't he?" Vera brought her hands together
"I saw him earlier—he's from one of the factories in the
south. Perhaps you'd think a tad old for you, but I'd say well-
seasoned. Yes," she giggled again.

"I don't think he's too old," said Margarita.

"You're blushing," said Vera, triumphant.

Margarita could not eat that night or the next morning. She
made some excuse of an unsettled stomach and Klavdia looked
at her as though she might be infectious. Anyuta helped herself
to her untouched portions. Would this be her final meal at the
prison camp? The next morning the shoe factory seemed no
different than before. The collection of ledgers on her desk
had not changed. Other workers arrived with regular greet-
ings. There was nothing that might indicate the propitiousness
of the day. She tried to appear busy but could not focus on the
ledgers. Midmorning, the manager arrived; he was alone. He
greeted the receptionist, then disappeared into his office. Ilya
was gone; it was as though she'd imagined him.

What did this mean? The numbers seemed to dart about
the page. Had she done something wrong? Had he changed
his mind? There was no one to ask. No one in whom to confide. She got up—where would she go? She almost sat down
again, then went to the small water closet reserved for the
office workers. She shut the door, sat on the toilet, and stared
at the back of the door. What did it mean?

Someone rapped at the door. "Have you fallen in?" a
female voice asked. Margarita opened it, edged past the
waiting woman, and went back to her seat. The numbers con-

tinued to swim about the columns. She closed her eyes. It was no good.

Just before lunch Vera appeared by her desk. "Someone made a very good impression yesterday." She and her husband had hosted Ilya to supper the night before.

"He has left already?" said Margarita. She measured her own voice; did she sound desperate?

"Look who's so interested," said Vera. "He'll be back in a month or so, I imagine. If the weather cooperates. Nice man. Newly assigned." She nodded as if she already approved of the match. She seemed to be assessing Margarita's appearance, her ability to entice a man. Suddenly Margarita felt lacking.

"I've lost so much weight," she said. "I'm sure I look terrible." She brought a hand to her hair. "We have no mirrors."

Vera invited her to her apartment for lunch. Once there, she went to her closet and removed several dresses. She held one then the other in front of Margarita as she stood in front of the mirror.

"This blue," she pronounced. Margarita went behind the screen and slipped it on. When she emerged, Vera had a tape measure around her neck; in her hands a pincushion and yardstick.

"This is perfect for your figure," she said. "Too big, of course." She pinned in the sides then stood back, considering the length. "It can come up an inch or two as well."

"You're so kind to me," said Margarita.

Vera studied her face. She went to her drawer and returned with several tubes of lipstick. She selected one, then applied it to Margarita's lips. "There!" She stepped back and they both looked to the mirror.

The color was more orange than she would have worn back in Moscow. She seemed altered in ways that she wouldn't have predicted.

"We tried to have children," Vera said to the reflection. "I'd always wanted a daughter." She gave Margarita a squeeze around the waist. "I'll take this in, but maybe not too much. We can try to fatten you up a bit these next few weeks."

Vera went to put aside the yardstick and pins.

Vera would deliver her to Ilya. Unknowingly, unwittingly, she would make her escape possible. There would be consequences to this.

Vera turned back. "Are you hungry?" she asked brightly.

"I am," said Margarita.

# Chapter 34

The trip to the camp took four days; they stopped each evening before nightfall and slept in huts similar to the first. Delilah remained behind at the last one and Bulgakov and the driver traveled the remaining half day without her. The camp was comprised of a series of long, low buildings; its size and the density of its structures and their implied population seemed anomalous in the relatively empty landscape. It was surrounded by a perimeter fence and intermittent towers, though he suspected these were largely unmanned during the winter months; anyone trying to escape on foot would not survive. He was escorted to a nondescript building, to a windowless room of gray-painted cinderblock, and left alone. It held two chairs and a table between them. The floor was cement; from the ceiling hung two lightbulbs, only one of which was working. The room was poorly heated, yet he still removed his coat, placed it over the back of his chair, and sat facing the door. The dark bulb flickered then came to life. It seemed as if anything could happen.

It'd been five months since he'd last seen her, almost half a year. He was nervous of her appearance.

Footsteps were heard, the door was unlocked, and he stood. It opened, a guard entered, then Margarita. Her surprise was immediate. The guard then left, locking the door behind him. They would have only minutes together.

How did she look? Fragile. Weary. Achingly thin. Words that could apply to the whole of her and also to each individual part: her skin, her bones, her wrists; even her hair, tied back with a piece of string. She was at once his Margarita and as well a person so utterly transformed. He recognized the blouse she wore and that seemed remarkable.

She hadn't moved. He picked up her hand. "Say something," he said. Be her, he thought.

"I can't believe it's you," she said. She seemed stunned by the sight of him.

He took her in his arms, though even in this he feared he would crush her. "What have they done to you?" He could not help the words.

"I can't believe you're here. How is this possible?" she said. "I was certain it was a trick."

He urged her to sit, then knelt on the floor before her. He studied her face. Shallow lines were apparent that he couldn't recall from before. She held his hands. Her fingers were cool hard things; her grip tight to the point of despairing.

"How is this possible?" she repeated, as though such information was important. As though she had lost all judgment of how time was to be spent.

He kissed her to reassure her; her hands loosened and he touched the cheek that had been battered in Pyotrovich's photograph. Its healing seemed a kind of miracle. But time could not account for other changes. The vague, unfettered fear he'd seen on that page had been transformed into something hard and shining: a desperate need, an unassailable hope. He was then overwhelmed by a singular thought as though it'd conquered his brain. She needed to escape this place. Nothing else mattered. And with that came a new kind of misery. She touched his face as if in seeing this, she wanted to dispel it.

"I don't care how you came to be here," she said. "You're here now." She kissed him.

She might forgive him his association with Pyotrovich, but he couldn't bring himself to tell her of it.

"I talked to your mother," he said. "I told her where you are." She nodded.

He didn't tell her of the growth that had been discovered on her spine. That would likely claim her before spring returned.

"And your play?" She smiled, hopeful for the news.

He was touched that she'd thought of it. "It plays to a full house," he said. "Every night." He didn't tell her that the censors had succeeded in closing it down weeks before.

"So you are now famous." She beamed.

He changed the subject. "Are you given enough to eat? Is it sufficiently warm?" Her temples had hollowed. He glanced over her wrists; the cordlike vessels were prominent. Her nails were whole though several were broken. A ribbon of grime where there'd once been white. She tightened her hold as though to hide them. He wanted to ask if they'd hurt her, then considered that perhaps like him she would give falsehoods for those things he could do nothing about.

She told him the food and the housing was adequate. If anything, she was bored.

"I miss our talks," she said. "I miss a lot of things." She shifted a little in the chair.

He thought of Mandelstam and wondered what he would find under her clothes.

She lowered her voice. "Have you been harassed any further?"

Her concern was both sweet and distressing. "No, no," he shook his head.

She kissed him again. "I feared I'd never see you—and here you are." Her happiness seemed sincere, yet in some way incomplete.

She would know of Ilya's plan; would she tell him of it? He could see these complexities encroaching upon her. He could see her wanting to push them away, wanting only to be happy.

"You are staying in Irkutsk?" she said. She looked more worried than curious.

"I have several rooms. Evidently the housing problems are not so keen here." he said. "It's not exactly what I'd dreamed for us, but there is a small garden adjoining." He let himself for a moment imagine her there and he added shyly, "I think you would be happy with it." She looked further troubled.

"I had hoped—when you are released." he said. She would think he intended her to wait out her sentence and he rushed forward.

"The neighbors are friendly. They know about you—I've told them and they are eager to welcome you, too."

"But you must return to Moscow."

"Perhaps there is a way, perhaps someday—perhaps soon."

"You shouldn't," she said, then he watched as the implications became clear to her. "You can't. It's too long." She looked at the door. Did she fear they were listening? She turned back. "Don't wait for me," she said.

But he was willing to wait. "You are all that matters. It doesn't have to be forever," he said.

She studied his mouth as though it was the impossible thing. What could he know of forever?

There was the sound of a distant door shutting; footsteps echoed then faded. His knees ached from the cement; the bulb flickered again. There was a purpose for his visit. Were they waiting for him? He'd not yet delivered his message. It seemed then that all things around them were strangely false. A stage made up with a flimsy set; walls painted to look like cinderblock; walls that could be toppled by a finger; the lights pulled down and with them the ceiling such that the rafters of a theater would be revealed. Even the winter and hardship of travel had been manufactured. The driver. Delilah. All imagined and dressed for their purpose.

He was to tell her what Pyotrovich had promised, he was to

convince her that it was genuine. But what if it was not? And then his next and most terrible thought—how could it be?

She'd been exiled not for her crimes but his. Had any of this changed? Would they let them both go without some warrant? If he vowed not to write, would they believe him? Not to speak—would it be possible?

Pyotrovich wanted only Ilya; the rest of them were a footnote. Promises made would not be kept if for so little as the untidiness of it all.

"Oh, my love." His voice faltered. There was no answer for them.

"They know about Ilya," he said.

Fear returned to her face. Certainty as well. She did not question him.

"I'm supposed to tell you that if you turn him in, they will release you," he said. "That we can then be together." He paused. "I'm supposed to convince you of this."

She waited. He knew she would trust whatever he told her.

It seemed impossible to believe that he would never see her again.

"Whatever happens, you mustn't be caught," he said. "Promise me."

The door opened and the guard returned. Bulgakov pressed his pocket watch into her hands. Her expression was a glaze of loss, even as she held it, and then he thought, in some small part there was relief. She could stop pretending that he could give her happiness.

He could stop pretending as well.

# CHAPTER 35

Anyuta asked her, repeatedly, what was wrong. She seemed to vacillate between concern and annoyance. What could Margarita say?

She wore Bulgakov's watch around her neck from a string. It touched her skin between her breasts. Could she wait? The dress was finished. She needed to decide. Eight years—the extent of that gulf was unfathomable.

In addition to its alterations, Vera had taken a scarf and sewn it with a scalloped stitch along the neckline. Up in her apartment nearly every day, Margarita was witness to its transformation. Now it was the last day. The dress hung over the side of the screen. She touched the fabric of the skirt, the scarf, its tidy track of stitches.

Ilya would arrive tomorrow.

Vera's husband was finishing his breakfast at the table.

"Come up in the morning and put this on," said Vera. "I'll make a special lunch for you here. Just for the two of you."

The manager put his arm around his wife's waist. "She's been so excited, planning this," he said, inclining his head toward Vera.

Vera suddenly noticed his coffee-stained shirt. "Look at this," she chided good-naturedly. "He'd go about like this if it weren't for me." She nodded to Margarita. "See what you may have to put up with yourself." She tried to shoo him behind the screen to change, but he wouldn't let go of her until she gave him a kiss.

Margarita looked at the dress as if it was this that over-whelmed her. "I don't think I can do this," she said.

"Of course you can," said Vera. "I'll hear no other talk."

"She's just nervous," said the manager. "He seems like a stand-up person." He grinned a little. "I don't think you'll need a chaperone."

Vera gave an exclamation of mock despair. She hugged Margarita, then propelled her to the door. "Don't listen to him," she told her. "It's just a lunch. No pressure." She regarded her kindly. "Smile and you will light up the room." She closed the door behind her.

Before descending Margarita paused at the end of the hall-way and gazed out across the snowy fields. The crisp expanse was untouched; it glittered in the morning sun. Bordering forests were less distinct; mists hovered among the dark tree trunks, stretching ghostly fingers of white across the perimeter.

She imagined the snow clinging to the hem of her coat as she waded through; she imagined looking back and seeing the path of her choosing manifest to the world.

It was March 3rd, International Women's Day, and it was decided the inmates would be treated to a single shot of vodka that night with dinner. No one, not the guards nor the prison-workers who went from table to table and provided the meas-ured taste into their cups, could say who had approved the directive or why. The guards joked about the women who'd be loaded up and "jollied" that night. Later, when it was determined the vodka had been laced with ethylene glycol, used as an extender since there was insufficient liquor, a brief investigation was launched by an assistant director of the local Chief Administration of Corrective Labor Camps and Colonies. Bureaucrats arrived at the camp unannounced one morning and interviewed guards and reviewed purchase orders and infirmary records for several hours before disappearing without a verdict. The camp director complained to the head of the district Administration and threatened to write letters up through the chain of officials at the Commission and, subsequently, the investigation was quietly terminated and the assistant director transferred. He would be later arrested on charges of sabotage and sentenced to hard labor within the GULAG system.

Most downed the drink without comment. A brief frown, then the cup was set aside. Some would not finish it. It was too sweet, they complained. They swirled their portions doubtfully. If they feared poison, they didn't say it aloud. A few, Anyuta in particular, drank their own then filled up on those that had been abandoned. Anyuta went to other tables, allowing the teetotalers to pour theirs in. When she returned and clambered back over the bench, her cup was brimming. Margarita told her this was a bad idea and looked to Klavdia for support. Klavdia watched Anyuta with a strange combination of amusement and disdain.

"Let the girl have some fun," she said.

Anyuta lifted her cup to Margarita. "Fun," she said, in pointed defiance. Her already small eyes had narrowed to slits and her nose and cheeks blushed with a glossy redness. "Do you even know what fun is, Comrade?" she asked with a feigned sadness then broke into laughter. She dropped her head onto her handless arm in helpless giggles.

Suddenly, Anyuta looked around, then climbed over the bench. She carried the cup; her other arm was straight and swinging hard, the fabric of the sleeve flapping loosely. Other women stared at her but no one moved to stop her. She jostled against another table unsteadily then continued. She headed toward a cluster of guards standing by the door.

Margarita turned to Klavdia. "There's something terrifically wrong with you," she said. The older woman continued to eat. Across the room, Anyuta was talking to the guards. They stood around her in grey jackets and fur-lined hats, nearly double her size, listening intently. One glanced toward the room as she spoke, vigilant, as if the girl might be a deliberate distraction. The others appeared not to concern themselves. Margarita went to her side.

One of the guards was speaking. "What are you asking?" he said to her. He seemed to understand her well enough.

"Isn't it obvious?" said a larger guard. He was a mountain of a man with a barrel-shaped chest and a face that rippled with old pock scars. His arms were crossed and he loomed over her like a ledge of rock. Anyuta stared up at him.

"I've been told a girl can measure the package by the length of the earlobes." She bobbed back and forth to examine his. "I'd say you were swindled out of a bit or more, Comrade."

He did not appear to react to her words.

"Really, Anyuta," Margarita chided. "Our worthy Guards are issued the same standard equipment." She looked up at the Ledge. "All manufactured with exceptional quality," she added sweetly.

He seemed no longer interested in Anyuta. "Did you enjoy your vodka?" he asked Margarita. "Did you enjoy it as much as this one?" The other guards were grinning quietly.

Anyuta was furious. She drove her shoulder against Margarita's, half-turning her. "No one asked you. You always step in. Go back to your precious desk job." Those last words resounded of Klavdia. Anyuta nearly fell as she stomped away, but recovered herself, her handless arm held aloft. She stumbled against a group of women. The vodka surged from the cup and sprayed across the backs of several. They erupted in protests but she continued past, waving them off with the dripping cup. She disappeared into the corridor that led to the barracks. Margarita turned to follow but the smaller guard grabbed her arm.

"I thought you wanted to inspect our equipment," he said, jeering at her.

"I'm certain I am unqualified for the task," she said. She pulled against his grasp but he held her as if by the bone.

"Let her go," said the Ledge. He appeared to have lost interest in the proposition. He turned to the other guards. One laughed at his subsequent comment. She followed Anyuta into the barracks. The girl was not to be found.

Margarita sat on her bunk board and watched the door. She suspected Anyuta was sick and in the latrine. Sick and drunk and angry. She'd get over all of this by tomorrow. Tomorrow. Margarita got up and looked through her clothes in her box. Tomorrow could well be the day. Could she leave this place? In her box she found a chemise. It was a summery thing. Embroidered in a green and blue pattern. Anyuta would like it. She'd make this a gift to her.

Other women were filing into the barracks. None of them had seen the drunken Anyuta since the dining room. Some looked more concerned than others. One commented on the temperature outside. Klavdia, who had been chatting with several women, said nothing. She turned toward her own bunk board. A planned retreat.

Margarita crossed the frozen yard between the barracks and the latrine, scanning the space on either side of the path for a crumpled figure. The moon was a hard white ball. It looked no different from the spotlights which illuminated the prison grounds at regular intervals. Between these there was only black sky. The wind lifted but nothing moved; the ground had already been scoured clean. Ahead, the latrine door was ajar. There were voices within. Margarita pushed against it.

Inside, a partial wall of greenish square tiles reflected a dim light. Margarita heard voices more clearly. A man's voice and she slowed. She touched the wall in front of her and looked past the partition's edge. The latrine's larger space was revealed. For a moment she didn't understand what she saw.

Naked bulbs dangled from a beamed ceiling. The same tile covered the interior walls, broken by a series of sinks along one side and toilets on the other. The cement floor sloped downward to a central drain that was absent its cover. A guard stood over it, urinating a thick yellow stream into its circle. He did not see her. He spoke over his shoulder to a second guard holding a rubber mallet.

"You will most certainly have your promotion, Sergei," he said. "By season's end. I'd wager a bucket of vodka on that."

A body was draped over the nearest sink—Anyuta; her pants were puddled around her ankles, her shirt pushed up and over her shoulders and down over her head and her arms; her bare white back, the doughy skin of her buttocks, spanned the breadth. The guard from before, the Ledge, stood behind her and held her hips cruelly in his great hands as he sodomized her. Sergei, carrying the mallet, stood nearby and waited his turn. She moaned and seemed to rise up, arching her back in protest. He clubbed her between the shoulders, and she went down. The guard at the drain shook himself and zipped his trousers. He turned and started to say something, but the Ledge spoke over him.

"You will have to tell us how our equipment compares." His voice stiffened with his last words and his thrusts became more forceful. Softer, muffled sobs came from within the shirt. Sergei made to beat her again, but the breathy grunts of the Ledge stopped him. His gaze shifted to Margarita standing in the background. Inexplicably, he looked away without reaction.

"Leave some for me," he said suddenly. He sounded entirely too serious and the first one laughed at his words.

"There'll be plenty," said the Ledge.

Margarita did not move. What was happening to Anyuta would happen to her.

The Ledge groaned; his fingers dug into the girl's flesh. He pressed forward and froze. His knuckles whitened. His skin as white as hers. For that moment they were one. Anyuta quieted; even he seemed to pause. Sergei lowered his mallet. When the Ledge pulled out, dark red clots dropped to the floor between his feet. Anyuta made a brief choking sound.

Margarita lowered her head. She crossed the room toward the pair. She put her arms around Anyuta's midsection and tried to pull her from the sink.

"What, what, what?" said the first guard. He took the back of her shirt and pinned her in his hand. Anyuta slipped to the floor and lay still under the sink. "Here's your fresh meat." he said. He shook her in his hand. "I should have let you go first." He slung Margarita over the bowl.

Her head hung down; she could see the underside of the sink. The blood pounded in her temples. A cold slat of ceramic cut through her thin shirt. Anyuta's motionless form was below her. Her pants were still bunched around her shoes. From her ankles to her neck she was naked. Her shirt, inside-out and pulled over her head, had fallen a bit. Margarita could make out the top of her head between its folds. The short, thick, uneven hair made it her. The legs of the guard moved past her. She waited for the hands. Someone pulled her back.

"Get out of here," said Sergei. He motioned with the mallet at Anyuta. "Get her out of here." In the briefest moment, their eyes met. Then in a strange display, like some halfhearted sculptor, he brought his mallet down on the sink's edge. A chunk of ceramic skittered across the floor. Nearby, the Ledge leaned against the wall, still breathing heavily.

Margarita lifted the semiconscious girl to a stooped posture, pushed her shirt down around her neck, and pulled up her pants. She hooked Anyuta's arm around her neck, and pulled the girl with her, toward the door. The girl cried out as she moved.

"Tell her to shut up," he said.

"Shh, shh," said Margarita. "Come now." Outside the wind

had quieted. Her head down, Margarita watched their feet move across the uneven ground. Anyuta's hard breaths were in her ear. A scraping sound, as if brushing fresh snow from frozen earth. The girl was crying.

Inside, Margarita cleaned her up and redressed her. Anyuta sat on her bunk board and let Margarita slip the fresh shirt over her head and arms. Margarita eased her flat then lifted her legs onto the board as well. Anyuta rolled toward the wall. Margarita crawled in next to her and wrapped her arm around the girl's waist.

"I'm sorry," said Anyuta. Her head was turned down against the planking.

Margarita stroked her hair. It was like fur. "Why are you sorry?"

"They did this to you." Anyuta thought she'd been raped as well.

It could have been her; perhaps next time it would be.

"That feels good," said Anyuta.

"Try to sleep," said Margarita. It was only hours until morning.

# CHAPTER 36

The next morning, while they were dressing, Margarita gave Anyuta the peasant blouse. Immediately, the girl put it on over her other shirt.

"It's for summer," said Margarita.

The shirt stayed on.

At breakfast, Anyuta showed it to Klavdia. Anyuta pointed out the colorful stitching around the sleeve. She urged her to touch it. Klavdia turned to Margarita.

"Where are you going that you give your clothes away?"

Klavdia wasn't the manager's wife. She was clever. And in some ways, she believed in the Soviet penal system. Even as it would eat through years of her life. She would feel no remorse in enabling it.

"Same place as you," said Margarita. "To the grave."

Anyuta thought that was a good one.

On the bus, Margarita and Anyuta sat together. Klavdia sat across the aisle. Anyuta slept, her head against the window. Margarita glanced toward Klavdia and found the other woman staring at her. Her expression was different than before; unshakable. Margarita tried to focus on the roadway ahead. She straightened to see past the top of the seat in front of her.

The bus slowed as it drove through the town and Anyuta woke up and rubbed her eyes. They stopped in front of the shoe factory. Margarita put her arm around her shoulders and squeezed her.

"I'll see you tonight," said Margarita. The lie came so easily. Anyuta seemed suddenly quite vulnerable.

Anyuta shifted away and for a moment studied Margarita with a frown as if unable to recognize her. Then she leaned toward her—Margarita thought to share some secret or observation—but instead she kissed Margarita full on the mouth. She saw only the blur of her face in front of her. The girl's lips moved with intention as if this was something she'd imagined doing before. Margarita pulled away and the girl sat back. Margarita felt the continued pressure on her mouth.

"I'll never forget you," said Anyuta in a shallow whisper. She stared at Margarita's lips.

Margarita stood quickly. "Tonight then," she said, alarmed. She tried to sound both cheerful and resigned. A compliant prisoner. Klavdia had already turned to the whitewashed window.

Margarita felt them both at her back as she walked the short aisle. Anyuta would be looking at her new shirt, brushing her fingers again over the embroidery. Klavdia would be watching Anyuta now. After a moment she'd move to the empty seat. Put a breath of time between Margarita and herself. She had time. She had the rest of the ride, the rest of the day. She would smile at the distracted Anyuta. Simple Anyuta. She would touch the colored threads of the girl's sleeve. She would admire them.

The bus door opened to release Margarita. She could leave Anyuta to that monster.

The cold sharp air touched her face. She stepped onto the uneven ground. There was the sliding squeal of metal against metal as the door closed behind her. The groan of the engine, the crunch of snow, a momentary breeze across her back as the bus moved away. The yard was white; the morning was quiet and lovely. They had let her go.

Later, as Vera had instructed and minutes after the noon

hour, Margarita opened the apartment door. It was the same sunny room it had always been. She was wearing the blue dress. Ilya stood near the table, motionless, facing her. His hair was longer and he was dressed more simply than before. He held his hat. It turned slightly as though his hands were eager to move, anxious perhaps. She closed the door, and locked it with the key. She left it in its place and turned around.

She could see from his face he was overwhelmed by her appearance. Her shoulder blades brushed against the door.

"Are you happy to see me?" he asked. She didn't answer and his expression changed as if some amount of his confidence had fled him.

He set his hat on the table. She touched his arm; she would urge him to wait. He brushed it away in a gentle motion, and gathered her face in his hands and kissed her, and it was as though he'd waited long enough, his lifetime in fact, guarding against all other trespasses and dalliances in order to spend that one moment here. Any disinclination on her part would be dealt with later.

He was then practical. "We should go."

He went to the bed and stripped its pillows of their cases. He held one extended to her. They would pillage the apartment for supplies they might need.

"They know about us," she said.

He didn't ask *who* specifically. Perhaps he knew better than she did. His arm dropped a little. "Have you changed your mind?"

There was a glint of light from the windowsill; the pincushion sat like a ripening tomato.

Margarita imagined Vera's expression, her tapping knock unanswered, her initial wonderment as she opened the door. Taking in the disassembled room, trying to make sense of it: the coverlet gone, the blanket that had been folded on top vanished as well. Half-open drawers in the kitchen area, their contents spilled on the floor. The meal, so carefully prepared and laid out on the table, untouched. The blue dress, crumpled in a pile at the foot of the screen. She would sit on the bed. The sheet resting beneath her hand would ball into her fist; her fingers would ache from its grip. There would be a new physical awareness, the sense of being acutely exposed as though her blouse had been stripped away. She would raise her hand to her chest to see if this were true.

They left by a back door and crossed the adjacent field along its perimeter where the snow had melted and their tracks would not show. Ilya had left the car less than a kilometer away. They didn't speak. There was only the sound of their feet trudging; occasionally a branch would snap. The whole time she thought: *I can undo this.*

The trees thinned and they crossed a road. Miles away, past other fields and other roads there was the camp. The guards would take out their rage on Anyuta. Their rage and their boredom. She saw them in the twilight prison yard, clustered around her. She heard their words. She heard Anyuta speak. At first, then she would quiet.

*I can go back.*

The car was there and they got into it. The engine turned over. Ilya set it in gear, then turned the steering wheel and the car eased onto the road. Trees and fields drifted past the windows, gathering speed.

Margarita awoke in the passenger seat wrapped in a fur lining Ilya had produced the night before. He'd driven into the early morning hours, finally pulling along an abandoned track into a stand of trees. He'd told her they'd be safe there; that was the last thing she remembered. Beside her now, he slept. A thin sheet of ice had formed on the inner pane of glass such that the outside world was a haze of dim blue light. She scraped her fingernail across its surface. The icy edges lifted and folded away in tiny pleats. She fully expected to see them surrounded by a regiment of police, their rifles trained on the automobile.

Outside, the dark grey timbers stood in peaceful guard as if they were truly safe. As if the world had shrunk to this tiny bite of land and sky. As if the rest didn't matter or could be forgotten. Or rather, as if their sleep had encompassed not hours but years such that those things that had mattered once were so distant and small in the enormity of time that they were no longer relevant and indeed one could indulge in the imagining that they'd never really existed. One could believe that one's actions hadn't diminished the lives of others.

Klavdia awoke in her bunk that morning, the dull pressure in her abdomen gone. The night before, after the one-armed girl was taken away, she had been escorted to a separate building for further questioning. Such was the ploy they had provided. There, in a windowless room, she had been given a meal of a grey-colored meat, turnips, and herring, similar to that received each night by the resident guards. She stared at the wall in front of her as she chewed each bite, rolling the food from cheek to cheek and over her tongue again. There was a crack in the wall; it ran from the ceiling in a ragged slope to a point about waist height. She studied the way the paint had separated on either side of the fault. When she was finished, she washed her skin and mouth in the latrine before going back to the barracks so the other women wouldn't smell the food. Still, she kept apart and said little when others speculated of Anyuta's fate. This they would discover the next day as they boarded the bus. Just past the latrine, the girl's body had been tied to the perimeter fence. She'd been stripped bare from the waist down; brown blood streaked her thighs. An eye had been gouged out. Her blouse had been tied around her neck, the rest stuffed in her mouth. She'd been shot once in the center of her forehead. A large crow sat on the single coil of barbed wire that stretched along the top of the fence. It cawed at the women. Perhaps telling them to hurry along. Or to take their time. The women stared as they waited, shuffling forward until, in their turn, each stepped onto the bus's lowest stair. No one spoke. Klavdia took her regular seat. No one sat beside her. She looked toward the painted window as though she could see beyond its whiteness. As though the spectacle of the countryside was hers to enjoy.

The trip back to Irkutsk seemed shorter to Bulgakov. Delilah had found other interests so it was just the two men. The driver appeared to mope over this; they conversed little and only about that which was necessary.

At the house, he found a police seal over the door of the apartment above his. The door was ajar; no one answered his call and he went downstairs. The steps had gone unvarnished.

Several days later, Pyotrovich came to his apartment unannounced. He was without his valise. He wanted to know if it'd been worth it, seeing her.

Bulgakov found his question curious. It seemed both personal and calculated.

"It can be startling, how quickly someone can change in a short amount of time. Sometimes to the point of being unrecognizable," said Pyotrovich. His knowledge of this sounded coldly intimate. He sat in the other available armchair. He appeared to have recovered from his head cold. "Do you mind if I smoke?"

Bulgakov indicated that he did not. Outside a light snow fell. The temperature within was only slightly warmer and Pyotrovich had remained in his coat. The fireplace was cold but both men ignored it.

A large bottle of vodka, nearly empty, stood next to Bulgakov's glass. He debated whether or not to finish it; that would require that he rise and get another. He debated whether or not to place his fist in Pyotrovich's face; that would also require him to move. The vodka seemed to argue against this;

it would argue instead for numbness; that in fact his arms and legs had already disappeared and the only fist that remained was the one in his chest. Vodka would argue for more vodka.

He filled his glass.

Pyotrovich seemed preoccupied with lighting his cigarette.

"I've applied for residency in Moscow," said Bulgakov. "Then Leningrad, then Kiev. All have been denied."

Pyotrovich wasn't surprised. "The movement of the population, the ethnic makeup of each region, it is a careful science." He then seemed to be encouraging. "This is an up-and-coming town. And it's been a number of years since the last real fuel shortage. You may like it here."

Pyotrovich still believed that Bulgakov could be the trap which would catch Ilya. "Why not arrest him immediately?" said Bulgakov. "Or better, take him in the act." The taste in his mouth was sour to the point of foul. "It makes no sense to wait. You make no sense." He raised his glass as though this was something to celebrate.

Pyotrovich reacted little. "We've made certain things easier for him, and that in itself is a risk. If Ivanovich senses any of this, any efforts of surveillance, then it is unlikely he will act. He has a brother in the area. Evidently there was a falling-out years ago, but we'll pursue every avenue of course." Pyotrovich muted his enthusiasm for arresting his colleague. As though this was the unpleasantness he must put up with.

"What's to keep him from disappearing into the countryside? He must know you will be looking for him."

"He'll try to leave the country with her. Likely Mongolia. By road. Or by train."

"Tell me, when you catch him, if you catch him, do you shoot him right away? Throw him up against a wall, or is there some process you must follow."

Pyotrovich hesitated. "Given the crime, there will be a trial."

No doubt it would be highly publicized; the Director's

efforts lauded. Promotions would offer themselves. Pyotrovich smoked as though this meant little to him.

"You are a bastard," said Bulgakov, as if he was amazed by the man. He went to the cabinet and brought out another bottle and glass. He set them in front of Pyotrovich.

Pyotrovich considered them before pouring. "If he's smart, and he is, he'll move quickly. He'll try to get them out of the country before she changes her mind. Men tend to look forward. It's the woman who looks back. Who reconsiders." He drank and set down the glass. "She will want to see you."

Bulgakov saw her then in front of a firing squad. A bag over her head. It was by her blouse that he knew her. The clarity of the vision stunned him as though it'd already happened. He could now only hope he would never see her again. The fist found its way into his throat. There wasn't enough vodka in this world. "Why didn't you arrest me in the first place?" he said.

Pyotrovich looked surprised, as though the imprisonment of writers was a novel idea. He raised his hands; he was helpless in all of this. "How do we arrest Stalin's favorite writer?"

Pyotrovich stood and pulled his coat around him more closely. Even in their brief minutes together, the room had chilled further. In the fireplace, remnants of writing paper, black from combustion, clung to the andirons.

"I can see that better fuel is delivered to you," said Pyotrovich.

"I have plenty," said Bulgakov.

"Manuscripts don't burn," he said, gently it seemed. "If they did, I could have a different job."

It had begun to snow and what little light remained was further diminished. Bulgakov did not light a lamp. He stared at the empty fireplace until it was only a dark shape on the wall. Both the vodka and the Nagant were his companions.

His hand rested on its cool lines; it felt like the hand of a friend.

If he'd not met Mandelstam that night. Perhaps he would have learned of his arrest the next day. Perhaps later. He'd have gone to Nadya as a grieving friend long after Margarita's departure. And if he'd seen her at the Writers' Union (indeed, would she have come?) he'd have recognized her, of course, but it was unlikely that anything further would have transpired. That avenue would have stopped short, like so many unexplored. He'd not have known the difference.

He stroked the Nagant. It wouldn't hold back the People's army, but it would do the trick. Yet vodka was his friend as well and he refilled his glass. He listened to the gathering liquid. He didn't want to die, but he didn't want to live. Vodka promised to help with this.

Pyotrovich had said that manuscripts don't burn. Yet people disappear. Whole countries of them.

Bulgakov went to his desk and gathered the final chapters. He knelt by the fireplace. He arranged some of the pages on the andirons; in the darkness, they seemed unaware of their new bed. With a match, he lit a corner. The paper held the flame poorly at first and he moved the match along its edge. As the flames caught, the orange light illuminated the words; he recognized a particular passage. He sat back a little; the flames progressed along the perimeter; then, growing, they leaned inward, cupping the pages. The edges darkened and curled; lifting up, fragmenting, more life to them than they'd ever known. He added more; again, the flames illuminated first, then consumed. The characters who'd lived there were gone. This seemed more than right. They should all disappear.

# CHAPTER 38

I lya had told her they were traveling to Irkutsk. There they would board the train for Mongolia.

He'd had false papers made for them. They were stopped only once. They sat in the car as the soldier reviewed them. Ilya maintained an air of disinterest and boredom. When the soldier bent down to look at her Ilya placed his hand high on her thigh, as if in absent gesture. The soldier straightened, his head disappearing, and concluded his business with them. Ilya's hand slipped away. She looked out the window and the car started forward.

Later she asked to see them. She made a face at the typeset of her new name. "Who picked this?" *Maryanka Vasileyna Solovyova.* Ilya didn't answer right away. He was driving.

"You don't like it?" He sounded sheepish and in part apologetic. It somehow pleased her that she could do that.

"It sounds like the name of an unattractive girl."

"No it doesn't." He looked to see if she could be serious.

"And you?" she said.

"Boris. Mikhailovich Solovyov."

So she was married. As though she'd dressed that morning in someone else's clothes. Of course, it was only paper.

"That is the name of a blacksmith," she said.

"Perhaps in my next life, Marya."

She stared ahead. The sky was a hard, steady blue.

"Are you all right?" he said after a moment.

She nodded. "The sun hurts my eyes," she told him, by way of explanation.

She could hear the voice of Anyuta in her head. It seemed a nuisance memory replaying itself. The girl had been talking on and on about nothing and Margarita had just wanted some quiet to think. *You're not as nice as you look*, Anyuta had told her, marching away. Was it a person's responsibility to live up to the promise of their appearance? An hour later, it'd been forgotten, Anyuta chatting endlessly, but the memory refused to leave her.

She asked Ilya what he thought would happen to Vera and her husband. When at first he was silent, she thought he was considering the question. Then she saw his acute discomfort.

"They had no idea what they were doing," she said.

"Some effort will be expended to find out if that is true." He sounded coldly technical, though perhaps self-conscious for that.

She remembered the sound of her feet on the stairs to Vera's apartment. The wear of the banister under her hand. All of the times she'd joined her at lunch. All of the ways she'd appealed to her nature. Criminal acts, every one.

"You spent time with them too," said Margarita.

"Any information they provide will put the authorities on the wrong track. At least for a while." He paused. "If they are forthcoming it might give us an advantage."

She could still feel Vera's arm around her waist. Speaking of the daughter she'd always wanted.

He stared at the road as he spoke; it was straight and unambiguous. As though to look instead at her would be a cruel thing. It seemed then he was taking them both to some terrible destination.

They slept in the car at night. Other than that first kiss he'd not touched her. She lay awake under the layers of fur and listened to his restless breathing.

Why writers, he had asked long ago. She'd asked it of herself.

The memory of a particular afternoon came back to her. It'd been raining and Bulgakov had returned to their apartment carrying its chill in the folds of his damp clothes. At first it'd seemed she wanted only to relieve him of his coat, but the fabric of his shirt beneath clung to him in a way that made him startlingly vibrant. She didn't stop at his coat, his shirt; she wanted to feel the warmth of his skin. He let her; he held his arms slightly apart and quietly watched. He was both passive and complicit. Then she pulled off her own clothes.

Later, she told him he wasn't such a genius. She was being playful.

"Actually, I am," he said. He was smiling.

She stopped teasing and became thoughtful. "You're a genius about people."

He wouldn't take her seriously. "I just pay attention. How else does one write?"

"Even the villains have their chance," she said

"Well—don't they?"

She reached across the dark car toward Ilya; her fingers stopped short of him.

*Why Bulgakov?* She thought back to Patriarch's Ponds—had she known then? Before everything, had she known of those things of which she could be capable? She withdrew her hand.

Write your most flawed character, she wished to him so far away. She squeezed her eyes shut until the darkness turned red. She strengthened her prayer. *Take all of your humanity and write your grandest villain, your most foul sinner. Write as though mankind depended on this. And render some parcel of that humanity for me.*

The next day shortly before noon, they came upon a line of wagons stopped on the road. The reason wasn't immediately apparent. The day was fine; the sky promised no difficulties. Much of the snow had melted; clover grew everywhere.

Children played along the roadway, chasing each other between the stopped vehicles; mothers stood in the shallow ditch and chatted in small groups. Ilya slowed as they entered the queue, then stopped the engine. Faces turned to them, the car a relative novelty, before returning to other conversations.

Ilya stared over the top of the steering wheel; he seemed certain yet tentative. Perhaps it was nothing. "Stay here," he said. He looked like he might say more but instead got out and began walking toward the front of the line. Effortlessly he took on the gait of a more common man, ambling, broad-based. He passed a group of children; he ran his hand over the head of one of the older boys playing. The boy glanced up, unperturbed; the old man appeared no different from any of those from his village. She thought—they needed to be forgettable. To disappear among the others. Perhaps he thought that she, like the car, was incapable of such.

There was a knock on her glass. A woman only slightly older bent low and beckoned her, smiling. Margarita lowered the window.

Had she brought something for dinner? asked the woman. Someone had suggested a picnic. The woman eyed the back of the car greedily. Surely someone driving such a vehicle would have something worthy to share. "I've never seen a car like this before," she said.

There was Vera's food. They couldn't spare any yet this would be a way to disappear—even for a few hours.

"Is that your husband?" said the woman.

Ilya was returning.

His hands were in his pockets. He appeared to give off a casual air, yet Margarita sensed the urgency in his stride. Something was wrong. She shook her head at the woman. "We didn't bring anything." She tried to seem disappointed.

The woman straightened. "How did you find yourself such a pretty young wife?" she said to Ilya.

"Ah," said Ilya. "But in the meantime I starve. She cannot cook."

"She will learn," said the woman. She smiled again at Margarita. "We all do."

Ilya got into the car and the woman drifted toward the wagon ahead of them.

"They're searching vehicles," he said. "I'm not sure for what." He looked at her then as though cataloguing her every feature. He paused at her midsection. "Can you make it so you appear pregnant?"

He reached into the backseat and gathered some clothes loosely in one of the pillowcases. She undid the clasp of her skirt and tucked the bundle under her waistband and blouse. She settled back in the seat.

Her arms circled the mound. It was a remembered gesture; a remembered loss. It was her younger self that seemed difficult to recall.

He nodded. "Try to look a bit more matronly."

Ahead, soldiers moved from wagon to wagon.

The occupants stood to the side while their belongings were examined. When finished, the soldiers moved to the next. They had not yet found what they'd come for.

"Try not to speak," he said as they watched.

The soldiers went through the cart in front of them. Several had climbed into the back, over irregular forms covered in tarps. They opened crates and bags of various sizes. Off to the side at the verge of the ditch, the woman from before stood watching. Several children clung to her. One of the soldiers broke away, walking toward their car. His rifle slung over his back, he didn't appear threatening. He knocked on Ilya's window. Ilya lowered it and the man's face appeared.

"This is quite a car," he exclaimed. He grinned openly. He'd get to talk about it for the next few days.

He was Margarita's age. Startlingly handsome. Eyes that were sharp blue. His hat was pushed back slightly on his head. He looked at Ilya first, then at her. His expression changed slightly. She was the type of girl he'd have pursued. She saw his recognition of this, then his slight puzzlement. Why was she here, with this much older man? He noticed her midsection then, and returned his attention to Ilya as though it'd always been there. "You'll need to step out," he said. The car was forgotten.

Margarita opened the door. Ilya's arm reached across her.

"Would it be all right if my wife remained?" Ilya patted her belly. "I think the midwife is overly concerned, but she wants her to stay off her feet as much as possible."

Ahead, the woman watched them. Would she notice the change should Margarita get out?

The soldier nodded; of course, if that was necessary.

Ilya opened his door and the steppe's breeze moved between them as though eager for the chance; it shifted her clothes. She cradled the bulk in her arms protectively.

The soldier asked a question about the car. Ilya got out and closed the door. She didn't hear his answer.

Several other soldiers approached. She listened to the muffled conversation. The more senior one wanted all of the vehicle's occupants removed in order to search properly. Ilya tried to appear apologetic, yet shook his head.

She got out of the car. "It's all right. I've been sitting too long." She hugged the bundle to her. They'd not fastened it in any way and she risked losing it.

The handsome soldier looked concerned for her.

"What an amazing day," she said to him brightly.

"It is," he said. As if they were anywhere but along this road.

She sensed Ilya watching this scene, disapproving.

She could tell the soldier that she wasn't really pregnant. That it was Ilya who'd made her disguise herself. Ilya who'd told her not to speak. Yet she could speak. She could say that all that had happened was his doing. The soldier would believe her. He would believe she was blameless.

The woman ahead saw her; even at that distance, Margarita could see her surprise. She lifted her arms away from the children as though to take a step toward them.

A whiff of fear rose through her. Then she thought, *Come to me.*

There was a cry from the back of the wagon ahead of them. One of the soldiers standing on the bed had straightened, holding a dark sack, and the soldiers left the car. The woman and her family were surrounded and escorted on foot toward the front of the column. Ilya motioned to Margarita to get in.

"Black market," he said, once the doors were closed. He seemed relieved, then he looked at her. "Leave that in place until we get past them entirely."

She touched the mound. It was as if she was incapable of disobedience. Her mouth, her hands were subordinate to him; she could hate them for that.

The column of vehicles began to move. Ilya followed the others. It was a slow exodus.

The soldiers had lined the family up in a row along the top of the ditch. Someone—the husband—had been given a pickax and a shovel. Rifles were trained upon him as he worked to clear the sod nearby.

The woman was watching her younger child, a girl, perhaps three or four years of age, crouched, her dress blossomed about her, picking buds of new clover, her small fingers working them into a chain. The woman called to her; she would want her close, the silkiness of her skin, the comfort of that, but the girl was intent upon a necklace to wear. There came the sound of the ax striking the earth behind her. Her son, older, understanding, gripped her other hand. She dared not move. She called again. She tried to sound sweet. "Come, child, come." Her daughter pretended not to hear.

Ilya told her to cover her ears. Margarita lifted her hands to her head.

When they stopped for meals, they stood as they ate, sharing a single cup, the corner of the car hood between them. Ilya would distribute their food. She would note the disproportion between them. "I'm not as hungry as you think I am," she complained, lightly at first.

"You are starved." This seemed a criticism and she did her best. She sensed they would not leave until she was finished; even should the People's Army appear over their horizon.

"Please, take some," she would beg. He would light a cigarette instead and gaze at the scenery as though something in it had changed.

After the family's arrest, when they next stopped, he took nothing for himself, providing her with a modest portion. She ate several bites, then pushed the rest toward him. "This tastes like sawdust."

"Taste doesn't matter," he said.

He made no effort to push it back; neither did she reclaim it. It lay between them like a forlorn thing.

He lit a cigarette. She as well could pretend disinterest. She sensed that any movement on her part, even the rise of her chest, was in revolt of him. Dry leaves scuttled across the road as though unaware. The breeze pushed her scarf across her cheek; it would set her into motion regardless of what she wanted.

"I won't eat it," she said.

He brought the cigarette to his lips.

"Why are you doing this?" she said.

"I've told you."

"I mean why are you doing this?" She extended her arms to the world. He could have left her in that camp.

He gathered the food, carried it to the side of the road, and scattered it across the ditch. He looked for a moment as though he would go further, even stomp it into the ground. He got into the car and started it. He would leave her there, she thought, and she got in quickly.

The car started forward. The forgotten cup flew across the windshield and then away.

"I want to see Mikhail," she said.

They drove in silence for several hours. He tried an old trail, then after a kilometer he turned and backtracked. He took another, less-likely road. Surrounding fields were still covered in snow; there were intermittent swaths of brush where animals might hide.

"Do you even know where you're going?" she asked.

Amid the darker grays of a stand of trees, the black timbers of a small hut emerged. The car's headlights danced across its walls. Its shutters were closed. It appeared abandoned. Ilya turned off the engine and got out.

She stared through the windshield. He pushed the door of the hut with his foot. The lower hinge was broken and it opened only partway. He disappeared into the black interior. The temperature in the car seemed to drop perceptibly and she followed.

Inside, he had lit a match. The orange glow around his hand penetrated little into the darkness, but he seemed to move with foreknowledge to a high shelf built around the room's perimeter and took down several oil lamps. He lit one, then, with a second match, lit several more. The lanterns extended fingers of light to the walls. There was a hearth, chairs and a table, a cabinet and a bed frame. The place had been left in good order, as if someone had thought to return someday. A small stack of wood remained and he built a modest fire.

He straightened and brushed off his hands lightly. "You should be safe here," he said.

"Where are you going?" she said.

He gestured to the flames; this wouldn't last, he told her, and he left as though to gather more. She heard the car engine start and she ran outside.

He'd backed the car across the path they'd taken to the door, then turned the car down the track. Would he leave her? She ran after him. The car bounced over the ruts, gaining speed. Within moments he was gone.

The silent land spread away as if this was all there was. She stared at the road, distant, where it was no longer discernible from the snow. There were no birds; nothing moved. She heard only her own breaths.

There came the howl of a wolf. She went back to the hut. Already the fire was dying.

Once when they'd stopped for petrol, she returned to the car to find a small bundle of daisies on her seat. The wife of the man who operated the distribution site kept a greenhouse. At first Ilya wouldn't admit to them, then said they'd reminded him of her. He refused to tell her what he'd traded for them. She held the bouquet for a time, then it seemed as though her hands and arms had become dotted with moving grains of sand. The undersides of the petals were covered with spider mites. Ilya tossed the clutch from the window as he drove. She tried to refrain from continuing to examine her arms, rubbing them instead as though it was the chill of the air.

He'd brought clothes for her. Not in her style but she only had those that she'd worn that day. He suggested she consider changing her style. She remembered a particular skirt she'd once owned. She could recall precisely where it'd hung in their apartment in Moscow. She remembered the occasions when she'd worn it. She mentioned it once, as though it was an amusing mystery. "I don't understand why I miss the thing," she said. "Was it a favorite of his?" he asked her. She couldn't remember. Perhaps she'd never known. What did it matter; it was not as though she was going to go back for it. Several miles had passed before she realized that she hadn't answered. The steppe could do that.

He wore a ring on his right hand. It was a simple band, braided silver. She asked him about it once when he was driving, touching it as his hand held the steering wheel. It'd been a gift, he told her. He'd been engaged at one time. "She changed her mind. I was not the love of her life," he added lightly. He glanced at her. "It was long ago," he said, as though she was the one in need of some comfort. Yet the wound seemed still fresh in some way. Perhaps it was the familiarity of the land they traveled which caused old memories to bloom.

"I didn't know," she said.

Ilya watched the road unfold. "It was long ago," he repeated.

It seemed she could not stop touching it. "Was she the love of your life?" she asked.

He smiled a little at the sky ahead as though it was the amusing thing.

It was utterly black outside. She added to the fire. The dark walls seemed to come to life, painted in folk art. Centuries-old and faded, stylized animals and birds and flowers paraded about the perimeter with flourishes of yellow and rust and blue. The images told an ancient story: wolves were chasing an abducted bride. The plot line disappeared behind the cabinet. This was a tale she'd been told as a child. Would the hero slay the beasts in time to save his beloved? She pulled at the cabinet's corner. It resisted; gripping the floor, too long in its place. She pulled harder. Something was there, written in the wood. She brought a lantern and held it near the wall.

In delicate script, by a woman's hand, were names in a tidy column, one atop the next, repeated over and over, and beside each, a short line and an age. Ilya at six, Pavel at seven. Ilya at seven, then eight. The lines formed an uneven ladder up the wall. *Youngsters bound across the room in hand-sewn overalls, knocking into walls, laughing, taunting as brothers do. Their mother calls them animals.* Pavel at ten. Ilya at twelve. *There is a girl whose name when spoken will cause Ilya to blush; Pavel takes his advantage with such knowledge.* Ilya at fifteen. *He finds it amusing that he must bend down to kiss his mother's cheek. He does this often to show off his stature to her.* Pavel at fifteen. There the names stopped. *Men are not measured by the hand of their mother.*

Margarita turned back toward the fire. Outside, wolves could be heard. The sound didn't frighten her. She and they would wait together. They would all try not to think too hard.

# CHAPTER 39

The concrete steps leading to the small regional police station hadn't been shoveled. A trail of boot prints had packed down a sullied path. Ilya smoked a cigarette and watched the building from a stand of trees. The glow from an interior desk lamp reflected in one of the windows.

He could hope it would be anyone but him. He crumpled his cigarette against the bottom of his shoe and flicked it into the snow.

The officer seated in the chair looked up as the door opened, then, as recognition widened his gaze, he pushed away slightly and craned his head back. His hair was flecked with gray. His face was broad and flattish in aspect, some ancient Nordic lineage; his cheeks were heavy yet his eyes remained powder blue. He smiled as though pleased for the visit; as though this was all it could be counted as. Ilya measured his expression for its surprise; he didn't appear to have anticipated Ilya's arrival, yet Pavel had always been difficult to read.

It startled him how much he resembled their mother.

Their mother told the story of once when they were small, she'd taken a switch in order to punish Ilya for some transgression. But before she could lift the piece against him, she would say, the younger Pavel had stepped between them and, with solemn eyes, asked that he might take the punishment instead. She was amazed, and with every retelling, this seemed new. As it would happen, she'd then conclude, no one was punished that day. Neither of them could remember the event yet they had never doubted her account. Only years later did Ilya reconsider it. He wondered why he'd not been made the hero of that drama. He wondered what she'd read on his young heart that she might want him to believe in some perpetual fealty owed to his brother. He wondered which son she thought she was protecting.

"I can't believe it's you," said Pavel. He touched the top of his head with his hands as though it was necessary in order to contain such news. Abruptly, he stood and hugged Ilya, kissing him on both cheeks and hugging him again. He gestured to the chair beside the desk, easing back into his own.

"How many years has it been?" he asked, as though such a thing must be incalculable.

"Thirty."

"Thirty." Pavel shook his head. The number itself seemed tragic. Half a man's lifetime.

There were only a few things that might estrange a brother from a brother. Perhaps only one. Yet Pavel smiled, as if determined to overcome any obstacle. "I will take you home," he said. "We will share a meal."

"Sure. I'll come," said Ilya.

They were both suddenly quiet in the face of his lie. Somewhere in the back of the small room, a primus flame hummed. There was no photograph of her on his desk. There was a telephone but Pavel's gaze passed over it. He could wait to tell her, thought Ilya. In fact, it was unlikely he'd tell her at all. Olga.

The wood grain of the desk was marred by a watermark. It'd been there when it was Ilya's desk. "You've done well?" Ilya asked.

"I've had the burden of trying to live up to the reputation of my older brother."

"Children?" It seemed a required question.

Pavel shook his head. "She couldn't." The years of heart-break that went with that would go unspoken.

"And Olga?" Was this required as well?

"She is fine," said Pavel. His brief smile sealed that avenue from anything further. "Did you marry?"

Ilya shook his head. What was there to say, other than it was long ago. Even that seemed needless.

Perhaps on this point Pavel agreed. He gestured expansively. "And now my important brother has returned for a visit."

Ilya had wanted information about Pyotrovich; he wanted it badly enough to risk this trip to the police station. To risk seeing his brother, though Pavel was not a threat. To risk seeing her—even in a photograph. He wondered vaguely if this visit might implicate Pavel in some way. It was unlikely the room was wired. Pavel appeared to have no concerns.

The blowing whistle of a kettle sounded and Pavel got up to prepare tea. Watching him go through the mechanics provided a breath of normalcy. His gait was lumbering, perhaps painful, and Ilya noticed a limp. This was new—new in the last thirty years, and he felt some small guilt for failing to know of it, for his part in the silence between them.

"I wrote you about Mother," said Pavel, his back turned. There was the mildest sense of rebuke in his voice.

"It found me eventually."

"I wasn't certain."

At the time it'd seemed to have arrived from a different world. "It was nearly summer when I got it," said Ilya.

"Mail was tricky then." He paused. "I've always wondered when I would see you again."

In his motions the sense of their mother returned more sharply. The quiet of her disappointment in his setting aside of family, her questioning of this; it would have been a personal thing. When his brother turned, he held a cup in each hand.

Pavel's gaze seemed to stop short; it focused on his mouth.

"Do you still take milk? I have some powdered in the cabinet," he said.

When they were children, Pavel had always been able to find him. Even when alone in the forest, desiring the quiet of his own thoughts; even then, Pavel would appear, as though his brother's wanderings were mapped on his heart.

Pavel set the cups on the desk. One covered the water-mark. He sat down heavily.

How easily they slipped into familiar patterns, as though they'd done this every morning. Time seemed a flimsy thing. What ran in one's blood that allowed for this?

Pavel sipped his tea. His lips retracted from the hot liquid. "You might want to let it cool a bit," he said. He glanced at the telephone.

Ilya fingered the cup. It had begun to snow.

For thirty years he'd thought his brother happy. The master of happiness. Supreme in this. It had been enough to keep him away.

But something was wrong. "What happened to Olga?" said Ilya.

Pavel watched the steam rise up from the cup. "She died about a year after you left."

All that time he'd imagined the world with her somewhere in it. How could he not have known? Behind them the whirring of some small office machine could be heard.

"Pyotrovich has been here twice," said Pavel, touching the cup's edge. "Unpleasant man. What is it they say about promotions? There is always one too many?"

He remembered her scarlet cap, a blot of blood in the snowy tableau. He remembered her slender arm extended, her gloved fingers holding the small ring, his betrothal gift to her. Her words had been forgotten. Snow fell between them; perfect crystals alighted on the velvet cloth as though grateful for that brief privilege, then were gone forever.

*Come with me,* he'd said. He meant, *If you love me, you will come with me.* It was then that he'd sensed another presence in the woods, a figure in the shadows. Someone waiting to take his place.

Ilya stood, all at once anxious to leave.

"Is she as beautiful as they say?" Pavel asked. He smiled a little, as though at long last happy for his brother. As though this was all he'd ever wanted.

What was the distance between having everything and having nothing? A span of decades, a matter of seconds? What was the difference between having everything and having nothing? He could not answer; he could not tell them apart.

The hut was dimly lit, the fire low amid embers. Ilya stood in the doorway. The night at his back, bitterly cold, was trying to get in.

"Marry me," he said. His voice hung oddly in the quiet room. He took his hat in his hand; the other held the doorframe.

She'd been sleeping, seated in front of the fire. She straightened slightly, blinking. She rubbed the back of her neck.

"I would go out and fetch a priest this moment," he said. There were no priests to be found, yet the binding quality of a bureaucratic seal seemed lacking for the task.

She was fully awake now. She looked achingly young and in this he felt aged. He could forgive her that. He went onto his knees before her.

"I can take care of you," he said.

"I never doubted that you would return." Her arms were crossed over her chest. Once again, he felt the need to take one hand into his, to separate it from the other, as though apart they could be more easily convinced.

"I can make you happy."

Could he? Her eyes carried that question.

He imagined a snowy forest as though it'd been his to remember; the quiet movements of a man and a woman toward one another. They'd always known, Pavel and Olga, since childhood; it'd run in their blood, yet they had been willing to allow for the grandest of cosmic errors. Perhaps he'd known too, and when he left, he knew that Pavel would blame himself.

"I can make you happy," he repeated. He could make someone happy.

She took his hand; he could see that she would try to believe him. But the gesture communicated something else. Surely she'd intended to give comfort rather than despair. His talent as an interrogator would not allow for misunderstanding.

# CHAPTER 40

Bulgakov was summoned to the Regional Office of the Chief Directorate of Frontier Guards and Interior Troops in Irkutsk. Pyotrovich had established a temporary office on its second floor. It was clear he was dissatisfied with the local contingent. After the clerk had ushered him in, Pyotrovich got up to shut the door himself. "They smile while they're slipping something unpleasant into your tea," he said. He sat down again. "At least in Moscow, no one pretends to like each other."

He expressed surprise that Bulgakov had not heard from Margarita. Pyotrovich did not say how he knew and he studied him as though the cause of this was some flaw which could be rectified by a reasonable improvement in personal hygiene or a new jacket. "It's possible she's more under his influence than I'd originally considered. That happens not infrequently—particularly in cases of prolonged *association*." His inflection seemed to give the relationship a bureaucratic tone. "Of course those of certain sensitivities are more prone," Pyotrovich added. These weren't just Bulgakov's inadequacies.

Bulgakov searched their last moments together at the camp; nothing she had said or done would support this, yet other images slipped willfully past these thoughts. He imagined Ilya and Margarita standing alone in the foyer of a comfortably furnished house; the light was low; perhaps they had been guests of some future happy evening, well-fed, the conversation and laughter of the gathering still clinging to them as they prepared to depart into the snowy night. Ilya offered her coat, holding it as she slipped it on; then, with practiced intimacy, lifting her hair so that it might spill over the collar. She turned and Bulgakov saw her ease, her grateful smile, as she buttoned it close. Ilya layered upon it her scarf; sometimes he wrapped it about her neck; this time instead he leaned in and kissed her lightly. She waited while he put on his coat; she looked to the window; her face held only patient waiting. Beyond her, the light from the street shone in halos through the glass. The threads of her scarf were frayed slightly and brushed the edge of her cheek. Her eyes glistened. Perhaps she was thinking of the quiet walk home.

Pyotrovich took him outside to a small enclosed yard; a collection of women of varying ages and ethnicities had been arranged to stand along a wall. The local police had been conducting regular sweeps of the train depot, he explained; his gesture was both effeminate and dismissive. Likewise in Ulan-Ude and Chita. Pyotrovich went down the line; it seemed more of a schoolyard inspection and he appeared unexpectedly pleased, as though these women were somehow a favorable reflection upon himself. He stopped before one; he removed his glove and stroked her cheek. She was young and sturdily built.

"Feel this complexion," he gushed. "That brow, that cheekbone." He drew his thumb along these. He then squeezed her shoulder. "She could plow a field single-handed."

Her gaze was stony. He pinched her cheek then slapped it. She didn't flinch and he laughed at this. "Any one of them," he swept his arm. He glanced at Bulgakov as though suggesting he might pick one for himself. They might both pick.

"We'll get them," he said. Bulgakov should not despair.

Bulgakov looked at the women—did any even resemble her? And if one had, would he have risen up in her defense? To save a nose of a similar tilt, a common complexion, hair that was styled in the same fashion? The women looked cold, the breeze moved across their coats; they looked frightened. He wanted to save them all, a triumph of her cause.

She must leave with Ilya. Both needed to disappear. He imagined them together in the train depot; anxiously looking to the timetables, listening for the approaching whistle. Would their hands be clasped? In mutual comfort or something more? How could she not love someone willing to sacrifice for her? For Ilya, this had never been a choice. What if he could warn them, ensure their escape? Would he not try? Was this even a choice?

What could Pyotrovich know of despair?

Bulgakov went to the train depot.

The interior was an open space with rows of benches. The wall adjacent to the ticket sellers had been painted black; the arrivals and departures were posted in chalk. The next train was due in several hours and the benches were half filled. Margarita and Ilya weren't there.

Ilya would anticipate the police surveillance of these stations. This one would be as good as any.

Bulgakov sat down.

Nearby a young soldier waited next to a woman who appeared to be his mother. Between them on the floor was a single suitcase tied with string like a parcel. His uniform was new; its cuffs were stiff and without wear. His hands, pale young things, rested on the fresh fabric of his trousers. He looked regularly to the board and to the windows overlooking the platform. Squares of blue promise. His face carried both uncertainty and excitement.

His mother looked away from the ticket windows, away from the chalkboard, from the platform, and instead to the doors which led to the town, to the street where they'd lived their years together. Bulgakov could only guess—perhaps seventeen or eighteen. She would know. She would try to recall some memory from when he was small and still needed her. She would wish she could talk to her own mother about it.

One of the conductors came with a cloth, and, climbing the short stepladder, updated the board with fresh chalk.

Their soldier was a good boy. He tried to look regretful of the approaching hour; she tried to seem brave.

He would get on the train; he would wave farewell and later would forget this day; others would take its place.

She would remember the walk home; she would notice not the other pedestrians, but instead their footprints in the snow and the way light shifted to blue as it passed into the shadow cast by the fragile rim. She would climb the stairs to the apartment they'd shared, a tidy room in the fading light, a lampshade made of colored glass, a figurine from another country, and she would wonder how any of these things could have ever held importance to her before.

Bulgakov looked about the depot—others, scattered figures lost to their own thoughts. Their hearts were available to him for his reading; the particulars of their defeats as though they'd been pinned to their coats like a written notice. Here was the real People's Army. He would be a willing recruit. He would come back tomorrow, and each day of those that followed. He would do what was necessary to safeguard her departure. He would join their ranks.

# CHAPTER 41

The next morning they did not start a fire. Ilya brought out clothes suitable for a young man and Margarita dressed quickly. Her breasts were camouflaged by the loose tunic. He handed her a cap. "Wouldn't it be better to cut it?" she said. She twisted her hair atop her head and put it on. He stepped back to examine her. He shook his head.

"This isn't going to work," he said. He took some ash from the fireplace and smeared it lightly over her chin. "It's hopeless," he said, in a kind of wonderment.

She looked at her reflection in the small mirror of his shaving case. She couldn't capture the entirety of her head in it.

"I can try to scowl like a teenager," she said.

He studied her; he seemed contemplative of something else.

"Perhaps you should cut it," she said after a moment. She removed the cap.

He looked away as though her gesture had unsettled him. "If I thought it would help, I would," he said. He went to manage the luggage. She put the cap back on.

Her other clothes and papers were placed in the hidden compartment of the suitcase. The new papers he produced made her his nephew.

Outside, the air was still. Fresh snow covered the ground and settled on the larger branches. The sky was pale with thin high clouds. The sun, hanging low in the east, was a tepid yellow ball. She got into the car with him. Today, he told her, they would leave Russia forever.

He smiled; they were nearly there.

He started the car. She touched the back of her neck where the chilled air had slipped past the collar of her coat.

They stopped along the roadside briefly. In the distance a town clung to shallow-sloped hills. It was cold and bright with a steady breeze. Ilya had brought some food and she spread a cloth across the hood of the car and laid out the small meal. He set a flask of vodka where their cup would have stood. She took a drink and he smiled at this. It felt like a dare and she drank again.

"When I become too drunk to walk," she said. "What will you do with me?"

"I will carry you home," he said.

His use of the word surprised her. She imagined a flat they might share, the cluttered messiness: stacks of books, dishes, shoes about the floor. Both his and hers. Did he make the bed or allow the sheets to collect in a mound at the foot? Would he measure first before hanging a picture or tack it askew? It seemed disconcerting that she didn't know such things.

She went on more carefully. "And when I become too heavy to manage?"

"I will pitch a tent around us and wait until your drunkenness passes."

"A tent?"

He seemed to feign surprise. "I carry one for just such occasions." He touched the brim of her cap; he smiled a little, as though it was remarkable in some way.

"And should I catch a cold from spending the night in your tent?"

"I will feed you tea and honey and aspirin until you are better."

She imagined them lying together, her pregnant with their child. She imagined him stroking her stomach, cupping the swell, talking to it, sternly at times. Counseling it on the finer points of hockey; assuring that it would know how to skate before it could walk.

*And if it's a girl*, she'd mildly protest.

*I see that it makes no difference,* he'd say. He'd put his daughter against any lineup of boys.

"And if I should become diabetic from the honey and my toes collect sores?" she said.

"I will clean and dress them until they are healed."

She imagined herself wasted with disease in a hospital bed. She imagined him arguing with doctors, sneaking portions of soups and casseroles past militant nurses. While she slept he would doze in the chair beside her. When she was awake he would tell her gossip of the neighbors, stories to distract. He'd hide his heartbreak from her.

"And if my toes fall off?"

He looked off, at the distant town. "I will give you mine."

When they were done she gathered the small cloth by the corners and shook the loose crumbs out over the expanse. In the distance, the hills were spotted with shadows cast from high white clouds. She wiped her eyes with the back of her hand.

The train depot in Irkutsk had been built in the time of Tsar Nicholas, shortly before the arrival of its first train in 1898. The ceilings were high and arched; places where its plaster had fallen revealed dark underlying timbers. The stone chosen for its tiled floor was overly porous and its former brilliance had been ground to a toothlike grey even in those few decades. It was poorly heated. Timetables were rarely adhered to and its rows of benches were filled. Some drowsed as they waited. Several grudgingly shifted to make room for them.

A few soldiers milled about though they appeared no older and with no greater seriousness towards life than teenagers. Their uniforms reminded Margarita of the camp guards and she was chilled by the thought that they'd been sent to retrieve her. She laid her glove over Ilya's and they sat hand in hand as a young couple might, despite their disguise. Margarita knew this could expose them. She hadn't counted on the pervasiveness of her distress, and she was surprised he tolerated the risk. Perhaps he felt a similar despondency; how could they succeed, in which case, what did it matter? Better to find comfort in their last moments. An old woman swathed in black stared at them. She lifted her hand in what Margarita thought would be a gesture of silence, but instead she crossed herself.

Nearby, a young girl played on the floor with a small and crudely made doll. When she saw Margarita she came over. Holding the doll in one hand, she stroked the sleeve of Margarita's coat. Her eyes were steel blue and unblinking; short, fair-colored braids could be seen from under a knit cap. She as well seemed unimpressed by Margarita's disguise. Who was this child—why did she choose Margarita for her attentions? "Someone's made a friend," said Ilya; he sounded more curious than concerned. "Where is your mother?" Margarita asked. The girl appeared not to understand or care to be helpful; she seemed to have laid claim to her.

"It's all right," said Ilya. His tone had changed. There was a hollowness to it. He was staring at the soldiers.

Where Margarita had counted two, there were now four; they'd coalesced and were moving along the benches, examining the travel papers of those waiting. Only one appeared to have any real interest in this activity; he carried a folded page printed with several photographs. He was shorter than the others, though built broadly through the torso. Despite his youthful face, a day's growth of beard covered his cheeks. He reminded her of a young bear. A woman was instructed to stand and remove her outer garments. He held the paper alongside her face and studied it, then moved further down the row. Another woman was told to similarly disrobe.

"You should leave," she said to Ilya.

"Where would I go?" he said.

She thought he meant that there was no world beyond this room; no existence to be counted without her in it. She wanted to tell him how absurd he was being. Then she saw the fifth soldier, standing at the station entrance, rifle in hand.

From the platform, the train's whistle sounded. The crowd murmured. The soldier carrying the photographs gazed over the heads of those waiting, then climbed onto a bench.

"You may not leave until your papers have been reviewed," he announced. He seemed unaccustomed to the possession of such authority. His comrades as well gazed at him in mild surprise. He repeated his words in a stronger voice. *You will not leave.* The crowd seemed to bristle slightly, perhaps at his youth, and he added, as though in a conciliatory way, that no one would miss the train.

He surveyed them once more as he stepped down and Margarita sensed his eye catch and with that there was the turn of decision—should he go straight to her or should he have her wait with the rest; her anxiety growing, he would know. One of the other soldiers had already instructed another woman to stand for examination and he stepped forward with the photographs he carried. It was simpler to go one by one. He would get to her momentarily.

As though he'd gained new confidence, he took his time over this next one. He held the photograph at her ear, then, taking her chin, turned her head to each side. She was young and slim. Would she be mistaken for Margarita? He gestured to a corner of the room and a soldier led her there. He ignored the protests of her family at first, then indicated that they should join her as well. Any remaining conversation was silenced. All eyes followed his every movement, and he, as though aware of this, seemed to harden his expression, his words harsher than necessary. The next young woman was similarly corralled with the first; this time her family let her go. She stood with the others, clutching her hat to her chest, her face stony in its fear, her hair still in disarray after he had had her unpin it.

"You must go," she whispered to Ilya.

He picked up the child and set her in Margarita's lap.

Nearby, there was a sudden eruption of sound and motion. A man stood, then stumbled back as though the floor had tipped up on him. *Oh dear god*—it was Bulgakov! How could this be? Had he seen her? How was it that she'd not seen him until now? All about him seemed unkempt—his clothes flapped loose as he moved, his hair long and uncombed. Was he intoxicated? Had he been there the entire time? He shook his fist in the air, then stumbled forward as though to wield it upon a waiting passenger. A woman shrieked and another man rose to his feet, his arms raised in defense of himself. The soldiers looked around as though skeptical of this disruption separate from their own; a measure of their authority had been lost; a rumble of concern from the other passengers grew. The soldier who carried the photographs nodded to another to go and subdue the drunkard. There was a flash of something in Bulgakov's hand and a shot was fired.

The crowd flattened itself against the benches. Plaster fell from the wall where the shot had lodged itself. The sound of its larger pieces could be heard littering the floor.

Only Bulgakov and the soldier with the photographs were unmoved. The soldier tucked the page inside his jacket and went over to him, his hands held up on either side; perhaps not in submission so much as to be calming.

"That's a nice piece you're carrying, friend," said the soldier. "I've not seen that model before."

"It's a Nagant." Bulgakov leveled it at him. His intoxication appeared to have passed. "It can do tricks. Friend."

*Oh*—why was he here? What could he hope to accomplish? The other soldiers had their weapons trained on him. This was too great a cost. She wanted to intercede, to take the gun with gentle suggestion. The child weighed upon her like a stone.

The soldier smiled stiffly. "Say, this is no way to behave."

Bulgakov seemed to feign mild bewilderment. "But I've submitted the correct paperwork."

"You're giving these good people a scare."

Bulgakov then looked amused. "I'd call it a chronic condition."

The soldier was reaching for Bulgakov's shoulder. Bulgakov stepped back and cocked the weapon, and the soldier withdrew. "What is it you want?" said the soldier. His face had paled.

Bulgakov looked at the Nagant as though it could answer. "I don't want clean windows," he said. He returned his attention to the soldier, though Margarita sensed his words were for her.

"I want what I cannot have."

A desperate man would have no price. The room was hushed. The child put the doll's head in her mouth.

The hand at Bulgakov's side trembled. Was he ill, thought Margarita? Was he in his right mind? Even in those few weeks since they'd seen each other, he seemed transformed. But his words were clear and his voice familiar. She recognized his watch chain; it hung loose from his trouser pocket much as a bewildered hanger-on from a gentler world that was being made to suffer these recent hardships. She put her hand to her chest; beneath her shirt, the dial was cool on her skin.

"What is your name?" said Bulgakov.

"Yury—Yury Vladimirovich," said the soldier.

"Yury Vladimirovich, do you believe in God?"

"Of course not."

Bulgakov considered him. "Even as your chest might at any moment become a stew of bone and muscle? Someone in your position should want to squeeze out a small miracle from a benevolent spirit if they could find one."

"No one believes anymore," Yury's voice seemed to fade.

"The ancients had a panoply of gods—for wood, for fire; one for wine, two for water—both salt and fresh." He seemed to count them in the air with the muzzle of the gun. "Is it possible none have survived?"

"Well, there is no evidence to suggest—"

"Yet every human culture ever to exist, even our first and most primitive tribe, has evoked some higher being—what is it about us that we seek a Creator? Is it our soul searching for its larger self?"

"Look—I'm only a soldier."

Bulgakov waved off his excuse. "You must admit we are different from other creatures. Can you name another that would stand as we do, one before the other, willing to kill—or to be killed—for something that is not food or property or even temporary dominance? For ideas as inconstant as principle or justice or *love*? Is this what makes us so wretchedly human? Dare we call it a soul? And why would we want one? Indeed, why would anyone want us to have one? Yury—think! How malleable we'd be if we didn't."

From some corner there was a murmur of assent. Every eye was fastened upon them.

Would Bulgakov look at her? One glance—that was all she wanted. One last—she couldn't think it. *Find me*—she thought fiercely. *Don't leave me.*

Yury looked about the room as though for some ally. Bulgakov gazed at him sympathetically. The Nagant never lost its aim.

"It seems a rather old-fashioned concept," said Yury; he appeared to take care with his words.

"Even dead souls have their value." Someone behind them laughed aloud.

"Is it your intention then to save ours?" Yury looked doubtful of this.

Bulgakov smiled. "There is only one soul here I have in mind to save."

Margarita touched her lips.

"Then you are a priest," said Yury.

"There was a time I'd thought myself a shaman."

"A professor, then? You seem to know a lot."

"One must concede that books have uses beyond that of a doorstop."

Another laughed; the sound quickly disappeared. The soldiers looked around.

"Perhaps if you tell me what you want?" said Yury. "We can talk like reasonable people. We can let these others go."

Again Bulgakov seemed sympathetic. "They may not be the ones you should be concerned about."

"I don't think you want to shoot me." Yury sounded both wistful and defiant in this.

Bulgakov put his hand on his shoulder. "Are you counting on my good nature? My compassion for the unlucky? My admiration for your courage—for I do admire you." He seemed almost caring. "Are you hoping that with insanity comes poor aim?" He tucked the gun under the soldier's chin. "Soulless creatures are not required to justify their acts, good Yury. Soulless creatures can stand in the sunlight without care for what they've done."

There was a gentleness to Bulgakov's embrace; an earnestness to the gun's gesture, its touch like a parent's, directing the chin upward, demanding good attention. Yury had seemed to have lost the capacity to blink. He stared into Bulgakov's eyes, first one then the other; fear had taken all reason.

Bulgakov leaned in. "They tell us not to believe. How easy is it then to take it from us?" His face turned grim. "It won't hurt, Yury. But I want mine back."

He looked at her then. At long last. His expression, his eyes, they held her in place. They carried his deepest apology.

He turned the piece toward his own chest. It seemed more a gesture than intent.

*No!*—had she whispered? Had she shouted? A woman screamed. The soldiers closed in around him. There was a brief tussle, then he was horizontal, midair, with one on each limb. He struggled more as a madman now. Margarita could see only the soles of his shoes. Would this be her last image of him? She let the girl slip from her arms and she stood. She took a step toward him.

Someone held her back; it was Ilya.

The soldiers disappeared through the station doors carrying Bulgakov. Once they were gone, those waiting for the train seemed to rise as one, their voices growing; could they believe what had just transpired? They gathered their various luggage and packages and children and funneled onto the platform. Ilya directed her there as well.

"Will they not search the train?" she said. Surely there was some reason he would need to release her. His expression was stern, unreadable. Outside, the crowd had separated into individual streams, climbing into the various carriages. He propelled her into one. She could have escaped the soldiers more easily. Once inside, he found an empty compartment, then shut the door behind them.

"Let me go," she said. He stared at her, uncomprehending. His back was against the door.

"I need to use the water closet," she said. She reached for the handle. He brushed her hand aside.

"You can wait until we are under way." He appeared then to work to control himself, to calm her down.

She turned to the window behind her.

"We'll be leaving soon." He was trying to sound confident, she knew. To invoke some anticipation for the trip. To appease her with the promise of safety and shelter and food.

"He made it possible for us to get away," he added then, more gently. Was she indifferent to this?

She touched the glass. It was cold through her gloves.

Bulgakov had let her go. He'd let her go. There would be no return once she crossed that border. It seemed the world beyond would drop into nothing. This was forever.

Outside the sun shone blindingly upon the remaining snow of the train yard. Discarded railroad ties lay scattered, rotting. Squat, unmarked, unpainted buildings ringed the space. A single line of graffiti ran along the bottom of one. The script seemed impossible to read; it could have been another language. Her breath on the pane caused the scene to blur. She struck it with her hands.

She would insist that she was simply going to the lavatory; that she would return. That they would travel together. They would again take on the guise of man and wife. Perhaps someday they would become those things.

She wiped the glass. Between the buildings and beyond them, a distant smudge of the ice-locked Angara could be seen.

She would tell him that she'd forgotten something in the depot. Something for which she had a great fondness. Something she couldn't imagine leaving behind. She knew exactly where it lay; she would be back in a moment's time. She would promise.

Distant, over the buildings, a solitary swan flew. Grey against the blue at that height. Following the waterway back to Lake Baikal. Its form wavered through the imperfections in the glass, then slipped beyond its edge. Her forehead touched the windowpane.

Ilya was waiting for her answer.

She would tell him that his eyes had always held a particular sadness, as though his view of the world was from some great distance.

She would tell him that she was aware of how much he'd given up, places and things to which he could never return.

That she knew how utterly unfair she was being.

She turned back. Her vision had darkened from the glare of the snow.

"I can't go with you," she said.

She could not know what he read on her face. His appeared to have greatly aged. He had carried on for both of them long enough; she would have to want this too. He looked away; it seemed he could no longer bear the sight of her. He stepped from the door as though this was his choice.

The platform was deserted. An attendant suggested she hurry; the train would soon depart. She went inside the depot; the benches were empty. A child's mitten, a scrap of paper. No soldiers—as though she'd been forgotten. She paused in the spot where Bulgakov had stood.

Once she'd suggested to Mandelstam that she should write poetry. He'd laughed at her, not unkindly. What on earth would she write about, he'd asked. He'd drilled a finger into her shoulder. You need to have died a bit, he'd told her. Maybe died a lot. He'd kissed her then, as if to say, enjoy your aliveness. One writes not because he wants to.

She went outside toward the street; it was bright and crowded with wagons and cars and people. A horn sounded, then another. It was bitter cold. She searched for soldiers or police and saw none. A man's coat brushed her arm. There were fragments of conversations. She pulled the cap from her head; her hair spilled about her shoulders. No one noticed.

The edge of the street was black from the collected soot of a city. An old newspaper lay at her feet, its print damp. A photograph of officials stared past her. Something about the opening of a bridge in a distant region. They had called it a triumph of the People.

Someone grabbed her arm. It was an older woman, her head covered in a faded print kerchief. She searched Margarita's face; her own was crossed by fine lines from years of sun; it was both disappointed and unrelenting. "I thought you were my sister," she said, as though still unconvinced that it could not be her. She released Margarita's arm and disappeared into the crowd. Margarita wondered if the woman had lost sight of her sister only moments before, or if it'd been many years. She still felt the pressure of her fingers through her clothes.

She could be someone's sister, someone's daughter. Someone's wife. She examined the faces of those around her. Most were preoccupied, indifferent. A few paused at her gaze; she could be anyone and in that they seemed untroubled. A taxi driver motioned hopefully to the door of his vehicle but she shook her head and went into the street.

The men in the photograph watched her pass; if only they had been able to see beyond the camera's lens that day. They would have applauded her if they could.

# CHAPTER 42

I lya watched the passing landscape from the train carriage. He sensed a change in the inertial force as it began to slow. They were still miles from the Mongolian border. There were no trees, only a vast golden plain, distant snowy mountains, and empty sky. It was easy to believe in a curious god, watching from above.

The train was stopped for five hours at the border. It was night; intermittent lights shone along the platform. There were interior lights from the station house. Ilya guessed a barracks adjacent to that. A handful of other smaller buildings. Beyond these, impenetrable darkness. Perhaps this god had lost interest.

There was a knock on the carriage door. A young soldier asked to see his papers. He traced a small light over the print, then handed them back. He glanced at Ilya as though he should recognize him, then quickly away. As though the form of this man had been altered, perhaps by fire or another past trauma, and though well healed, the soldier was unsettled by it. Later, the soldier would believe that it had been the poor light which had made for the sense of unworldliness. In any case, this was not the man for whom they'd been searching; earlier that day they'd been told that he'd been found.

A short time later the train pulled away from the station. The lights in the window retreated, leaving only Ilya's reflection. He turned down the lamp as though he would sleep.

He and Pavel had been fishing. It was late spring with the water at its highest and Pavel had ventured in too far. He laughed the first time he slipped as though this was a game between him and the rapids. He gave no shout of surprise when he disappeared. Ilya had thought, if he'd looked away at that moment, it would be as if he'd never had a brother. Ilya called to him; tossed aside his rod and clambered in, his voice lost to the pounding water. His brother's face appeared only once, not far from where he'd been. Grey, determined, as though set upon the task of drowning. Their eyes met before he sank again.

Ilya embraced the water, slipping below; cold gripped his chest, muffled throbs filled his ears. Some limb touched his hand and he grasped it, pulling it to him as a fisherman hauls in a loaded net, then fighting for his footing on the river bottom, back to the shore.

Pavel told everyone how his brother had saved him. It was then that Ilya applied for service in Moscow.

Perhaps Pavel had made some promise to deliver Ilya, thinking this would deter Pyotrovich and give his brother a better chance. Perhaps he'd considered none of this, but it wouldn't matter. It was enough that they were brothers. Agents would take him to the quiet of a snowy woods. The shot would echo, followed by the quiet tramping of boots. Papers belonging to an Ilya Ivanovich would be left on the body. A final shot to the face would disfigure it. Pyotrovich would have his promotion.

# CHAPTER 43

Bulgakov wasn't arrested but rather hospitalized for several weeks. He was diagnosed with delirium tremens, given fluids and potassium salts, and discharged with the admonishment to avoid liquor and protein-laden foods. When he returned to his apartment, the necessary approvals for his relocation to Moscow were waiting. He never saw Pyotrovich again.

Those with whom he shared a train carriage nicknamed him the "professor." He'd purchased a ream of writing paper and sat with it for hours each day, pausing for meals and tea and sleep. The paper had seemed something of a habit he wished to acquire. He would finger his pen and watch the landscape pass.

He considered the balance of what had transpired. Why had he only been hospitalized rather than arrested? What price had been paid that made this a reasonable exchange? The physical laws which governed the world seemed untrustworthy.

He wondered about Ilya and Margarita. They were distant, floating in a vague realm of grey light. He tried to place them on the streets of a Cantonese city, or on an eastward boat to another land; but always the sea was becalmed and the sky swathed in mists. He couldn't see her future; he wondered if she was happy.

The pages before him remained hopeful in their whiteness: surely he would conceive of something worth saying. Even better, he might write something funny.

In Moscow, Bulgakov returned to the apartment on Sadovaya

Street. As he climbed the stairs, he startled a medium-sized black cat lurking on the landing. "A new tenant," he said, scratching it behind its ears, and when he opened his door, the animal trotted in. "So you've taken over the place," he said.

But the room was unchanged, simply dusty. One of the curtain panels was still half hung. He would buy more pins, he thought. Her boots stood by the door, her book on the table. The cat leapt onto the armrest of her chair. Bulgakov picked up the book, examined it briefly, then returned it to the shelf. Its binding was unremarkable among the others. One might wonder why it'd been picked. He went to unpack; no one would know. Eventually it would be forgotten.

Several weeks later, a letter came. He recognized the script. The envelope was slender; it held a page at most. Its postage was Soviet. He sat on the edge of the bed and opened it carefully.

She was safe, living in a town she did not name. Working as a house cleaner.

*I've learned to disappear. If I passed you on the street, you would not see me.*

He finished reading then folded the letter and returned it to the envelope.

Outside, the afternoon was unusually warm for mid-spring. Patriarch's Ponds was nearly empty. The linden trees were a pale green, their leaves still new. He took a bench in their shade.

Along the path that bordered the water, a figure approached. At such a distance and with the humidity of the air, it seemed to shimmer like a mirage. As it drew close, it gained substance and an older gentleman emerged. He walked with a cane; more from habit, Bulgakov would surmise. His posture was straight and his gait appeared sound. He slowed as he neared, then, with a nod of acknowledgment, he sat on the other end of the bench. He was dressed entirely in black. He held the cane before him, planted between his feet; both hands rested atop its handle. His wrists were pale and thin; his skin was mottled with age. He was clearly much older than what Bulgakov had guessed.

"Take care," said the man, nodding toward the other side of the pond. "The light can play tricks—it's played many before."

Across the water, as though materializing from the heat, another figure took form. Slender, young; a woman; she turned to stare at him. He recognized the clothes: buttercup yellow. The hair, the shape of her face. He couldn't perceive her expression. Could it be her?

"A perfect afternoon," said the man. He looked about as though the weather was a performance that had been staged for him specifically. "I should think God would want to spend more time here."

"I imagine he has other concerns," said Bulgakov. Who could know what a deity might find important?

"Perhaps so—perhaps he is in *America*." The man nodded, laughing silently at his own joke. After a moment, though, he tapped the pavement before him with the tip of his cane and drew a more serious tone. "I, on the other hand, am more inclined to this place."

She had written: *To disappear is my freedom; for you, my dearest, it would be your prison.*

The man went on. "Typically I offer food to the starved, power to the weak, love to the lonesome; but I suspect you want none of those things," he said.

Across the water, the woman was gone. The water rippled outward as though it'd been disturbed. Likely it was fish feeding on surface insects.

"There's nothing you can offer me," said Bulgakov.

The man got up stiffly, as though to continue on his way. "Then write us a good story, Messire Bulgakov. Give us something enjoyable to read."

ACKNOWLEDGMENTS

My principal literary debt is clear, however those familiar with Mikhail Bulgakov's *The White Guard*, *A Country Doctor's Notebook*, and *A Dead Man's Memoir* will no doubt enjoy some echo of those writings herein. Likewise I am grateful to Johann von Goethe and Christopher Marlowe and Charles Gounod for their particular interpretations of the Faust legend. Of those who were emboldened to tell their stories of this time, I'm indebted to Nadezhda Mandelstam (*Hope Against Hope*) and Anna Larina (*This I Cannot Forget*). Similarly, to the many individuals, hundreds in fact, who, as expatriates in the early 1950s, allowed their narratives to be captured in the faint and bluish hues of vintage mimeograph and to the Harvard College Library that has made them accessible (the Harvard Project on the Soviet Social System Online).

I am grateful for the warmth and empathy of James H. Billington (*The Icon and the Axe*), Orlando Figes (*Natasha's Dance*), and Sheila Fitzpatrick (*Everyday Stalinism*) which taught a foreigner an abiding regard and love for this people's character and history and fortune.

I am grateful for Joseph Himes, who in his resolute passion to help first the Soviet Union, then the countries of Ukraine and Russia, advance their nuclear safety, traveled frequently to those places, learned their language, and introduced me to *The Master and Margarita*.

To those who dutifully read (and I believe in affection for me) those early and highly unsatisfactory versions of this story, Susan Tacent, Robin McLean, Krishna Lewis, Susan Robison, Dona Bolding, Robert Anthony, Priya Balasubramanian, and Claire Burdett, I am unbounded in my gratitude. And further, to my teachers, who through no fault of their own other than to be unflaggingly generous and remarkable in their teaching and their personage and their friendship and whom I call my mentors: Margot Livesey and Jim Shepard.

I am grateful for Dani Shapiro, Michael Marin, and Hannah Tinti.

For Christopher Castellani and Sonya Larson.

I am indebted to the patience and astuteness of Adam Schear. Likewise I am wholly grateful for the editorial wisdom of Michael Reynolds.

And finally, for those who have abided for years (yes, years), those souls who are my best mirrors of humanity and myself, I am grateful to Kristen Lekstrom; to Chris Thiem; to Vivian and Elie Aoun; to Inez Mostue; to Paul, Ryan, and Mark Himes; and above and beyond, to the one for whom I am most thankful that he roams the planet with me, Daniel Himes.

## ABOUT THE AUTHOR

Julie Lekstrom Himes's short fiction has been published in *Shenandoah*, *The Florida Review* (Editor's Choice Award 2008), *Fourteen Hills* (nominated for Best American Mysteries 2011), and elsewhere. This is her debut novel. She lives with her family in Marblehead, Massachusetts.